The
MESMERIST

By Felice Picano

SMART AS THE DEVIL

EYES

THE MESMERIST

Felice Picano

The

MESMERIST

Delacorte Press/New York

Published by
Delacorte Press
1 Dag Hammarskjold Plaza
New York, New York 10017

Designed by Giorgetta Bell McRee

Library of Congress Cataloging in Publication Data

Picano, Felice, 1944–
The mesmerist.

I. Title.
PZ4.P5925Me [PS3566.I25] 813'.5'4   77-9529
ISBN 0-440-05542-3

To Jane,
with red roses

Then save me, or the passed day will shine
Upon my pillow, breeding many woes,—
Save me from curious Conscience, that still lords
Its strength for darkness, burrowing like a mole . . .

(—From the sonnet "To Sleep" JOHN KEATS)

BOOK ONE

The Warning–
Spring 1899

H ENRY LANE IS DEAD."
The boy had just darted in and was teetering on the
dining room lintel of Mrs. Page's Board and Hotel for
Gentlemen in Center City, Nebraska. It was the late spring of
1899, and the boy was breathless, tousled, and excited: something had finally happened in his young life.

"Mrs. Ingram found him in the stable, or what used to be the
stable before Mr. Lane got that motorcar. Sheriff Timbs said you
should come right away."

James Ransom didn't even look up from his mutton stew. Not
that he cared for it so much tonight. Mrs. Page hadn't displayed
her usual culinary skill, he thought. Something was missing: an
herb, a spice—something. It nagged him not to know exactly
what. And now this news. No, he was going to finish his plate,
even have a cup of coffee, and possibly a brandy and cigar too
before leaving the table tonight.

"Tell him I'll be there after dinner."

"He's hung himself."

"Hanged himself," Dr. Murcott corrected.

Amasa Murcott had stopped eating at the boy's words, even
if Ransom hadn't. He looked across the big table at his fellow
boarder and friend, expecting more of a response. Nothing at all.
Just the two empty plates on either side of them staring up at him,
one for Mrs. Page, the other for Nate, who was already so filled
with his news he'd never be able to eat.

"They want you there too," the boy said. " 'Cause he hanged
himself. Left a letter for Mrs. Lane and everything. Just like in
a penny novel. Floyd said he must have thrown a noose up over
a rafter and stepped into it off the fender of the horseless."

"I will accompany Mr. Ransom."

"Don't you want to see him all strung up? They'll be taking
him down soon."

"Have you seen him?" Ransom asked.

"Sure did." Said proudly.

"Well, I guess that's good enough for me." Then, to the doctor, "I don't see why it's any of my business."

"When the town's most prominent citizen steps up and hangs himself out of a clear blue sky it seems to me it's everyone's business."

"You're the county coroner, Amasa. I can understand why . . ."

"You're the county prosecutor, James. Timbs must want you there for some reason."

"You know as well as I do that fool won't sign his name without having a dozen witnesses around."

There was a rustle of skirts behind him and he was quiet.

"Should I say you're coming?" Nate pleaded.

"Stay right where you are, Cincinnatus Page." His mother loomed large in the opposite doorway. Despite her flushed face, drenched with perspiration, and the tray of biscuits she had just taken from the oven, she looked dangerous.

"But ma'am, Henry Lane . . ."

"Don't you ma'am me. You get yourself to the pump. Wash up. Get a clean shirt on, and back at this table in three minutes."

"Yes, ma'am."

"He's been out all day," Mrs. Page said, setting down the smoking biscuits and sitting herself down. "I had to fetch all the coal for our dinner myself. I'll tan him for this."

"Henry Lane's dead," the doctor said, forking open a biscuit. "Hanged himself at home. I'll have to go take a look."

"I knew something like this would happen," she said.

"Something like what?" Ransom asked. Mrs. Page looked anxious. She seldom looked anxious.

"Nothing, I suppose. Just a woman's silliness." She served herself from the stewpot but didn't eat. "Here. Have some biscuits. I don't want word going out that Augusta Page doesn't feed her gentlemen."

Ransom wondered what she meant by "woman's silliness." Should he pry? Or let it go?

"Perhaps you ought to hold the coffee until we come back," he said.

"You're going too?" she asked.

"Why not. It's not every day that someone hangs himself. Besides, the drive will draw up an appetite for that pie I smelled cooling outside my office window all day. Apple?"

"Strawberry and rhubarb." She was still distracted.

Ransom wondered why he had hidden from her that he was wanted there too. Probably because of what she'd hinted of. Professional wariness too; just in case he actually was needed there, much as he doubted that. Mrs. Page was discreet. And she'd discover the truth sooner or later anyway. Still . . .

"You be careful," she said.

"Careful?" He was so amazed he stopped the forkful from reaching his mouth. "The man's dead. Not that I ever had to be careful of him when he wasn't."

"Now, I know better," she said. "I know how you felt about him."

Nate came in then, his hair combed, wearing a clean shirt, and that ended conversation until his mother stepped into the kitchen. Then Ransom looked at the doctor, and asked: "What do you think she meant?"

"Who knows?"

Five minutes later Nate fetched the doctor's medical kit. It was a warm evening, too warm for coats, the men decided, awaiting the boy on the big front porch. So they found their hats and gloves, hitched up Ransom's little shay, and drove off.

———————————●———————————

IT HAD GROWN DUSK by the time they reached the long dirt alley that ran parallel to Grant Street, forming a service road for the stables and back doors of the half dozen largest homes in the town. Others had heard the news; a dozen or more buggies were drawn up alongside the road, the horses tethered to branches or fence palings, right up to the big stableyard behind Lane's house.

The stable doors had been thrown wide open. Two canister-shaped headlights hung on either side of Lane's tall, glittering, metallic Reo illuminated the inside and the crowd of onlookers with their dull, sickly yellow glow.

"Looks like we missed seeing him strung up," Ransom said. He smelled honeysuckle all around them. Driving, he'd looked up and watched the stars coming out. It was too balmy, too beautiful a night for death. He wished he hadn't come, but instead stayed talking at home with Mrs. Page on the porch.

"I wish to hell they would have waited for me," Murcott said, bristling forward in his irritation. "Those fools always make more work. Hello, Floyd. I see you finally found something to get you off your rear end."

Floyd—no one called him anything else, or even recalled his last name anymore—was a wry, grizzled, talkative old-timer who'd been in Nebraska since it was a territory, and, for all anyone knew, had been alive and active when the Louisiana Purchase—of which the state had been part—was first made. Years before, he'd been manager of Lane's public stables, but he was old now and sometimes drank too much. Lane had pensioned him off—a typical act of charity, Ransom thought, to cover some of Lane's more dubious works, and now Floyd passed his time on courthouse benches looking over the big lawn of plaza, gabbing with the other old men.

He winked at Ransom. "It's a bad business, Mr. Prosecutor."

Damn! That was the second time someone had reminded him of his position today. "Sure is. Let's take a look."

"Last thing in the world I expected from Lane," Floyd went on, joining them.

"You or anyone else," Ransom agreed.

" 'Cause money ain't everything. Can't buy you happiness, as the Good Book says. Now take me. I ain't had a silver dollar to my name most of my life. You wouldn't catch me doing a fool thing like that, though."

Ransom wondered how often tonight those words had been repeated. "I wasn't aware that Mr. Lane was particularly unhappy," he said, lightly probing.

" 'Tweren't. Least not that I knew of."

They pushed through the crowd of men blocking the body. Murcott had impatiently gone ahead and was bending down over the corpse—gesturing for the onlookers to clear a space for him. The familiar leather bag crackled like mica in the carlamp's light.

Ransom detached himself from Floyd, nodding hello to a score of familiar faces before he spotted the sheriff. Might have known that when something finally happened in town Timbs would take the opportunity to act like a big shot. He was leaning his considerable bulk against the Reo's back tank, gesticulating and blabbering on to Mr. Jeffries, that transplanted easterner who was publisher and editor of the Center City *Star*. That fool would believe you if you told him cows could fly.

"First suicide we've had in fifteen years," Timbs was saying when Ransom joined them. The doctor was suddenly at his side. Jeffries, busy scribbling on a pad of foolscap, looked up.

"Would you gentlemen care to comment on this tragedy?"

"Hell, we just got here," the doctor said. He was annoyed by the crowd, by the body's having been moved, by having been dragged away from his dinner. Most of all, Ransom guessed, the doctor was annoyed by Lane's death; it had an element of the unexpected about it that the rational, bustling little man hated.

As usual, whenever Murcott was angry, Ransom was calm, even amused, taking his time feeling things out. His experience had taught him that nothing was unexpected—or everything was.

"Mr. Timbs here was kind enough to give me a great deal of information about the deceased," Jeffries said. The way he screwed up his face reminded Ransom of a woodchuck.

"Oh? I wasn't aware Henry Lane's life was a closed book to anyone," Ransom said.

"We're here," Murcott said. "What more do you want, Timbs?"

"An autopsy."

"An autopsy here? With this Fourth of July crowd?" He didn't give Timbs a chance to answer. "I'll take another look if that's what you need. Go on!" he ordered an onlooker, "clear the way for me."

"While he's doing that," Ransom said, "I'd like a word with Mr. Timbs." He moved past the editor, taking the sheriff's arm. Jeffries followed.

"Don't take too long. This is big news, you know. I have to get back to the shop and print it for tomorrow's front page."

"I understand," Ransom said, dripping courtesy. He was rougher with the sheriff, leading him deep into the stable like a boy he was about to whip.

"Now what's this all about?"

"He hung himself."

"I can see that. Why did you want me here?"

Timbs mumbled something under his breath that Ransom didn't catch. But even in the dark, he could see the sheriff's eyes were fearful, darting from side to side, as though begging help or seeking escape. Ransom got to the point. "Where's this letter he left to his wife?"

"Letter?"

"Nate said he had a letter. Where is it?"

Timbs fumbled in several pockets of his coat, vest, and pants. "I forgot. I gave it to Mrs. Lane."

"Well, what did it say?"

"Nothing much. How he was sorry and all. But it would be better this way."

"Better with him dead?"

"I guess."

"Better than what?"

"I don't know. I don't recall. In all the excitement I didn't read it too well."

The crowd began to murmur behind him. Ransom guessed Murcott was moving the body. Timbs looked over his shoulder to see what was happening. Like an overgrown boy, Ransom thought.

"You know that we don't prosecute dead men in this county."

"I know that. I just thought someone ought to be here. Judge Dietz is up at the state capitol."

"Looks to me like you have enough people here. You thinking of selling admissions?"

"Admissions?" Timbs asked.

How did he ever get to be sheriff, Ransom wondered again. But of course Henry Lane had backed Eliot Timbs in the last election. That was how. Well, here's your boy now, Lane.

Murcott joined them again: "You had him cut down."

"I couldn't just leave him up there for anyone to see," Timbs said, looking trapped now.

"You could have closed the stable doors. Never mind. Just tell me how much you rearranged him when you cut him down."

"Didn't touch him."

"Not even the hand?"

"Nothing. His hand was like that. I got to go there now," he said.

Murcott wavered, then moved aside to let him pass. The sheriff went to the crowd and gave orders in a loud voice for everyone to clear out, then turned to talk to Jeffries again.

"Poor bastard. Looks like he changed his mind at the last minute," Murcott said.

"Lane tried to save himself?"

"Looks like it. His thumb is stuck in the noose knot, as though to keep it from closing. Didn't help. Just cut off blood circulation in the thumb too. Go look."

"I don't have any stomach for pop-eyes, thank you."

"His aren't," the doctor said, lighting the pipe he'd stuck between his teeth as they'd come in.

"How come?"

"Don't know. Damndest thing I ever saw. His eyes were closed when he died. That doesn't happen in hangings. Sure, sometimes a lynched man will close them tight from fear. Lane's weren't like that; they weren't tensed. Wasn't tension in any of his face or body at all that I could make out. His tongue was stuck out and black, naturally. I put it back in. But Lane must have been calm and collected when he stepped off that horseless. That's my belief."

"No man is calm and collected when he hangs himself," Ransom replied. "Not even Henry Lane."

"Take a look," Murcott said, puffing.

Everyone was out in the yard. Someone had drawn the doors partly closed. They knelt down.

"Look."

"I see what you mean."

It wasn't the contorted mask of despair and strangulation Ransom had expected. Simply Henry Lane's big florid face, the eyes closed as though in sleep. A young face for someone who'd pushed and shoved for more than half a century. Honey-red mustachios just touched with gray. The unlined face reflecting good living and self-importance, right down to the laugh lines around his big eyes and generous mouth; laugh lines accentuated now, as though he had gotten the last laugh.

Relaxed, natural except for his hand twisted up above his head, his thumb stuck into the noose. That was pathetic. Accidental? Instinctive? Or, as Murcott thought, a last-minute change of mind.

It didn't make sense. Not from what Ransom knew of Henry Lane. The man had everything: the hotel and public stables on Lincoln Street, a thriving feed and grain business on Butler Avenue, a large ranch outside town with a hundred or so head of cattle, some fifty acres of sorghum and rye farmland, this big house, several carriages, the motorcar, stocks, bonds, cash. Position too—probably the best position in town. Whenever the state senator visited Center City he stayed at Lane's hotel, and dined at Lane's home. Whenever Lane visited Lincoln—several times a year—the generosity was reciprocated. He had power too, the sort of power that enabled him to make friends easily, and to be certain those friends would be in office to help him in turn. The kind of power Ransom had always called corrupting power, but which he'd been wary of crossing, little as he had to do with Lane in his lifetime.

What problem could have led him to take his own life? Problems with his wife, perhaps? Absurd. They were considered a love match, despite the difference in their ages. There had never been a word of rumor about them since the time Lane had gone to New York and brought her to live in Center City some twelve years before. They had no children; but that hadn't made any

difference. Lane had all his businesses, and Mrs. Lane had all her
charities, her teas, her dinners, her "at homes." She brought to
all these occasions her own special beauty and charm, and in
addition, an enviable New York stylishness she'd been bred to,
which had quickly made her the town's social leader, a position
recognized even by the very independent Mrs. Page. No, it
couldn't be marital problems.

Ransom would have to see the letter Lane had written. That
might hold some clue, not that Ransom expected it would explain anything. Getting it might take some doing too. Especially
now that Timbs had just given it to *her.* The fool!

As though he were thinking the same thing, Murcott said,
"How's Mrs. Lane taking all this?"

"Can't say. Timbs isn't overtactful."

"Better take a look. Care to join me?"

Ransom hesitated. He couldn't say why. She had the letter. As
prosecutor he had to look at it. Still. . . .

Murcott undid the noose. A large, silk handkerchief dangled
out of Lane's front vest pocket. The doctor tied it to hide the raw
hemp welts like wagon tracks on Lane's neck.

The crowd was dispersed into small groups now; standing
around the yard or by their conveyances. Timbs and Jeffries were
still busy jawing.

"Keep those doors closed," the doctor said. "I'll be back."

———————————●———————————

A SERVANT WOMAN neither of them knew answered their knock
on the back door. She must have been borrowed from a neighbor, Ransom thought, for the crisis. They were led past the
pantry and dining room, through the central hallway of the huge
two-story house, into a large front parlor, stuffily formal with
horsehair furniture, antimacassars, and gilt bronze—not much
used except for calls like this. Mumbling something in a heavy
Scandinavian accent, the woman bobbed and disappeared.
Where was Mrs. Ingram, the omnipresent housekeeper? Ransom
wondered.

They had only a minute to peer into the deep frames of a half dozen stiffly posed photographs hung on the walls or placed atop chests before Carrie Lane came into the room. The last photograph Ransom looked at was of her alone, years before, on her wedding day, trailing yards of lacy stuff over the steps she stood on, looking regal and blank and very young despite the grainy paper.

"Good of you gentlemen to come," she said, greeting them as freshly and indifferently as though she had stepped in from a garden party. At first sight, she seemed more distant to Ransom than her image in the picture frame. "Won't you sit down?"

The doctor must have been as amazed as Ransom by her attitude. Not making any move to sit down, he said, "Before I do, ma'am, I'd like to take my professional prerogative."

"By all means. Sheriff Timbs will show you . . ."

"I meant with yourself, ma'am," Murcott said, swiftly going to her, taking one hand for her pulse, placing the other lightly on forehead.

"Oh, I'm fine," she protested with a little laugh. "It's Mrs. Ingram who's ill, I'm afraid. It's been something of a shock for her. You see, she was in the stable when . . . well, it was she who first found Henry."

Evidently Mrs. Lane wasn't ill or in shock.

"Aase." She went to the doorway for the servant. "Please show the doctor to Mrs. Ingram. And stay with him in case he needs you."

Murcott gave Ransom a puzzled look, but he followed Aase.

"Please sit down," Mrs. Lane repeated.

As he did, she perched on the edge of a heavily embroidered, deep-cushioned chair.

Aware that he was staring at her, Ransom murmured his condolences. As he spoke, he became more conscious of his accent, a remnant of his Georgia childhood usually not noticeable except when he was nervous or uncomfortable. He never drawled like this in front of a jury or when pleading a case in inner chambers.

"You're very kind," she said, then looked down at the muted Turkey carpet.

Ransom had always been taken with Mrs. Lane's manner—so refined in this town composed mostly of rough and impoverished first- and second-generation immigrants and settlers of dubious background. It was her manner more than her considerable, very special beauty that had always appealed to him and had made him feel a bond—however slender—between them. He too had come from the East, from a genteel and educated family, from a tradition of courtesy and tact and, above all, good manners. This, even after the Union Army had destroyed the way of life that had fostered such manners; even when Ransom and his mother were left starving like the poorest of sharecroppers in a few downstairs rooms of the family's abandoned plantation house.

Today, however, Carrie Lane's formality irked him—it was inappropriate; and after all, aptness was what manners were about. He'd expected to see her grief-stricken, in tears. He hadn't really expected to see her at all, thinking she'd be confined to her room. Instead, except for a bit less color on her already pale complexion and two loose strands of curling auburn hair from behind her flat coiffure, she was as untroubled, as composed in the face of her husband's death as a stranger would be.

Ransom assumed she had loved her husband—everyone said she had. Why else had she allowed herself to be drawn away from the bustle and glamour of a big city to live in a town most railroads didn't stop at? Ransom had reasons for being here—but for the first few years he had desperately missed the stimulating urban life. Why else had she come, why else had she married a man twice her age; married him and lived with him without a flicker of gossip in a town where everyone knew each other's business, if she hadn't loved him? And if she had loved him, why was she acting this way now?

"Henry always said one could rely upon friends in a time of emergency," she said gently, breaking the silence.

"I confess I've come in a professional capacity," Ransom said. He hardly considered himself—or the doctor—a friend of the Lanes'. "Like the doctor."

"Of course," she replied.

She held her small head high, but looked down, away from his gaze. He'd noticed this in her before—at official functions, at formal dinners, even meeting the Lanes in the street. Modesty, he'd always thought it. A modesty charming in one so beautiful and well-to-do. Could it be evasion? All those times and now too?

"Henry always preferred the best solicitors," she said now. "He was always careful and fastidious in his business affairs." She rose. "If you'll come with me, I believe you'll find his papers up to date and in the best of order."

Ransom also stood up.

"I've no doubts," he said. "May I remind you that your husband has not used my services for the last few years."

Not since the last elections, in fact, during which Henry Lane had not even bothered to disguise his power-broking, but had openly supported fools such as Timbs, and opposed far worthier men all for the sake of influence. Most of the town had taken sides, and although there had been no violence, Ransom and others had been disgusted enough to sever all professional connections with Lane and his businesses. "I believe Mr. Applegate . . ."

"Yes, of course. How stupid of me."

"The business I referred to was as representative of the county, of the courts. I understand you received a letter from the deceased."

At first she seemed puzzled. For the first time since she'd entered the room she looked him full in the face. Her eyes were large and brown, soft but flecked with gold like a puma's. They questioned him, embarrassed him.

"You want to read the letter?"

"I don't want to read it. I don't read gentlemen's letters to their wives."

"Of course not."

"However this is an irregular situation, and just to be certain that no other irregularities are . . ." He was drawling so much he could hardly understand himself.

"I do understand," she said, saving him. "You have to read it."

"Naturally as soon as I'm satisfied that . . . it will be returned."

"You have to take it?"

"It has to be notarized and filed with the doctor's and sheriff's reports."

"Others will see it?"

"Probably not. Unless of course . . ."

But she had already turned from him, and he had to content himself with following the high line of her shoulders and stately drop of her back down to where the russet-colored shot silk opened up like the calyx of a flower as she quickly left the room.

He didn't have long to look once more at her wedding portrait to see how little she had changed since then. She came back holding the tip of a long pale-gray envelope in her outstretched hand. Automatically he reached for it. She held on to it.

"It's mostly for court records," he said.

"I'm certain I can rely on your discretion in such a very personal letter," she said as if, he thought, his tact were a requirement of her giving it.

"I can assure you. I will copy it over myself." Without opening it, Ransom put it inside his long vest pocket. "As for the other matters you mentioned, I'm sure Mr. Applegate can be relied upon . . ."

"Yes of course," she said, still uncertain whether to trust him or not. "Ah, Dr. Murcott. How is poor Mrs. Ingram?"

"Sleeping now. I gave her a mild potion. Should she awaken and still fret, have the girl give her more. Two drops in a water-glass. Tincture of opium. Perhaps if you have difficulty sleeping . . . ?"

"Thank you. I've used it before. Thank you, both of you."

It was so clearly a dismissal that both men put on their hats and allowed themselves to be shown out the front door.

As soon as they had cleared the house, Ransom turned to the doctor. "Had she used some of that stuff tonight? Before we came?"

"Can't say. Sure seemed calm enough."

Only a few men remained of the crowd. The doors were shut tight. No light flickered from the windows. The motorcar lamp had been extinguished. Timbs and Jeffries were gone.

"I want to take another look at him," the doctor said when they reached the stable. "Do you mind?"

Ransom went to the shay and stood against it, seeing a lamp waver on again through the stable windows.

In the dark, he could smell honeysuckle all around him. He knew it grew clustering all around the Lane house, right down to here; more pungent in the sudden spring warmth than it would be in high summer—when it would be almost sickly sweet. He breathed it now. It reminded him of Carrie Lane.

It was a moonless night; but very clear, with a ceiling almost white with stars, especially the band of Milky Way that twisted across the sky like a ribbon in a woman's hair. Carrie's hair.

The stars were high, though. High and distant. Cold and almost dizzying to look at, compared to the pungent sweetness of honeysuckle and the powdered earth beneath his nervous boot heels. Distant. As she was.

The envelope seemed to fill his vest pocket, like a second heart; pulsing with possibilities. He was warmed by it, then embarrassed by how much he had insisted on it: and how little she had wanted to part with it. Embarrassed too at how he had behaved so differently with her now that Lane was dead. He'd been a bachelor all his life. Not that he had wanted to be: but there had been "circumstances"—that's what he always called them—surrounding the one woman he'd loved when he was a young man, circumstances that had made him a bachelor. Since then he'd been with women, naturally: harlots, widows, even a married woman in Chicago, but he'd always thought of himself as a bachelor; one as contented with his lot at forty-one years of age as the doctor, some twenty years older, was with his. But there came days like this overripe spring evening when he didn't feel content, when he would think of how it could have been if Florence Poindexter and he had married, back there in D.C.— or he would give himself up to fancies of sitting on the porch as he did, but there would be another woman instead of stout Mrs. Page, a beautiful woman with a soft voice and gentle manners, with long-lashed speckled eyes that both bathed and challenged, the long concave sweep of her back. . . . Best to not think of it. He'd get all jumpy and have to take a night ride to the widow living outside of town, over an hour's ride away.

"Well, there's nothing more for me to do there," Dr. Murcott said, startlingly near.

Ransom got into the shay, grateful the darkness hid his musings.

—————————●—————————

"QUITE WELL," THE DOCTOR REPORTED to Mrs. Page over coffee and pie. "Mrs. Lane has taken it all quite well. That was to be expected. A fine lady. A bit sad, naturally, but resigned to it. Quite nobly reserved, I'd say," the doctor went on. "Reminds me of those wives and daughters we read about in the classics— Andromache, Iphigenia, Lucretia Tarquina. Noble women, all of them."

Ransom added nothing. He didn't mention how surprised both men had been at her attitude. Nor did he say a word about the letter. Mrs. Page was too inquisitive tonight.

"I wish I could feel comfortable about Lane," the doctor confided later, when he and Ransom were alone bidding each other goodnight outside their rooms on the second floor. "I don't like the way Lane looked. It's just not natural somehow. Reminds me of someone else. I wish I could remember who."

—————————●—————————

THE WAKE TOOK PLACE two days later in that same front parlor of the Lane house. Despite Lane's manner of death, and because of his wealth and position, no one questioned his right to the plot in the cemetery yard adjoining the Episcopal Church, or the services to be said over his remains. Everything would be done with all due respects, as though his passing had been natural. The wake set the example for this, as Ransom, Murcott and even Augusta Page saw for themselves.

To begin with, Mrs. Ingram had recovered and had taken up her duties, orchestrating the wake with the usual good-natured brusqueness and big-boned efficiency she had used to manage the Lane household for the past twelve years. At nine thirty that morning she opened the doors of the house to those townsmen who hoped to get a look at the corpse; they saw nothing but Henry Lane, a little paler but looking as though he was merely asleep in the big coffin set on two chairs at one end of the parlor.

Thereafter Mrs. Ingram could be seen greeting newcomers, sharing confidences with some of the women, making certain the elderly found a seat and the children were kept quiet in the back parlor and outside yard as they waited for their parents. It was difficult to believe she had collapsed upon seeing Lane's body dangling and had to have been sedated almost forty-eight hours. She was all business now, moving around the room quickly, jerkily arranging some flowers in an ornamental urn, turning to give an order to Aase—still on loan—smoothing down the skirt of her serge dress as her big periwinkle-blue calf-eyes scanned the room for any errors or improprieties; and her thin lips seemed to remain pursed over her large teeth even in the midst of the most animated conversation. Woven around the ribbon that held up a bun of her lustrous ash-blond hair was a twine of funereal crepe which scandalized some women as very frivolous, but which many of the men liked. Despite her overlarge features, or possibly because of them, Mrs. Ingram was much courted by the town's bachelors, even though she'd never given so much as a hint of interest in any of them for over a decade. Possibly those very qualities which seem fussy in a younger woman—thrift, economy, organization and good sense—made Mrs. Ingram, in her mid-forties, desirable. She'd been widowed so long most people couldn't recall Mr. Ingram at all. She couldn't stay unmarried forever: a buxom, active woman like that, the old men on the courtroom benches said, and would wink and dig into each other's ribs.

In contrast to the omnipresent Mrs. Ingram, Carrie Lane was scarcely seen throughout the long day of visitors. She appeared twice: in the morning, pale and distant but as always cordial, according to reports, and not again until after three o'clock to read the telegrams she'd received—one from the state senator; one from Judge Dietz, who was already on his way back from the capitol to Center City; and another from the County Chamber of Commerce.

Ransom, watching, couldn't help but notice how much more upset she seemed this day than she had at first. Of course she was able to read the flowery official rhetoric of the condolent messages but her voice had a flutter to it he hadn't heard before.

He took that opportunity to ask to speak to her alone in the library and to return the envelope containing Lane's last letter. Before he could do more than wonder if she only now realized her bereavement, they were invaded by other townsmen seeking a closer interview, and she fled to the second floor.

Talking to her the following day at the graveside was also impossible; and he couldn't even much see her, as she appeared shrouded in several layers of veils, and with the exception of two striking moments she seemed not to be present or attentive.

The first came when in the service Reverend Ritchie cast a handful of soil upon the box already lowered into the grave. She appeared to suddenly come to attention and then began to sob quietly, leaning upon Mrs. Ingram's arm.

The second came soon after when a small, dapper, handsome man pushed through those gathered behind Mrs. Lane and took her arm. She turned to see who it was and for a second seemed to shrink away from his touch. Ransom saw the stranger say something in a whisper, and Mrs. Lane then leaned into his arm. Minutes later, the rite completed, she allowed the man to lead her away from the grave.

Ransom assumed the stranger was a relative. But not for very long. As soon as the sexton began to shovel over the grave, he heard Mrs. Page's shocked voice:

"Do you see that?" She pointed her umbrella to the other side of the cemetery where Mrs. Lane and the stranger were stopped, evidently conferring, by her carriage.

"What?"

"That man. He has no business being here."

"Why? Who is he?"

"That dentist. That quack. Dinsmore."

Mrs. Page took Ransom's arm and firmly led him closer to Mrs. Lane. The stranger stood just behind her, leaning against the closed phaeton, with one patent leather boot lifted in back on a wheel spoke. He had an air of ownership, of very much exercising a right, as if, indeed, he had every business being there.

"Was he a friend of Lane's?" Ransom asked.

"I can't believe he was close enough to give himself such airs," Mrs. Page said. "He's a quack. He operates out of some rooms above a saloon in the South End. Ask Amasa. He'll tell you all about him."

His curiosity piqued, Ransom said, "I want to get a closer look. Go say something to her. I'll join you."

Augusta Page went up to Carrie Lane; and Ransom sidled alongside, using her bulk to hide how closely he was looking at the stranger.

Dinsmore was intent on rolling a cigarette, which his long fine fingers accomplished dexterously. Ransom remembered he was a dental surgeon, which accounted for the clean, manicured hands; however it didn't explain a large ruby ring on one index finger, or the extremely fine, eastern-cut clothing the man wore so jauntily. He wore a bowler hat, not a stetson variation, and he managed not only not to look absurd in it, but instead quite good. When he looked up and lighted the cigarette, Ransom's first impression returned—he was handsome, but in a pretty, feminine way: soft white complexion, curls of dark hair on either side of his face, a short immaculately clipped mustache, fine black eyebrows, and long eyelashes. But it was his eyes that most attracted. They were only medium sized and perfectly set on either side of a straight little nose, but they were of a blue that seemed to have had an electric current run through them. He didn't so much gaze as flash his eyes, and where they landed they stopped for a second as if taking in every detail of an image before moving on to the next. When they finally stopped at Ransom, the eyes seemed to cloud over for an instant as they rested, reminding Ransom of the almost invisible inner lids of a desert lizard's eyes.

Ransom nodded, forcing the man to do the same, then to look away to Mrs. Lane. There his eyes rested for a long time. Ransom too turned to her, as she now declined an offer of aid or company from Mrs. Page. Absently, she raised a hand to the back of her collar. Just then Dinsmore leaned forward and spoke.

"You must be quite fatigued." Taking Carrie Lane's arm, he turned to Mrs. Page. "Thank you for coming." Ransom was surprised by the deep bass of the man's voice, its unruffled tone of a doctor to a patient in duress.

Mrs. Ingram joined the two of them in the carriage a second later, and as the phaeton lurched forward, Dinsmore leaned into view, tipping his hat, and flashing one bright blue eye at Mrs. Page.

"The impudence!" she snorted and, gathering up one end of her dress, moved away.

"A dental surgeon, eh?" Ransom mused out loud.

"A low-life. What's he doing in those women's company?"

Ransom guessed the question to be rhetorical and remained silent all the way back to the Center City Board and Hotel.

———————————●———————————

"WHAT WAS HE DOING in those women's company?" She repeated her question the following day, after all the boarders had completed their large Sunday afternoon meal and the "family circle"—including Murcott, Ransom, and Isabelle Page, Augusta's grown daughter—had gathered as was customary in the large second-floor parlor. This time Mrs. Page's question was not rhetorical, but quite direct.

Ransom ignored her. He was engrossed in Frank Leslie's *Illustrated Weekly*, with its cover story of a huge fire that had swept through a Boston sweatshop killing dozens of teen-aged girls.

He knew that questions would continue to be asked about the Lanes for the next few weeks. Center City was astir with Henry Lane's death and all that pertained to it, and it would remain that way until the fall elections or some other topic replaced it.

In the parlors and dining rooms of Grant and Lincoln avenues, and in the shabby kitchens and back porches of the South End, people were busy remembering what Lane had said, or was reported to have said; what he had done, or planned to do or never thought to do—as Ransom knew, people always did when a well-known man died.

Reverend Ritchie had that Sunday morning preached a sermon using the words of Christ: "It is easier for a camel to pass through the eye of a needle than a rich man to find the way to heaven"—an undisguised reference to the deceased. And, in the storefront Baptist Church on Van Buren Avenue, the minister asked his shoddy workmen and half-black congregation to say a prayer for Lane's immortal soul, recalling to them how many jobs Lane had provided in his stables, his hotel, his business, his farm, his ranch, and day work loading and unloading dry goods and feed at the railroad station.

Rumors persisted about why Lane had killed himself or even whether he had killed himself. The other boarders had provided a good cross-section of public opinion on this at the dinner table. Some believed Lane had discovered an incurable, debilitating disease, and had ended it quickly rather than linger on an invalid. Others, who couldn't believe he had hanged himself, but who were aware of how ambitious Lane had been for innovations, believed he'd had a stroke cranking his horseless carriage into starting up—a lesson to others who supported such newfangled contraptions. Almost everyone had accepted his demise. He hadn't been a young man after all. Far younger among their own friends had died, and Lane had led a full rich life.

Almost everyone but Mrs. Page, it seemed, who still had questions to bother Ransom and Murcott with. She laid down her *Peterson's Fashion Catalogue* on the tea-cosy and asked, "Well? What do you make of it, Doctor?"

"It says here," Ransom interrupted, hoping to change the topic of conversation, "that the girls couldn't get out of the fifth-story windows because there were no outer stairwells. Two or three jumped, but of course they died."

"Was Simon Carr there?" she asked Ransom.

"Who? Where?"

"Old Simon Carr. Dinsmore's assistant. Was he at the stable Thursday night?"

"I don't know. I guess I don't know the man."

"Doctor?" she persisted. "Was he there?"

"No, and neither was that quack Dinsmore," Murcott said. He dropped his volume of Lucretius' *On the Nature of Things*—a dog-eared old copy he read whenever he had spare time, declaring it as up to date on science and medicine "as Darwin, Mendel, and all the rest of 'em since"—and lighted the ubiquitous pipe.

"What would Dinsmore be doing with Mrs. Lane?" she asked, having his attention.

"Who is this Dinsmore anyway?" Ransom finally asked.

"A quack!" Murcott said. "Calls himself a dental surgeon. He's no more a dental surgeon than you are."

Dinsmore had slipped into Center City with little publicity some three years before, the doctor filled in. With him had been his older, frowzy wife, and Simon Carr. All three had lived in a shanty among the black day workers by the railroad station. Then Dinsmore had set up an office above Bent's Saloon on Llewellen Street. Murcott heard he was treating the people of the neighborhood, putting it out that he was a fully educated and licensed general practitioner, which was hardly the case. The man had no medical or personal references that Murcott knew of, despite the reports that he did perform the most "Anti-Septic, Painless, Dental Surgery" in the "Newest French Manner," as the shingle outside his downstairs door said. In the last year or so, people of a better class—tradesmen and such—had gone to Dinsmore for their dental surgery and declared that it had been as completely painless as advertised. Which was probably how Henry

Lane had gone to him, poor as Murcott knew Lane's teeth to have been from sucking so much sugar beet as a child.

"A man with no degree, no past." Murcott declared in conclusion, "A fraud, I'm sure of it, and most certainly a scoundrel."

Which still didn't answer their landlady's question. But after a moment or two of silence and strenuous puffing of his brierwood the doctor suddenly said:

"Like her, like the quack's wife. That's how Lane looked."

"Dinsmore's wife?"

"Remember? She was found drowned in the public reservoir on the other side of shantytown. It was believed she'd been to the Bixby farm on some errand and slipped on the muddy banks on her way into town."

"That was last year, wasn't it?"

"Seven or eight months back. I was at Mrs. Bent's tending the youngest boy, who had the croup. I stopped in at the Baptist Church where the woman was laid out. She had that same look on the face—as though she hadn't put up any struggle while drowning, but had just let go of her life. A look of relief, I'd call it."

"From what I heard," Mrs. Page said, "it was a relief."

"Because of her husband?" Ransom asked.

"That I can't say. But from working so hard, and for so little. Always picking up and moving on every few years. She had been a fine lady. From Cincinnati, I believe, before she married him. Though it was hard to credit, looking at her. She was ill too. Consumption."

"Which *he* was treating?" Murcott asked.

"Who can say?"

"Perhaps it was a relief then," Ransom suggested, going back to his weekly.

"Well, Henry Lane didn't have consumption," Murcott declared, "nor any other illness either, despite what people say. I know. I examined the man myself not three months ago. As fit as he ever was."

"Calm and collected?" Ransom teased.

"Now don't start that again."

"I don't know how calm he was," Mrs. Page said. "Isabelle told me an incident last week concerning the Lanes I found curious. Why don't you tell the doctor, Belle?"

"I don't like to speak ill of the dead," the girl said, looking up from her crewelwork. At nineteen years old, Isabelle was a contrary mixture, all shyness and reserve among her elders, free-thinking and free-speaking among her friends.

"It's not speaking ill," her mother declared.

"If you say not," she said. "Last week Mrs. Lane came into the shop," Isabelle began. She worked as a notions clerk at Mrs. Brennan's on Center Street, the only store in town to sell tailored clothing cut from Sears' and Peterson's catalogue designs, as well as Mrs. Brennan's own "Paris Originals."

"She was with Mrs. Ingram as usual. I waited on them. They were there to pick up an amount of summer clothing Mrs. Lane had ordered made in February. Lightweight things, straw hats, open-work gloves. Lovely things. She buys as much every summer, I was told. Everything had been fitted the week before. There were a dozen or so boxfuls of different sizes, and I helped the ladies place them all into the back seat of her surrey when Mr. Lane came up to us on the street.

"He didn't say hello, which I thought unusual. He looked at all the boxes. 'What's all this?' he asked Mrs. Lane. 'More money wasted? You know we can't afford it.' "

"I could have died. Not only because of what he said, but how he said it. I never knew Mr. Lane to be discourteous, least of all to his wife. Why, he worshiped her."

"Was he agitated?" Ransom interrupted. "Nervous?"

"Oh, very. Angry too. He grew quite red in the face. I'm afraid Mrs. Lane did too—though from mortification I'm certain. But even more curious, his anger didn't last. Just as she was about to say a word to him, he stopped her. 'Don't mind me, dearest,' he said, completely changed. 'Buy all you want. Look as pretty as you ought to. I won't grudge it. It's too little and too late to make any difference now.' Well, you can imagine how that struck me."

"Did he appear to be confused?" Ransom asked. "As though he had other matters on his mind?"

"He must have. He just walked off without another word. Down Center Street and into the barbershop."

"The poor woman," her mother clucked. "With all he had."

"It was terrible," Isabelle said. "Just mortifying."

"Do you know if Lane was meeting his bills at the shop?" Ransom asked.

"You can be sure I asked Mrs. Brennan that very question. She laughed at me. She said Henry Lane always paid early and in full."

"That sounds right," the doctor said. "His credit was good all over. Any bank in the state honored his name. Caspar Bixby, old Bixby's boy, said he once rode the Topeka Line down to Austin, Texas, on Henry Lane's signature."

"Well, that *is* curious, then, isn't it?" Isabelle asked.

"Very," Murcott said.

Ransom held his peace. At the wake two days before, he had gently probed the exact nature of Henry Lane's finances, cornering first Cal Applegate, then Noah Mason, owner of the Mason Centennial Bank, founded 1876.

Lane's finances were excellent; his business booming; his savings large, his holdings secure: even his few speculations were bringing in revenue. Carrie Lane said her husband was a fastidious man, and that had been corroborated. No one had doubted it for over a decade.

But Ransom had discovered something else talking to the two men. Applegate mentioned in passing how Lane had only recently become extremely cautious in speculation, and how he had wanted to leave off all further investing in stocks and bonds. Mason confessed that Lane worried about how safe his bank was, going around it one day to point out how defenseless it would be in a large-scale attack. He'd fretted about the silver standard being discussed in the Federal Congress and had even talked about how much he might lose by the conversion from gold.

What was worse, Lane had never given more than the necessary practical thought to such matters before. Not only had his attitude changed, but he seemed to be worried all the time, calling on the banker and solicitor day, noon, or night with a new anxiety, a new worry, and never completely satisfied with any reassurances they gave.

Now Isabelle's anecdote seemed to confirm what Ransom had come to believe—in his last days Lane had believed he was bankrupt or about to be bankrupt.

That was what—so surprised Ransom had to read it twice—the letter Henry Lane had written to his wife in his dying moments had said. That was why Carrie Lane had been so hesitant to show it to anyone, why she had asked Ransom's utmost discretion. She believed that her husband was deluded, or deranged. Why else would he declare in writing that he had failed to provide her the rich, secure life he had promised her? Why else would he have called himself a ruined man?

What was Ransom to think of it? Given Lane's character, if he had believed himself ruined, he might have easily enough hanged himself. But what could make him think a thing so contrary to the known facts? Unless in the last few months he had gone insane. That would explain his anxieties, the way he'd suddenly begun pestering his solicitor and banker, his words to Mrs. Lane about her buying. It had happened to other men—though not so quickly—not in a few months, but over years, as they grew miserly and misanthropic. Lane might have changed that quickly if he'd had a tumor in his brain—the doctor had explained to Ransom—putting pressure on it all the time. But Lane had died without any tumor. He had been fit and healthy.

It was curious, almost unprecedented. The sort of thing that Ransom loved to cogitate about in his quieter moments, like freak storms in which lightning struck two people, killing one and not scratching the other at all; like the two-headed cows shown at the county fair; like anything eerie, out of the usual which had to be swilled around in one's mind, sipped at like a fine French brandy.

"There's one good thing to be said about Henry Lane's passing on," Mrs. Page said now, interrupting Ransom's reverie. "When Judge Dietz steps down from office, there will be no one to oppose our Mr. Ransom from taking it."

"Whoa! Hold on now!" he protested. "Henry Lane had no intention of becoming county judge that I heard of."

"No. But if he had a mind to it—and you know he had a hand in everything that happened here—someone else would be put up and run in the election."

"Well, that's what an election is for," Ransom argued. "To select the best man."

"Don't be foolish. You know as well as I what elections are like in this town," she said. "You've talked about it enough. This time it will be a real election."

"If I decide to run for it," Ransom said, "and if—which we don't at all know except for the rumor of it—if Judge Dietz decides to retire. Meanwhile I'm not going to think about it. I'll have more than enough to think about in the next few months with that land-grant business coming to a head up at the capitol. I might even have to be out of town a month or more to make sure the case is handled properly. That is more important to me than any pie-in-the-sky judgeships."

"I hope it doesn't take so long you decide to stay at Lincoln," Augusta said.

"Don't you worry. No matter how long it takes. I'll be back and I'll just go on living here in the Center City Board and Hotel until Isabelle here has children her own age."

"If only for the cooking," the doctor put in.

"Not to mention the fine feminine company," Ransom added.

"Georgia charm closes the conversation," Mrs. Page said, not displeased, "as it usually does around here."

She went to the window and pushed the second pane out. It made little difference. It was warm and still outside, silent but for the crickets' mechanical whir. Fresh young leaves from the big front-yard elms were bursting into leaf. New-mown grass and sap rising. A fresh smell, like beginnings, like new things.

"It's almost summer," she said.

"Soon it'll be too hot here," Ransom said, "and we'll have to sit on the outside porch with fly swatters."

"I wonder if Henry Lane thought he'd die before the summer came," she mused.

"Now, Augusta," the doctor said gently. "Don't you go getting melancholy on us. By autumn you'll have forgotten all about Henry Lane. We all will."

"I suppose," she sighed.

Not all of us, Ransom said to himself. I won't have forgotten. There are too many questions, too many untied ends, more than usually occur when a man dies suddenly. No, I won't forget it. Nor, I think, will Carrie Lane.

Thinking of her, he couldn't help but picture her as he had last seen her, standing at the curbstone talking to Mrs. Page, in front of the glossy black phaeton. And next to her, a blur, a sort of shadow.

"Musing?" Isabelle asked timorously.

"A little. Now, that's a fine piece of crewelwork. When are you going to make a motto for me to hang on my wall?"

"Which one would you like?" she asked, blushing.

BOOK TWO

The Descent–
Autumn 1899

M URCOTT STILL HADN'T ARRIVED with the shay by the time the Topeka Line Local pulled out of the station.

Ransom stood for another minute at the deserted platform, and leaving the large brass-studded and black leather trunk where the conductor had helped lift it off the train, he picked up his lighter traveling bag and went to sit on the bench in the shade of the overhang.

It was three fifteen in the afternoon by his vest-pocket watch. As usual, the train had been some ten minutes late arriving in Center City. It wasn't like the doctor to be unpunctual. Perhaps a patient was keeping him—Ransom knew how some of the older women patients liked to drag out a simple office visit forever. Especially if no one had been in the waiting room when they had gone in.

If it weren't such a stifling hot September day, Ransom would have walked the half dozen blocks to the Center City Board and Hotel. But it was all he could do to just sit down and look at the heat rising in waves along the horizon of fields on the open side of the station. It had been a sweltering five-hour ride in the Pullman down from the capitol. He hadn't gotten much sleep the night before, having to attend the large testimonial dinner given in his honor. He was hot and thirsty, and a thin layer of yellow dust covered every inch of him, not only his clothing, but his hands too, and, he was certain, his face.

No one else had gotten off at Center City. There was no life to be seen anywhere in the vicinity of the station: no one on the platform, no children waiting to bother the locomotive engineer with endless questions. The stationmaster and ticket seller weren't even there. The roll-gate windows of the little office were shut. As though it were a ghost town.

A hell of a way to be welcomed home after being gone four months! Not that he'd expected a brass band. But he had at least expected the wry, spectacled little figure of his friend, muttering at the world's vices and follies from within the safety of his professional excellence and his eternal, shiny-sleeved, black frock coat.

Ransom remembered he had brought some lemon drops as he had boarded the train in Lincoln, and searching in one vest pocket he found the cone of white paper they'd been wrapped in. They were stuck together with the heat, half melted—but refreshingly tangy once he had popped one in his mouth.

Not a person to be seen—not that one could see much from here anyway. The station faced away from the town, not toward it. Still . . . he'd wait another minute more. Amasa might be playing with his microscope up in the room on the second floor he'd set up as a sort of laboratory, looking at those animaculae, or whatever he called them, that he insisted caused illness. He must be up there, so involved he'd forgotten Ransom.

There was a tiny figure running up one side of the tracks, coming from the south. A child. He'd fall over running in heat like this. A breezeless, plains-style scorcher; worse today than it would have been in mid-July. The month he'd expected to spend at the capitol had stretched to four, but nothing seemed changed. What had he expected to change? Nothing had much changed in Center City in the nine years he'd been here.

Then the running figure was much closer—climbing up the concrete platform ramp—and familiar too: Nate Page.

The boy shot over to where Ransom sat, and with one glance at the trunk upended some feet away, began sputtering something.

"Hold on, boy," Ransom said. "Catch your breath first."

"Doctor . . . can't come . . . emergency . . . called out as he was on . . . his way . . . I followed him . . . then came here fast as I could . . . up to the Lane house . . ."

"Who's ill? Mrs. Lane?"

"No . . . Mrs. Ingram . . . taken suddenly . . . taken real bad . . . yelling, carrying on in the middle of Grant Street."

"That's very unlike her."

"That's what the doctor said."

"Well, I guess there's no shay for my trunk here, then," Ransom said, getting up slowly, seeing he would have to walk home. "I suppose I'll just leave it here and come back later."

They walked out to Emerson Street. No one was there either. The boy tagged along.

"You see the stationmaster?" Ransom asked.

"No, sir."

"Well, let's go then."

He strode faster now, feeling a slight twinge of anxiety. Mrs. Ingram, eh? What was that all about? He'd felt irritated all the way down on the train. Couldn't have said why. Like having a splinter under your fingernail you could barely see to get at.

As they crossed Williams Street, the boy spotted the stationmaster. Still wearing the ebony eyeshade on his forehead that all but hid the upper half of his face, the man was standing just outside the open doorway leading into the offices of the Lane Dry Goods Store. He was gesticulating and shouting. Ransom couldn't make out his words. But they didn't sound peaceable.

"Pardon me, Mr. Maxwell."

Maxwell turned, still annoyed, then cracked a half-smile. "Day, Mr. Ransom. Didn't know you was back in town."

"Just arrived. I'm leaving a trunk on your platform. See that it doesn't get sent out to Oregon, will you?"

"Will do." Maxwell turned, looked back at the office doorway with a scowl, and began limping away toward the station.

"Pardon me," a voice said, preceding a figure out of the shadow of the office.

Ransom turned to the voice. It was that Dinsmore fellow. Dressed as nattily as he'd been at Henry Lane's funeral: bowler hat and all.

"Yes?"

"I couldn't help but overhear that you have some luggage at the station."

"That's right. I was to be met by a shay."

Now Dinsmore emerged from the darkness, at the same time

tilting his hat to shade the sun's glare from his eyes. Even in the shadow of the hat brim, they were a sparkling blue. He didn't look hot. Cool. Neat.

"Perhaps I can be of some assistance. There's a buckboard on the side ready to go with some other lading. We could easily fit your trunk on."

Before Ransom could thank the man and tell him not to bother, Dinsmore called out:

"Millard! Move that buckboard over here!"

A sweating, mahogany-skinned black, dressed only in heavy oversized denims, appeared around the side of the building.

"Sir?"

"This gentleman has a trunk at the railroad station. Bring it to where he lives."

The black man looked blank for a second, then disappeared, returning a moment later leading a large buckboard drawn by two horses.

"I'm much obliged to you . . ." Ransom began.

"No trouble at all. Dinsmore's my name. And you're Mr. Ransom, the attorney."

"That's correct."

"Always willing to do a turn for one of our more prominent citizens." Dinsmore put out a hand, and Ransom took it, surprised by the softness of the skin—like a woman's, treated with cold creams and lotions it seemed—and, contrarily, the firmness of his grip.

"Much obliged," Ransom repeated. He gave Millard directions for delivering the trunk. When he turned back again, Dinsmore had disappeared back into the shadows of the office.

"He work there now?" Ransom asked the boy as they walked on.

"I suppose he runs it."

"Runs it? When did that happen?"

"Don't know. Ask Ma."

First with Carrie Lane at the funeral, now here at the Lane Dry Goods Store, giving orders. What was that all about? Ransom thought about the man for another minute or so. He seemed obliging enough, willing to be of help to others. Still, what was a dental surgeon doing managing a dry-feed business?

He hadn't reached a conclusion when the familiar three-story corner building of the Center City Board and Hotel for Gentlemen came into sight. There! That wasn't changed. That was as it ought to be. The square roof with its large top-story gables. The wide roofed-over veranda, a dozen stone steps up from Williams Street. The big trees in the front yard looking a bit withered with the heat, but still leafy, thick, green. Ransom's pace quickened seeing it. When he entered and dropped his hand-held bag in the front hallway, Nate disappeared.

Late-afternoon sunlight checkered the floors and table of the big dining room.

"Everybody gone fishing today?" he called out from the dining room doorway, taking off his hat and jacket.

Mrs. Page turned around. She was red-faced from work, and held up two hands covered to the elbows with flour.

"There you are! Did Nate find you?"

"Finally. The trunk is being sent over with one of the Lane Feed and Grain wagons."

"Well, come here and I'll hug you. You've been gone so long I almost forgot what you looked like."

"I'll pass up being covered with flour on top of dust, if you don't mind," Ransom said. But seeing her good-natured, beaming face, he went closer and allowed her to peck his cheek.

"You're looking tired," she said. "Thinner too. Don't they feed people up at Lincoln?"

"Not as well as you do."

"Well, come into the kitchen. I'll fix you something."

"As soon as I change. I feel like a plaster-of-Paris statue in this gear."

"Your rooms are just as they were," she said, still looking at him fondly, as though he were a long-lost child. "Except that I dusted it all today. Hurry on down, I'll fix you something nice."

Once he had washed up and changed into a light seersucker suit, Ransom felt much better. Mrs. Page had cleaned herself up too, as though he were company, Ransom thought.

Despite the hot weather, she'd been baking, and the kitchen was so sweltering with it, they moved onto the back porch, where it was a bit breezier and where the sun couldn't reach them. They'd just settled into big wicker-work chairs, when Nate appeared with a pitcher covered over with a cloth napkin—lemonade. In a few minutes, Ransom felt cool, relaxed, at home, almost as though he had never left Center City at all. They sipped their drinks, pulling the liquid tartness over shaved ice, and were silent.

"You glad you went to Lincoln?" Mrs. Page suddenly asked. "Amasa said you've done well there."

"If I may say so, without meaning to boast."

He went on to explain how he and another attorney representing the adjacent county had joined forces with the state's own lawyers to sue the Federal Government against selling certain of their lands for livestock use only. Now these areas—including a large tract due west of Center City—would be opened to new settlers as farmland, the land sold by the state and irrigated with its help. It had been a complex suit, involving much work of an investigatory nature—which Ransom had personally done—and which everyone assured him had won the suit. He was proud of that personal achievement. He was equally proud of the friendships he'd made with several legislators and state government officials, now important allies. It didn't hurt to have such allies, he said, and should he ever decide later on to enter politics. . . . But that was as far as he allowed that topic to go with Mrs. Page. All she had to know was that he'd been involved in a landmark case with many implications, that he'd helped win it and done well by it, and that he was glad to be back home in Center City.

"So am I glad," she declared. "And Amasa's so proud of you. Been telling everyone about you. A shame he couldn't come to meet you. But he'll be back soon enough."

That led her into detailing all that had passed among the people they knew in town since he had been gone. Most of it was of the birth, marriage, new-barn, new-field, new-store variety. Banal enough, and comforting to Ransom for that very reason.

But the morning's anxiety he'd felt hovered somewhere in the background of it all: causeless, senseless.

They were interrupted by the arrival of the trunk. Millard carried it up the stairs and was repaid by a shiny new quarter dollar, which occasioned many thank you's. After he'd gone, Ransom explained:

"The new manager of Lane's Feed and Grain sent it over. Very obliging fellow."

"Dinsmore?" she asked.

"I believe that's his name. He been there long?"

"There and everywhere else too."

"Where else?"

"The Lane Hotel. The Dry Goods Store. Everywhere you can name."

"You mean he's running all of the Lane businesses? Wasn't he a dental surgeon?"

"And the ranch and the farms too. And . . ." she hesitated, biting her lip to silence herself.

"And . . . ?" he prodded her.

"I don't like to talk about other folks' business, James. But some matters are, well, just not right."

"You mean because he was a dental surgeon?"

"It's more than that. He lived out at the Lane ranch all summer. He and that old man who worked for him, Simon Carr. That wasn't so bad, even though everyone knew he spent most of the time at her house."

"Whose house? Mrs. Lane's?"

She didn't answer directly. "At least that was showing some propriety. She's only a widow a few months, you know. And she's not a girl any more. But at the end of August, he just plain moved in. Closed down the rooms on Winter Lane, and moved right in. He lives there now. Why, even an Emerson Street seamstress would know better than to break a year's mourning like that. It's a scandal!"

"You mean to say Mrs. Lane is keeping company with this Dinsmore?"

Mrs. Page almost shook her head with frustration at his lack of comprehension. "You make it sound like two children who don't know any better, James. He's with her all the time now. Why, at church this Sunday, she and Harriet Ingram and he . . ."

"Well, if Mrs. Ingram was with them, I don't see what's so wrong about it," he reasoned.

"It means nothing that she was with them. It's a sin and it's a shame and I'm surprised Reverend Ritchie didn't throw them out of church. I would have."

Ransom saw there was no way of extracting more information from Mrs. Page without getting more of her outraged sense of propriety as well. He'd ask the doctor about it later on.

But as he let the subject drop, and while Mrs. Page talked on and on about other matters pertaining more closely to herself and her boarders, he couldn't help but think about it.

Ransom had assumed nothing had much altered in Center City while he'd been away. Instead it seemed as though a great deal had changed. Not openly, perhaps, but just beneath the surface. . . . He wondered if that was what he'd intuited, coming down from Lincoln. Could that explain his anxiety, his irritation? Or had it merely been not enough sleep, too many brandies and cigars the night before, and the interminable, stifling train ride?

He decided he would call on Carrie Lane some time shortly. It would be a natural enough thing to do: he hadn't seen her since her bereavement. A purely social call, asking after her, and —he had to admit—to see for himself what all this talk about the dental surgeon was. If Mrs. Page wasn't jumping to conclusions based on rumors . . . after all, it was one thing to hire such a man to manage a business; she couldn't be expected to do it herself . . . but, Mrs. Page evidently thought it went further than business. It was even possible that Carrie Lane didn't know how people were talking about her, that Dinsmore had moved into her house to be near for business matters and. . . . Not upstairs, of course. He couldn't believe that. Probably in one of the spare bedrooms at the back of the house, by the kitchen, near the servants' rooms.

Ransom tried to picture Carrie Lane, to bring her into focus, and by seeing her in his mind's eye, to see for himself if all that Mrs. Page said wasn't just gossip and rumor. No sooner had he gotten an image of Mrs. Lane, however, than he saw Dinsmore too, one boot raised on a wagon-wheel spoke, rolling a cigarette, and those eyes flashing like the shutter of a camera.

"That sounds like Amasa now," Mrs. Page said, shattering Ransom's disturbing experiment in visualization. "We're back here!" she called.

The doctor's heavily lined face lighted up immediately. After a half hour's greetings, apologies, and small talk, Mrs. Page went into the house, and Ransom broached the subject that had intrigued him from the moment he'd arrived in Center City that day.

"What's all this about Mrs. Ingram?"

Murcott frowned. "I had her take a sedative."

"What was wrong with her?"

"Who's to say. When I got there she was crying like her best friend had just died, rushing back and forth, repeating some nonsense about not knowing what she was going to do next."

"What had she done?"

"According to the Mason's gardener, she suddenly started acting like a crazy woman. One minute she was down by the well near the back of the house drawing water, the next she was screaming and running out into Grant Street, stopping traffic there. She'd been brought back into the house and quieted a little by the time I got there, but she was quite upset. Hysterical is what that Viennese psychologist Breuer calls it. A classic case of effect with no apparent cause."

"There must have been *some* cause?"

"Nothing I could make out examining the woman. I don't know, James. Could have been she was out too long and got a touch of sunstroke wearing all that heavy black clothing. Might have been her stays were too tight. Might be anything. Who's to say? She'll be here tomorrow morning. I asked her to come in for a more thorough examination. The woman is frustrated, is what I believe. Too many years without a man, if you ask me, and not such an uncommon problem either. That Frenchman,

Charcot, did studies that suggested it was responsible for most female hysteria and I think . . . but here's Augusta. We'll discuss this later, James."

Mrs. Page came out to refresh their glasses of lemonade. When she'd gone in again, Murcott said in a lower voice, "Some folks say she *has* got a man. That dental surgeon. 'Course I don't know that for sure, you understand. And I have no intentions of asking either."

"And Mrs. Lane? How is she?"

"Well enough, it seemed to me. A mite sad still. That's to be expected. She doted on that husband of hers. And now he's left her with all this business a woman can't know how to deal with. I wouldn't be surprised if it all collapses in a year, with this mountebank in charge of it. Now, I've talked enough. Tell me all about Lincoln. I hear the capitol building is finally completed. What's it look like?"

———————————————●———————————————

RANSOM PLANNED TO DEVOTE all of the following morning to reviewing the backlog of work that had accrued while he'd been in Lincoln. This turned out to be a more considerable task than he had expected. Only a few of the envelopes and papers stacked neatly upon his desk every day by Isabelle Page referred to county prosecution matters. The bulk of it was from his private clientele. Writs, deeds, mortgages, bank loans, suits to be filed, subpoenas to be answered—it was a formidable testament to how much the town was growing, enough paperwork to last until Christmas. He was surprised that more of his regular clients hadn't gone with their business to Cal Applegate. But why would they? Most of them were tradesmen and small farmers, and Applegate had a reputation as a "rich man's lawyer," not interested in the smaller pieces of business that, along with his small salary as county prosecutor, were Ransom's bread and butter.

By eleven o'clock, the day was proving as much of a scorcher as the one before. Ransom took off his waistcoat, rolled up his shirtsleeves, and undid his shirt collar and tie. It wasn't much help. The one open window in the office provided no circulation, so he opened the office door that led directly to the foot of the stairs. Now, anyone coming or going in the Center City Board and Hotel could look in and disturb him, but it was worth it for the breeze.

He was in the midst of a particularly complex land deed when there was a timid knock on the open door. He assumed it was Mrs. Page or Isabelle. Without looking up, he said:

"Come in. I'll be with you shortly."

Someone did come in and immediately sat down in the straight-backed chair by the doorway. Ransom reread the questionable phrase again and again; and finally penciled a clarification into the margin. Then he pushed it aside and looked to his visitor.

It was Mrs. Ingram.

"Pardon me, ma'am," he said, rising for his waistcoat and collar. "I wasn't expecting company today."

She stood up too, but said nothing to stop him from hastily trying to dress himself. "I was downstairs. In Dr. Murcott's office. I thought . . . well, I saw your shingle on the door outside the house, and I thought . . . I see that you're busy."

"Not at all. Please have a seat. I hope you are quite recovered."

"Yes, thank you."

"This chair would be more convenient if we are to talk," he said. She had been about to sit by the door again. Instead, he motioned her to a large horsehair-covered chair. She sat down stiff-backed, pale, tired; yes, quite exhausted-looking. Meanwhile, Ransom snapped together the collar and wrapped on the tie. He wondered about putting on a jacket and decided against it. "You'll pardon my casual attire, I hope. The heat, you know."

"It does seem awfully warm for this time of year," she said. But she didn't seem to suffer from it. From the little pork-pie hat that nestled atop the mound of her abundant light hair, to the longsleeved buttoned-to-the-neck pale blue cotton dress, down to her twenty-laced boots, she seemed unaware of the blazing temperature.

Ransom went through his papers, looking for a blank sheet of foolscap in case notes were required. When he glanced up again, she was looking aside. Yes, she was quite pale, not so much ill as . . . well, as distracted. She didn't seem herself at all.

"Now," he said. "How may I be of assistance?"

She turned back to him, startled. "Quite well, thank you. Dr. Murcott suggested it was merely the sun being so hot and all."

"Of course," he replied, bewildered. "I hope all is well with you and your employer, despite the tragic loss you both sustained."

"Loss? Oh, you mean Mr. Lane. Yes. As well as could be expected I suppose. I don't know that I ever really recovered from the shock of finding . . . the doctor thinks that it must have been such a recall that yesterday made me . . . but I'm quite well now and I don't believe I'll suffer a relapse. Might we . . . ? I know it is very warm today, but might we speak more privately?"

She was so distracted, he was curious. Once the outer door was closed he asked if that would do.

"Yes. I think so." But she glanced about as if she weren't sure.

"And Mrs. Lane?" he asked. "How is she finding her new situation? I'm sure your being with her is a great source of strength and consolation."

"I suppose. It's of her, actually, that I've come to speak. Not that I specifically came for that purpose, you understand. But being downstairs anyway and so near . . ." She trailed off.

Ransom remained silent, waiting for her to go on. When she didn't, he prompted her. "It must be a great burden, with all the enterprises Mr. Lane was involved in. More than enough for any woman, I should think. But I'm certain assistance has been found to manage it all. From what I understand, Mrs. Lane has already secured such assistance. I speak of Mr. Dinsmore."

Her air of distraction vanished in an instant. "It's actually of him that I wanted to speak to you," she whispered intensely, suspicious still that someone might be listening.

"I'm afraid I don't know the man," Ransom went on, "but if I may be of help . . ."

"He's managing it all," she whispered. "It's not right how

much she's put into his hands. The hotel. The farms. The stables. The stores and warehouse. Everything.''

"I trust he knows how much effort that will entail. It certainly kept Henry Lane busy enough."

"He can handle it," she said with a private laugh. "Oh, he can handle that and plenty more too. But ought he be doing it?"

"That I can't answer. I know his previous occupation . . .''

"She's put it all into his hands! I know she didn't know what else to do. What with no family here to turn to. All she has is a mother and her sister's husband. But they're miles away. In New York, in the East. Don't you think she ought not have done it?''

Ransom wondered what Mrs. Ingram was saying. Was she sincerely concerned for Mrs. Lane's interests? Was she jealous of this Dinsmore fellow? Or what? He couldn't comment until he knew. He had to tread carefully, and try to discover what was really bothering her.

"I couldn't really say, ma'am. I'm not familiar enough with either the business or with Mr. Dinsmore's capabilities. I do know that someone was needed. I can't see Mrs. Lane prepared to suddenly deal with it all herself."

"I agree. I'm not a feminist, you know."

"Then, what . . .''

"I don't know," she sighed. "It's simply that he seems to have such an influence over her."

"Over Mrs. Lane? What kind of influence?"

She sighed again. "I can't exactly say. But it's uncanny. I see how she's changed because of it. Not that she isn't still the sweetest and loveliest lady in Center City . . .''

"Perhaps you ascribe the wrong reasons. Perhaps her bereavement continues strongly. It had to have been shocking, coming so unexpectedly."

"Perhaps," she said, sounding unpersuaded by his argument. Then: "No. It's him. It's his influence."

"If he's helping to manage her affairs, I would hope he had some influence," Ransom reasoned.

"Yes. But so much?"

"How much?" He had to ask.

She began to say something, but stopped herself. "Perhaps it was wrong of me to come here. I don't want you to think that she sent me here."

"I understand. But, if you wish to enlist my aid, you must be a bit more specific, Mrs. Ingram. If, for example, you believe that Mr. Dinsmore is taking advantage of Mrs. Lane's ignorance in business . . . if he's, say, embezzling from her, or mismanaging in such a way that . . ."

"No. No," she interrupted him. "I'm certain all he does is well within the law."

"Then what is it you believe of him?"

"He's ambitious. Very ambitious. I know. I've watched him. I've seen him."

"Ambition is commendable in a man, so long as he doesn't break any laws. We depend upon great ambition for the development of the nation."

She stared at him then, her calf-eyes seemed to look not at him, but just beyond. Her lips were curled up in scorn.

"I thought you were her friend!" she whispered.

That took him aback.

"I respect and admire Mrs. Lane, naturally. All of Center City does. But I'm afraid I can't claim I was either Mr. or Mrs. Lane's personal friend."

"The worse for her. She could use a good friend now."

"Hasn't she a good enough one in you?"

"Not good enough. Not enough for *him.*"

Ransom tried another tack. "Have you been to see Mr. Applegate? I believe he is still Mrs. Lane's attorney."

"Applegate? He'll do whatever the money that pays him says to do."

"You take a poor view of our legal fraternity, I fear."

"I didn't until now. Nor, of you," she said bitterly, and stood up. "That's changed."

Even more puzzled, Ransom stood too. "Believe me, Mrs. Ingram, I'd like to be able to help you. But unless I know of some specific misdeed or broken law, I can't see how I can."

"That's how he will get his way," she said in a furious whisper. "Because none of you sees beyond your little laws, beyond your papers and your dispositions and your technicalities. You have no vision."

His face flushed. But he said, "If you'd like, I'll talk to Mrs. Lane."

"She'll say nothing. He has her. Has her completely. No. I *was* wrong to have come here. It's best that you forget it altogether. Good day."

"May I see you down?"

"Don't bother. Go back to your books and papers, to your orderly little laws that won't make a bit of difference when you most need them." She flung open the door and left.

Stunned, he followed her. Halfway down the stairs she turned to him, grabbed his shirt and whispered:

"Make certain to tell no one I've been to see you. Don't tell her. And especially don't you breathe a word of it to him!"

———————●———————

AFTER MRS. INGRAM HAD GONE, Ransom went back to his desk. But however much he attempted to concentrate, he found he couldn't. Her words—in fact the entire encounter—kept returning bit by bit, nagging at him with its strange tone and curious urgency. He tried shrugging it off, tried to think she was merely jealous of Dinsmore, afraid he might be invading her managerial precincts in the Lane house, of having Mrs. Lane's confidence. That must be all it was.

But if that were all, why would Mrs. Ingram come to see him? Though she obviously didn't have Cal Applegate's ear, he was the person she ought to see. Then too, Mrs. Ingram had intimated a closeness between Mrs. Lane and Ransom that simply did not exist. Or had Mrs. Lane talked of him? That took another five minutes of distracted thinking. When it seemed to be going too far, Ransom steeled himself and went back to work. He stopped again, though. What if Mrs. Ingram were—well, what if, for whatever reason, she were going mad? Her speech had been disconnected, even irrelevant at times. She had seemed almost obsessed. Could the shock of finding Lane's body have set off some lurking derangement that had existed all the while? Murcott would be able to tell him. He'd seen her earlier.

But the doctor wasn't in his office when Ransom bounded downstairs to talk to him. The waiting room was open, but the surgical and examination rooms were locked.

Back in his office again, Ransom heard noise outside his doorway: Mrs. Page, dustcloths in hand. She stopped in to ask when he would have lunch. He was the only boarder to eat in that day.

"Where's Amasa gone to?" he asked.

"Out of town all afternoon. To Swedeville. He goes every Wednesday to look after those folks."

She referred to some twenty small poor farms owned by recent immigrants, about fifteen miles west of Center City. Some of the farmers scarcely spoke English. They would come into town once a month or so to buy and sell goods, and from all appearances most of them were barely eking out an existence. Murcott tended them free of charge—another example of the many contrarieties in his nature.

Ransom said he would lunch when it was convenient for her. That was a half hour later. Afterward, refreshed, he was able to return to work and to put Mrs. Ingram's visit out of his mind. At four thirty, he stood up, stretched, and decided he needed a rest. His eyes were no longer focusing from reading so much finely printed legal copy. A walk might rest his mind and exercise his limbs.

North of the Page Board and Hotel, three grassy blocks formed the central plaza of the town. Ransom crossed Center Street and strolled beneath huge old elm trees. Judge Dietz's house on the corner of Center and Dakota Streets had been whitewashed recently: it looked larger now. Across from it, the line of small shops seemed unchanged. Lane's Hotel, on the next corner, was still the highest building on the plaza—five stories of it. But the needle-shaped steeple of the Episcopal Church opposite was almost as tall. The whole plaza was dominated by the Greek-Revival–style courthouse, the only edifice fronting the green on McKinley Avenue: handsome, cool-white, and most imposing.

No, nothing seemed changed at all. The town was as clean and quietly handsome as it had been some nine years before when he'd first come there to visit Amasa Murcott, whom Ransom had met in Chicago. The doctor had talked of Center City as if it were Paradise. He'd exaggerated, of course. Enthusiastic as he sometimes was, he often did exaggerate. But he hadn't been that far off the mark. Ransom had visited Murcott for several weeks back then, and a year later had resettled here. If Center City wasn't Eden, it was the first place Ransom had felt comfortable in since he'd been a child. The pace of life and the closeness of the people were similar to what Georgia had been like before the war. He'd never really liked living in cities—and Washington D.C. had quickly grown into a city in the ten years Ransom had lived there, as a law student and apprentice attorney. Chicago was the worst, with its industry and its smelting, with its meat-packing stench filling the air weeks at a time. Slums on the South Side. Tenements that seemed to stretch for miles. No, Center City was his home now. He was pleased with it—especially freshly returned from Lincoln, which seemed to be on its way to becoming a smaller, uglier Chicago.

Ransom crossed McKinley Avenue with these thoughts in mind. Floyd was on his usual perch—the courthouse bench—a copy of the Center City *Star* in his hands.

"Not much changed in town since I've been gone," Ransom said.

The older man was delighted to have company. He dropped his newspaper, ready for a good, long jaw.

"Not much a-tall. If you've been here as long as I have, you'd seen this town sprout like alfalfa in April."

"I guess it doesn't make that much difference that Henry Lane passed on."

Floyd pulled a calico handkerchief out of his pocket and tugged at his nose with it.

"I guess," he said. "Yes. Everything about the same. One man don't make a hell of a difference, you know."

"That's true. I understand some stranger is managing all of Lane's property these days."

"Stranger?"

"Name of Dinsmore."

"Ain't a stranger. He's been in town for years. Was a dental surgeon, down on the South End."

"So I've heard. What kind of fellow is he?"

Floyd narrowed his eyes. "No one much knows."

"In three years?"

"Well, then, I don't much know."

"Who would know?"

"Can't say. Kept pretty much to himself, this dental surgeon. I guess Jack Bent would know. Why you interested?"

Ransom knew better than to be open with Floyd. "Curiosity. After all, a man comes from nowhere into managing all that much. Makes you kind of wonder."

"I thought maybe you wanted to know for some prosecuting business," Floyd said, squinting again.

"Not at all. But it is a little bit curious, don't you think? And what's even more curious is that old Floyd, who can tell you what kind of inexpressibles most of the ladies in town are wearing, can't tell me anything about him."

"I ain't never heard a word against him. 'Coursen he'll be making some enemies now with the Lane properties in his hands. Of that I can assure you."

He already had, Ransom wanted to say: Mrs. Ingram.

"Nat'rally Jack Bent could tell you better than me," Floyd went on. "That office Dinsmore had was right above the Bent saloon in the corner of Van Buren Avenue."

Ransom decided he just might go have a little talk with Jack Bent. Not for a while, of course. He didn't want to arouse any further suspicions in Floyd. The old man had his nose in too much business around town already. So Ransom changed the topic for another, then another, until he was certain Floyd had forgotten it. When Ransom got up to leave, the old man said:

"Nice fellow, that Dinsmore."

"You've met?"

"Met? Why I went to him to have a tooth pulled last year. He's an easterner, you know. Though I can't tell from where by the way he talks. Educated too. Uses big words I never heard before. Soft hands. Like he never lifted a bale of hay or put a foot to the shareplow. Most accommodating though."

"Which tooth?"

"The one that was right here," Floyd said, lifting one side of his mouth with an index finger, and revealing soft whitish gums with a few rotten stumps.

"Looks like you may be going again," Ransom said.

"Hell, I don't mind. It didn't hurt at all. Better than that old butcher of a barber who took out t'other one. Why he'd wrench at me for an hour, and I'd have to keep my mouth stuffed with cotton for a week with all the bleeding. This here tooth came out like it was walking out to take the air. Not enough blood from it to cover a fingernail. Anti-Septic too. He swabbed at it with some nasty kind of lotion."

That must be the painless dentistry Dinsmore's shingle advertised. "You mean it didn't hurt at all?" Ransom asked.

"Not once he was pulling on it. It sure hurt plenty all week before that. Ask that old Dutch bastard at the grocery store. I took a bottle of brandy a day for it."

"I suppose I wouldn't feel much pain either with a bottle of brandy in me."

"Could use some right now," Floyd said, crackling and fingering one rheumy eye. " 'Cept I'm off it for a whiles. But it 'tweren't the brandy, I tell you. That dentist made it so's I didn't notice a thing. Yes, sir, that's what I call dental surgery. Mark now, you go to see him if you've got teeth trouble."

He had to call out his last words, as Ransom had already waved good-bye and was threading through the carriages and wagons on Lincoln Avenue. One brightly painted lorry, going north— a milk truck—stopped for Ransom to cross, then the driver waved him over.

It was Sam Burgess, a dairy farmer who delivered his own products to customers' homes.

"Hello, Burgess."

"Got to be careful, Mr. Ransom. Otherwise they'll knock you over."

"Thanks for the tip."

"Want a ride?" Burgess offered.

"No, thanks. I'm going the opposite way."

Burgess looked sheepish. "Actually, I wanted to talk to you. About making out my will."

"Why don't you come by my office some time," Ransom suggested.

"I keep meaning to. But I never can seem to find the time to do it. You wouldn't have a minute now, would you?"

People behind the milk truck were shouting for it to move.

"I'll just be going up to the Hill to make a few deliveries," Burgess prodded. "Why not git in?"

Ransom didn't hesitate now. He knew he would be able to do business with Burgess as effectively this way as with the two of them sitting in an office. And in the few minutes it took them to reach the High Street delivery alley they had more or less concluded their business—all but the drawing up and signing of the necessary documents. They were at the Masons' house now.

"Just one more," Burgess said, "and I'm done. I'll drive you down to Miz Page's."

"Don't bother. I think I'll take this opportunity to pay a long overdue social call," Ransom said. He had that very moment decided to see Carrie Lane, to find out exactly what all this fuss about Mrs. Ingram and the general manager was about.

He walked with Burgess up to the kitchen door, was let in by the cook, and his presence immediately forwarded to Mrs. Lane. The housekeeper didn't seem to be at home today: he hoped Mrs. Ingram was out and would remain out until he had gone.

Once again, he was led into the large formal parlor to wait for Carrie Lane. He hadn't been there since the day that Lane's body had been on view. The room seemed unchanged, as stuffy and overdecorated as in the past. This time, however, he only had to wait a minute before she came in, wearing a tan smock over her dress, removing a large, rough-textured gardener's glove to take Ransom's hand.

"Pardon my apparel, Mr. Ransom. I wasn't expecting visitors."

"Pardon me for calling on you so precipitately," he replied. "I hope I haven't interrupted you."

"No," she lied politely.

"It seems," he said, looking at her gloves, "that I have."

"Well," she laughed a little, "then I admit it. I've been in the conservatory. The plants need such looking after."

"I have no intention of keeping you from them, then. The Lane conservatory is the most famous in the state. I wonder, may I join you as you work?"

She only hesitated a second before agreeing. Despite the frock and work gloves—and her hair tied up from her face and neck like a young girl's—Carrie Lane was as elegantly beautiful as he had ever seen her. She was pale, as usual, a paleness set off as always by her coppery colored hair, and as restrained and graceful as ever, but today there was a difference in her. What was it? Ah, yes. Her eyes, her golden eyes, had a brightness, an excitement that added a new luster to her. Were they so bright because of his visit, or some other, unknown reason? What difference did it make. Ransom was pleased and excited by her, by her eyes.

"I wasn't aware you had returned to Center City," she said, leading him through a mazework of corridors.

"I only returned a day ago. My work at Lincoln was done. But even if it weren't, I would have felt compelled to return, if only to pay my respects to you, ma'am."

She ignored the compliment. A minute later, she said, "Here we are. As you can see, it's only a common winter garden."

It was anything but common. Ransom had seen the conservatory being built, but had never before been inside it. The room was a story and a half high and wrapped around the east and south of the Lane house like a huge veranda, only it was glass-enclosed, right up to the angled glass roof. As he had said, it was famous all over the state. With good reason too. Not only because of its size and expense, but because nowhere else would one see such a vast sun-flooded room so filled with tropical plants and flowers. Meandering gravel-strewn paths led between tubs of huge-leaved banana trees, around groves of palms of many varieties, through sandy areas of cacti of all shapes and sizes and grotesqueness. The center of the room held the only open space —a circular area about thirty feet across, where wicker furniture was placed among planters holding a profusion of flowers: lilies, irises, gardenias, camelias, orchids, birds of paradise, and many varieties Ransom had never seen before. The entire room—but most especially this center part—was filled with a damp, fetid, sickly sweet odor, as though a perfume wagon had fallen over and all the musks and scents had been indiscriminately mixed. Ransom found himself slightly dizzy with the odors.

"Henry loved these plants and flowers," Carrie Lane said, leading him out of the center of the room. "He spent the last two decades collecting them. Wherever he went he would ask to look at rare and unusual examples of the local flora, and would invariably get a seed, a shoot, a root, or whatever to bring back to Center City."

She paused amid a dwarf grove of pine trees no higher than her knees set in low, rectangular tubs, looking like a giantess among a miniature forest which was perfectly proportioned in every detail—needles, gnarled branches, even the tiny pine cones that dotted the trees with color. "These are called bonsai. They come from Japan, where they're considered very precious and handed down from one generation to another. This grove of trees is over two hundred years old. Henry heard about them and had the captain of a China trade clipper buy them for him. They were purposely stunted as seedlings, then bent to imitate natural growth."

Ransom admired the curious trees, and another ten minutes or so were passed in the identification and histories of various other plants. He had almost begun to wish he hadn't asked to come into the conservatory when a lapse occurred in their talk and he quickly said, "I was not certain whether or not you would be receiving."

She seemed startled and not at all pleased. "Whoever told you that?" she asked sharply. Then changing her tone: "Whatever gave you that idea?"

"No one said a word," he answered, surprised by her sudden, inexplicable intensity. "No one at all. I merely thought that because of your mourning and all . . ." He let that dangle for a while, incomplete, then said, "And Mrs. Ingram. She's well?"

"Yes, quite well," Carrie said, as calm as before, but now somewhat guarded.

"I asked because I didn't see her. And I had heard she had recently suffered an illness. It would be a great shame if her condition were a chronic one," he offered, testing her reactions.

"What condition? Surely you don't mean to suggest that what occurred yesterday is a condition of any sort? She was merely out in the sun too long. I've warned her about it a score of times. But you know how strongheaded Harriet can be. And she is the most conscientious of employees, always having to check after the other servants to make certain their chores are done well. She's resting now. She's been ordered to rest an hour or so afternoons."

"Then this was the first time she displayed such an attack of bizarre behavior?" Ransom asked, choosing the words carefully.

Carrie stopped watering the miniature trees and looked at him. She seemed a bit perplexed. But she didn't say a word.

"What I mean," Ransom said, "was that this sort of thing has never happened before?"

"No. Never," she said, as if picking up a challenge.

Well, that answered any question he might have about Mrs. Ingram. Or did it? Carrie Lane seemed to resent his even asking. Could she be hiding something?

"Then, Mrs. Ingram is quite well," he said.

"As I first said, quite well."

"Then there's no cause for concern."

"None at all." She was becoming colder and more guarded with every word.

"Fine. I'm delighted to hear it," Ransom said, sounding unconvincing even to himself. "I also trust everything else is fine too. I mean regarding the estate Mr. Lane left. I hope you have encountered no problems there?"

"None but what is usual, I'm told. It's really hardly my concern. Mr. Applegate and others see to it all."

"Naturally. And it must be a great relief to you to have found a general manager," Ransom said, probing her attitude toward her steward.

"Yes. Mr. Dinsmore seems quite satisfactory." Like all of her answers in the last minute or so, this was spoken dispassionately, indifferently.

"Mr. Dinsmore must be a man of great experience and competence to take on so much responsibility."

"I suppose," she replied languidly, turning away from Ransom to prune some nearby bushes she had earlier identified as kumquats.

Her unconcern told Ransom that Mrs. Ingram's allegations of the new manager's influence on Mrs. Lane were probably more jealousy than anything else. But did that explain Carrie Lane's evasions about Mrs. Ingram's health? He decided to make one more attempt.

"I have to say, Mrs. Lane, I'm extremely pleased to find all is working out so well. To be completely frank with you, I had suspicions that you might encounter rather serious problems in adjusting to your new situation." As she didn't respond, he went on. "It appears that all is going admirably well, as well as could be hoped. I hope that will continue to be the case."

"I don't see why it shouldn't," she replied, not taking the opportunity he had opened, not even turning to face him as she answered, still snipping away at the branches of the kumquat.

"Once before, Mrs. Lane, on the sad occasion of your husband's death, I offered you my assistance. I offer it again."

"Thank you, Mr. Ransom. You're very kind. I trust I will not be forced to bother you for your considerate offer."

Ransom found himself at a loss for anything else to say. She had checked him at every point, checked him, yet left him feeling that nothing was settled at all. He stood watching her go about her gardening as though he weren't even in the room, until, after several minutes, she looked up at him. She seemed surprised he was still there.

"I beg your pardon, Mr. Ransom. Did you say something?"

"Only that I'll take my leave of you."

"You must be a busy man. I'm sorry if I've wasted your time pottering around here. May I have you seen to the door?"

Without waiting for an answer, she called for the cook, who might have been listening at the door, she appeared so quickly. Ransom was not offered a hand—gloved or ungloved—but merely nodded and found himself out the front door, striding rapidly down High Street, more puzzled and unsatisfied than when he had arrived.

———————————●———————————

IT WAS ONLY FOUR BLOCKS down to Van Buren Avenue and another four west to Emerson Street, but they were long blocks, and within only a few the character of Center City changed rapidly, large homes on tree-lined streets yielding to a huddle of smaller frame houses, and finally to rows of two- and three-story attached wooden buildings. This was the South End, the oldest area in town, the first to be built up when Center City had been only a stagecoach rest with a post office and a small cluster of ranches around it.

Jack Bent's saloon was one of the first buildings that later on became Center City. Up until quite recently as the White Star Saloon, it had remained one of the central attractions for travelers. By then, of course, the real center had moved farther north, amid parklands, where the courthouse and churches and where Lane's Hotel were located.

The saloon still had the look of a Wild-West gambling bar, complete with gaming tables, a half-horsehoe–shaped oaken bar, upstairs rooms, and even a sort of kitchen. The private gaming rooms had been closed almost a generation ago, boarded up from the barroom, and reopened on the street as the Baptist Church's meeting place. The upstairs rooms had been sealed from inside too, and were only open to the street hallway, let out by the month, mostly to large immigrant families trying to earn enough money as day laborers to set up small farms up in Swede-ville.

Inside, the bar carried its age like a fine patina, as though it weren't so much real as a chromolithograph taken some thirty years before and untouched by the intervening years. All colors were faded, all surfaces were smoothed and glossy, all shines were dulled and tarnished including the two dozen pier glasses backing the bar wall. Even the rowdy portraits of seminude dance hall favorites from a half century before still adorning the higher walls, seemed to have aged: the brazen, roughly charac-terized faces softened and mellowed, the way aging courtesans would look.

No cattle managers, or flashily dressed gamblers, or traveling buffalo hunters reeking from fresh pelts filled the large open room now. Those breeds of men were vanished—gone farther west, to Wyoming and Montana. And the more elegant visitors to Center City no longer even saw the saloon. They arrived by railroad and put up at the Lane Hotel, sensibly placed in the middle of town.

Ransom wasn't a stranger to the South End, nor to the White Star Saloon. Not exactly a familiar face either. He'd come before on business—away from the trappings of a lawyer's office—to meet with struggling farmers and out-of-towners. He was recog-nizable though not well-known, and that might be helpful now.

He walked around the outside of the saloon to the stairway entry where Dinsmore's shingle was hung. If he was right, the man wouldn't be in. Just to be certain, he went up and knocked on the frosted-glass office door. As he'd thought, no one in.

Inside the saloon itself, there were two men in the far corner of the room at separate tables, one of them reading a yellowing newspaper, the other sleeping with his head thrown back, his mouth open. Two other men, dressed like farmers, occupied the far end of the horseshoe bar. Ransom perched himself at the other end and waited for the bartender.

"Hey, 'Manda," one of the farmers called in a loud voice. "You got a customer."

A woman stepped out of the doorway a few inches, then

ducked back in again, and finally emerged buttoning the top button of her blouse. She must live in those rooms.

"Yes?" she asked, drawing out the sibilant.

Ransom ordered a brandy and water. When she'd brought it, he asked, "Where's my old friend Jack Bent?"

"Got the stomach cramps," she said indifferently, probably lying. She tossed aside a mist of thin auburn hair that surrounded her pushed-in little face in a disordered halo. "I'm the missus."

"Glad to make your acquaintance, Mrs. Bent."

"I'll get Jack, if you want him," she offered unpersuasively.

"Don't bother."

She looked at him closely, then sort of flounced off to talk to the two men at the other end of the horseshoe. A few minutes later she was back, making a pretense of wiping the brass rim of the bar with a cloth rag when it probably needed steel wool to clean it, and a lot of that too.

"Sorry to hear Jack's feeling down," Ransom said. "I confess I'm feeling poorly myself. Not the stomach. Teeth," he said. "I hoped to see that dentist fellow upstairs. He's not in though. Second day in a row I've come by looking."

"Mr. Dinsmore hasn't been in his office lately," she said.

"He still in business?"

"He's still up there every once in a while. But he only sees by appointment now. He's very busy otherwise."

"Must be a good dentist. He really painless like it says?"

"Absolutely! 'Course he's not busy with dental surgery as much as with other matters. Managerial and the like," she said with a confidential air. "He's bettered himself, in fact. Not like that heap of cramps and aches in there," she said, scowling toward the doorway from which she'd emerged. "I told Jack when he first moved upstairs, I said, 'Jack. That there is an educated and an ambitious man. He won't be a renter here for long.' Sure enough. He bettered himself, he did."

"You know him that long?"

"Ain't so long. Three years at the most. A few months over maybe. Why, we was the first place he looked for a room for his office. He took what used to be called the family suite—three

rooms with indoor plumbing. He insisted on that. For the sink
and all. Very neat tenant too. Very clean. He's Anti-Septic, you
know. Those rooms never looked so scrubbed clean. 'Course she
did it all when she was alive, his wife, that is, bless her and may
she rest."

"He lives up there too?"

"Never. He lives up on High Street these days, which I have
to say is certainly a step or two up from Winter Lane. That's
where they used to have rooms. In the house of some nigrahs if
you can believe it. Though I must say everyone in that house who
wasn't a child was employed. Old Yolanda Bowles saw to that.
My what a woman she is! I sometimes wish she'd take a switch
to my Jack, as she's reputed to do with her own sons—some of
them forty-five years of age and with grandchildren of their
own."

It didn't take Ransom long to gather information from her.
Mrs. Bent was talkative by nature, admiring of the dental surgeon and eager to reproduce for him the days and works of every
person within a five-block radius. Getting her back onto his
subject without arousing any suspicions was only slightly difficult.

"I'll bet he charges a lot, if he's that good a dentist."

"Not at all. Regular fee. Two dollars for an extraction. One
dollar for an examination. One and a half for every silver alloy
filling he gives you. Worth it for the relief, I say. Lord knows,
Jack is blessed with teeth like a beaver. Not me. And that's the
marvel of it, why that Dinsmore wouldn't take a nickel from me.
Treats other folks that way too, those what are too poor to pay.
He deserves his good fortune, I say. A charitable man like that."

She went on to relate other examples of Dinsmore's good
works, such as his lending of much needed funds to more indigent patients. This was followed by an encomium on his personal
looks and grooming, with vivid, unflattering comparisons to her
husband and most other men too. The dentist's manners came in
for their share of praise too. She finally had to mention how
deeply he had been affected by the lingering illness and death of
Mrs. Dinsmore. She was so busy talking to Ransom, she shushed

the farmers when they demanded another round of drinks. She might have been an advertisement for Dinsmore: all she said threw more fully into doubt Mrs. Ingram's fears and suspicions. Ransom was ready to believe those anxieties had been completely fabricated, when Mrs. Bent, still jabbering on, finally offered a less flattering statement.

"Only thing I can't understand is why now that he's doing so well and all, he doesn't have Mr. Carr with him. Poor old man, he served Mr. Dinsmore hand and foot all the time they were here. Doting on him like a father would."

"Where is Mr. Carr?" Ransom asked.

"Don't know. Not in town, I can tell you. Otherwise he would have come by."

"He's not in Mrs. Dinsmore's rooms on Winter Lane?"

"They've been let to another family."

Ransom recalled Murcott's mentioning this old Carr some time before. He'd been Dinsmore's assistant, hadn't he? Had there been another connection? Mrs. Bent suggested a closer relation between them. Why else would she so deplore their separation?

That little mystery decided Ransom. It was nearly six o'clock, but only a short distance to Winter Lane, where they had all lived. Perhaps he would find a differing set of opinions concerning Dinsmore there.

"If you want your teeth taken care of, leave your name," Mrs. Bent said, hesitant to let him go. "I'll see to it he gets it and you can make an appointment."

Ransom declined and she shrugged. "You won't be sorry if you do go to him. Why he just says a dozen words or so to make you feel real comfortable and you won't feel a single turn of the drill. Believe me."

"I think I'll check back tomorrow," he said.

"Suit yourself."

As he was going out the double doors he saw someone emerge from the other rooms.

"Here's Jack now. Wait a minute, mister," she called out. "Jack, a friend to see you."

Ransom ignored her, closing the door behind him just in time.

———————————•———————————

"THA'S CORRECT. They all three lived there. Him and her and the old man too. In those four small rooms. I don't know how they made out in such little space. Didn't cost them but four dollars and change a month."

The huge, old black woman turned around in the rickety rocking chair and called to one of the numerous younger women inside the house to bring out some iced tea for the gentleman.

Yolanda Bowles hadn't been that friendly when Ransom had first stepped up to the front porch veranda to ask if Mr. Dinsmore lived there. She had looked at him hard, frowned at him, and tried to send him away. When he had persisted, she had called her two grandsons from the backyard yam patch, and with them standing guard beside her, as though over some tribal queen, she had demanded what Ransom's business with Dinsmore was.

He had fallen back on the bad-tooth ploy, which she didn't believe.

She told him Dinsmore had moved out. She didn't know where.

Still Ransom lingered; the two grandsons moved toward him in a vaguely threatening manner.

It was then that he decided on a new tactic.

"Pardon me, ma'am. But would you happen to come from the state of Georgia?" he asked. Even after so many years her languorous plantation accent was unmistakable to him.

"What business is that of yours?" she asked. "Haven't you heard of Mr. Lincoln's emancipation?"

He had, Ransom said. But he too happened to hail from Georgia. Atlanta and environs, to be specific. And he'd always thought his home-staters would receive him more cordially.

"Atlanta? What's your name?"

"My father was William Cassius Ransom."

"Tha's correct," she said slowly, and seemed to be thinking. "I seen that man. I used to work over on the next plantation. The Cabots, you know them?"

"Very well."

"What are you wanting with this Yankee, Mr. Ransom?"

He told her about his bad tooth. She still doubted that, but she sent her grandsons back to the yam patch and invited Ransom to take a seat with her. When he was closer to her, she seemed even more enormous than before. Not all fat either, he figured, especially if she'd been a plantation slave in her youth. They sat and talked for a few minutes about the various families he'd known and what had happened to them after the war. Meanwhile, behind the panes of windows opening out onto the veranda, three curious faces appeared and reappeared, vying to see whom she was conversing with.

Yolanda still disbelieved his intentions, but she was more ready to speak of the Dinsmores now that she knew who Ransom was. She suddenly asked: "What's he done wrong?"

"Dinsmore? Nothing. Least not that I know of."

"Your father was a lawyer man, if I recollect. And so, by your apparel, are you, Mr. Ransom. That means you ain't got no bad tooth at all, but instead are investigating this man."

"All right. But let's say it's a private investigation."

Pleased to have been correct, she talked about her former tenants.

"He ain't done nothing wrong that I could ever make out either. Otherwise he wouldn't have stayed here. I can tell you that. I don't brook no criminals in my home, of no color. Nat'rally I 'spected that man had him a history that weren't all gold. Why else would he come to live here? I didn't ask him, of course. I jes' warned him a bit, and left him alone. He was a tolerable good tenant. Paid on time. Didn't bother no one at all. Didn't have much truck with him in all the years he was here. Not with the old Professor either. I couldn't say he was a bad man at all, the old man. And soon enough, Mr. Dinsmore made himself a good enough name among the other nigrahs so's I wasn't afraid he wouldn't run out without paying his rent."

It was a recommendation, though a grudging one. She began
to say something, then stopped herself, and instead asked:

"This investigating about a woman? He planning to marry?"

Ransom admitted it concerned a woman, although it hadn't
gone so far as marriage yet, to his knowledge.

"Well, tha's what I figured. The kind of man he was. Oh, I
don't begrudge a man his partying. All of you men are such
snakes when it comes to the ladies. But I felt real sorrowful for
Mrs. Dinsmore. Why, that poor woman would come and cry on
my shoulders about his gallivanting so. 'What you expect,
woman?' I'd tell her. 'Why, tha's the prettiest and most enchant-
ing man you done married. You must be a fool to think no other
woman can see it.' And her always feeling so poorly with her
health and all. She'd cry all week long if it weren't she had work
to do, cleaning and sewing and cooking. Poor darling. But it was
true. A man that pretty ought never marry. Eyes like blue sap-
phires. You ever see 'em? And a voice that could charm the birds
off the trees, never mind a woman. Why he'd just start talking
to you real soft and gentle and in no time he'd have you fetching
and carrying and doing jes' about anything he wanted. Well, I
didn't cater much to that. Not for myself, and not for those fool
women inside the house either. So's we all kept to our separate
businesses, he and his and me and mine. 'Cept Mrs. Dinsmore."

"You never heard anything . . . well, anything at all about
him?"

"Nothing but what I figured out myself. And that was that he
was a ladies' man. Tha's what he was doing, living here in Centah
City. Must have had to hightail it out of a bigger town on account
of that. Poor woman. And what was worst of all, the poor thing
got crazy in the head after a while. Died from it."

"I thought she drowned?"

Yolanda laughed. "You *is* an investigatin' man, ain't you? She
drowned all right. Threw herself into the reservoir. Thought she
was dying of the consumption. Now, I ain't no medical doctor,
mind you, but I've lived these eighty-one years and I've seen
blackfolk and whitefolk alike with the consumption. She never

had no consumption. 'Course toward the end she looked poorly enough. Never eatin' but a few scraps of greens. Never sleeping. Fretting about a disease she didn't have. I tell you she never once spat no phlegm, not to mention no blood at all. Consumption, indeed! Why, and him being almost a miracle man, and not being able to cure her from such craziness. I jes' don't know what good he was for her."

"You mean she really wasn't sick?"

"Never saw no doctor nor anyone who said she was. Poor thing was just crazy with longing and jealousy. Fool that she was."

One of the younger women brought out a tray with large glasses of iced tea; and Yolanda insisted on chastising her, and then demanding specifics of the work supposedly going on inside the house. During this lengthy cross-examination, Ransom sipped his drink and wondered about the new information he'd received. He still had a question to ask, and when the girl went back in, he asked it.

"Why did you call him almost a miracle man? Because of the painless surgery?"

"That. And other things too. 'Course I didn't trust the man, so's I didn't put much belief in what Reverend Sydney of the Baptist Church and all his fool parishioners said and thought. But he was a painless dentist from what I did hear. And when my Millard had his leg half taken off in the open-work thresher, Mr. Dinsmore did fix it up so good it's as though nothing ever happened to it. That was almost a miracle."

"Millard's your son?"

"Grandson. You want to see? Millard! Millard! Nancy! You there, girl? Fetch Millard out here!"

Before Ransom could say she needn't bother, the girl had run back through the house. In another minute or so, Millard came, limping slightly, from around the corner of the house.

"C'mere," she ordered. "Show the man where your leg was gashed up and fixed up again."

Millard came up onto the veranda and lifted one trouser leg.

A deep, twisting wound spiraled around the muscular, dark-skinned leg—a central white inner gash, outlined in two layers of pinkish skin.

"It goes right up above the knee," Yolanda said. "Tell the gentleman about it, Millard."

"Goes right up to here," Millard said, marking a spot high on his thigh. "Good thing that Mr. Dinsmore was here. Y'landa's Billy got him back to the barn soon as it happened. I was bleeding like I was fit to die. And hollering so much I thought all my breath would leave me. My leg was all bloody, right up to here," he said, touching his groin.

"Dinsmore stitched that?" Ransom asked.

"Yessir." Proudly declared. "He stitched it up with some catgut thread Y'landa's Billy fetched for him. But first of all he made it to stop bleeding. That calmed me somewhat."

"How? With a tourniquet?"

"Don't rightly know. Unless a tourniquet means to talk. Tha's what he did. Held me by the throat real hard soon as he saw me, like as he was to strangle me, and talked to me real good until I wasn't so scared and stopped hollering. Then the bleeding stopped to nothing at all. And by then Y'landa's Billy had fetched the doctor's bag what belonged to the old Professor, and Mr. Dinsmore made it all Anti-Septic with spirits of alcohol which didn't burn at all like it usually does, and then he jes' sewed it up with the catgut."

"Hadn't Dinsmore tied the leg to stop it from bleeding?" Ransom asked. No, Millard insisted. Had he lifted it up? No, Dinsmore hadn't touched the leg until after it had stopped bleeding. And then only to clean it up with the alcohol and to stitch it up. That seemed odd to Ransom. Had Millard lost consciousness during the time? Perhaps that was how he had missed seeing the tourniquet? But Millard insisted he had been awake all the time, and Y'landa's Billy would corroborate everything he said, just ask him.

It was certainly an unlikely story. Even stranger that the leg had been so well stitched, brilliantly stitched in fact. And, within a week, Millard said, he'd been walking on the leg. If it weren't for the scar, he wouldn't even remember that he'd almost lost it.

Yolanda dismissed her grandson, then she and Ransom finished their iced teas.

"You see now why I said almost a miracle?" she asked.

"I do indeed. But Millard seems to think it was one. Who else does? You mentioned Reverend Sydney?"

"That old coot! He'll believe jes' about anything so long as you put something into his poorbox at the church. But go talk to him. You'll see for yourself exactly what kind of fool he is."

Ransom said he thought he would do just that. He thanked Yolanda for her information and for her conversation. When he'd reached Van Buren Avenue again, he had a start. The figure of a woman darted out of the upstairs doorway of the White Star Saloon and into a waiting carriage at the curbstone. Too fast for him to make out her features. But the slim, high-shouldered form was familiar to him: Carrie Lane. Could he be certain of it?

He toyed for a second with going upstairs again, then decided against it. Instead he went into the storefront Baptist Church.

Reverend Sydney was in his office—a closed space to one side of the larger, congregational area—reviewing some ledgers.

Yes, he said to Ransom's first question, he knew Mr. Dinsmore. No, he replied to the next one, neither he nor his wife had had any dental work done. But others they knew had, and they had nothing but praise for the dental surgeon's cheap rates and good character. He repeated to Ransom what Mrs. Bent had said about Dinsmore sometimes giving free services and even ready money to some of the poorer patients. The Reverend—a thin, vigorous man, somewhere in his late fifties, with a childlike face and random tufts of white hair scattered among baldspots on his head—explained Dinsmore's method of treatment to Ransom as a "gift from God." Without being asked to elaborate, Reverend Sydney did so, saying that Dinsmore's ability to eliminate pain was not by any satanic, scientific methods, but merely by the use of the voice and the spirit.

"It is a gift that Joseph of the parti-colored coat enjoyed at Pharaoh's throne, and that the young David commanded in Saul's chambers," Sydney said, then quoted whole passages verbatim from the Old Testament to bolster his attestations. This gift and the man's humanitarianism had endeared Dinsmore to many of Sydney's congregation, he said.

Ransom soon discovered the preacher was an enthusiast and a Bible-thumper. Sydney asked no questions of Ransom and once begun on a topic, he seemed to find threads of relevant testamentary verbiage which he proceeded to orate at his listener as though Ransom were a great sinner in need of extra-rapid conversion to the faith. Still enveloped in a hail of oratory, he made a quick good-bye and a hasty escape from the storefront church.

By the time he'd reached the Center City Board and Hotel he had sorted out in his mind the strands of complex individual opinions he'd heard about Dinsmore. He certainly knew a great deal more about the man than before, but he still hadn't answered his primary question: had Harriet Ingram been justified in her fears about the man, or had she simply been overwrought? For all the good he'd done in that area, Ransom might as well have stayed at home. And the afternoon mail had arrived when he reached his office, in it scads of new business from those who had waited for him to return to town before sending it. A wasted afternoon. He rolled up his shirtsleeves and set to work.

———————●———————

THE INTENSE HEAT CONTINUED throughout the evening. Murcott was in such an irascible mood after his visit that day to Swedeville that Ransom decided to put off questioning him about Mrs. Ingram until a better time suggested itself. Later that evening, unable to sleep because of the dense humidity, Ransom decided to drop the matter altogether: it couldn't be so important: merely domestics squabbling among themselves.

Just before dawn a storm crashed overhead and raged for about a half hour. Despite the great noise, Ransom fell asleep. When he awoke, it was ten o'clock in the morning and quite cool. As all the other boarders were long gone to work, he had a quick breakfast downstairs by himself, then, instead of going to his desk, he decided to take a walk to the courthouse. He gathered a half dozen folios containing papers pertaining to court business he had looked at the previous afternoon and set out.

Neither Judge Dietz nor Alvin Barker, the court clerk, was in his office. Ransom didn't much mind. He'd just leave a note for Barker to look at the papers and he'd come back the following day.

Passing the courthouse façade, he made out the figure of old Floyd, draped as usual on the courthouse bench. For a second, Ransom thought to simply nod and pass by: then he decided to tease the old man a bit.

"Nice and cool after that storm last night," Ransom said, sitting down.

"I s'pose. Some lightning hit that elm, side of Judge Dietz's house. Cracked some of the roofing over the breakfast room when it fell," Floyd said.

"I heard that already. At breakfast time. Seems to me your information is getting a little stale these days."

"My information? Why, old Floyd knows everything and anything that occurs in this town as it occurs."

"That's what I used to believe too. But an old nigrah woman living down on the South End knew a volume more information about that dental surgeon than you did. I'd say you've been on a few too many benders lately to hold your position as town crier."

"Well, wasn't I the one who told you all about him?"

"Not a word I didn't already know."

"What's she know that I don't."

"Heaps. Everything. And then some."

"About Dinsmore?"

"That's correct."

"Well . . . well, I know something neither she nor anyone else but one person knows. I know where his old coot of a friend is."

"Simon Carr?"

"That's correct!" Floyd said, imitating Ransom and looking sly. "I got it from Paddlebrook Pell. Sitting right here on this bench yesterday. Probably at the same time you were frequenting that nigrah woman."

"Well? Aren't you going to say?"

"Ah! So she didn't know that!" Floyd smiled a toothless grin and settled himself. "I will say, but only to you and to no one else. Everyone thought he'd left Center City when Dinsmore went to work for Mrs. Lane. Well, it so happens he did—sort of. Paddlebrook was just out there three days ago, so he knows. He had what you lawyers would call the ocular proof."

"Out where?"

"Out on the Lane Ranch. Carr's been there since he moved out of the rooms on Winter Lane. He's dying out there, Paddlebrook said. Though I can't say that's certain. And he and that Dinsmore don't get along a-tall anymore. So's he'd be able to tell you whatever it is you want to know."

"I already know what I want to know," Ransom said, watching Floyd cock his head and half shut an eye, as though that would allow him to hear better. "Dinsmore's as good a dentist as you said. But I need an appointment to see him."

Floyd spat on the grass between his feet. "Yeah. Well, in case you want to know 'xactly how good, Carr'll tell you, thanks to me."

"Well, good day to you then."

"You know how to go there?" Floyd asked.

"I know."

"You want me to go with you?"

"I'm not going. Don't need to. Dinsmore's here."

Ransom believed it then, believed there was no cause for further bother about Dinsmore. Certainly not cause enough to take him all the way out to the Lane Ranch. He returned to his office instead, got a great deal of work accomplished and even saw a new client.

It was only at teatime, with dinner some three hours off, that he began thinking about Carr again. It wouldn't be such a long ride—only twenty minutes or so either way. He'd take his horse instead of a pair and shay; that would shorten it even more. Who knew how much exercise the animal got at the public stables. Golden always did like a good run. And if the old man was as ill as Floyd said he was, he might not mind company.

In minutes, Ransom was dressed and out of the Center City Board and Hotel. Another few minutes were required to get to the stables and to get his horse, Golden, saddled, then he was riding, heading north, past the Lane house on High Street. A few blocks more and he was outside the town, cantering along on the old Pony Express route that would take him to the Lane Ranch.

Only once did he have any hesitation. Closing in on the turnoff to the ranch, he saw two horsemen coming his way. Could one be Dinsmore, just coming from the ranch? He really didn't want to meet the man out here. But no, it turned out they were the Bixby brothers riding into town for the night.

The ranch was down in a gully, bare but for a large clump of some sort of berry bush to one side. The ranch house was a sprawling, half-wood, half-adobe building hugging the ground. Beside it was another adobe building, even more ramshackle— the ranch hands' bunkhouse, Ransom supposed. In the clear, ringing blue sky and brightness of sunlight, every architectural detail was highlighted, throwing deep, well-defined shadows onto the trodden dirt ground. The whole place looked in need of whitewashing, reshingling, and repairs. The front door was closed, not a window thrust open for the afternoon breeze to enter.

Ransom thought to take a look around before dismounting. He turned Golden toward the back of the ranch. As he passed the bunkhouse, he saw a woman in heavy aprons and skirts bent over a small vegetable patch.

"Hello," he called to her.

She looked up, red-faced from exertion, and, shading her eyes with a soiled hand, stared at him.

He rode right up to the vegetable garden.

"I thought no one was here."

She continued to stare, without the shading hand now, as he blocked the glare of the low-on-the-horizon sun. She wore a multicolored kerchief around her head, almost down to her eyes, and she had the ruddy skin and doughy features he associated with the few women he'd seen at Swedeville.

"*Svensk?*" he asked.

"Nein," she answered, in a harsh voice. *"Deutsche.* Cherman. *Nein* English *spricht."*

"Is the old man here?" Ransom asked. How to say it? *"Ein Mann? Ein alter Mann?"*

"Der Alte, ach ja!" was all he could make out in the sudden, affirmative torrent of her words. But she pointed to the ranch, so he thanked her and rode to the front door, dismounting and tying Golden loosely to the hitching post.

Knocking on the front door brought no response. He tried the handle and found it opened.

Entering, he had to bend under the low, upper lintel. There was a little platform, then a few steps down into a dark hallway. He called out "Hello," twice.

The second time a voice responded.

"In here. Where are you? Turn left. Third doorway."

The voice was strangely accented, and surprisingly spry. Ransom followed the directions and found himself in a small adobe-walled bedroom, bare but for an old brass bed and a darkwood bedtable that held a flickering candle. In the bed, covered to his chest by a quilted blanket, was an old man with pale but sharp and eager-looking blue eyes. His thin white hair was grown past his ears, a whitish stubble on his face about to become a beard. A long, hawklike nose dominated the drawn and desiccated features.

"Mr. Carr? Mr. Simon Carr?"

"Yes. Who are you? I was expecting someone else."

The man attempted to sit up more fully to get a better look. Ransom went up to him, and helped prop the pillows behind him so he could sit up. All the while Carr stared at him birdlike, his curious, watery-blue eyes like those of an aged bird of prey, his hawklike nose seeming to grow and hook even as Ransom looked at it.

"Well?" Carr asked. "Who are you? Are you a doctor?" His voice was clipped, surprisingly young, and very British. "If you are a doctor, you may leave this moment. I don't trust you. Not a one of you."

"I'm not a doctor," Ransom assured him.

"Who are you? What do you want?"

"Let's just say I'm from the government. Although not on official business. I heard you were ill here and decided to pay you a social visit." As he spoke, Ransom attempted to instill every bit of charm he could muster into his words. The room was airless, stifling. "Surely these windows ought to be open a bit."

"Don't touch them. It's cooler this way."

"But it's cool outside now. Quite cool since the storm."

Before Carr could comment, Ransom opened out one of the hinged double windows. The sunlight streamed in, and with it, fresh air. Ransom took a deep breath. Better. Especially for an invalid.

"There. How's that?"

"What government?" Carr asked, querulously. "What have you come here to tell me?"

"Not a thing."

"Well then, what is it you want to know of me?"

"For one, how are you feeling?"

"Poorly. But that's not a stranger's business. Government man or not. Where are your papers? Show them to me."

"I said it wasn't official business."

"You're lying. You're from him. You're some new friend of his!" He almost spat out the last words. "You've come from him, admit it. To torment me. To kill me, perhaps. Yes, that's it."

"Whoa now, Mr. Carr. Wait one second. I'm not from whomever you think. I'm here entirely on my own. So don't go and upset yourself over nothing."

The old man had grown quite purple in the face. His creased, chicken-thin neck was uncovered down to his breastplate now. His Adam's apple continued to bob, even though he no longer said a word.

"Well then, where are your papers?" Carr demanded.

Ransom saw he had no choice. "I'm the county prosecutor," he said, showing the old man the marshall's card he'd been issued when he'd been appointed, but careful to cover his name with a finger. "There. That make you more comfortable?"

Carr didn't answer.

"I'm here to help you, Mr. Carr."

"I want no one's help."

"From what you just now said, it strikes me you might need some help. If you'd care to confide in me . . ."

"I do not care to."

"Has someone been threatening your life? You said before . . ."

"I said nothing at all."

"Who is it? Mr. Dinsmore?"

"No one. I said nothing."

Ransom sat down on the edge of the bed. As he did, the old man moved away from him. In motion, even under the quilt, the thinness of his body was apparent.

"Is that German woman the only person here besides you?"

"At night the others come. They have dinner and then I don't know what they do."

"You can't have everything you need here?"

"I get what I need. I speak German."

"But you're ill. What's your illness?"

"My heart. I had a stroke a week or two ago. I couldn't even talk very well then. I'm better now. Much better. I even walk now. I'll show you."

Ransom got up to let Carr out of bed. Wearing only a yellowed nightshirt down to his knees and heavy woolen socks, the old man looked even older and more frail, but his movements were spry enough.

"I know how ill and how well I am," Carr said. "Hand me those trousers."

Ransom found them hung on a nail behind the door. Once the old man had them on, he hunted around the room for shoes, found a battered pair of lace-me-ups and worked them only half up.

"You see. I'm completely able to care for myself."

"Good. Perhaps now we can go somewhere more comfortable."

"I'll make us a pot of tea. That's what's needed," Carr said and led Ransom back down the hallway to the entrance and then into a primitive kitchen.

Ransom hovered about the old man, as much to be certain he didn't injure himself lighting the old wooden stove and putting on the water to boil, as to try to get more information from him. But Carr was so intent on his work that he brushed aside all questions until the tea was set on the kitchen table.

"You don't have many visitors?" Ransom asked.

"Not many. The ranch hands, occasionally. Infrequently."

"Doesn't Mr. Dinsmore visit?"

"Sometimes. He's very occupied these days I believe."

"And Mrs. Lane?"

"Heavens no!"

"Well, it is her ranch. She had a right to come here, I would think."

"Yes. Quite," Carr said. "I merely meant, well, we don't really know each other. Not to say more than a cursory meeting or two."

"Did you know Henry Lane?"

"As well as his wife, which wasn't very much. I'm afraid Mr. —what did you say your name was?"

"But Mr. Dinsmore knew Henry Lane very well. He was a close friend of the Lanes', wasn't he? He must have been to be one of the chief mourners at the funeral. Right-hand man to Mrs. Lane since then. Her general manager and property foreman. For all that, he must have known the Lanes awfully well. Wouldn't you say?"

"I'm afraid I'm not privy to Mr. Dinsmore's business."

"But you were. For years."

"His dental business only. Which is quite different."

"If you say so," Ransom sipped the tea, disliking its bitterness. "People are saying some funny things about Mr. Dinsmore, you know."

"How can I know? Being out here, so isolated?"

"Well, I know. People are wondering how come it is Mr. Dinsmore is suddenly in a position of such importance."

"He's a capable man."

"As a dental surgeon," Ransom qualified. "Why, I don't know that even I would do all that much managing as he's doing. And I've considerable experience. Unless, of course, Henry Lane showed him all the intricacies of it before his death."

"I couldn't say," Carr said succinctly. Ever since they had sat down to tea, Ransom had decided to wage an all-out war of questions. Carr hadn't flinched or lost his calm once. He reminded Ransom of the illustrations he'd seen of Livingstone among the natives—the calm, tea-drinking Englishman among the barbarians. His attitude riled Ransom.

"Could you say how Henry Lane died?"

The cup and saucer rattled in the old man's hand. He set it down on the table.

"He committed suicide. Or so everyone says. I was not present."

"Do you know why?" Ransom persisted.

"I? I scarcely knew the man."

"Do you know why he killed himself?"

"No." Very clipped now. "No. I do not."

"Well, I do," Ransom said, and let the words just hang there in the still, sun-filtered room as he watched Carr's look of surprise crumple into haggard exhaustion.

"I see," Carr said after a minute, looking down at the table. "In that case I don't know why you're asking me." As Ransom still didn't answer, he went on, "I'm afraid I'm rather less well than I thought at first." He got to his feet shakily. "I thank you for your social call. I'm sorry not to be more helpful to you."

Ransom stood up too, ready to take the old man's arm if it was needed. But Carr edged past him.

"Do you know why Henry Lane died?" Ransom asked again. Then, "Is that why Dinsmore's threatening you?"

"No more questions today. No more. Good day, Mr. Government Man." Carr edged past the door and back into the hallway. Ransom followed a bit, then said so clearly that the old man could not help but hear:

"I'll be back, you know. I'll be back to hear the truth. I don't know when. But you can rely on it."

Carr walked slowly to his room, supporting himself with one hand touching the wall as though he were a blind man.

———————————•———————————

"THERE SHE IS, JAMES. Finally. My, she looks lovely!"

Ransom had been immersed in a political conversation with Amasa Murcott and Ludwig Baers, the candidate for the county seat in the Nebraska State Senate, when Augusta Page tapped his elbow. He looked up and, following her eyes, gazed toward the oversized entrance to the west parlor of Judge Dietz's house.

Carrie Lane was just removing the pins that held in place a heavy, black mantilla that covered her head and draped half of her upper body. As the servant woman lifted off the wrap, Mrs. Lane stepped forward a bit as though freed from its weight, then went to the full-length mirror to ascertain whether her coiffure had been disturbed. It hadn't. The little black-stoned tiara nestled steadily in her rich, auburn hair.

As Mrs. Page said, she looked lovely. Almost regal, with the little, finely wrought tiara, and the floor-length black gown, cut square in front to reveal a soft, white expanse of neck and shoulders, and high-sleeved to accommodate a pair of arm-length meshwork gloves as jet as the trim of her flowing skirts. Regal, Ransom thought, but like a queen in mourning for some fabled consort.

She turned facing the doorway. In a minute, Ransom made out the object of her ambiguous look: Dinsmore, as blackly resplendent as she, in dinner clothes complete with what had to be pearl buttons on his shirt front and cuffs, from their refracting gleam. Dinsmore, too, glanced at himself in the mirror, and turned back to sweep her from from head to foot with his photographic-lens eyes. Then, with a small satisfied look on his cupid's-bow lips, he went to her and took her arm.

The conversation Ransom had been so interested in a moment

before, and which continued inches away from him, seemed to
recede a hundred yards as he watched Carrie Lane allow herself
to be taken by the arm and led into the west parlor, where Judge
Dietz and his corpulent wife, Lavinia, stood to receive their
guests.

"With him again," Mrs. Page whispered into Ransom's ear.
"Always with him. How I pity her tonight!"

Ransom tore his gaze from the doorway long enough to look
at Mrs. Page. "Why?"

"You'll see, soon enough. There! Look! She's approaching the
Masons. Watch!"

He turned in time to see that Dinsmore and Carrie Lane had
been greeted by their hosts and had stepped fully into the room
as another party took their place with the judge and his wife. The
Masons were standing close by, the banker in conversation with
someone, Mrs. Mason beset by ennui. As Carrie Lane moved
toward her, she did not meet her gaze, but looked about as
though searching for a way of escape. Mason himself greeted the
couple, but Mrs. Mason contented herself with a few words, then
quickly bustled away toward a group on the other side of the
room.

"What's happening?" Ransom asked.

"She'll be snubbed by all her so-called friends tonight. You
just watch."

"But why?"

"Why? Surely, James, you don't expect someone like Mrs.
Mason to be on social terms with a woman who couldn't even
wait the traditional, required year of mourning before throwing
herself at a mere dental surgeon? Oh, it's all right for her husband. They have a business connection. No one will speak to
Mrs. Lane tonight. Except, I suppose, the men. How mortifying!"

As his informant explained, Ransom could see that Mrs. Lane
had stood quite still to watch her friend walk away. If not mortification, then she at least suffered from the realization of her
position. That was evident in the sudden spots of red that appeared high on either cheek of her pale face.

"Is she his woman?" Ransom had to ask.

"Who knows? He does live in the same house. He does go about with her all the time. He certainly acts as though she is. And most important, everyone assumes she is."

Ransom continued looking at Carrie Lane. She was perfectly still, as though a subject in a mysterious portrait, while around her the room bustled with activity. Ransom felt a blush begin to rise to his own face as he shared her humiliation.

"I'll go to her," he said.

"Go. What difference will it make? You're a man."

"Then you go to her."

"But she hardly knows me."

"You're afraid of what they'll think. Aren't you? For all your talk of being so independent, you're afraid of what Mrs. Mason and those other women will say."

"Calm yourself, James."

When she said that, he realized he was inappropriately angry with her. He apologized, but looking toward where Mason and Dinsmore were conversing, he begged Mrs. Page to go to her.

"At least come with me," he pleaded, standing up and drawing Mrs. Page to her feet too.

"It will hardly make a difference, James. I'm a boardinghouse keeper. It'll be worse." But she rose anyway and fussed a minute with her own voluminous skirts. "One simply can't trust a man to not interfere," she said. "Exactly what is your interest in doing this, James?"

"Justice. That's all."

"Isn't it a bit naïve to still believe in justice at your age?"

"I still believe in it. It's the only reason I'm a lawyer."

She shook her head, but said, "All right. Take me to her."

Ransom took her arm, but neither of them moved. Mrs. Lane was no longer alone, but now surrounded on one side by Robertson Sloan, the Nebraska state senator, and on the other by a rather dowdily dressed middle-aged woman who must be Sloan's wife. Mason and Dinsmore had moved to the wood-paneled wall, still in animated conversation. Carrie Lane was smiling and

talking as though nothing were amiss. But the two spots of color
had not left her cheeks.

"Saved!" Augusta Page said. "And how beautifully for her.
To be shown such marked attention by the senator's wife. Now.
May I resume my seat?"

Ransom didn't reply immediately, and Mrs. Page went back
to sit with Dr. Murcott and Baers. When he turned aside, he was
face to face with Judge Dietz. The big doors to the parlor were
partially closed, the receiving line was broken; all the guests for
the annual pre-election dinner must have arrived.

"Well, Mr. Ransom. Another fine crowd, don't you think?"

Before Ransom could respond, the judge had looked past him
at Carrie Lane. "She'll be surrounded by suitors tonight. And I
don't blame them either. If I were single, and if I were in your
position, James, I'd make certain to be close by her too."

"I thought Mrs. Lane had an escort tonight?" Ransom asked.

"Her manager? Hardly an escort. She couldn't come alone,
could she? I wouldn't let that stop me a bit."

"I thought you above matchmaking, your honor."

They began to walk. "Let's just say I think it in Center City's
best interest that Mrs. Lane be well married just as soon as her
mourning period is over. There are important considerations
involved. Economic and political considerations. One might almost say the future of this town depends on it."

He looked at Ransom with his large, wrinkled face, and his
shaggy-browed, penetrating gray eyes.

"You're joking," was Ransom's response.

"I'm completely serious. Whoever marries her will carry a
great deal of weight in the county. As much as Henry Lane did.
That's why it ought to be the right person. Good evening, Mrs.
Brennan. Hope you're well tonight. Let's move on, James, I
don't want to talk to that old crone. Heed my words, though,"
he said, steering Ransom toward the massive double doors that
opened onto the formal dining room where dinner would be
served. "I've been in Center City since it began. I know the
intricacies of these matters."

"What makes you believe I'm the right man for such a position," Ransom asked, half amused now.

"I don't exactly know. You don't seem to have a hell of a lot of ambition. But you've done everything right so far and nothing wrong in the time you've been here. That's good enough for me. Sloan talked of you tonight, you know. You made quite an impression at the capitol with that land-grant business. They've all got their eyes on you. They're waiting to see what you'll do next."

"A romance will hardly . . ."

"More than a romance," Dietz interrupted. "It shows good sense. Both personally and professionally. Don't you think Sloan doesn't know that too?"

Ransom inspected the judge's face again to be certain he wasn't being toyed with. No, the man was in dead earnest. He'd known Dietz long enough to determine that.

"Well, then," Ransom said lightly. "If you present it as a civic duty . . . I just might go pay my respects."

"Begin right now. She's out tonight. Catch her."

"In the few minutes left before dinner?"

Dietz considered a while. Without answering he called to his wife, who was passing nearby.

"Mr. Ransom," Lavinia said, greeting him.

"Lavinia, Mr. Ransom has some urgent business with Mrs. Lane this evening. How are they placed at the table?"

"Apart, I'm certain."

"Place them together."

"I've seated her between the senator and her escort."

"He's just her steward. Move him."

"Carl, I couldn't."

"Move him into James's seat."

She looked questioningly at Ransom, who looked away. "Well, if you insist," she said.

"I insist. Have it done now."

She was evidently ruffled by his command, expecting no interference in social matters, her domain. But she walked off and found a servant to relay the message to.

"Thank you, your honor. I hope . . ."

"Better start in right now," Dietz said gruffly. "She's alone now. Go."

He almost shoved Ransom forward. Propelled as much by his own sense of the impending interview, Ransom went to Carrie Lane just as she was turning away from Mrs. Robertson Sloan.

She seemed startled to see him.

"Mrs. Lane," he said, taking her hand.

"Mr. Ransom."

"I hope you won't mind some Georgia complimenting, ma'am, but tonight you make bereavement so beautiful it almost seems a desirable state."

She was taken aback by that and could only utter, "I'm afraid it's hardly desirable."

"Perhaps I chose my words poorly. What I meant was . . ."

"Thank you, I think I understand." She let go of his hand.

"I haven't offended you, I hope."

"Not at all. Thank you for your kind words." She looked away from him, at the wall where Dinsmore and Mason were still conferring.

"I had intended," Ransom began again, aware that he was beginning to drawl, "I had intended, I say, to call on you again and to reiterate my offer of assistance."

"Thank you again. It's all working out somehow." She looked toward the two men again. Was she waiting for Dinsmore to come lead her into dinner? Ransom determined to do that. But he first had to have her undivided attention. How?

"It's a fine turnout for the dinner," he began, aware it was small talk.

She agreed succinctly.

"Luckily, there are no important elections this year here in town. What with all the vehemence over state politics."

Again she agreed. He was making no progress at all.

"I understand the sorghum crop is the best ever," he offered.

"Up at the capitol they all say so." Even worse. He sounded like a hayseed.

"You've done rather well at the capitol," she suddenly replied, surprising him. "I'm amazed you even bothered to return to our little town."

"My friends are here, ma'am. At least I hope those I admire and respect will allow me to call them friends."

"I'm certain they're honored to."

"I would be more certain of that, if you would consent."

"Consent?" she asked, clearly confused.

"To allow me to call you a friend," he explained. "Especially now that both of us very much need friends."

"You less than I, I'm afraid."

"All the more reason then, that you'll allow me to call on you shortly to persuade you of my intentions."

She looked even more confused at this. "Your intentions?"

He was about to explain these intentions, when the doors to the dining room were thrown open from within, revealing the enormous gaslit room and the candelabra-studded table set for two dozen guests. There was a shuffling as people stood up readying to enter.

Ransom saw Mrs. Lane cast another glance toward Dinsmore. Before she could do more than that, he took her arm.

"May I escort you in?"

"I . . . yes, I suppose so."

Holding her, he felt the hard meshwork of her glove and the cool softness of her skin under his fingers. It almost sent shivers up his spine.

They passed a bottleneck of people immediately within the doors, and Ransom led Mrs. Lane to the far end of the huge room where Judge Dietz was standing, talking to Cal Applegate. Ransom noted his name was directly to the left of hers, and only a seat apart from Senator Sloan's. Evidently this end of the banquet table was reserved for the most prominent guests.

"How fortunate," Ransom said, pretending surprise, and pulling out a chair for her. "We're to be dinner companions."

She allowed herself to be seated, and when he had taken his own seat, she was talking to the senator. Ransom contented himself with greeting those just sitting down, and watching the rest of the party seat itself.

Mason and Dinsmore had entered the room still talking. The banker found his place, directly opposite Mrs. Sloan. His wife was already seated two places away. But they couldn't find Dinsmore's name, and had to ask a dining room servant, who directed Dinsmore farther down, between Mrs. Mason and Dr. Murcott. Dinsmore stood still, facing Ransom's side of the table.

Carrie Lane put her hand to the back of her neck, as though arranging her hair there, then looked up to face her employee. His bright eyes flashed at her, and Ransom could swear the red spots appeared instantly again on her cheeks. Then Dinsmore bowed, and unable to be heard over the talk, gestured to her where he was to be seated. She looked toward the empty seat he pointed to, down at her plate, then sharply up again, just in time to see Dinsmore take his place.

"I do hope the speeches will wait until after dinner," Ransom said in a low voice, leaning over to her. "I'm quite famished."

"I beg your pardon," she replied.

He repeated his words, watching the color leave her cheeks.

"Ah, yes," she said this time. "So am I. It seems as though most politicians can nourish themselves on words alone."

"Ah, we're in luck. Here's the soup," Ransom said. *"Bon appétit."*

A flurry of waiters appeared, setting out bread and butter and serving the soup: the Center City Annual Pre-Election Dinner had begun.

———————————●———————————

IT CONTINUED FOR ANOTHER three hours—no surprise to Ransom, who had attended four previous such occasions. Only half the time was given over to actual dining. Once coffee and dessert were served, the various candidates and their supporters stood up at the head of the table, vacated by the judge, who served as chairman of the evening, to speechify. They explained their platforms, denounced rival policies, and complimented various members of Center City for a multiplicity of reasons.

Even before the rhetoric had set in, Ransom was beginning to find himself far less comfortable at the table than he had expected. As course after course was laid out, devoured, cleared away and replenished, he seemed to steadily lose ground with his companion rather than gain it.

Why had he thought she would be pleased with his attentions? Because of the judge's words, yes. Because, also, of some still infant plans of his own, he had to admit. Plans still too undeveloped, he now realized, to be nourished into much this evening. He might as well have sat where he had been originally placed for the amount of response he was receiving from Carrie Lane. True, she was talking to him every once in a while, between delicate nibblings at the surplus of turkeys and hams and sides of beef that filled the table. But it was small talk. And she was talking even more to Robertson Sloan, on the other side of her. Naturally enough, as she knew the senator better than she knew Ransom.

His own companion to the left, Mrs. Robertson Sloan, was not making matters any less difficult. So intrigued was she by anything Ransom had to say that she insisted on drawing out his responses to the simplest of questions with the skill of a cross-examiner. He ought to tread lightly with her. For all he knew, it was she, rather than the jovial, blustery senator, who wielded all the power and influence that Ransom wished to retain.

So he chatted amiably with her, all the while watching Mrs. Lane, and it became increasingly apparent that she was keeping her eyes on her escort—even seated so far away. She would turn to look at Dinsmore—not only when he had regaled his area of the table with some pleasantry which had drawn a highly vocal response, but also as he simply helped himself with great relish to the feast laid out before him. He seemed to be a bright point at his end of the table: Mrs. Brennan, Mrs. Mason, and even Amasa Murcott—who'd earlier called him a "quack"—listened as Dinsmore spoke, then burst out into peals of laughter.

Yet there were other moments, when Dinsmore's bright blue eyes would flash past the candelabra and serving ware to seek out those of his employer. Always she responded to these looks, Ransom noted, even going so far as to interrupt a conversation to turn and look at Dinsmore.

Then she would become quiet, as though chastened. Once she faltered in the middle of a trivial remark, hung her head, and only looked up again as though for guidance when Dinsmore had returned to his dinner.

The frequency of his looks and of her immediate responses was unnerving. Ransom was reminded of a mother watching a mischievous child. Or was it merely a jealous man watching his flirtatious lover? Whatever the cause, Ransom realized his own influence over her was feeble in comparison.

Influence. Yes. For wasn't that what Mrs. Ingram had ranted on about—about Dinsmore's influence upon Mrs. Lane. What was it she had said? *Dinsmore had her completely.* Watching the two of them tonight, Ransom could well understand those words in a way that he never could have with all the information in the world about either of them. It was uncanny, though. Like a marionette master and his doll—he would look, she would look in turn, become quiet, he would look away again. Over and over again. Especially uncanny that she would stop talking to Ransom, to look at Dinsmore.

At the head of the table Judge Dietz had just introduced Ludwig Baers, and the big German had begun to speak, when Ransom noticed the influence again. He decided to interfere by any means at his disposal.

"The blueberry tarts," he said, at the same time moving his entire upper torso forward and putting one hand to the side of his face, thus effectively blocking her view of Dinsmore. "I've had Lavinia's tarts before. I recommend them highly."

Poised on the other side of the gilded tray of pastries held by a servant standing between them, Carrie Lane suddenly looked directly into Ransom's eyes. Was she aware of what he was doing?

"Try one," he insisted.

She hesitated, then said, "Yes, I think I will," looking not at the waiter, but at him.

"You don't mind my deciding for you?" Ransom asked.

"Not if you decide well," she answered and poked at the flaky edge of the dessert with her fork.

"I assure you my decisions will always be in your best interest."

She looked directly into his eyes again. Was that fear? Or relief?

"Unlike others," Ransom added quickly, "whose own motives may not be so worthy."

She tried then to look past him down the table. Finding her view blocked, she looked back at him. "Can I be absolutely certain you don't possess motives of your own?" she said without a hint of emotion. "Motives that may be self-interested to a high degree."

"No. You can't. But at least I would never expose you."

"Expose me? To what?"

"To what has been happening this evening. That, I assure you, would never happen."

She colored as she realized what he was implying, then turned back to her plate. "You presume a great deal, Mr. Ransom." She tried looking past him again. He angled his elbow out even farther. "A great deal," she said. He could swear her eyes were as grateful as her words were stern.

"Perhaps. But can you deny what I say? You'd be received again."

"Don't say it."

"Received again among respectable people in this town . . ."

"Don't continue."

"Do you think it's a secret? Or that no one has noticed? Everyone has."

"Do you really care what everyone notices?" she asked.

"About you? Yes. Especially when it becomes so scandalous that even I, who know nothing and care nothing of these matters, am informed of it."

"I can't really see how it concerns you."

"Do you deny it concerns you?" he asked pointedly. Keeping her questioned, even annoyed at him, seemed to be breaking the uncanny contact she'd had all evening. He had to keep it going, no matter where it led to.

"You mean my not being received?"

"You're becoming a pariah," he said harshly. "Because of ignorance, I believe. Innocent ignorance, I'm certain. But that's hardly an excuse to others."

She was methodically forking open the tart. The berries gleamed blackly through the golden crust.

"When I asked if I might be your friend," Ransom went on, "I was hoping I would be able to take the liberty of finding out how aware you were of your position."

"Oh, my position!" she said, sounding disgusted. "What is my position, that it's everyone's concern?"

"Whatever it is, it does not include being known as the mistress of your own employee. Especially in the light of that employee's own dubious character and qualifications."

She tried looking past him again, and succeeded. But, as Ransom saw, Dinsmore was looking away. No contact was being made now.

"Please don't interfere," she said. "This is no concern of yours."

"I'm afraid it is."

"I don't give you permission to interfere," she said.

"I take it anyway."

"You cannot presume that I ever gave you reason to hope . . ." she began, but stopped.

"I presume nothing. If I interfere it will be for professional reasons."

"What professional reasons?"

"As prosecuting attorney of this county court district. Surely you are aware that your permission is not necessary in such matters."

Her hand went up to her mouth. "What will you do?" she asked.

"Much of that depends upon you. Upon how much you choose to trust me."

"I cannot trust anyone."

"You can't if it means hiding the truth," he replied.

She seemed to be on the verge of tears. She turned away, looking again toward Dinsmore, who still didn't respond, then back to her plate, where the blueberry tart lay crushed. She had not taken a single bite.

"I knew I ought never have given you that letter."

"You had no choice. I would have subpoenaed it."

"If I'd known it would bring me to this, I would have burned it first."

"If you haven't done wrong, you have nothing to fear."

"How can you say that? What do you know of it?"

"Not as much as I intend to know."

"Is that why you had him displaced tonight? So you could sit here and question me during dinner?"

"Is that what you believe?" he asked.

"I don't know what to believe."

"Then believe in me. Trust in me," he insisted.

"Leave me be," she whispered fiercely.

"It will be easier all round," he wheedled now. "Easier than having to be snubbed."

"Do you think me that shallow? That what a gaggle of women thinks could bring such anguish?"

He was stopped now, as much by her tone as by her words. He had managed to wrest her from Dinsmore. In the last few minutes, she hadn't once looked toward the man. Yet he was paying a price for such supercharged conversation—the price of her possible affection.

"Help me to know what to think of you," Ransom pleaded then, hoping to placate her. "That is all I ask of you."

She seemed to understand, for now she turned away and said, "Why must you too torment me? Haven't I enough to bear?"

"Let me help bear it."

"It's none of your concern," she said with finality.

"Then I'll make it my concern," he answered, as unrelenting.

He heard her sharp intake of breath, then watched as she struggled to stand up in her place, pushing her chair backward away from her. It began to topple; Ransom reached out to catch it. As he did, she stepped away from the table, and in seconds was gone from the room.

Even with Baers' table-thumping speech, her retreat was noticed by many present. Ought he follow her? Once away from the specious, flashing eyes of her steward, could he hope to explain what he had been trying to do? Before he could decide, Ransom saw Dinsmore rise from his own place. That decided him.

"Mrs. Lane . . ." he whispered to Mrs. Robertson Sloan, as he got out of his seat. "Feeling poorly . . . I'll go see."

"Ought I come too?" she asked.

"I think not," he said, and made good his escape out one of the small side doors of the dining room.

It led to a larder. Ransom surprised a woman servant who was picking at the remnants of a Virginia ham. She hastily wiped her fingers on her apron.

"How do I get to the big parlor?" he asked.

"There," she pointed to another doorway. "And then left again."

He passed out the door into a small back corridor. This must be the door that opened on the west parlor. As he gripped it, he heard voices coming from another direction. Going a few steps toward them, he saw the corridor narrowed past a stairway, then opened out again into the large entrance foyer. Keeping himself in the shadows, he edged forward until he could see who it was. Ah! Carrie Lane. Her mantilla was already drawn around her shoulders. She was alone.

He was about to step into the foyer, when the front door opened and Arthur, the Dietzes' butler, came in to tell her the phaeton was waiting.

She thanked him and opened her small black reticule, as though searching for something. Before she could find it or Ransom go to her, a figure stepped out of the west parlor, blocking Ransom's view. It was Dinsmore. He spoke so quietly, Ransom couldn't hear his words.

"Tell them anything," Carrie Lane answered, audibly enough. "Tell them I'm ill. I am now, you know. I told you, I ought never have come here tonight."

Dinsmore spoke again: a murmur.

"Leave me be!" she said. "I feel ghastly. I do."

She started toward the door. Again Dinsmore murmured. She stopped before the door, but did not turn around. In a low voice she said, "Yes. I'll wait. I'll be awake."

Dinsmore stood watching her go out the front door and descend to the phaeton. Then he shut the door and went into the west parlor.

Ransom came into the foyer. He heard the horses rattle off into the night. He could see Dinsmore standing by the fireplace in the big room, lost in thought, smoking a cigarette.

His meditation lasted only a brief moment. As soon as he became aware that he was being watched, he looked up at Ransom, then seemed to shake off his pensive mood, and advanced, smiling.

"I came looking for Mrs. Lane," Ransom explained. "Is she recovered?"

"Evidently not," Dinsmore replied. "She insisted on leaving. Wouldn't let me accompany her."

"Was she ill?"

"Who knows?" Dinsmore offered a cigarette. The fine, slender gold cigarette box was held open between them. Ransom went on:

"Has she been ill lately?"

"Again, I can't answer you. The housekeeper would know. I'm half tempted to go after her." He offered the cigarettes again, and this time Ransom took one and even let it be lighted.

"Women!" Dinsmore said, looking—or pretending to look— worried. "Who can say if they are ever ill, or merely being moody? I certainly can't."

The man's poise fascinated Ransom. He seemed to have decided on a role to play and was keeping fast to it.

"I'm afraid Mrs. Lane still hasn't completely recovered from her recent loss," Ransom suggested.

"Not at all," Dinsmore agreed. "It's positively morbid the way I find her lurking about. She sometimes comes into the office as though her husband were still there. I must say, the first few times it thoroughly chilled me."

They remained in the west parlor, Ransom trying to decide how it was that this ordinary-seeming man—quite ordinary-seeming, in fact—could have so extraordinary an influence over Carrie Lane. His attitude was that of a hired employee, not of a lover, not of a . . . of a what? She had seemed almost enchanted at the dinner table. What was the explanation for it?

They talked until their cigarettes had been smoked down to their fingers and there was no further question of following Mrs. Lane.

"What do you say?" Dinsmore asked brightly. "Shall we go in and hear the rest of the speeches?"

In the few minutes of their conversation the man had become so familiar, Ransom felt resentful of him. But he allowed himself to be slapped on the back, as he said, "Why not?"

It would be all that much time that Dinsmore would be away from Carrie Lane. And suddenly that mattered tremendously.

———————◆———————

THIS TIME SIMON CARR was already out of bed when Ransom rode up, sitting in an old rocking chair at the back of the house, amidst dry ground sparsely vegetated with sagebrush, and littered with rubble and debris. No one else was about the property, not even the German cook.

Ransom decided to waste no time on civilities.

"Feeling better?" he asked the startled old man as he dismounted, pulled over a wooden crate, and wedged himself against Carr's knees, effectively trapping him in place.

"Somewhat," Carr replied.

"Glad to hear it. Now I want to hear more. I want to hear all about Mr. Dinsmore. Everything. Including why he's Mrs. Lane's manager, what his connection with her is, what role you played in that connection, and in his life altogether, what you and Dinsmore had to do with Henry Lane's death, and why you're out here on this ranch. Everything. Right now. In full detail. With no evasions. Otherwise, so help me God, I'll come out here this afternoon with a court order, and by sunset you'll be sitting in judge's chambers, before a grand jury, under oath, and with the penalty of imprisonment hanging over you. Is that clear?"

Carr did not react until Ransom was done. Then his scrawny neck drew in on either side of the prominent Adam's apple, the heavy eyes lidded over, and the hawk nose seemed to grow even more beaklike.

"I'll tell you nothing, Mr. Government Man."

"You're an old man, Mr. Carr. How would you like to spend the rest of your days rotting away in the state prison?"

"You can't frighten me. You can't compel me either. Not you, not any judge, not all the grand juries in the nation. Whatever I happen to know is my concern. It'll go to the grave with me if that's what I choose."

"And that's your choice?" Ransom asked, standing up.

"That's my choice," Carr said proudly.

"I respect and admire your determination," Ransom said then, watching Carr's face register surprise. "Now, if you'll be so kind as to set out some tea for me as you did the last time I visited you, perhaps I can persuade you otherwise."

"Nothing in the world can persuade me otherwise," the old man declared. "But I'll be happy to fix you a cuppa. I just might have some too."

He got up spryly enough from the rocker, but he looked even thinner, even more wasted than when Ransom had last seen him.

Inside the kitchen, Ransom was quiet, watching Carr putter about. Once the tea was ready, the cups set out, the tea poured, the first sip taken, Ransom began to tell Carr what he had witnessed the night before between Dinsmore and Carrie Lane: his growing realization of the influence Dinsmore had over her; her words, her actions, her awareness of the scandal she was creating, her anguish over it, and what she had said to Dinsmore in the foyer, leaving the Dietzes' house.

Carr's initial pleasure at what he thought would be a social report of the big pre-election dinner dwindled as he realized what he was being told. His face became grim. He interrupted Ransom to ask one or two specific questions. When Ransom mentioned Mrs. Lane searching for something in her reticule, Carr had him repeat that. When Ransom was done, he finished the cold tea remaining in his cup and said:

"Now you see why I have come out here. Will you tell me what I must know?"

"Do you love this woman?" Carr asked.

Ransom had edited his account to avoid relaying any of his personal feelings or intentions. He was taken aback by the old man's question.

"Perhaps you don't quite understand why I've told you all this, Mr. Carr?"

"Simon. Call me Simon. For like that other Simon, I too have denied the truth three times, to my eternal shame. Yes, Mr. Government Man, I understand all too well what you've told me. And now I'm asking you if you love this woman."

"I don't see what that has to do with anything."

"If you don't, you don't have a chance with her. She's lost. But if you do, I'll forgive your rudeness to me before and pity you instead."

"Lost? What do you mean lost?"

"Lost. He has got her. This influence of which you spoke, and so well described, goes far beyond what you noticed last night. That was like the top leaves of those little plants whose entire root system lies underneath the ground, covering hundreds of yards in all directions."

"How can that be?" Ransom asked. The old man's image seemed fetid, moulding, crepuscular to him. It seemed so rotting, so dead. "I don't believe it. No one can influence another person to that extent."

"They can. *He* can."

"How?"

The old man shrugged and mumbled something under his breath. Aloud he said, "You want to know everything. Isn't that what you said? I was like you once myself. So eager for knowledge no matter how terrible it might prove to be, or how strange. But let me tell you, Mr. Government Man, some things are better left unknown. If I weren't so curious when I was younger, so avid for forbidden knowledge, you wouldn't have to be curious yourself today. Believe me. I made Dinsmore what he is today. I'm the one responsible—the one to blame, if you will. Before he met me he was a ruffian, a huckster, a carpetbagger, hawking phony miracles on street corners. Now look at him! That's all because of me. I curse the day I met him. And not only for this precious little bit of half-concocted community on the edge of the frontier. No. I curse myself for more, far more than that."

Ransom tried to follow the old man's words. They were passionately enough spoken, no matter how rambling, how incoherent. Ought he let Carr talk on and hope to glean what it was he was saying? Or should he question the man more closely?

"Have you ever been to a traveling show?" Carr suddenly asked. "To a carnival?"

"Yes, but . . ."

"And have you ever seen a Mesmerist in the show? You know, the man who induces animal magnetism into a subject?"

"Once, yes. Briefly."

"And the Mesmerist did something foolish to show the powers of animal magnetism, didn't he?"

"Very foolish," Ransom admitted. "He convinced a man that he had lost the use of one leg. The man pretended to hobble off, calling for a cane. Of course it was a complete fraud."

Carr didn't comment on that. After a second's silence he simply said:

"Mr. Dinsmore is a Mesmerist, Mr. Government Man. So, for that matter, am I a Mesmerist. Or at least I have been one. I don't know if I possess the ability any longer, it's been a long time since I've used it. But not your carnival, side-show variety of Mesmerist, Mr. Government Man. Not at all. For I was a colleague of the great Sir James Braid, of the Royal Academy of Medicine. He is the man most responsible for introducing mesmerism into the practice of surgery. He called it hypnotism. Now, do you understand what I'm talking of?''

"Not completely,'' Ransom said. In fact, he didn't understand at all.

"Well, then, have another cup of tea, and so will I. Then I'll explain, and at the same time answer your questions. I'm not afraid of prison, you'll discover. It's not because of threats that I'm telling you this; I want that to be clearly understood. But because you ought to know exactly what Dinsmore is capable of. I suppose I owe it to someone to speak what I know. Especially now that he's so far on his way. Not that it will make a great deal of difference, I'm afraid. But at least all of you won't be completely taken in by him.''

"I'm ready,'' Ransom said.

————————————•————————————

"SUFFICE IT FOR ME TO SAY I was born the younger son of a wealthy, untitled family in Yorkshire,'' the old man began. "Raised and educated to resemble one of my more aristocratic classmates at the Kings College at Oxford, I soon joined society as one of them: frivolous, superficial, a dilettante, determined at all costs to entertain myself. That I felt little real pleasure in this course of life I can best explain by how quickly I was able to throw it over for a life of dedication and consuming interest.

"The cause of this was Sir James Braid, whom I met one evening at one of the best salons in Mayfair. There, in a drawing room that I remember to this day, I first fell under the spell of Braid's voice and words. He was at that time a magnetic man, blooming with vigor, at the peak of his life and reputation. A brilliant surgeon, he had just rediscovered the science of mesmerism and had begun employing it with great success in operations where drugs proved dangerous or ineffective.

"Braid called the technique hypnotism—from his belief in its similarity to sleep. *Hypnos* is the Greek word for sleep. He needed a listener, and I was more than willing to listen. Only a few such drawing-room *tête-à-têtes* persuaded me that I had found what it was my life had so badly wanted—a purpose, a goal. Medicine became for me the highest aim of an educated, cultured man. I threw myself into its intricacies heart and soul, studying and finally learning enough through the university course and hospital internship to knock on Braid's door one day and offer my time and talents to him.

"I discovered it was a poor time for me to be calling on him. Braid's clientele had fallen off as a result of his own growing obsession with the uses of hypnotism in matters outside the elimination of pain during surgical operations. Blind to his eccentricities, I entered willingly, fully into his research, after a while becoming as practiced as he, becoming myself a Mesmerist.

"That word is the more common one for this sort of practice, used to describe not only illusionists in circuses and traveling side shows, but also highly respected men in scientific academies. It derives from the name of its founder, Anton Mesmer, a Frenchman at the court of Louis XVI, who used it in the most elegant salons and boudoirs of Paris. Mesmer claimed it was a natural, although invisible, ether, like electricity—but more refined. He tried to connect it with the other fledgling sciences—electricity and magnetism—and to harness mesmerism, collect it in barrels surrounded with magnetically charged metal rims. Amid all this balderdash, he effected some rather marvelous cures.

"Mesmer did not realize that it was not animal magnetism but instead a method of entering the mind of another person. Sir James understood this immediately. The force—if one could even call it a force—was merely that of suggestion, but suggestion of a closely controlled kind, and inductible to another only when that person was free of any other distractions. Thus the necessity for placing the subject into a nonconscious state, a sleeplike trance. Braid discovered that this trance could be easily induced and that it resembled the sleep of somnambulists, who walk about and even perform tasks. Thus this choice of the word hypnosis. He later discovered, however, that the sleep he induced was not like somnambulism. For his subjects, once

awakened, remembered all that had occurred to them in the
trance, except when he suggested they not recall it; then they
recollected nothing. He also discovered that suggestions instilled
during the trance were effective afterward too—day after day of
the subject's waking life. For example, a young man known to
Braid had, as a little boy, been attacked by a large Labrador
retriever. The young man's fear of dogs was continual, unreasoning, often embarrassing. Braid discovered the cause of this
unreasoning fear, and during a trance the young man was
brought into contact with a series of the canine species, which he
petted and even fondled. After only two such sessions, he was
cured of his fear.

"Like Braid, I too saw the implications in these experiments,
and foolish as I was, I was not in the least bit horrified, but instead
decided to carry on my own research into this area even after
Braid had drawn back.

"By this time Sir James's own health and fortunes had considerably worsened. There was some sort of misunderstanding
about a young female subject. It was blown into a scandal out of
all proportion. The doors of Belgravia were shut in his face; he
was reproved by the Academy of Medicine, and then—when he
persisted in arguing for his discoveries—forced to resign from
that august assemblage. Reluctantly, Sir James abandoned his
practice and retired to an ancestral estate far from the caprices
of London.

"I continued his work for several years, perfecting methods of
inducing the hypnotic state most rapidly and effectively; learning
that I could induce suggestions into trance states which were not
at all sleeplike, but merely arrested consciousness. I experimented with other aspects of the mind—habit, despondency,
anxiety, elation, even hysteria. I worked with the insane and the
semi-insane, with neurasthenics and melancholiacs, convinced
the work was of the greatest importance to mankind. A Dar-
winian, I stood by mesmerism as the key to our next evolutionary
state—the perfection of mental control.

"During this time, my bills steadily mounted, for after my
inheritance was spent securing volunteer subjects for my work,

I became so immersed in my research that I scarcely noticed that Braid's old offices were foreclosing about me. When I did finally look about me, I was financially ruined, socially ostracized, personally a laughingstock, and professionally as dishonored as Braid had been. It did not require a great deal of deliberation for me to decide to leave England for less constraining parts. I wrote to universities with medical schools all over the continent, giving my background, and especially my connection with Sir James.

"Unfortunately, the reaction that I had experienced in my own country had begun across Europe too. All my applications were rejected, save for an unremunerative post at Heidelberg, where I would have so many classes I could not find enough time for my own work. Like so many of the oppressed I decided to immigrate to America.

"Once arrived in Boston, however, I found my hopes instantly dashed. The New England temperament does not take kindly to the unexplainable, unless it be theistic or philosophical. It was the same in all of the large eastern cities—Philadelphia, Charlestown, New York. I was offered surgical positions, once my association and tutelage under Braid was known. But under no circumstances would any medical institution finance or approve my research in mesmerism. Principled fool that I was, I eschewed their offers and went off, brooding like Satan after his great fall, among the indigent and despondent.

"This lasted some months. I was only brought out of my proud and gloomy contemplations by the need of another. A woman neighbor in my shabby lodgings suffered from an abscessed tooth. She could not afford to see a dentist. I examined her and found the tooth had dangerously infected her nasal, sinal, and Eustachian cavities. Prompt action was called for. With the most primitive of instruments remaining in my much depleted medical bag—for I had pawned many of them to live—I operated, first mesmerizing her, then removing the tooth, and afterward draining the infection. She recovered and there—I thought—the matter stood.

"Within a week I had people from all over the tenement

knocking on my door, timidly clutching coins in their hands, requiring—no, begging for—my services. In this way, I became a dental surgeon while remaining as much as ever a misanthrope.

"One patient's recommendation led to another's, and I soon found myself out of the garret and living in Chicago, with wealthy and socially prominent patients. I had all the worldly goods that I needed, more than I had ever expected, but my life remained as empty, as meaningless as it had been before I had met Sir James Braid. It was at this crucial time that I first met Mr. Dinsmore.

"He didn't go by his own name then, but instead by a crude, though admittedly poetic one—Father Francis Truth.

"Father Francis Truth stood on a sort of easily erected platform against the wall of any well-traveled street in the center of Chicago's business district, surrounded by banners proclaiming his pseudonym and the various abilities he claimed to possess. He was assisted at that time by a grubby boy of indeterminate age and despicable manners. And from morning to night, standing upon his little platform, Father Francis Truth hawked panaceas for all the ills of the flesh. He sold a patent elixir of some sulfurous mess which he claimed cured anything from migraine headaches to foot corns. For the more gullible, he sold handkerchiefs of a cheap linen, with curious stains on them, which he declared came from the healing waters of Baden-Baden and Siberia. His business was a poor one: faith healing often is. His cuffs were frayed, his trouser knees and jacket elbows shiny with age and usage, his linen unspeakably yellow, his mood alternately entreating and mocking. I passed him three times a week before I realized what continued to draw me to him.

"Not since Sir James had I heard a voice so perfectly pitched, so beautifully modulated for inducing mesmeric trances. It was as fine an instrument as a great singer's—dark, clear, of an almost colorless timber. Yet so flexible and liquid it could enter the mind and once there remain forever. And indeed, in some primitive fashion, he was already using mesmeric techniques. On two separate occasions I watched and listened as a prospective purchaser for one item was convinced of the necessity for purchasing several others. It was not mere salesmanship, for Father Francis Truth, in his grimy, semiclerical garb, would select his subject from among the small audience he had gathered around him, and using his magnificent eyes to fix a stare, would work on that one person with his voice until he had gotten him.

"I immediately thought what an asset he could prove in my own research. I had not done any experimentation for more than a decade. Yet I was inspired by his eyes and voice to begin once more. With the aid of such an assistant, I need not throw myself so completely into it as I'd done before. I might retain my prosperous dental practice and still experiment. But how to approach him, that's what I pondered day after day.

"An opportunity soon presented itself. Passing him yet another afternoon, I witnessed his forced removal from the street corner by the police: evidently a common mischance for street hawkers such as he. I followed him to the nearest saloon, where he began muttering his troubles. I engaged him in sympathetic conversation and quickly outlined my need of an assistant. Cautiously, for I did not mention mesmerism, fearing to come against some initial preclusive prejudice. Watching him later on during that encounter, while he was playing cards, I also noticed that he had clever, facile hands. He was young, not unintelligent and quite optimistic. Opposites attract, I suppose, and so I thought I had found precisely the man to aid me as I had once assisted Sir James so many years before.

"He proved a quick study. He attended me assiduously during surgery and examinations for nearly two years. Once my professional business was done for the day, we would resume our research. Here, Dinsmore proved an even better student. Unlike myself, he was able to instill suggestions into a subject with great facility—almost naturally, it seemed—and, most important, without requiring an object for them to fix upon. Both men and ladies were only too happy to sit back, to talk with this clever, polite young man and to stare at his remarkable blue eyes until they had been all unawares fixed into a trance. For Dinsmore had another ability I lacked, that of inducing a trance so gossamer light that one couldn't be certain one was in a trance. These abilities were demonstrated to an extraordinary degree in our late-afternoon experiments. In a trance so light the subject would be giggling at jokes, Dinsmore would, in quite offhanded a manner, suggest something absurd to be accomplished at a later point. He could snap the trance apart as easily too—a word or two, a hand passed over the subject's eyes, even a wink of his eye would do it. Then the real efficacy of his power would be proved, time after time, as the absurd, prescribed action was performed by the embarrassed subject; often to our great amusement.

"At this point, I ought to have taken greater care. But my obsession had now returned with undiminished force. Once again I hoped to set the world on its ear with my discoveries and proofs. Once again I was to have a startling recognition of the truth of the matter.

"This occurred one day as I was standing behind a new subject whom Dinsmore was testing for depth of trance ability. You ought to know that about ninety-six out of any hundred people can be hypnotized—but of them, only a third are capable of attaining the deepest of trances, that most resembling sleep. Another third can attain an intermediate trance, and almost all the lightest trance. What was remarkable this day was that the initial hypnosis did not take at all. One only does it a few minutes at a time—up to six or seven minutes at the longest. Well, I thought, here we have one of the rare ones: a workingman of some fifty years who was not subject to any trance. He was clearly unaffected, I could see that. But Dinsmore continued to test him anyway. 'Lift your right arm,' Dinsmore said, and the man did so easily, laughing at Dinsmore, who had only a moment before suggested the subject would not be able to. You may guess my own reaction when I discovered that while the subject could lift his arm, I could not move my right arm an inch. It's almost impossible to describe how I felt. Naturally I did not say a word at the time. Dinsmore then made a few more demands of our subject. As before, the workingman did as he wished, and I was bound to follow all of the suggestions. It was a stupendous feat, I realized: Dinsmore had mesmerized me by proxy. The subject was dismissed and paid his fee, and I was taken out of a trance so light I scarcely knew I had been in one. That night Dinsmore and I celebrated his ability over a fine dinner and champagne.

"The following day, on my insistence, Dinsmore again mesmerized me by proxy. Once the subject had departed, I was brought to again, with many congratulations. Not ten minutes later, we closed the office. I remember very little about it, except that I removed my trousers and, otherwise fully clothed for the outdoors, walked out to the street. That was the first taste I had of his power—a grotesque introduction to the new shape of our connection. And an appropriate one, for it would soon prove humiliating in other ways.

"Dinsmore claimed he had only been having some sport with me. But this sport soon became tiresome. He would mesmerize me as easily, as instantly as one breaks the knuckles on one's hands in cold weather—he even utilized that method once or twice. When I was convinced of his strength he stated his conditions: he would have one half of my business profits, one half of all I possessed. Furthermore, I would introduce him as my full partner in the dental practice, with his own choice of patients. The experiments were to be continued, no longer under my direction, but his. He was to be named co-author on the title page of the treatise on mesmerism I was then completing for publication. Remonstrance proved impossible. He soon used his powers to find out why I had left Great Britain: discovering this and a great deal more while I was under a deep trance he had induced. He threatened to use this information to destroy my reputation, and whenever I would rebel, as quickly as a safety match struck on a rough surface, I would be quieted.

"Several times I found myself in peril. Once tottering from the tiny workmen's balcony of a high church steeple I had climbed unawares. Another time leaning over the edge of scaffolding thrown across a river. Whether I was prevented from death by his inability to wield control over me even to that extent or whether strangers had both times seen me and come to my aid, I do not know to this day, and would not care to speculate. Whatever the case, I saw my alternatives most lucidly after these incidents, and I bent to his domination.

"That lasted only a few more months in Chicago, due to one of his own demands and its consequences. In selecting his own patients, Dinsmore made certain most of them were ladies, and all of them, whether married or not, attractive. How base he was to them was only revealed when one of the single young ladies became mysteriously with child. Unfortunately for Dinsmore, the smitten young lady had never hidden her feelings about him to her family, going so far as to fabricate a relation which while as intimate as the one he enjoyed was hardly Dinsmore's real interest, i.e., she told them he had asked to marry her.

"The young lady's father was an industrialist with a great deal of money and as taken in as she by Dinsmore. I assumed it had been Dinsmore's purpose to force a situation which might not have gone his way by less controlled methods. After all, he had talked often enough of how well he could get on in the world with a rich wife and good relations. So I was amazed when he said he would not marry the girl. Could not marry her was closer to the truth, for I discovered that Dinsmore was already married, and though I don't doubt that he would have scrupled to commit bigamy if his wife weren't in Chicago, she was, and so he was prevented.

"When told of his decision and its cause, the pregnant young lady went up to her bedroom, locked herself in, and hanged herself with a knotted bedsheet. Enraged, her father swore vengeance. Both Dinsmore and I—as his accomplice—were arrested. We were charged with a number of crimes from fraud to manslaughter. Thanks to Mrs. Dinsmore's timely intervention, we were released on bail she had managed to raise.

"Only two courses were now open: to watch the devastation of my fortunes once more and hope to remain a free man while fighting the court case; or to flee.

"This latter was Dinsmore's only view of the matter. He must take me and his wife with him too. Not that he cared a bit for either of us, but he feared that we would stand as witnesses against him. For the next few days, she and I were forced to pawn all that could bring ready money, delving into neighborhoods where we were not known so as to not arouse any suspicions. That accomplished, we left the city one night by stealth.

"I won't weary you with our wanderings or with our travails. Whenever we attempted to settle or I to set up a dental practice, difficulties cropped up. Too often, we were justly regarded as dangerous. Larger cities soon became prohibitive—for it was between them that news of us traveled most rapidly. We were forced to move to smaller towns, farther south and west, forced to remain half-hidden wherever we went, in the poorer sections, for fear we would be known and hounded once more. Dinsmore was now the dental surgeon, and I—broken in health and more than that, in spirit—was his slave.

"It fared even worse for his devoted Margaret. It was she who was blamed for our distresses and calamities; she who had cheated him of the industrialist's daughter, caused him to be arrested, and consequently to lead this life of vagabondage, poverty, and shame. He beat her on occasion, he humiliated her far more often, he ignored her for weeks at a time. She told me she had been the child of a wealthy family in Philadelphia when she had first met him. Even without my own tutelage, he had mesmerized her using other, less subtle means. She had come to him willingly. They had married. But the expected reconciliation with her family had not happened. Since then, Dinsmore had sometimes stayed with Margaret, but more often had kept away from her. He often left her, and it was only after years and great hardships that she found him again. He saw this devotion as his crown of thorns, his cross—and he bore it most unwillingly.

"It was thus, three bound together by forces both natural and unnatural, that we came to Center City. And thus that we remained here, once more eking out a living, living half-hidden from the daylight or from any proper people. Once more we set up a dental office, once more I assisted whenever I was able to. Increasingly, I could not even do this. My heart had already begun to trouble me; now it began to fail me more seriously. I could feel its erratic beat grow weak. Knowing medicine as well as I did, it was impossible for me to not recognize every sign of its malfunction. I soon became invalid.

"Margaret, too, began to decline, though not from any such evident cause, and in a far less dramatic manner. And always, I came to believe, under the direct suggestion of her hateful husband. He was healthy enough—a virile, active man. He visited many women. He never sought to hide it from her. He desperately wanted to be free of her. He said as much many times. I firmly believe she withered under his neglect, and came to think of herself as consumptive under his direct mesmeric control. His control of both of us was that extensive, that enveloping.

"Margaret was a good woman, gentle, courteous, but she could show spark and fight, and sometimes she did so. He liked that about her; said it was the only mark left of her fine breeding. He liked fine ladies; the finer, the more high born, the better. Ladies who had that spirit bred into them. But even more, he liked to crush that spirit. As he crushed her. As he crushed me too.

"I was deeply bereft when Margaret died. She had been kindness itself to me. It was only a half year later that Dinsmore came to me and told me to pack up and get ready. He'd gotten rid of one burden; I was to be the last.

"I was brought here at the beginning of the summer in a state of near collapse. Minna—the cook—takes care of me as well as she can. I am regaining my health away from him. But not my will. Every once in a while he comes to visit me, to regale me with his new position, to warn me to not say anything to anyone about him or our shared past.

"As though I would! I had half forgotten it until today, or had hoped I'd forgotten it. For though he seldom comes anymore, I know he has me watched. I don't care. I feel free of him, even if it is not true that I am. Just to be at a distance from him is enough. Yet it is somehow worse too that I cannot be with him, for I often thought myself a restraint upon his worst instincts— almost a conscience.

"By talking to you today, I have probably put my life in the gravest danger. But I had to tell this to someone. Not to the cook —she's a good-hearted woman, but ignorant. To someone who would understand, as I think you have. Dinsmore is a dangerous and ambitious man. I can shed no further light upon what you have told me. But I recognize his past failures are now matured into triumph for him.

"I can tell you nothing at all of Henry Lane, but that he was a patient of Dinsmore's for over a year. Of Mrs. Lane I know even less. But these are new pieces, and surely you can fit them in somehow, given the frame and pattern of his life. Now, do you have any further questions?"

Ransom had a score of questions, a hundred questions to ask. He had had no idea when he first sat down to listen to Carr that the old man would tell his life story—a story as strange and full of wonder as a tale from *The Arabian Nights.* He'd listened in silence, more from not wishing to interrupt and thus miss a word of it, than from any politeness. And, as he'd listened, Ranson had found himself unable to find the right questions to ask.

Was the old man throwing out an ingeniously constructed barrage of words to serve as a screen between them? To confuse Ransom? To throw him off the trail altogether? Toward the end of his narration, Carr had finally answered some of Ransom's demands for explanations, but they now seemed insignificant in light of the whole story he had told. Had that been done on purpose? Nothing of Carr's narration had been wandering or inconsistent, nothing at all indicative of oncoming senility. Yet it was all so exotic, so alien—and still so well formulated—that it was difficult to believe it hadn't been thought out beforehand. Worst of all, the whole thing hinged on this mesmerism business which Ransom had never seriously thought of before as anything but a fraud.

He could, probably should, laugh it all off, take it as a grandly conceived evasion. Several times during the old man's talk—at a loss for any other appropriate reaction—he had almost done exactly that. But he'd always stopped himself, let himself listen on. If only because of Carr's utter conviction as he spoke. Only a consummate actor could do all that Carr had done today—shudder to recall his near escapes from death, wax indignant over how badly Margaret had been treated, curse himself for his folly, for the blindness that had led him to become Dinsmore's tool—without having lived it. But wasn't it as easy to believe Carr a has-been Thespian from some itinerant traveling troupe as it was to believe him an associate of the knighted Sir James Braid, or a psychic explorer? Easier than believing him a Mesmerist, at any rate.

So, for a while he asked nothing important, merely a half dozen questions relating to their arrests and the legality of their leaving Illinois. Then another half dozen on the method of mesmeric induction. The old man answered fully, in detail.

"Is that all?" Carr asked.

"That's all for the moment."

"Well then, good day to you. And hope I shall still be alive should you chance to call again, Mr. Government Man."

He said the words lightly, almost bantering. Since he had talked, his spirits seemed to have lifted considerably. As though the chains of the past had been lifted from his shoulders and he felt their release with pleasure. He even smiled now, and accompanied his visitor outside.

When Ransom had mounted, he rode to the back of the house to say good-bye. Carr was sitting in the rocking chair amid the rubble and the dry earth, enjoying the sun, almost serene.

———————————●———————————

THE BURDEN SIMON CARR LIFTED off himself with such relief did not come immediately to rest on Ransom's shoulders, nor when it did, did it rest easily.

Riding back to Center City from the Lane Ranch, Ransom did not ask himself how much of what the old man had said he believed, but rather how he could believe any of it. For to believe any single strand of the story meant to take the whole cloth of it—it was that closely woven.

When Carr had asked if Ransom had ever seen a Mesmerist, and he'd admitted it, Ransom had quickly pictured the illusionist's little side show: the canvas tent held up by two tilting poles, the stage made of rough planking, the crowd of faces made

grotesque and ambiguous by the flickering light of several tor-
ches framing the stage, and the Mesmerist himself—a
broken-down Medicine Man with five days' beard, a whisky
voice, and few of his wits still about him. It had been a fraud. Of
that Ransom was certain.

Now Carr had told him it hadn't been, that mesmerism had
been experimented with by great physicians, studied and found
to work on almost anyone. A science, Carr had called it, admit-
ting at the same time that it was beyond science too. A black
science. From what Ransom had understood, an insidious, nefarious method whereby men were convinced that what was, was
not; and what was not, was. Whereby men and women were
manipulated like puppets, controlled like slaves. A black art.

Ransom had heard testimony often enough before to know
fairly certainly when a person lied or fabricated, and when he
told the truth. If people lied for a reason, they also told the truth
for a reason. One reason was fear. Another to unburden themselves. Carr had not lied. He'd told the truth. Ransom knew it,
knew it instinctively—yet he still couldn't believe it.

What, too, of the way Carr had prefaced his story? Asking if
Ransom loved Carrie Lane. Saying how far Dinsmore now had
her under control. Implying that control was as great, as deep as
Dinsmore's control over his wife, over Carr himself in the past.

Until now, Ransom's motives had been unclear even to himself. Despite his coming back out to see Carr, he hadn't been
entirely certain it wasn't merely out of jealousy—and the fear
that the influence he had seen so clearly the night before wasn't
simply a passion between Mrs. Lane and her manager. Especially
after the brief scene he'd witnessed between them in the judge's
foyer. Now he had confirmation of Mrs. Ingram's fears. Of
course he would have to see how this mesmerism worked. For
without knowing it at first hand, there would be no knowing if
it could do all that Carr claimed.

Amasa Murcott was extending his lunch hour when Ransom
joined him at the boarders' table, and began questioning him
about mesmerism.

"I don't rightly know how it works," the doctor admitted.

"Some of the medical journals have articles on the subject. I've read one or two. An Austrian has used it on hysterical patients. I could show them to you."

"Right now?" Ransom asked. Then seeing Murcott's surprise, "Is it ever used in surgery?"

"I believe so."

Ransom followed the doctor into his office, and hung over his shoulder as the older man looked into a large, morocco-bound index.

"Dinsmore uses it," Ransom said. "For his painless dentistry."

"You don't say," Murcott looked up, a finger poised on the printed line of the index. "I thought he was using Nitrous Oxide. What people sometimes call laughing gas."

"That's what his former assistant said: mesmerism."

"Here you are, James. There are five or six articles," he said, ticking off several lines. "That looks most relevant. The journal is behind you," he added, pointing to a shelf full of morocco volumes similarly bound. "Help yourself."

Ransom spent the next half hour finding the articles, and toting the big volumes up to his second-floor office. He shut his office door to any interruptions and read through not only the six articles Murcott had suggested but every other one listed in the index. He was done at dinner time. After they had eaten, he asked the doctor to join him upstairs for a brandy and a smoke.

"Well," Ransom began, patting the volumes. "I've read them all. Now, I would like to know your opinion on the subject."

"I don't have one. What do they say?"

"None of the articles seems to say a great deal." He paused. "Mrs. Ingram came to talk to me after she saw you for her examination. She was extremely disturbed. Acting very unlike herself. Is it possible that she had been mesmerized the day before?"

"All I can report is that she was physically fit. What's the point of all this, James? Or oughtn't I know?"

"You're going to have to know. I need another view on it."

In a few minutes he had told the doctor what Mrs. Ingram had said of Dinsmore's influence over Mrs. Lane. Then he described what he had witnessed between Mrs. Lane and Dinsmore at the pre-election dinner. A longer time was required for him to relate what Simon Carr had told him.

Murcott did not respond at once. He tamped out the ashes from his pipe, packed in a third pipeful, and lit it. "Now, you're sure all this isn't just a tall tale? Because if it isn't, it's sure going to take a lot of bother. You have nothing to go on but suppositions."

"What if it isn't a tall story?"

"Well, then, it goes some way toward explaining some mighty curious matters. But first of all you're going to have to find out if this mesmerism business actually works."

"I know that. I'm going to see Dinsmore in his capacity as a dentist. I'm going to allow myself to be mesmerized, just like one of his patients. That's the only way I figure I can find out if it isn't malarkey."

"Won't he be suspicious? Your teeth are all in good condition."

"I've thought of that. I'm going to have an abscessed tooth when I go, so he has no suspicions. And you're going to help me. I want you to remove one of my silver alloy fillings. It oughtn't be too long before the tooth gets infected. I'll go to him, have him mesmerize me, and have positive proof."

"Positive proof that he's a painless dentist. Nothing else."

"We'll see. I've thought about it, Amasa. Will you do it?"

"Seems foolhardy to me. Why go messing up a perfectly good tooth?"

"I suppose I have to do something foolish to prove something foolish. Will you help?"

"If you insist."

"Another thing. I'm writing to William K. Reese at the capitol. I owe him a letter anyway. I'll express curiosity about Dinsmore's past. A few rumors and suchlike. He'll understand what I'm aiming at. He's not the state district attorney for nothing. But I'd like to ask a favor of you, too. I'd like you to write to some of these fellows"—stroking the volume in front of him—"Write in your professional capacity, and ask what they know about mesmerism, and if what Carr says had happened, can happen. Would you do that?"

"I'm a busy man, James," Murcott said. Then, "All right. Draw up the letters. I'll sign 'em." He stood up. "You better have another glassful of brandy for this operation. I suppose I'll have to improvise down there. Don't blame me if something goes wrong."

"I won't."

As both men reached the door, Murcott hesitated.

"Just one question, James. What will you charge Dinsmore with?"

"I'm not certain of the details, but it will be murder."

"Henry Lane?"

"And Margaret Dinsmore."

———————●———————

RANSOM STRUGGLED TO AWAKE through a vague but ghastly dream. Once his eyes were open, he wished he were asleep again. Sitting up, he felt pain like hammer blows strike his head, neck, shoulders and back, all along his left side as though someone were trampling on him.

It was worse when he attempted to stand up. The pain was so sharp, and he so dizzy, he almost crumpled to the floor. Grabbing the dresser ledge, he was able to stand up, and inspected his face in the oval shaving mirror.

His left eye was half-shut, puffy and red. Tiny globules of perspiration stood out on his forehead. His left cheek was swollen to almost twice the size of the other; it was puffy and red, the skin stretched hard. The abscess had taken, taken well in the four days since Amasa had removed the filling. He hoped to hell Dinsmore could see him today. Every move caused him to wince. He dressed in slow motion.

Only Murcott and Mrs. Page were at the breakfast table. Ransom hardly greeted them. Now that he was more fully awake, he felt worse than before. The veins on the left side of his neck throbbed like snare drums. His hearing seemed dulled, his head filled with a buzzing. Had he let the abscess go too long, too far? He hoped not.

Food was impossible. Even eating with his head on an angle to avoid touching the left side of his mouth, he felt every morsel as if it were a dagger point. The corn muffins—Mrs. Page's speciality—tasted like sand today. Coffee was a little better: strong, black and hot. He hardly felt its heat, and swilling it around the area of the bad tooth, though shocking at first, later on seemed to dull the pain a bit.

There was no note from Dinsmore confirming their appointment, which didn't help his mood. The afternoon before, Ransom had sent Nate to the Lane house with an emergency message. Trying to blank his mind to the pain, Ransom now went over the words he had written. "I'm told you're the best dentist in the county, though no longer practicing. I hope you will make an exception for a recent dinner companion with Job's own trials to bear in an infected lower molar." Ransom had signed his name to it with no apprehension that Dinsmore would associate him with the government man Simon Carr had talked to—in the unlikely event he'd gone out to see the old man. Ransom hoped the familiar tone of his words would draw Dinsmore the way an extravagantly designed fly on a fishhook would draw even the most reluctant carp.

Nor was he disappointed. Before breakfast was over, a day laborer he recognized from the Lane Feed and Grain arrived with Dinsmore's answer. He would see Ransom at noon. He gave an address: the office above Bent's saloon.

"Eureka!" Ransom said, showing the note to Murcott.

"You look awful, James."

"That's how I have to look."

"Are you in much pain?"

"Don't ask."

"Why don't I give you a pain-killer? Just to hold you over until you go there?"

"Much as I would beg for it under other circumstances, I can't. I have to know if mesmerism works. I have to see how he does it. I need proof. You can see that, can't you?"

"Bull-headed," Murcott muttered. "Suit yourself," he added, and stalked off to his office, Ransom to his.

Work was out of the question: he could scarcely read. Even lying down, fully dressed on his bed, was no help. The pain seemed to grow minute by minute. It seemed a malignant force. He hadn't had a bad tooth in a dozen years. Curious, he hadn't thought how bad it would be until now. But then pain itself was a curious matter. One could not remember it very well, and one couldn't really anticipate it either. In his condition, in bondage to his torment, he felt less than human.

It will be gone soon, he told himself then, and later on, walking down Van Buren Avenue and ascending the shadowed stairway to the familiar frosted green-glass door.

This time it opened when he knocked.

"Ah, Mr. Ransom. Come in. I've just arrived myself. I'm getting ready for you."

Dinsmore had his jacket off, and after directing Ransom to do likewise, he tied on a white, spotlessly clean frock that reached to his knees, but which had no arms or collar.

"Anti-Septic," Dinsmore explained. "We can't let you become more ill than you already are."

Ransom mumbled his appreciation that Dinsmore had decided to see him. He hoped he wasn't causing any problems.

"None at all," Dinsmore replied. "Consider it my pleasure. Now, shall we go into the other room?"

The other room was a bit larger than the waiting room, and although that chamber only held a few chairs and lamp tables, this one was even more sparsely furnished. In the center was a large ancient barber's chair, with padded-leather head and foot rests, and an adjustable back. Next to it was a small, free-standing porcelain sink, stained green from dripping water. On the opposite side of the chair stood a tiny metal table on rolling casters —like a tea caddy—littered with surgical instruments. Against one wall was a high wooden cabinet, painted dull yellow, with perhaps a hundred tiny drawers. The two windows before the chair were blocked over with oilpaper shades. The room was lighted by a hanging gas lamp which sputtered whenever there was movement around it.

Ransom sat down and opened his mouth as directed.

Dinsmore was in sparkling condition today, fresh and cheerful. He looked into Ransom's mouth with the concentrated gaze of someone trying to put together a jigsaw puzzle. This close up, his eyelashes were remarkably long and thick, they fluttered as a young girl's would, flirting with her beau. His small mouth, half hidden in his evenly cropped fine, black mustaches, formed a little *moue* as he inspected Ransom's teeth and hummed. His eyes were so brightly blue, Ransom had to look away from them.

"I do hope you were not particularly fond of this lower molar, Mr. Ransom. I'm afraid it's quite far gone and will have to be removed."

Ransom mumbled that he didn't care.

"Don't worry about the extraction hurting you. In a few more minutes you will no longer feel any pain. Trust in me. That's all I ask of you. Ah, here's the water."

Someone came into the room behind Ransom and placed a lidded kettle on the little rollaway table. Before he could turn to see who it was, or the newcomer see his face, the figure was gone, the office door shut. Dinsmore opened the kettle lid, and as the steam mushroomed upward, he placed several of his glinting metal tools into the boiling water, then once again shut the lid.

"That's part of our battle against Sepsis," Dinsmore said. "Sterilization of all instruments. Now, don't be anxious. You won't feel any pain. No pain at all. Now, Mr. Ransom, I would be very gratified if you could relax a bit. I'm afraid you're not at all relaxed, and I understand the pain you're suffering is the reason for that. But that will soon vanish. In the meanwhile, I want you to attempt to relax, to loosen up all of your limbs. That's right, just stretch them out a bit. I want them to be loose, dangling, relaxed. Now, your head too. Yes, I know. The pain is most intense there. But that's already beginning to subside. That's right. Loosen up from your back and shoulders, right up to your neck and now the head."

He lifted up one of Ransom's hands, and dropped it. It fell into Ransom's lap.

"That's fine. And already the pain is beginning to subside."

Ransom didn't comment.

"Good. It will soon vanish. But you'll have to relax more. No. Don't close your eyes. Look at me. Look at my eyes. That's right. Now, just relax. Pretend, oh, let's say, that you're by the sea and it's so relaxing. You're from the East, aren't you?"

"Georgia."

"Ah, Georgia. Beautiful state. Well, there must be a great many lakes and ponds where you were growing up in Georgia. Let's pretend you're on one of those ponds. Out in the middle of the pond in a little wooden skiff. It's a sunny, hot, restful day. So hot even the flies are buzzing lazily. So restful, you're feeling lazy yourself. Lying out in the skiff, in the middle of the pond, just resting. There's no current to the water at all. It's so restful. The fish are all resting too. So restful. The sun is hot. Restful. The sky is so blue that you have to close your eyes, close your eyes, and rest, just rest, rest, just rest, rest, just rest, rest, just rest, rest, just rest, rest. . . .

———————•———————

". . . NOW. THERE. THAT'S BETTER. How do you feel?"

He heard Dinsmore's words, then opened his eyes. Dinsmore stood at the foot of the barber's chair, a half-concerned, half-triumphant look on his face. Nothing about the room had changed in the meantime. There had been a meantime. Ransom was totally certain of that. A time, a space that had not been, which he could not remember, but which he instantly missed, tiny, noticeable, like a dropped stitch on a piece of knitting.

"I must have dozed off," Ransom said.

"No problem. Easier to work that way, as a matter of fact." Dinsmore's concern was gone, even his triumph had been short-lived. He was all business now, tossing the instruments he'd used into the pot, removing his white frock.

"You mean you took the tooth out?"

"See for yourself."

Dinsmore held up a bloody ivory-colored object in a pair of thin wire tweezers.

"Slipped right out. Must have been a bad one," Dinsmore said. "Want it as a memento? I'll have to wash it first."

"You keep it," Ransom said.

Dinsmore dropped the tooth to the table. "How are you feeling?"

"No pain. Not even a throb."

"Good. It was a very simple extraction. There now. I'm just about ready."

But Ransom wasn't. He was still trying to puzzle out what had occurred. He'd sat down in the chair. Someone had come and rapidly gone. Dinsmore had boiled the instruments against Sepsis. Then he'd talked. Was that all?

"Are you feeling all right?" Dinsmore asked. The concern had returned.

"I guess," Ransom said, making it seem doubtful.

"Are you feeling any pain?"

"No . . . but . . . a little strange."

"You're feeling strange? How? Not dizzy?"

"No. Let me think for a moment."

The eyes. He'd looked into Dinsmore's eyes. Wait, start from the beginning. He'd sat down. The instruments had arrived, were put into the kettle. His entire body had been throbbing with pain, trembling, sweat breaking out every few seconds. He didn't feel drained now as he ought to feel. As though the past four days—and especially all this morning—had never happened. He'd looked into his eyes, blue as the little pond at the plantation. That's right! He'd said to relax. Just rest. Talked about Georgia and fishing from a skiff. The sun. The sky blue as Dinsmore's eyes, sparkling on the water of the pond. He'd closed his eyes then . . . then, nothing. A few words, and his eyes had opened again. That's all that had happened. Bother Dinsmore and his concern! This was what it meant to be mesmerized: a hole in the texture of his thought, a gap in his consciousness, that time just gone.

Dinsmore was closing drawers, fastening his waistcoat button, straightening his tie. "Feeling better?"

"I'm feeling a bit slowed down, is all," Ransom said. If the man could doubt—if only doubt a minuscule amount and for only a second—then perhaps he might hesitate mesmerizing so quickly again. That struck Ransom, preventing him from leaping right up from the chair, thanking Dinsmore and going off. He could do all that, if he wanted to. Amazing as that seemed; he could.

"Perhaps I lost so much blood . . . ?"

"There was no blood. A thimbleful at most. I've put a septic pack on your gum. Keep it there for a day or so. Change it once before bed. Spirits of alcohol on a cotton wad will do. You're not headachy, are you?"

"No. Not really." Ransom got up from the chair, and walked a few steps. "No. I suppose not."

The dentist led him to the outer office and handed him his coat and hat.

"I guess I'll get a ride," Ransom said.

"You don't feel well enough to walk?" Dinsmore asked, and put a soft palm to Ransom's forehead. Then he took his pulse at Ransom's wrist. "You seem all right."

"Maybe I could sit here for a minute or so?"

"I don't see why not. I have an appointment, I'm afraid. Otherwise, I'd join you. Yes. Do sit down until you feel ready to go."

"If it's trouble . . ."

"No trouble at all. I'll tell the woman who cleans to wait a bit. No trouble at all."

Dinsmore looked quizzed now. He began to ask another question, thought better of it, and with a parting, still puzzled look on his face, was out the door.

When the sound of his footsteps was no longer audible, Ransom felt more at ease. It had been eerie being in the same room with Dinsmore, with the man who had so effortlessly eliminated —how many minutes was it? Forty or so, by Ransom's pocket watch. Forty minutes gone from his life. Just like that.

And Dinsmore had simply talked to him. That's what Carr had said he would do, what Yolanda Bowles and Millard said he had done. Just talk. And his eyes too, reflecting and refracting the gaslight, not like the pieces of jelly and blood that Ransom knew they actually were, but as though made of some hard, faceted material. The talk mostly, though. The eyes had simply been a fascinating focal point. The voice had done the work. Extraordinary.

Unless there were something else to it. Some contraption in the inner office. Ransom hadn't noticed any. And Millard had been mesmerized away from the office, in a barn. Still. There was no one about. It would be worth a look.

The inner office was as Ransom had thought: bare but for the chair, the sink, the little rolling table and the cabinet. The oilpaper shades were up now, the gas lamp extinguished. Perhaps a gas in the lamp? He sniffed the fuel cone. Nothing. Just kerosene.

Where those footsteps outside? Dinsmore returning? The cleaning lady?

Ransom quickly left the office and had just closed the inner door when the outer office door opened. He had expected someone, anyone but who appeared.

It was Carrie Lane.

She hesitated in the open doorway, clearly confused.

"Mr. Ransom?"

"Mrs. Lane," he acknowledged, making a half bow.

"I don't understand," she said, but came in anyway and shut the door.

"I had some dental work done. An extraction."

"Ah." She walked across the room to the inner office door.

"He's not in."

"Not in? But we were to meet here."

"He left, not three minutes ago. He had another appointment."

Her presence here, so far from her own world and her own social sphere, in this shabby office, in this run-down neighborhood, startled Ransom. Then it decided him. He would have it

out with her now, here. He knew what it was to be mesmerized.
He'd tell her how much he actually did know.

"I don't understand," she repeated, almost ignoring Ransom
and talking as though to herself. "Unless we were to meet at the
hotel. No. I'm certain he said here."

"Mrs. Lane," Ransom began. "I didn't come here for an extraction."

She looked up from her own ruminations. "You didn't?"

"I mean I did have a tooth extracted. But I needn't have."

She looked so completely baffled he wanted to take her violet-
gloved hands in his own, to hold them as he explained.

"Why did you come then?"

"Mrs. Lane, I want very much to apologize for my behavior
that night."

"But why come here?"

"I hadn't meant to goad you, you know. I simply had to know
how matters stood."

The bafflement still hadn't left her face. Lord, how golden and
tawny her eyes were. How silken her cheeks . . .

"You're not making a great deal of sense, Mr. Ransom."

"You're in a great deal of trouble," he said calmly, softly.

"I am?"

"I want to help you. You see, I know a great deal. I know
everything."

"Everything? What are you talking about?"

"You would best know that. I've intimations so far. You see,
I've been to Simon Carr." And, as she didn't register any change
of expression: "He's Mr. Dinsmore's former assistant. He lives
out at your ranch. You knew that, didn't you?"

"I suppose. But what has that to do . . . ?"

"He's told me everything about Mr. Dinsmore. How he met
him, how he taught him mesmerism."

She backed away from him.

"That's really why I came here. To see what mesmerism is, to
find out how it works. I know now. It's ghastly. Horrifying."

She turned away from him to the shabbily papered wall.

"It was a stroke of fortune that you came here today," he said. "I almost believe it wasn't a mistake. Now that I know, I want to help you, to save you. I can now, you see. But in order to do so, to free you from his pernicious influence, I have to have your assistance. I need your own words. You must believe me that I will do all I can to protect you. Trust in me, ma'am. That's what I was attempting to ask you that night."

"You were a beast that night," she said quietly.

"I admit it. But I didn't know what else to do. I had to know."

"Know what?" she suddenly asked, her voice hard now. "You know nothing. Even now. Nothing at all. You have some bizarrely mistaken idea . . ."

"Persuade me that I'm mistaken. I beg of you. Persuade me you aren't enchanted by this man, that you aren't his tool, his slave."

"Mr. Ransom!" she almost shouted as the blood drained from her face. "Mr. Ransom, must I remind you to comport yourself like the gentleman I had always assumed you to be."

"Won't you let me help you?"

"How you presume to comment on my private life, I'll never understand. Whether here—or so shockingly, in public."

He turned away now, utterly frustrated. Why did she persist in these petty formalities? In these evasions? When so much was at stake.

"It was only in the light of such great danger, that I took any liberties," he said.

"There is no danger, Mr. Ransom."

"I wish I could believe that."

"You must believe it," she said, raising her voice. "You have no other choice. To do otherwise would embroil us both in . . ."

"In what?" he asked as she faltered. "In further danger?"

She was startled. He heard the footsteps too.

In a low voice, she said, "You were very foolish to come here, Mr. Ransom."

There were two knocks on the frosted glass.

"Come in," she said airily.

"Oh, pardon!" It was Mrs. Bent, dilapidated, carrying a bucket and rags. "I heard noises. I thought . . ."

"Mr. Ransom has just had a tooth extracted," Carrie Lane said in that same superior tone. "Did Mr. Dinsmore leave any message for me?"

Mrs. Bent looked at each of them. "He said he was meeting someone at the Lane Hotel dining room."

"You see," Carrie Lane said, superficial, peeved, "I did make a mistake. I don't know what I was thinking of." Then, to Mrs. Bent: "You're here to clean up? Good." She headed for the door.

Ransom caught up with her on the stairway. She pulled away from him and kept to one side of the stairs until they had reached the small hallway. Ransom looked up. The office door was closed.

"I'm not mistaken," he said. "I know I'm not."

Her diffidence vanished. "Stay out of my affairs, Mr. Ransom."

Ransom opened the street door, but held it long enough to say, "Anytime at all you want to see me, to talk to me, I'll be willing to listen. Anytime at all. Believe me, Mrs. Lane, this man's influence . . ."

But she had already pulled the door from him, and fled through it to the street, where the phaeton was waiting. She got in, tapped on the inside window, and drove off without looking back.

"Damn!" Ransom said. He'd come so close to having her trust. So close.

———————●———————

DISAPPOINTED AS RANSOM WAS at first by Carrie Lane's refusal to place her trust in him, he was to discover how much that refusal would color his moods over the next four weeks.

For the first few days following their encounter in Dinsmore's office, Ransom had the completely unsubstantiated belief that she would change her mind and seek him out. And with that belief was a corresponding elation—although of a quiet kind. He returned to the work he had at hand and disposed of it firmly, all the while feeling an undercurrent he could only characterize as expectation. Nothing he could—or even would—put into words, but an attitude which he couldn't recall in himself for almost twenty years—the belief that he had a future, an undefined one, but one significantly different than his present, and intimately tied to the successful prosecution of Dinsmore and, more important, to Carrie Lane herself.

Quiet as it was, this expectation had the power to disturb. He'd been excited this summer by a prosecution, and the magnitude of his accomplishment in settling the intergovernmental dispute over land use had given him a feeling that he was finally, however slowly, working toward some end approximate to the aspirations he had once held for himself.

Those hopes had been astronomically high, naturally. All young men had such hopes. But two decades of experience had changed that. Twenty years of minor decisions had pushed him off the main track and onto what seemed to be an endless railroad siding. A score of years of such derailment growing out of one decision many years back in Washington D.C., when—as a matter of principle—he'd discovered he could not defend Calvin Poindexter in the antitrust suit against him. Not defend him, even though Ransom and Florence Poindexter were engaged to marry; not defend him even though Ransom knew the textile magnate would never forgive him for his defection.

Ransom had been a man with a future then. One of the young Turks of the nation's capital, rubbing shoulders with Lasters, Claytons, and Adamses; a protégé of Antonia Herbst, the most influential woman in the city; a young attorney with his own offices around the corner from the Supreme Court building, his own private practice, and through it, connections with legislators, diplomats, administrators, and millionaires. By the time he was twenty-seven years old, Ransom's future seemed as secure as any young lawyer's in the country. He would marry Florence, continue to practice law, probably come to own a large share of the Poindexter mills that dotted the Virginias and Carolinas and more than likely would end up in a profitable judgeship, demanding little application but involving much honor.

That future had been blighted by what Ransom had discovered while investigating Poindexter's management. He'd been appalled to discover that his future father-in-law—a man as smooth and amiable as aged bourbon, a man who could quote Cicero to charm a woman into a waltz—had a business dependent upon crimes a Nero would blush at: power-broking, extortion, blackmail, the defrauding of widows and orphans, even murder. Nothing had stopped Poindexter in his effort to obtain and control the huge cotton mills in the four-state area. Ransom's decision had been firm: he'd met with Poindexter, told him what he knew, resigned the case, and then found himself unengaged and ostracized.

Only Antonia Herbst had understood Ransom then. Only she had supported his belief that justice was not to be bought and sold. Ransom had not been able to bring himself to reveal what he had discovered to Florence—to do so would be to break her heart, he knew. He had to suffer her scorn, then her neglect. His friends had mocked his naïveté. Surely he'd been aware of Poindexter's methods? And, besides, what difference did it make? The old magnate would be dead soon. Ransom would be in charge of the business. He could right the old man's wrongs then, if he wanted to; or more likely, let them slide into oblivion.

Ransom hadn't seen it like that. He'd seen the forces of good and evil launched in relentless battle. Any concession to the one, any swerving from the other was a total defeat.

He'd held himself apart during the course of the trial, not caring that his practice had dwindled, believing he would be shown to be right. But he'd been shocked the prosecution never once mentioned what he had so easily found out: surely he'd only scratched the surface of the corruption? Poindexter was powerful, and though the government won its case against him, they'd shown him the courtesy of not revealing what a scoundrel he'd been. After the trial he was no less rich or powerful. He'd taken a month-long air-clearing vacation with his family to Saratoga

Springs, then had returned to the capital to consolidate his power. One detail of that was the destruction of Ransom's career —a not difficult task, as Ransom was already considered a hardhead, a principled fool, a man of no loyalty to his class or to his own best interest.

That reputation and Poindexter's malign influence spread as far north as Boston and New York, and as far west as Chicago, where Ransom had once more attempted to set up a law practice. It was Amasa Murcott who had convinced him to try once more here in Center City. He'd done well since then. But only now did he believe he had a real future. Reese at the state capitol thought so, so did Carl Dietz, here in town. But it was necessary that Carrie Lane be involved in his next step, whether only as a witness for the prosecution, or—as he had come to hope—as a more lasting element in his life.

He could begin again, even at his age, when most men were beginning to wind up their affairs. With a successful prosecution of Dinsmore, he could win not only the honor and position so long denied to him, but also Carrie Lane.

He knew she had a more than ordinary interest in wanting to please him. He'd seen her conflict clearly enough at the preelection dinner, and also in Dinsmore's office. She had not been able to come to his way of thinking, yet. But wasn't that partly his own fault? He'd been so sudden, so abrupt with her. He hadn't given her enough time to assimilate his knowledge of her situation, and the honesty of his intentions. But she would come round; he knew she would. And then . . . and then Ransom would find himself painting pictures in his mind of a future with Carrie Lane. As though only she, and no other woman, could possibly mean a future. Not the widow Rogers, not a half-dozen other marriageable women he knew, not even the increasingly attractive, maturing Isabelle Page, who'd done nothing to hide her own interest in him.

But as the days passed into weeks, expectation changed to anxiety, then to impatience, and finally—by Thanksgiving and the first light snowfall—to frustration and disappointment.

The trees were already bare outside his office windows. He

could see the frieze of the courthouse building clearly now, and
Carrie Lane still hadn't contacted him. Every week brought news
of some new improvement completed, or innovation planned by
Lane's new manager. With every rumor and piece of gossip,
Ransom felt a chill enter his life that even his room's excellent
Franklin stove could not thaw. Autumn was flitting by; winter
beginning an early set—and Ransom saw the seasonal change as
a metaphor for his own situation. Matters would stop now, freeze
over, remain as they unhappily were, unchanged for months.
Would he have to wait for spring to come before anything would
happen? Wait, when each day brought new information on Dinsmore to confirm his belief that the dental surgeon was hardly the
man to be trusted with an estate worth hundreds of thousands of
dollars? Not that the man had a criminal record in Nebraska: he
didn't. But Reese had understood Ransom's carefully worded
request, and had sent for information throughout the country. As
this data was received, Ransom saw a pattern of criminality
emerge, ranging from loitering and petty larceny to assault with
a deadly weapon, from fraud to breach of promise. The record
stretched like a tentacle from the slums of Boston and New
York's Lower East Side, to the middle-class drawing rooms of
Cleveland and Evanston. It was these last few crimes which
seemed most promising to Ransom—the statute of limitations
was not yet half over for a half-dozen Cook County warrants,
copies of which, forwarded by Reese, sat in a separate folder of
his growing dossier against Dinsmore, even now.

Difficult as it was to think of the sparkling-eyed, dapper dental
surgeon—with his cupid's-bow lips and ruby-ringed manicured
hands, with his courteous demeanor, his familiar attitude and
professional assurance—as a petty criminal almost from the cra-
dle, the proof was becoming irrefutable. With it, the peril to
Carrie Lane all the greater. Whatever manners Dinsmore had
learned, they only served to mask his real self—a man as used to
exploiting others, especially women, as irresponsibly and dexterously as Calvin Poindexter had exploited those around him.

If the legal evidence was mounting, the medical evidence
Ransom was receiving through Dr. Murcott was more ambigu-

ous. One out of all the medical men contacted—a Dr. Clark, from Brattleboro, Vermont, who had been using mesmerism in surgery for years—understood the implications of its use as clearly as Simon Carr. The others equivocated: they wrote in veiled terms, refusing to commit themselves, but in each instance, eagerly relating an incident or two involving the use of the technique which had astonished them. Almost every letter suggested Murcott write to European colleagues, especially those in Vienna, where the greatest amount of experimentation had been done, and where the younger branch of psychology was beginning to develop new and exotic growths.

None beside Clark even came close to suggesting the kind of manipulative control by a Mesmerist over a subject that Ransom was searching for. Although one New York surgeon did send a copy of George du Maurier's recent novel, *Trilby,* calling it a sensational and obviously fictional treatment of the subject.

This was dispiriting, but hardly enough to stop Ransom. It was generally known that since the pre-election dinner certain ladies in town no longer received Carrie Lane. She no longer attended social functions at which she had once been the major ornament. She hadn't been present at the Dietzes' Thanksgiving dinner, a far more intimate affair than the October political dinner—only a dozen invited guests. And when Ransom talked to his landlady, he discovered Mrs. Lane would probably not attend the Masons' Christmas party, or the Chamber of Commerce's New Year's Ball.

Of course she could claim continued mourning for her absence at these occasions. But Ransom suspected a far less dignified motive: she needed Dinsmore's presence and control far more than her own reputation. It was a shocking, an intolerable situation, especially since without her aid, he really could do little more than continue to gather information and prepare for what might never arrive—her trust in him.

Every glimpse he'd had of her since the day in Dinsmore's office was embedded in his mind: There had been a moment just outside Baers' Pharmacy, when Carrie Lane had emerged from within, stopped on the broad stone lintel looking pale and confused, a tiny dark-papered package dangling from one wrist, before she had seen him and turned away. Another time, as he'd been passing by the Lyceum on Taylor Avenue one night just as the Center City Women's Club was dispersing, Carrie Lane had walked out of the building, solitary among the groups of ladies, with her head held high, but her brows knitted as though in deep consternation. She had seen the waiting phaeton, and quickly gotten in. Ransom had stopped in his tracks, watched the phaeton rattle off, seen the other women huddling together, and had heard their disparaging remarks. He had felt then what Mrs. Page once called "a tug at the heartstrings"—something he'd never expected to feel.

Objectively, he was being foolish, acting on a feeling. He admitted it. But look how far his feelings had taken him. If he hadn't shared a feeling of the wrongness of Henry Lane's death, or of Mrs. Ingram's odd behavior, if he hadn't gone on a feeling out to Simon Carr's would he now know as much as he did of Dinsmore and of the agony Carrie Lane must be undergoing? Not at all. So what better than a feeling to go on, to continue with?

He'd been out to visit with Simon Carr again, especially as the road from the Widow Rogers' where he'd once more begun to spend a night or two weekly, took him just past the turnoff to the ranch. Carr had been glad to see him these times. He felt less pressured now that Dinsmore had still not left town to come bother him. Carr reiterated his story, filled in a few more details and after much haranguing from Ransom, finally agreed to testify against his former employer if the matter were ever brought to trial. This was an important asset to Ransom: he needed Carr's testimony to convict Dinsmore. But he secured the old man's agreement only at the price of conditions. Carr wanted his own complicitous warrants from Illinois waived, and to have adequate protection from the dental surgeon while he was in Center City. Ransom suspected he could gain both points, but he told Carr he would have to discuss them with Judge Dietz.

In order to do so, however, he first had to present the case to the judge. He hadn't so far: he had waited almost a month for

Carrie Lane to come to him before he made any move. As she continued to elude him, and as he became increasingly persuaded of her danger and the need to save her—even against her own wishes—he decided to talk to Dietz anyway.

The opportunity came unexpectedly, a relatively intimate dinner at the Dietz house he oughtn't even have been at but for a cancellation and Lavinia's insistence he join them. As the remainder of the guests were women, after dinner he and the judge retired to Dietz's library, while the ladies went across the hall to the sewing parlor. The situation seemed perfect, if Ransom could only find the right way to use it.

As they talked, he was reminded how often Carl Dietz told attorneys and witnesses alike to get to the point. He decided to do exactly that.

"Thank you," Ransom said, accepting a cut-crystal liqueur glass filled with a homemade peach brandy. Then, "By the way, your honor, I will need a warrant waiver for Simon Carr. He will be a most necessary witness for the prosecution, but he has to be assured he'll be protected. It's only a technicality. I'll draw up the required papers tomorrow morning."

Judge Dietz tried not to look astonished. "What prosecution?"

"Oh, that's the other matter I wanted to discuss with you. I'm going to ask the bench for an indictment against this Dinsmore fellow—you know, the one who's managing all the Lane businesses?—for the murder of Henry Lane."

"Very amusing," Dietz said, and pulled on the thick cigar he'd been smoking until its flaky ash threatened to fall off.

"I didn't say it to amuse. You'll have the papers tomorrow."

"What in the sam hill are you talking about?" Dietz said, sitting up so suddenly in the Windsor chair that he knocked the cigar ash onto his lap. "What?" he repeated. He reminded Ransom of a great horned owl suddenly spotting its prey.

"It's all in the testimony. You'll read it soon enough. But as we're here, and if you have a minute or two . . ."

It was three-quarters of an hour before he had explained it to the judge, who sank by minute degrees further down into the big Windsor chair, threw away the butts of first one then another, then one more well-chewed cigar, and took on a look of increasing gloom, as Ransom's case, which he'd mulled so long, flowed forth. Every once in a while, Dietz would wince at some statement—criticism against some specific rhetorical ornamentation Ransom had used, best held in reserve for the jury. But this was oratory after all, the need to inform and above all to persuade. He was certain Dietz would pick apart the written indictment with the sharpness of a mountain goat picking its way up a mountain.

When Ransom was done, Dietz looked even more gloomy. Then he cracked a tiny smile.

"Did you really have a tooth pulled?"

"Here, look," Ransom replied showing the space.

"Oh, hell! For all I know that tooth has been missing for years."

"The gum is freshly healed, isn't it?"

"I suppose. You're more of a fool than I ever thought," Dietz said, and now there wasn't a hint of mirth. "You remind me of an old friend of mine, a prospector, name of Jarrell. He's gone most of the time, off somewhere in Wyoming or Colorado. But whenever he's in town, he comes by. Lavinia don't care for him at all. He's kind of grimy. Got worse manners than a sow. But I like him. He tells me yarns about all of his adventures prospecting. Even shows me the scars. Some of them have been ascribed to the claws of a grizzly, to a Cheyenne tomahawk, to a rock slide. The same scar. He gets the stories mixed up sometimes. But I don't mind. You know why? Because I like a good yarn, and because he never takes any of them too seriously. I liked your yarn, too, James. But you're taking it far too seriously."

"Is it that you're afraid of Dinsmore?" Ransom asked, hoping to get a rise out of Dietz. "Or of the Lane money?"

"I'm not afraid of either. Nor am I of you, James."

"Good. Because Dinsmore *is* the Lane money now. And a hell of a lot of people are afraid of it."

"What's the point of all this?"

"I wouldn't go to all this trouble if I weren't sure of it, would I?"

"Sure of what? Hocus-pocus? What is it you expect a jury made up of farmers and livestock men and shopkeepers to understand? Witchcraft? Or what?"

"It's called mesmerism. I have testimony that it works. Simon Carr . . ."

"Carr is newly alienated from his former employer. He's a hostile witness. His testimony hardly makes a case."

"There are others too. Yolanda Bowles. Her grandson, Millard, Mrs. Jack Bent."

"Nigrahs and saloonkeepers. A fine lot for character witnesses. Whether for or against."

"We could cross-examine Mrs. Ingram. It was she who first brought it to my attention."

"Has she admitted to being mesmerized?"

"Not exactly. But it was she who spoke of his influence."

"Influence. That's the strongest point you have, isn't it? That a respected and very wealthy lady has given the reins of a financial empire to her manager because of some romantic attachment. It's happened often enough before. The baroness and the stableboy."

"You approve of it?"

"You don't see them in my house anymore, do you? Of course I don't approve of it. But I admit to its reality." He hesitated, then said, "You know that some folks will say it's all sour grapes. You know that, don't you? I won't. I know better. But they will."

Ransom suspected that was true. He'd been seen with Mrs. Lane at the pre-election dinner. It had been commented on. That much had come back to him. There were plenty of loose tongues in Center City spinning their own yarns, only needing an incident or two to embroider it into a sampler. Did that matter? Not in the final tabulation. Not at all.

Ransom felt he had to make his point more clearly. As a last, desperate chance he said, "What if she'll testify?"

"Mrs. Lane? Against Dinsmore? That she's been mesmerized by him?"

"Mesmerized and controlled by him."

Dietz thought for a moment. "It's more to go on. But unless

she implicates him in Henry Lane's death . . . Does she implicate him?"

"Not yet," Ransom said, hedging. "You see, it's because of the mesmerism."

"You mean to tell me Dinsmore just waved his hands and Henry Lane stepped up on that motorcar and hanged himself? You'd better come to court prepared with a library of medical evidence to prove it, and a practical demonstration. No, don't interrupt me, James. I have something to say to you. Here, have a bit more of this brandy, sit back and listen. Go on, sit back. You're as excited as a schoolboy. It isn't like you.

"Now, I do understand your feelings about Mrs. Lane. It is a shame. And, I must say, a great shock to me. I know you Georgia folks like to settle a woman's honor when it's been compromised, and I applaud that. But not in court. And especially not in my court. Understand that. And, if that isn't the real question, then I think it has to do with this past summer at the capitol.

"You had a taste of success there," he went on. "Well-earned, deserved success. I'm not at all surprised that you'd like to consolidate that into something more concrete. People in Lincoln have their eyes on you. Many prosecutors have had sudden advances through successful cases before. Some have even manufactured cases or blown up absurdly small ones into bigger ones. I'm not saying this because I believe that's what you're doing. If you were, you wouldn't be such a fool as to give me this mess. You'd find an important one, one that had importance to the town, to the country."

"This is important," Ransom interrupted. "Dinsmore's influence . . ."

"No interruptions yet, James. As I said, you'd find a case that could be won. Not a jackass race like this. Now just relax. I'm telling it to you straight because I'm as interested as you in your advancement. I am, James, which is why I mentioned Carrie Lane to you at the night of the big dinner."

"You also said that whoever married her would affect all of Center City," Ransom said. "Doesn't that include Dinsmore?"

"It does. It does. But he hasn't married her yet. We have to wait and see if he does. So far he's doing a little bit of this and a little of that, but mostly he's marking time."

"He's looking around to see where to strike next," Ransom said. "Looking to see precisely how many people will kowtow to him. The more that do it because of his position the less he'll have to mesmerize to do it."

"Do you really believe that?"

"I have proof of it. Forty minutes of my life are vanished. It's not much. But they're gone. Where to? One moment he was talking, the next nothing . . . nothing at all. This man is dangerous. Especially in the position he holds."

"Which he got to by mesmerizing the Lanes?"

"Yes. And others, too. Is that what you want for Center City?"

Dietz was silent for a long while. Then he said, "I'm sorry. I just don't see it."

Exasperated, Ransom stood up. "You'll see it. You'll see it and hear it for yourself. Mrs. Lane will tell you. I promise it. She'll sit right here in this chair, and tell you yourself."

"Don't be angry, James. James! Where are you going?"

Ransom was already in the foyer, getting on his coat.

Dietz came out and stood by him.

"You'll get the waiver papers tomorrow," Ransom said.

"Crazy Reb," was all Dietz replied.

Ransom walked home in the same heated mood: a protection against the frosty, moonless, star-studded night. Ice crackled like old wagon traces between branches of frozen trees. A horse neighed in its sleep in a distant stable and sounded ghostlike in the cold silence. The icy points of starlight were massed above him like a curtain pulled over the blue-black sky—they seemed to penetrate his vision like gelid stilettos, aloof and disdaining.

He had expected to win over the judge too quickly. He now saw that. But what else was he to do? Wait, while Dinsmore gained more power, more influence? It angered him. Angered him so much he'd thrown out a challenge he couldn't even partially fulfill without Carrie Lane. Ironical that he didn't possess what he so much needed. Ironical that lack had led him to act tonight. If he could only produce her, and her testimony, all of Dietz's arguments would be as nothing. Once Carrie Lane stood in the witness box, all else meant nothing at all. She would carry it through. He knew that. It had been proved time and again, given human nature and the judicial structure.

He reiterated these arguments all the way to the Center City Board and Hotel. It was darkened now, except for a tiny gas jet in the downstairs foyer, thoughtfully left by Mrs. Page to light his way. Even Murcott had gone to sleep. Too bad, he had wanted to talk to Amasa tonight. He'd need his friend's help in putting together convincing medical evidence.

Ransom shut off the gaswick, and was halfway upstairs to his room when he caught a white gleam out of the corner of his eye.

Descending again, he lit a match and went to the slim foyer table where messages and mail were placed. The white gleam had been a shiny-papered envelope. It hadn't been there when he'd gone out this evening. Another match and a closer look still revealed nothing. Then he caught a faint aroma from it, and holding it closer to his face, recognized the scent.

Even before he tore it open, he knew the letter had come from Carrie Lane.

———————————•———————————

HE WAS TO SEE HER AT TWO O'CLOCK in the afternoon. She specifically dwelled upon that. Curiously, as nothing else in her short note was very specific. She merely wrote to say she would allow him the opportunity he had so persistently requested, provided he at no time forgot their respective positions by untoward violence of speech or action. And he ought not arrive before two. A few minutes after would be best.

Ransom pondered her neatly written words; but he could not hide his exhilaration. He found himself more than once wondering what had prompted her decision after such a steadfast silence. Could it be an example of how much of an outcast she had become, shown so clearly the other night outside the Lyceum? Or was it something far worse?

It made no difference. He was to see her, to save her, and restore her name. Shortly. Shortly.

He would have to be more prudent with her this time; allow her to take her own time, draw her out slowly when needed, tug only a bit whenever she hesitated. None of his earlier aggressive tactics would serve. It must be accomplished gently.

Ransom reminded himself of this as he walked the sloping gradient up High Street toward the Lane house. He'd purposely set himself many tasks that morning to avoid thinking of the upcoming interview; he'd even made a lunch appointment in the Lane Hotel dining room with a prosperous sorghum farmer who had some small business to discuss with him; again so he wouldn't spend time idly spinning out the possibilities of the forthcoming meeting.

The large Lane house was the next but last on the ridge of land between High and Grant streets. More trees and bushes covered "the Hill," as it was sometimes called, than any other part of Center City, the result of a great gardening fashion among the Masons, the Wheelers, the Lanes, and, afterward, the other families of the area who had joined their privileged ranks. Compared to the flatness of the rest of the town and its surrounding land, the ridge was indeed a hill; the rooftop gables of the houses and the tallest trees could be noticed from anywhere in Center City.

The second-story gables of the Lane house were the most visible, as the house sat atop the flat back of the ridge at its greatest height. Even from the sloping concrete sidewalk (one of four such innovations in town) he had to climb a series of broad stone stairs to the entrance. Last night's frost had damaged the bushes that zigzagged up from High Street on either side of the walk, they were half brown and partially stripped of leaves.

Ransom knocked twice with the heavy wrought-iron knocker, then turned around for another look out over the town. A wonderful sight, even with the trees going bare. He could see clear down to the Lane warehouses on Williams Street, and just make out the shingled roof of the railroad station. Easterly, he saw the back of the courthouse, the steeple of the Episcopal Church, one cylindrical wing of the huge Dietz house, then the cemetery, smaller houses and farms. Directly before him was the wide, flat basin across High Street, consisting of a strand of uncultivated forest stretching north, then pasture lands giving way to a bog —iced over now and silver in the sunlight with rime. Farther away, beyond that and just visible, was the central hall of Swedeville, then fifty-five miles farther, beyond sight, the Platte River, and Grand Island, the only other considerable town between here and Lincoln. But what was taking Mrs. Ingram so long to open up?

He turned to knock again, but the door was open. Carrie Lane stood there as though she'd been watching him for some time.

"It's a beautiful view," Ransom said, after his initial surprise. "Wonderfully comprehensive."

"Even more comprehensive from the second story," she said, inviting him in with a motion of her hand. She didn't offer to take his hat and coat, but immediately led the way up the carpeted stairs.

"We'll sit in the reading room," she said, once they had gained the upper floor. "It's much brighter up here. Much more cheerful." She led the way past some paneled doorways into a large room surrounded on three sides by windows that rose almost from floor to ceiling, covered only by thin gauzy curtains. Two armchairs, a small sofa, a few small tables and a cigar tray kept the room airy and uncluttered, quite a change from the overstuffed furnishings of the rooms downstairs.

She gestured for his outer clothing now, and placed it in a small closet. In order to avoid questioning her immediately, Ransom went to the windows and looked out. As she had said, it was a more comprehensive view. He could now make out the railroad yards and the Bixby farm to the south. Only the northwest was hidden from view.

"I had no idea such a view existed," he said, determined to be polite no matter how urgent their business.

"Few enough people have seen it. This is my favorite room. My own rooms are nearby."

From the next window he could make out his own office

windows, far away, in the Page Board and Hotel. Had Mrs. Lane ever looked in that direction he wondered.

"If you wish to sit and look," she said, "I could move a chair . . ."

"This will do." He sat in an armchair facing where she stood offering him a cup of coffee from what appeared to be an ancient and much battered urn.

He accepted and she seated herself opposite, intent on the business of sipping, offering tea crackers, refusing, sipping again. Meanwhile, Ransom made no attempt to hide the fact that he was looking at her closely, and was surprised by the changes that were evident.

She was gaunter. Not thinner really, but her cheekbones seemed to have a pallor upon them, and the stark November sunlight outlined with cruel clarity hollows around her eyes that only an excess of powder and rouge could disguise. This was accentuated by the dark royal blue and white striping of her watered-silk bodice and the voluminous deep blue skirts, as though these tints had been chosen to take up the very hues of her complexion. A striking, though saddening effect, if a conscious one, he concluded. Her auburn hair, with a metallic glint in this light, was gathered in a loose bun, contrasting to all the blue.

She looked as though she had been seriously ill and was now convalescing. Yet strangely alluring too, as Ransom discovered to his disturbance. More alluring than he had ever found her before when she had seemed so much healthier. As though her gauntness somehow brought into greater relief features ordinarily not sensual. Her tawny, gold-flecked eyes seemed wilder, like those of a hungry mountain lion, the curve and fullness of her unpainted lips more ripe, fallen curlets of auburn behind each ear all the softer given the severity of the rest, the sharp rise and fall with each breath of her collarbone, of her sternum and her small full breasts beneath the tight-fitting bodice . . . hard and soft interwoven. But she was saying something now. He must attend.

". . . chose this time because Mrs. Ingram was to be out all afternoon. And naturally, Mr. Dinsmore too."

"I appreciate your discretion, ma'am."

"Only fitting. Given your own discretion, Mr. Ransom."

Was that meant as sarcasm? Had she talked to Judge Dietz?

"I was quite prepared," she said, "to find your visit to Van Buren Street a critical one."

"It was a critical one."

"For myself, I meant. I was afraid you would take steps. I expected an explosion of some sort."

"And now that there hasn't been one?"

"Well, I do want to thank you."

"You didn't ask me here to thank me. Little as we know each other, you know enough of me to know I never let matters go. That I worry them like a beagle with a quail."

She seemed to pale. "You do have that reputation."

"Well, then?"

"What you said the night of the big dinner . . . about Henry. Are you still taking steps in that direction?"

"I needn't tell you, but I will. I've prepared an indictment. I was about to hand it in, but having gotten your message, I decided to wait a day."

"I see. Am I implicated—is that the right word—in this indictment?"

"That depends upon you, Mrs. Lane. You were his wife. You knew the man, and I assume were privy to some if not all of his feelings and beliefs. To that extent you would be required to give evidence in court. Including, I'm afraid, his last letter."

"In public?"

"At a public trial, ma'am. I know you would prefer not. But I cannot see how it is to be avoided."

"Especially since my name is already quite worthless," she said, showing a bit of anger.

"I never said that."

She got up and went to the window. "No. Of course you didn't."

Ransom let her stand there, looking out over the town, her hands clasped in front of her. After a few minutes, she turned back to him.

"You wanted to save me, you said. What are you willing to do to save me? How far are you prepared to go?"

He didn't hesitate. "I'll do whatever has to be done."

"I almost believe you. I don't know why. Please keep your seat, Mr. Ransom. We can't both be stalking about." She turned back to the window, as though seeking assurance there. "You'll have to go very far, I'm afraid."

"Trust me."

"Can I trust you not to despise me?"

"But I don't. On the contrary . . ."

"To not despise me after I've told you what you so badly want to know?"

"I've been mesmerized. I've an idea . . ."

"You haven't a glimmer of an idea." She turned and almost fell into her seat. "Not a glimmer, of what I've become. It's like one of those awful illustrated police weeklies you men pore over at the barbershop. Are you prepared for that, Mr. Ransom? After hearing me out will you still be so eager to save me?"

Ransom wondered what he ought do to convince her. Before he could think of anything, she had begun to talk in a low voice. All he could do now was listen.

"I suppose it's all my mother's fault," she said. "She insisted that young girls be kept out of the world and its affairs. Oh, I know that's not such a terrible thing to do. I don't know that I wouldn't have done the same if I had my own child to raise. We always want the best for those we love. . . . We always want the world to seem a better place than we know it to actually be.

"So I was raised in ignorance. The widespread, common ignorance of girls from families of my kind. Even though, I suppose being brought up in a city made a difference. Then, when I was about fourteen years old, my father passed on. We were a close family, so associated with my natural grief was the knowledge that much of the fortune we had lived on would not much longer be with us. My mother was as ignorant of business as anything else having to do with the practical side of life. In no time at all —between creditors and partners—we were impoverished, living in a state that can only be called shabby genteel. The one

escape open to my sister and me—as my mother made so clear
to us—was a good marriage.

"My sister was already engaged by that time. She hastened her
wedding, and in time, she joined her husband's family in Pennsylvania. Relieved of one burden on our finances, my mother
decided to give me a freer rein. I led an easier life, though not
much at home, I must admit. For it was found expedient that I
visit with our many relatives, and as I enjoyed traveling, that was
how I spent the next four or five years. I lived in Newport, on
Long Island, and even farther west, spending almost a year with
my Aunt Neal at her home in Grosse Pointe.

"That's where I met Henry Lane. He also knew my aunt's
family, and he visited one summer too. He was a man in his
mid-thirties then. I thought quite handsome, intelligent, and
very, very kind to me, especially whenever I was feeling a bit
homesick. I soon heard from my Aunt Neal that Henry was a
very successful businessman here in Center City, which I naturally had never heard of, thinking every place west of the
Mississippi inhabited by riverboat captains and Indians. Those
few weeks of his summer stay at the Neals' were enough to
convince Henry that he wanted me for his wife. That was always
Henry's way—not so much impulsive as decisive, strongly decisive in everything he did.

"I wasn't aware how decisive until after I had returned to New
York, and began receiving his letters. All of them mentioned our
stay at Aunt Neal's, and little by little, they all pointed to an
unspoken proposal.

"I know it is not unusual in the western states for a woman to
marry a man twice her age, nor even in the east: but not among
the people I knew. It was for me, however. I had qualms. I
hesitated. Worst of all, I knew that I would have to leave my
home and all those I cared for, to come live in a strange, and,
I was certain, primitive village, far away from anything I had
encountered in my experience. These questions were put into
my own return letters to Henry. For I didn't know how else to
refuse him.

The following spring, he came to New York. I knew how

difficult it must have been for him to leave everything in Center City to come pay court to me, fourteen hundred miles distant. He never complained of it, but he pressed his suit with a charm and a vigor that wore down what little resistance I still had. He soon won over both my mother and my godfather—my closest advisors—and I was truly unable to deny that he affected me in a way no other man ever had. For his part, Henry said he was aware of the sacrifice I would have to make in moving here, and would promise me ample compensation in every way.

"So I accepted his hand, and came to live in Center City, a girl of nineteen with no experience of life other than picnics and parties and concerts and summer resorts and promenades along the East River.

"You don't mind my speaking so personally of all this? I have to do so, you will soon understand.

"Henry Lane loved me. To the day of his death he loved me. In a sense, I'm responsible for his death, because of the extent of the love he bore me. But I hadn't been married and moved here to Center City long before I discovered exactly the nature of that love. It wasn't the romantic love I'd read of in stories or heard told by servants. Nor was it the mere physical passion that I and all the other girls I knew feared and talked of only in whispers. Henry's passion was more for his many enterprises, and for Center City, and later on for wealth and politics. Which is not to say that our marriage was never consummated. It was. But Henry never remained in my room an entire night. From the beginning, he merely visited a while, and we slept apart. And then, as the years passed and I still hadn't conceived, even those visits became infrequent, and finally ended.

"I was more like a younger sister or an already grown daughter to him than a wife. I was his companion, but also the person he worked and planned and made decisions for. My duties were few—to him, to the home, and later to society. Knowing no better, I accepted this for almost a decade. It had many rewards, I assure you. For I had married into position: indeed a far better position than I had dreamed of. There were parties galore, as many as there had been in New York. There were meetings,

dinners, balls, clubs to attend, luncheons, charities. I had a carriage of my own—and might come and go freely. I had gowns,
jewels, hats, shoes, furs, books, whatever I wanted, and the best
and most beautiful. I soon had made tenuous connections with
other women in the town, and prided myself on their association.
Oh, I was still seen as an outsider, but we were all comfortable
together, and that was all I wished. I had Mrs. Ingram to take
care of the house, and other servants for the house and grounds.
I came to enjoy my life. If Henry did not give me his greatest
attention, he at least gave me more than anyone else. That too
seemed enough. He threw himself into the hotel, the farms, the
grains and baling businesses, and I knew that was all done for me,
for him to make good the promise he had made me.

"I ought to have been blissful instead of merely content. But
I soon discovered I could not forever thwart nature. Once, on
one of our many visits to Lincoln, I decided to visit a physician
Henry knew. After a lengthy examination, he told me that I was
perfectly healthy, and as well as he could determine, able to
conceive and bear. At the same time he hinted that the problem
lay with Henry; and that he, the doctor, had known about it for
years, and in fact that it was one reason why Henry had waited
so long before marrying.

"At first I didn't understand. When I did, I was shattered by
the discovery. I only lacked one thing for my life to be perfect
—that was children. It was evident that as long as I remained wed
to Henry Lane, I never would have children.

"This, too, I came to accept. I had never felt completely comfortable in our most intimate relations, and had never
complained as they lessened. I consoled myself with the examples of young widows, or spinsters who perforce shared that lack
in life with no dwindling of their vitality and happiness. If they
could, so could I. Having Mrs. Ingram in the house as a daily
example was naturally most helpful.

"Yet I became dissatisfied, restless. I developed curious, un-
detectable ailments—headaches, rashes, things that would come
and go with no warning, regardless of treatment or medication.
In my sixth year of marriage I became an insomniac.

"If you enjoy your sleep, Mr. Ransom, then thank God for it. To be denied the comfort of daily oblivion is a woe, I assure you, I would not wish on an enemy. I know the folk saying 'the bad sleep well.' Many times I wished I were a Messalina, a Lucrezia Borgia, if only to enjoy a complete night of restful slumber.

"You cannot imagine what it is like to suffer such an ailment, to go to bed with your body and mind exhausted from a full day of events and activity, and to be unable to sink into sleep. Hour after hour, no matter how you rearrange your pillows, no matter how many blankets you put off, how many cooler sheets you put on. The finest goosedown and feather beds might as well be granite ledges and slate boulders. All about you gas lamps are trimmed and put out. Every house is darkened around you, as you search outside through the window. All are sleeping but you. A dog barks in a dream. The streets are silence itself. You go out into the hallway, hoping someone, even a servant, is still awake. The hush of slowed breathing comes at you from every bedroom doorway, either that or the soft guttering of snores. Even that you envy.

"Everything but you and the house itself seems unconscious. Every noise you make is magnified tenfold in the great quiet of the night. You envy the poorest scullery her rest. The floorboards crack beneath your slippered feet as though mocking you. It is worse than a nightmare of awakening in a house filled with the dead. For the nightmare would happen and be over. But this goes on night after night. You go into the kitchen and light a fire, and warm some milk to drink, for this is an old wives' tale that often works. It soothes you, calms you, and you return upstairs to your bed thinking, well now, it will come. But you lay there hour after hour. You light the light again, you read until your eyes are bleary, you shut the lamp. You still cannot sleep. Idle thoughts rage about in your skull. It's almost dawn now. The night has passed and with it, you're certain, all hope. The curtains have to be pulled. You're angry. And then, without your noticing it, sleep does come, for a half hour or an hour or two. Never more. Just a tantalization, nothing more. Day after day, week after week, for months, until you become ill or crazed or both.

"Well has the poet called it the 'soft embalmer of the still midnight/Shutting with careful fingers and benign,/Our gloompleas'd eyes, embowered from the light,/Enshaded in forgetfulness divine.' Well has he bade it, 'O soothest Sleep! If so it please thee,/Close in midst of this thine hymn, my willing eyes.'

"There are medications devised for this problem. All of them share one common ingredient—the poet names it 'poppy'; it is sometimes called laudanum, sometimes tincture of opium. Taken in the proper quantities it is a mild sedative. Of larger quantities —but you already know, Mr. Ransom, what it is like. I used the smallest possible doses at first. Nevertheless, they had to be incremented. The dosages became larger every month. For three years I used the sedative—for more than three years I lived like this: sleeping more than before, I admit, sometimes for five or six hours a night, but enslaved by the drug.

"You're not wavering yet, Mr. Ransom. That is a good sign. Horrible as these revelations are, worse follow. I told you we would go far.

"Henry knew about this, of course. I would never think to hide it from him. Sometimes I wish I had, not only because of his almost infinite concern for me. He had borne with me during the worst times of my insomnia. As much as he deplored the solution, he bore with me through this too. But I must say I gave him ample cause for disturbance. Use of the drug had unanticipated effects—even during those hours I was not directly under its influence: mental abstraction, distraction, forgetfulness, a growing distance between myself and others, often a slurring of my speech, a marked slowing down of my movements—all of which could be embarrassing at the social functions we so often had to attend.

"It was about this time that another solution offered itself.

"Healthy as Henry was, he had grown up in the poorest of families. He had suffered from poor diet, and in the matter of his teeth only had this deprivation caused lasting effects. To a lesser degree than my insomnia, yet still quite chronically, Henry had serious toothaches. All the time we'd been married, he had gone from dentist to doctor to dentist, seeking to care for his teeth. Half of his natural ones had fallen out or been pulled. He was determined to salvage the remainder.

"When he told me of his first visits to Mr. Dinsmore, I was naturally pleased. I knew very well the torments Henry had suffered in dental offices. Within less than a year, Henry's remaining teeth were saved, and a set of false, ivory ones, put in a comfortable vulcanite plate installed. All of it accomplished painlessly. All of it done better professionally than any previous work. As you must know, Mr. Dinsmore's methods evoke the greatest compliance on the part of the patient, making his work a great deal easier; and as he is quite skilled, the effects tend to be longer lasting all around.

"Henry was never terribly clear about how it was that Mr. Dinsmore discovered my problem with insomnia. At the time, I merely assumed the topic had come up in conversation between them. At a later time, I discovered that he had found out about it as he had so much else in Henry's life—by mesmerizing him, then interrogating him in great detail during the trance. You see, you ought not doubt his capacity in managing all of the Lane businesses, Mr. Ransom. Henry tended to be a reserved, even a secretive man where his business matters were concerned, but Mr. Dinsmore soon knew more details of that too than I or anyone else.

"Whether Mr. Dinsmore had already seen me by then, or whether he merely wished to eliminate any possible opposition from me and to extend his control, I cannot say. I was hesitant about being mesmerized, and doubtless I see now that Henry insisted I try the method only because of increased pressure put upon him. Looking back on it, it was as though Satan had persuaded Adam to offer the apple to Eve. With, I'm afraid, results as disastrous for us.

"In one session, I was mesmerized in a matter of minutes into a deeper and more relaxing sleep than I had experienced in years, even using the drug. After the second session, I was able to enjoy that same sleep for an entire night. I was then mesmerized a third time, and after it I was able to sleep deeply every night for three months, without the use of any drug. After that, the insomnia returned as though it had never been gone. What he was doing, I now understand, was testing his own control. To this very day, Mr. Ransom, I do not know if I am sleeping nights or lying awake, as I sometimes do, upon his express command or not. That is how deeply influenced I am.

"If it were only that, however, I would have been an easy enough object for his domination. But he scrupled as little with me as with Henry, and during those false states of sleep, he also interrogated me. Doing so, he found out what I had never confided to another being—that my husband had not touched me in several years; that no man had.

"I am persuaded now that he might have taken his pleasure of me without my knowing of it. He chose a crueler and I suppose a more satisfying way of torturing me. He made love to me until I submitted of my own will.

"Yes, while Henry was still alive, I bartered the enslavement of a drug for the sin of adultery. And while I was doing so, further enslaved myself in still other and more terribly subtle ways.

"Do you recall my prefacing this confession by saying how ignorantly I had been raised by my parents? I did not know how ignorantly until Mr. Dinsmore entered my life. I suspected I knew all there was to know about the relations of men and women, simply because Henry had visited my bed for a half hour or so at a time, years before. I was to be disillusioned soon enough.

"It did not help that Mr. Dinsmore is an extremely attractive and, when he chooses to be, a charming man. I am not alone in that feeling. I have heard enough other women say so. I know their envy of me partly accounts for how I am now being treated by them. If Henry Lane in no way fulfilled the girlish requirements I suppose I still had for a romantic partner, Frederick, I'm afraid, more than fulfilled all of them.

"Unlike Henry, too, he possessed a physical passion that seemed to have few limits. I'd scarcely been touched by Henry. But when I'd leave that office over the saloon on Van Buren

Avenue, every muscle of my body would be aching, every nerve stimulated, sometimes with real bruises and welts on my flesh I would have been hard pressed to explain. He seemed to draw a never ending source of pleasure by causing me the most exquisite kinds of pleasure and even of pain. Some days I would be sprawled beneath him for hours at a time, until I thought I would lose my mind. Other days, I would scarcely open the door and be inside the office when he would take me, upon a chair, the sofa, a lamp table, against the wall, almost fully dressed, then send me away again. He probed every inch of my body, caused every crevice, every niche, every opening to become an organ of gratification. He took particular delight in watching me, without sometimes touching me, as he gave command after command for me to degrade myself before him in lascivious poses and gestures. He commanded me to dress in outlandish costumes that only the most obvious strumpets would be seen in, and then would order me to pose in the manner of French postcards he showed me. He commanded, and I obeyed. He was like some barbaric deity to me—I could never hope to understand what new humiliation he had planned, or what new pleasure. I went to his body as though it was the altar of a god, and I spent all my time adoring at that altar, even seeking new ways by which I might titillate or gratify him. He brought me various devices he had somehow or other gotten—false phalluses and the like—and we used them upon each other almost as though we no longer possessed separate genders, becoming both of us man and woman. He produced other devices capable of inflicting pain—these too we used upon each other. Every meeting we had, we became less and less God's chosen creatures, and more and more like animals floundering in their own sweat and filth and bile. I could not, I sometimes still cannot, believe two people can use each other as we have done and still remain sane. My own degradation has gone beyond any limits. Whatever the most degenerate of prostitutes have done from necessity, I can bitterly assure them, I have done too, and worse, and taken much pleasure from it.

"If those women who have snubbed me knew this, I would be

thrown to the dogs like a Jezebel. I have betrayed my own sex far more than any feminist they accuse of doing so.

"You are aghast, Mr. Ransom, as you ought to be, if only to share the same room with the monster that I have become. Do not think I do not despise myself as completely. But know that now this swinishness has ended. He has taken some dance hall girl. It is she and no longer I whom he is now degrading. How I pity her. And I have been cast aside as easily as though I didn't exist. He is civil to me, never really courteous, nor could I expect him to be after the horrors we have shared. I must be as contemptible in his eyes as he is in mine. Nor—I have to say in my own defense—did Henry ever know of this; as fine a cruelty as that would have been for Frederick to perpetrate, it did not fit his scheme to do so.

"So you see, Mr. Ransom, his control over me is quite complete. I am under his rigorous grip in all that I do. Not a step may I take without wondering and indeed fearing when he will again mesmerize me and discover it. You were witness to how much he enjoys exercising that control in public. It amuses him to see me a toy to his whim. He is capricious in that way. If he ignores me now, it is because he knows he can exercise dominance over me whenever he so choses. Under this influence, he knows, I will sign any document put under my eyes. He also thinks that I will never reveal him, for fear of revealing my own despicable weakness.

"I have no doubt that he caused Henry to hang himself. I am proof enough that even without being in a mesmeric trance I will act as he wishes. I fear Mrs. Ingram does also. I think that whenever she acts willfully in opposition to him that he has her cause some mischief to herself without her knowing what she is doing or why. Once, after an argument with him, she cut her forearm quite deeply with a breadknife, then came rushing into the parlor, demented by her own act. He laughed at her, and told her to be certain to behave herself in the future or she would suffer worse lapses. Only then did he aid her.

"Henry was under his influence longer and more deeply. He went to him several times a week. During the past winter,

Henry began to worry. He had come to believe that he was becoming bankrupt. No one could convince him otherwise. Any minor mishap that occurred in his enterprises, which a year before he would merely have shrugged off, was now seen as part of a colossal conspiracy by the government, by the stockbrokers, by other financiers, by anyone and everyone to ruin him. He never noticed the gains he made. Only the losses. He became distraught over those. He remained in the warehouse offices late at night trying to prove that he was being embezzled. He once counted every piece of linen in the Lane Hotel, certain he was being stolen from. He persecuted Mrs. Ingram over her monthly accounts. He went so far as to humiliate me in public about spending money. It was a horrible situation. Henry had grown up poor, and was afraid of dying a pauper; and Dinsmore was persuading him that this was about to happen, that it was happening. That is how he destroyed Henry. For he could bear anything else but that. Destroyed by his own worst fears, exaggerated beyond all sense, by another man's control.

"As I have been destroyed by my own fears and lusts, again under his control.

"Now, Mr. Ransom," she said as though completely exhausted by her words, "if you don't mind, I think you ought to leave. Mrs. Ingram will be home soon. I do not wish her to know you've been to this house. The poor woman would reveal it under his interrogation, and I fear she would suffer because of it. I will take the burden of that upon myself. I cannot shake it now." And for the first time since they'd sat down that afternoon, she could no longer disguise or restrain her utter misery. The detached, almost emotionless tone she'd used to detail a dozen appalling incidents vanished. Her voice fluttered, on the edge of a sob. Ransom could barely make out her last words.

"I am already so deeply involved I do not know how to shake it."

———————————●———————————

RANSOM WAS ALMOST AT FILLMORE AVENUE before he came to his senses. The numbness that had settled over him listening to her words, watching her face, chilled him as thoroughly as though he'd been walking naked through a blizzard instead of sitting inside a heated house with a cup of coffee within reach.

He had expected her words to gain his compassion, to bind the two of them more closely through shared sorrows—but he'd not expected to be quite so horrified at the abyss Carrie Lane had opened at his feet. As an attorney, he'd thought he had come to know all there was to know of human nature—its passions, its lusts, its twisted reasonings and petty motivations. But he'd never expected to hear firsthand, and from such a one as Carrie Lane, such depths of anguished depravity. Much as he had put on and held on the professional mask of the inquiring lawyer during her confession, she had seen through it to his shock. And had not been shocked herself. That was amazing. As though because of what she'd experienced Carrie Lane now had the same cool, privileged, unimpeded view into the human soul that he had always prided himself on. That had been the reward of her experience—terrifying as that had been. He had to admit she was a magnificent woman, as glorious in her confession of unspeakable vices as she'd been as merely the town's social leader. He knew now that to save her from Dinsmore meant saving her from herself—the self she had admitted to being: a woman of aberrant, untrammeled sensuality.

By the time he was back in his office at the Page Board and Hotel, the idea impelled him even more. Energized, Ransom took off his jacket, stoked the wood in the Franklin stove, asked Mrs. Page if he might have his dinner sent up, and set to work on Carrie Lane's evidence. This had to be presented in such a way that any judge in the country would accept it—yet certain details had to be glossed over, kept to a minimum, suggested. This would be a public document after all, and it had both to hide and reveal information, which if necessary could be given verbally in the judge's private chambers.

Simon Carr's testimony had to be reworked too, and then, the shorter dispositions of Mrs. Bent, Millard, Yolanda Bowles, and Reverend Sydney. The medical evidence would have to wait. For now, only those letters and articles from the medical journals which supported the most perilous uses of mesmerism would be included.

Dinner arrived, was eaten almost unconsciously by Ransom as he worked, and was removed. He called for a pot of coffee, and that was brought up by Isabelle, who noted the Franklin stove would need more wood if he were to be up much longer. Little Nate brought up armfuls in two trips, and stoked it for Ransom who hardly glanced up at the boy. Around him the house became quiet as everyone retired to bed. The coffee—left on the stove —was cooked to a tarlike sludge, the stove was only a glowing chunk of rapidly cooling black metal, and daylight began to break out of the eastern sky with long yellow fingers through jagged black clouds, when Ransom read over all he had written, then went to bed.

His first thought upon awakening some two hours later was that during the night Dinsmore had mesmerized Carrie Lane and had discovered all. Ransom ought to have warned her to lock herself in her rooms. Or would that be of any use? Couldn't a voice travel as easily through a keyhole? She was in danger even now, and what was he doing about it?

While shaving, he heard Nate on the stairway and called the boy to his room. Ransom quickly scrawled a note to Carrie Lane, and giving Nate a quarter dollar, bade him deliver it before he went to school and await a reply.

The boy was so impressed with his tip, he ran out of the house without eating breakfast. He was back in fifteen minutes, having gotten a ride from the Lane house in Caspar Bixby's produce wagon. Ransom tore open her answer in the downstairs foyer, unconcerned that Mrs. Page and Isabelle were observing his unusual activities.

She was well, she wrote. Dinsmore hadn't been home that night. He'd probably spent it at his suite in the Lane Hotel with his dance hall woman. Carrie had slept well. She thanked God for Ransom's concern and for his past persistence.

He wanted to crow like a rooster in triumph. Instead, he put the note in the inner pocket of his vest and finished his breakfast under the expectant gazes of all at the table.

A half hour later, he was in the foyer of the Dietz house insisting to Lavinia Dietz that the judge's morning reading be disturbed. She emerged from the library asking for the bulk of Ransom's disquisitions; the judge would not see him until it had been read and pored over. Had she conveyed his urgency? he asked. Yes, she assured him, she had. Would he have some breakfast? she asked; at least some coffee?

Reluctantly, Ransom joined Mrs. Dietz in the breakfast room. With impatience, he answered her questions, listened to her domestic conversation, and wondered why Dietz was taking so long. Ransom had put Mrs. Lane's testimony first, stressing her peril in his own covering letter.

After an hour or so, the library door remained firmly shut. Ransom dressed for outside again and, promising to return in a half an hour, left the house.

It was midmorning, and the traffic of wagons and pedestrians seemed at its height at the corner of Dakota Avenue and Center Street.

Ransom pondered whether he ought to go to Carrie Lane. But he'd already written instructing her to keep her distance from Dinsmore until he could come to her. She trusted him—finally, thankfully. Still, he oughtn't stray too far from the Dietz house.

So he slowly walked about the central plaza, idly inspecting the goods displayed in the haberdashers on Taylor Avenue, passing the post office, noting that the Lane Hotel was being refitted with new rain gutters on its roof, passing by the courthouse, the bench in front already occupied by Floyd and his cronies, arguing over some piece in the Center City *Star,* stopping into the pharmacist's for a nickel's worth of sour-lemon drops, one of which he sucked on his way back to the Dietz house.

Arthur, the judge's butler and general handyman, let him into the foyer, took his hat and coat. No, the judge hadn't come out of the library yet, he said. Ransom was about to ask for his outer clothing again when he heard female conversation in the small east parlor, and turned to see the ample figure of Lavinia. But in her own plump hands, she held the finer-boned, gloveless fingers of Carrie Lane. She must have just arrived: she still hadn't removed her large, veiled black hat.

"There you are, James," Lavinia said.

He was about to step into the parlor when a door opened from farther down the hall.

"Arthur. Get Ransom for me," Dietz said from the doorway. Then, "Ah. There you are, James! Don't stand there, come here. You've disorganized my morning already as it is."

Ransom gestured to the ladies that he would return and went into the library.

Dietz sat wearily in his big black-leather Windsor, behind a desk littered with Ransom's indictment.

"Has the Lane woman arrived yet?" he asked. His mood was dark; his voice angry.

"She's in the parlor now."

"I don't understand you, James. I really don't understand why you insist on opening this . . . this Pandora's box. No. Don't answer me. I do know why. But you don't seem to understand exactly how far this will go, what it will mean to Center City."

"It will mean the removal of an usurper, the restoration of order."

"Ah, if that were all. It's going to be like cutting out a cancer."

"It has to be done," Ransom said.

"There are ways it can be contained."

"Not even you can contain it now. The rot is spreading right to the state capitol. If Dinsmore has a tenth of the influence Henry Lane had there, it's far too much. You know that."

"It's going to be a battle, you know."

"I'm ready for a battle."

"Spoken like a man half your age, James. You Rebs never do grow up, do you? All right, send in Mrs. Lane."

"Will you accept the indictment?" Ransom had to ask.

"I said I will speak with Mrs. Lane," Dietz repeated, frowning. "Has she read this?"

"She knows what's in it."

"Get her," he ordered with a scowl.

Ransom tried to encourage her as they walked to the library door.

"You needn't worry," he assured her. "I kept your most confidential matters to myself. It was only necessary to point out the nature of your liaison with Dinsmore to clarify how over-whelming his influence is. All details remain between us. So you needn't fear to be embarrassed."

She pressed his hand. "You make me feel brave. You also make me feel unworthy of your goodness. I've done nothing to merit your help."

"You've done everything," he whispered, opened the library door, then closed it behind her.

She remained closeted with the judge most of the afternoon. An hour into it, Dietz called for Arthur and instructed him to have the court clerk come. A short while later, Lavinia was called into the library. She came out, telling Ransom to return that evening for dinner. Then she called her housekeeper, a small wary Norwegian woman named Rina, and sent her to the Lane house with a message for Mrs. Ingram to pack an overnight bag: her mistress would remain here for the night.

Ransom returned to his office in a disgruntled state. Though certain wheels had been set in motion, which would protect Carrie Lane and ultimately lead to the indictment, he felt he had little control over any of it. Dietz was as capricious and tyrannical a man who'd ever sat on a county judicial seat. He could move with lightning speed on some matters, and with the slowness of sap oozing from a frozen tree trunk on others. He was a sturdy ally but an inscrutable one. As an adversary he was as polite as a courtier of Louis XIV, and as deadly as a rattlesnake. Ransom had known Carl Dietz as a man and jurist for almost a decade— he knew that to cross him at any point before a trial was to make of him a martinet on the bench. The first criminal trial Ransom had prosecuted in Center City, some eight years before—an obvious case of Wild-West assassination—had evoked a passion for detail and a rigor for the letter of the law in Judge Dietz which had threatened to extend the proceedings from a few days to a month. As Dietz said afterward, before he hanged a man, he wanted to count every strand of the rope that would do the work: a prudence not always expressed west of the Mississippi, Ransom had to admit.

Ransom shifted some papers around on his desk for fifteen minutes, then realized how his concern had disguised real exhaustion. He slept in his chair until it was time to dress for dinner.

If he had expected Dietz to hand him a signed indictment as he went in the door, he was to be disappointed. Only four of them were to dine, but it had the air of a more formal affair. Carrie Lane looked fatigued, but somewhat calmer. The judge made only one reference to the matter that lay over the meal like a pall—and that was a Latin epigram he translated to the effect that food and business had nothing in common.

To Ransom's annoyance, that eliminated any questions he had, and dinner proceeded in a stately, unexciting fashion: silences broken by conversation of the most trivial importance. There was one consolation—that Carrie Lane, so recently excluded from this house, now sat at the judge's right hand at the table, as though her honor were already restored.

Once dessert had been eaten, Lavinia suggested that she and Carrie remove themselves upstairs. Alone with the judge, Ransom sulked, unwilling to open up the subject.

Dietz did it for him.

"You have made a very fine presentation, James. Very thorough, of the highest professional caliber."

"Then you'll accept it?"

"Ordinarily I would without any question. It wants a few details yet, the signature of the witnesses to their testimony, for example. I've no doubt these can be obtained."

"I'll get them tomorrow."

"Fine. Fine. As I said, ordinarily, all this would be enough. But we're dealing with a rather extraordinary situation, and that requires extraordinary methods, doesn't it?"

Ransom didn't comment.

"I believe you, James. I believe Mrs. Lane too. Poor woman.

I believe Simon Carr and the others. Or at least I'm prepared to believe them once under oath."

"Then what's the problem?"

"The problem is that I don't believe in this mesmerism business. The entire case hinges on that, James. You're going to have to convince twelve men, who live very much in the here and now, in the hard reality of crops and irrigation and feed and animals and pests, that this hocus-pocus is as effective as you claim it is."

"I'll persuade them."

"How? You haven't persuaded me yet. I told you I wanted a practical demonstration that it works. Until then, I can't sign this indictment."

"What am I supposed to do?" Ransom asked. "Call Dinsmore over and explain the problem to him. And maybe, just maybe, he'll be amused enough to demonstrate it?"

"I have to have it, James."

"I've experienced it. I'll go under oath and testify."

"You never had any of the postmesmeric effects the others had. That's what your case is so logically built upon, you know that. Or have you?"

"No. But . . . wait a minute. Simon Carr is a Mesmerist too. Would you consent to having him demonstrate? It's almost the same as having Dinsmore do it. Carr taught it to Dinsmore."

Dietz thought a few minutes. "Bring him here."

"I can't, he's very ill. We'll have to go there."

"In the morning, then."

"Can it wait that long? What if Dinsmore finds out that Mrs. Lane is here? He's certain to suspect something. What if he leaves Center City?"

"I see you'll give me no rest today," the judge said. "Arthur. Hitch up the carriage. No. Let's not. I never did like being in a touchy situation inside one of those lumbersome things. We'll ride, James."

When Ransom had gotten Golden at the Lane Public Stables and rode up, leading a large, well-broken gelding for the judge, Dietz seemed in an even fouler mood.

"It's cold as Minnesota tonight. This had better be worth all the trouble, James."

"It will be," Ransom said, but as they rode out of town and into the freezing night, he wondered whether Simon Carr could provide the practical demonstration the stubborn old jurist required. If not, where would that leave the case? And Mrs. Lane? It had to work, if Ransom had to threaten Carr to do it.

Even with the biting wind and the sharply icy ground underfoot, Golden seemed to exult in the ride—the first he'd had with Ransom in several days. Once out of Center City, there was only the sight of a sliver of moon alternately hidden and visible through a scudding scrim of black cloudlets to guide them. The horse reared toward the flat horizon as though challenging the wildness of the night. Ransom let the stallion have its way, but when he turned around to see how far behind him the judge had fallen, he was surprised to see Dietz had kept good pace with him. Like most of the old-timers who'd lived here since the place was a territory, Dietz rode as though it were second nature.

Halfway to the Lane ranch they slowed down so the horses would not sweat into a lather and chill up as they waited outside. Only because of the absolute, unbroken flatness of the land was the silhouette of the ranch at all visible. All the lights were out: the place looked forlorn.

As they tethered their horses, Ransom noticed a dull rectangle of light emerging from a side window on the adobe side of the building. That must be Carr's room. Ransom went to it. Wooden shutters shut, but behind them a weak light.

"Simon! Simon!" he called, tapping at the wooden shutter.

Silence. He called and tapped again. One shutter opened and in the dim light, Ransom made out the old man's buzzard features.

"It's me, Simon. I have to talk to you."

"You must be daft," Carr said. "I'm in my nightshirt."

"Open the front door. I have the county judge with me. He wants to talk to you. To settle up the warrant waiver."

"Now? Like this?"

"It's all right. We'll be at the front."

"Can't it wait?" Carr asked again, but Ransom had already turned to the front of the ranch, where Dietz was waiting in the small shelter of the overhanging roof, stamping his feet and breathing mist into the air.

"He'll be right here," Ransom said.

Dietz scowled. "So this is Lane's ranch. Looks like a cattle rustler's hideout. With all his money, you might think he would've put up a proper place."

"It's even worse by daylight. Nothing but rubble, broken furniture, and a tiny garden over there."

"My place at Plum Creek is paradise compared to this."

"I guess he didn't much use it."

"Too busy politicking around," the judge said. The dialogue had been the first criticism of Henry Lane Ransom had heard from Dietz. Perhaps they'd been more than the polite adversaries Ransom had always supposed? Perhaps the judge wasn't so unhappy that Henry Lane was dead after all? Could that be why he was stalling so much on this indictment?

They heard the bolt shoot open, then the big oak door was pulled to. Carr had thrown some sort of patterned serape over his longjohns and had put on a pair of shoes. All he needed was a few feathers to look like a demented medicine man of the Pawnee tribe. Without a greeting, he let them in, rebolted the door, and holding a tin candlestick aloft, guided them to his room. As he was closing the door, the worried face of Minna, the housekeeper, appeared in the hallway. Carr dismissed her in her own language so summarily, all Ransom caught was *schlafen*— sleep. Then they were alone.

Ransom watched the two men evaluating each other as he introduced them. They didn't shake hands, but Carr offered the judge the only seat—the spindly, slat-backed rocker brought inside—and himself sat on the edge of the bed. Their silence continued until Carr looked up at Ransom, as though questioning him.

Before he could say a word, Dietz began: "Are you willing to sign the testimony I have received to the effect that Frederick L. Dinsmore utilized a species of mental manipulation to control yourself and others? Will you agree to give that a testimony under oath? And will you then explain the circumstances of your flight from the state of Illinois with Mr. Dinsmore into Wisconsin, Indiana, *et cetera,* until your arrival here, in Center City?"

"He forced me to go with him," Carr said with no hesitation. "I would have stayed if I could have. I was guilty of nothing in Illinois. Nothing at all. He forced me and his wife so we wouldn't testify against him. By all justice, I ought never have been charged. He said as much himself," pointing to Ransom. "He said it could all be waived."

Their positions now stated, it was somehow easier. The judge even chuckled.

"It'll be waived if you'll testify," he said.

"I'll testify. Don't concern yourself. If I have to walk to the courthouse barefoot to do it."

"Fine. In the next day or two we'll have a written testimony for you to sign. It will be read to you if . . ."

"I can read, all right. I mightn't look like a great deal, but I was educated at Oxford University and I can read as well as you or anyone else in a half dozen languages, the classics as well as the modern languages."

"I don't doubt it," Dietz said, evidently warming to Carr. Obstreperousness usually did please him in others. "I don't doubt it at all. In that respect, I'm afraid you're superior to me. I only know Latin, from my legal studies. Now tell me about this mesmerism business. How is it that one can be controlled by it even with the Mesmerist not present?"

"It's very difficult, yet really quite simple," Carr began. He went on to explain how the subject is placed by the Mesmerist into a semiconscious state, not asleep, yet not awake. In this sort of half state, the subject is extremely impressionable, open to any suggestion or series of suggestions given. Since, as in sleep, ordinary concepts of time no longer exist for the subject, it is possible for the Mesmerist to make a suggestion which does not have to be carried out immediately: but which he can set off by a phrase, a word, a gesture—much as detonations are set off from a distance. If the subject has been tested to show this depth of suggestibility, it is impossible for him to not perform the suggested action. And if the Mesmerist has stipulated that it not be remembered, then, naturally, the subject has no way to understand what it is he has done. In some cases it's easily enough incorporated into a logical framework, and explained away. In others, it's totally inexplicable.

"You said a series of suggestions?" Dietz asked. "How does that work?"

"I ought to have said a chain of suggestions. For that is how it goes, each one forged to the other." Carr explained that in the trance state it is often impossible for a suggestion to be carried out, if only because of previous suggestions—beliefs, moral teachings, empirical discoveries—which held a longer and stronger place in a subject's mind. "Thus, in a mesmeric trance, I might tell you this man is your enemy and will certainly kill you if you don't kill him first. But he may be your closest friend, tried and trusted for the last twenty years. That knowledge, a lack of motivation, and an excess of religious teachings condemning homicide would work against my one suggestion."

Dietz agreed to this.

"But," Carr went on, "if, over a period of days or weeks or months, I probed your memory while you were in a mesmeric trance and discovered small incidents of discord—common even in the best of friends—I could turn these incidents into a pattern of secret odium and conspiracy. Then, using your growing unconscious distrust, fan it up by my suggestions and forge in you an ineluctable belief—circumstantially acceptable to you—of his enmity and his desire to have your life. This is Dinsmore's nefarious genius at work. I may have discovered how well the posthypnotic trance works; he uses it as though it were a black art."

"On you?" Dietz asked.

"No. Not so far. But on his wife, certainly. And, I've come to believe, on others."

"On Henry Lane?" Dietz asked.

"It's possible. No, more than possible: likely. I cannot say I've witnessed it with Mr. Lane. But I've seen it often enough to know that it works."

Dietz was silent for a while. Then he said, "I have to be certain of this. Three of you have testified to it, but I have to know it myself. Mr. Carr, I want you to mesmerize me, and suggest to me an action which I will then perform upon the given cue."

The old buzzard face screwed up. "I don't know. I don't know that I can. I was never as good as Dinsmore at it."

"Try it," Ransom insisted. "Do you want Dinsmore to be able to control you whenever he wants to?"

Carr stood up, tiny and ridiculous in his longjohns and serape. "I don't know if I can. Must I?" he pleaded. "I swore I'd never do it again."

"To him?" Ransom asked.

"To myself."

"Just this once. Otherwise I have no case against Dinsmore."

The old man thought for a moment, then sadly said, "I suppose it will do no harm to attempt it once. I'll need the candle closer though. As a focal point." He brought it closer to them.

"How will I know what it is you suggested?" Dietz said.

"I'll tell him," Carr said, pointing to Ransom.

"No. I need firmer proof than that. Write it down. Here. Here's a pen. And here"—tearing a sheet of paper out of a small vest diary—"here's some paper. Write down precisely what you'll suggest me to do, then seal it. I'll have no questions in my mind about this."

Carr agreed, but he held the paper, thinking, looking as though he were trying to recollect something. Finally he scribbled something on the paper, folded it in quarters, and sealed the edges with candle drippings. The judge inspected the seal, found it satisfactory, then put it back into his vest pocket, along with the diary.

"Now, Mr. Carr, if my friend is not needed, he will kindly wait outside the room. I assure you that will best prepare me for the experiment."

The housekeeper had lighted a candle in the kitchen. Ransom sat down at the table and stared blankly at the window, watching the setting moon now and again covered by clouds. A mackerel sky. Rain tomorrow, or if this cold kept up, snow. It was awfully early for winter to take hold in so tight a grasp. They seemed to be taking a great deal of time in there. He'd been mesmerized in minutes. What if Dietz were of that few percent of the population who were not subject to its power? Wouldn't that be just like him. What if Carr couldn't do it? Oh, bother it all! Hadn't Carrie Lane looked wonderful at dinner! A little tired, but the despair that had contorted her features had vanished. She had seemed younger, far more handsome. Difficult to believe all she had said.

His mind began to wander then, and he dropped his head onto his arms crossed atop the kitchen table. He must have dozed for a short while, because suddenly he was being shaken awake. He looked up groggily.

"Let's go, James," Dietz said, then looked at the still sealed note Carr had written. "Does this appear as it was before?"

Ransom inspected it. It seemed the same.

"When am I supposed to open this," the judge asked Carr.

"After you've entered your house and greeted someone," the old man said. He looked unsure, exhausted.

"Have you been mesmerized?" Ransom asked.

"I suppose. There's a period of some fifteen minutes I cannot account for."

Dietz strode to the door, and did not say good-bye, but waited silently for Carr to unbolt the door. He remained silent as they mounted and rode off.

After his short nap, Ransom felt extraordinarily alert as they rode, noticing, he thought, every object touched by the last light of the moon's ghostly pallor. He tried to concentrate on the cold night air, on landmarks they passed, on the low horizon, on everything and anything so as to not have to think whether or not the posthypnotic effect would work on Dietz. If it didn't? Ah, but they were already approaching town, and now they were entering it. All dark, of course, except for the few gas lamps on Center Street, and the flaming gas jets outside the entry to the Dietz house. Curious how much faster return journeys always were.

Ransom tried to calm the flutter of expectation he felt as they dismounted. If he only knew what it was that Dietz was supposed to do, he might somehow or other urge it on, help it to occur.

Arthur opened the door for them without a word, and took their outerwear. Nothing had happened yet.

Dietz fumbled with his vest to get the sealed note.

"Now, we'll see what this is all about," he said gruffly, and was about to tear it open, when Lavinia Dietz glided out of the shadows of the stairway into the foyer.

"You're back!" she said. "Thank God. I was so worried, why didn't you tell me you were going out?"

"Bonne nuit," Dietz said, bending over the foyer table to hold the note. *"Laisse-nous, s'il te plaît. Ces affaires sont très importantes."*

"Why, Carl! she exclaimed. "When did you learn to speak French?"

He looked up. "Did I?"

"Of course you did. Surely you heard him, James?"

Before Ransom could comment, the judge had torn open the paper and was reading what it said.

"Damn!" he swore, threw the paper onto the foyer table, and rushed off to the library. "Arthur! Get on your streetclothes, and come in here."

"You did hear him speak French, didn't you?" she asked.

"I certainly did," Ransom said, picking up the paper Dietz had dropped. In a crabbed script common to doctors and pharmacists, it read:

> Upon reaching home, you will address the first member of your family to greet you with the following words: *Bonne nuit. Laisse-nous, s'il te plaît. Ces affaires sont très importantes.* I will speak these words to you several times so that you will correctly pronounce them.

It was signed, Simon Carr.

Ransom went into the library, where Dietz was now writing furiously.

"Carl, will you tell me what's happening?" Lavinia said with anguish in her voice. "James. You tell me."

"There you are, Arthur," the judge said, sealing an envelope. "Bring this to Eliot Timbs. If he's not at the sheriff's office or at home, go find him, wherever he is. I want this order carried out tonight. Immediately. Make certain he knows that. Lavinia, is Mrs. Lane still in the house?"

"Yes. But what's happened, Carl?"

"Mr. Ransom has gotten what he wanted."

"What he wanted?" And still in the dark she looked at Ransom.

"Yes. And, Lavinia, your dear husband has been roundly and soundly mesmerized," Dietz said. "Show her that paper, James. I've never spoken a word of French in my life."

She read the paper, and still looked confused. "But what does it mean?"

"It means," Ransom translated, " 'Good night. Please leave us alone. We have important matters to discuss.' "

"You heard," Dietz said, and slumped in his chair. "Go to sleep, Lavinia."

———————————●———————————

BY NOON OF THE FOLLOWING DAY, the dark, scudding clouds that had blocked the moon the night before had gathered to an all-enveloping bleakness of low-ceilinged dove-gray sky. Every hour the temperature rose or descended five degrees: it was difficult to predict which way it would go next.

"Snow weather," Augusta Page said, stomping into the kitchen, carrying a leg of smoked ham from the outdoor larder. "It's so damp out there, you can lift a bare hand and have it rimed in a minute."

This was said by way of admonition to Ransom, who was in the hallway, preparing to go out. He took the warning to heart, still avoiding a closer contact with his landlady, lest a conversation develop and with it questions about his still unexplained overwork, haste, and mystery of late. Murcott might have already told her enough to satisfy her curiosity; the doctor was shrewd enough to piece together Ransom's comings and goings into a coherent whole.

Still, it would spoil the almost perfect mood Ransom was in to have to talk of it. Like a youth of twenty, he'd told himself, earlier that morning, whistling at his image in the shaving mirror as he chose a pin-striped shirt, an unworn collar, and, despite the season, knotted on a jaunty red bow tie. Like a youth going courting. Which he was, in a way: going to call on Carrie Lane, safe at Judge Dietz's house, and doubly safe now that Dinsmore had been arrested.

His jaunty, high spirits continued on his walk to the Dietz house, despite the threatening weather. The front door was answered by Arthur, and Ransom went directly into the east parlor, not wanting to disturb the judge after all the time he'd taken the day before, but simply to see the ladies.

Only one lady was there to receive him: Lavinia Dietz. Ransom evaded her barrage of questions and asked if Mrs. Lane could be told he was in the house.

"She's gone," Lavinia said.

"Gone? Gone where?"

"Back to High Street. She went with Rina this morning right after breakfast. I miss her already. What a jewel she is, James. An absolute jewel."

As he was asking her for details of the unexpected departure, he heard the judge's authoritative voice in the foyer.

"Hello, James," he said, coming into the parlor. "Well, we've done what we could."

What did that mean? "Wasn't Dinsmore arrested last night?"

"Finally. But that fool Timbs put him under house arrest. At the Lane Hotel suite. Naturally Applegate was here at six o'clock asking for bail to be set."

"You've let Dinsmore go?"

"What else could I do? Applegate had a blank check drawn on Lane's name. He must have her pre-sign them a dozen at a time. No amount was too high. I saw that soon enough. I set a high enough bond, and I have to say Applegate blanched when he heard it, but he signed it over anyway. James! Where are you off to in such a hurry?"

Ransom already had his coat and hat on. "I don't believe it. You've let him go. Then let her go too? Knowing he was free?"

"Wait a minute. You are headstrong. He won't be free until twenty-four hours are passed. That won't be until midnight."

"Now or midnight? What's the difference? He's out and more of a danger than ever to her. You can see that."

"What do you want me to do? Put out an order to keep him away from the Lane house? How am I supposed to enforce that order with one idiot sheriff and one nigger deputy?"

"She's got to be brought somewhere safe."

"That's already been done. She'll go out to Plum Creek. To my lodge there. She's already agreed to it. Rina will go stay with her. Now, don't worry. Even if Dinsmore knows where she is, he won't be able to leave Kearney County under the bond. Plum Creek is across the county line. If he does, I will personally deputize half of Center City and clap him into jail until trial time."

"Why did you decide to set a bail?"

"Had to. State law. Only in cases of an acknowledged public menace can I not set one."

"He's broken bail before," Ransom argued. "I have proof."

"Five years ago. And in another state. Listen, James, this Dinsmore isn't the petty criminal you think he is."

"Who knows better than I exactly what he is?"

"Applegate's making a big to-do. Jeffries too. Neither you nor I are going to look very chivalrous once tomorrow's edition of the Center City *Star* comes out. That fool easterner wrote an editorial blasting us, James, blasting us. He read it to me. He says we're playing class politics, territorial politics, politics against newcomers. I told you there would be a battle. That damn printer's been fixing to go at me since he got into town. He thinks this is his big chance. He called the indictment a threadbare tissue of trumped-up lies and hocus-pocus allegations. More than Henry Lane ever was, this Dinsmore seems to be the man fools like Jeffries and Applegate and Mason are looking for to knock down what little power I have."

"Mason, too?"

"You want to read the letter he just sent by messenger?"

"Can't you charge them with attempting to impede justice?"

"Sure I can. I can charge the whole county with it. But I'm not about to do such a thing. Dinsmore won't break bail, believe me. He's too sure of himself. And I don't blame him. They're all over there at the Lane Hotel confabbing right now, having a sort of party over it. Prepare this case well, James. Take all the time you need for it. Get all the details that are necessary. But I want you to make sure it will stick, stick like horsefoot glue."

"I'll make it stick," Ransom said, then he was out the door.

Once on the street, he wished he'd brought Golden. He wanted to run to Carrie, but he contented himself with a break-neck, lunging pace. Ordinarily, he'd pass the Lane Hotel to get there. Instead, he walked up Dakota Street right to McKinley Avenue, then cut through the frozen pastureland to High Street. He was out of breath when he reached the top landing of the flight of stone steps. He had to stop and rest before knocking.

He thought he heard some noise in the hallway, and knocked soundly a half dozen times.

"What is it?" he heard. "I'm coming."

Mrs. Ingram opened the door. She had a thick shawl thrown over her shoulders and a very unfriendly mien.

"Well? What is it?"

"I'd like to see Mrs. Lane," Ransom said, put off by her manner.

"She's busy right now."

"Will you let me in?" he asked. And as she made no move to do so, he pushed his way past her, into the hallway. There were two large trunks sitting upright at the foot of the stairs. "Would you be kind enough to tell Mrs. Lane I'm here."

She looked at him, then said, "She won't see anyone. She's busy."

"She'll see me," he insisted. "I'm expected."

Her mouth twisted, she looked suddenly awakened, as though just realizing a fact of some complexity. "So it's you who's behind all this packing business."

"Just go up and tell her, will you?"

"Perhaps you'll tell me what's going on around here," she said, obviously annoyed, and having found a listener. "First she stays away from the house for the night, which she hasn't done in three years. And never alone. Sending for an overnight bag. Then, this morning, she comes back and immediately says she's leaving for the country. In the winter? I ask. Which is only natural. Well, she just rushes upstairs and starts throwing clothing out of closets and onto the bed, giving orders. Then, while I'm trying to pack those without getting them ruined, she sends that Norwegian tart to the room, who orders me—mind you, me!—to send up some larger trunks to be filled."

"I'm certain Mrs. Lane will be glad to explain," Ransom said, trying to conciliate her. "All I can say, is that this is a crisis. And you ought to do all that is possible to aid her."

"A crisis? What kind of crisis?"

"Now, don't get upset. It's merely that Mrs. Lane will be safer away from Center City for a short while. So, I believe, would you be, Mrs. Ingram."

"Safe from what?"

"From Mr. Dinsmore. You know he's been arrested and is to be released on bail at midnight."

"*I've* nothing to fear from him," she declared. "And if she does, that's her own foolishness."

More than he could ever recall, Mrs. Ingram was contrary and exasperating. He was tired of arguing with her. "Will you please tell Mrs. Lane that I'm here."

Before she had ascended as far as the first landing, Rina, the Dietz maid, appeared at the top of the stairs, a valise in one hand, some hatboxes in the other. She called up in a high voice. Mrs. Ingram stopped where she was and turned to him.

"Look at her. She thinks she lives here."

Rina ignored the older woman and flounced past her on the stairs. Behind her, dressed in a mocha-brown velvet traveling outfit, was Carrie Lane, a hatbox dangling from one hand, a smaller bag from the other. Her carriage, her step, her complexion, were all bright and light. She seemed more like a young girl about to set off on a long-anticipated adventure than a widow being forced from her home for safety's sake.

"Good morning, Mr. Ransom. How nice of you to come to see me off."

Ransom went up to meet her, took the bag, then took her free hand in his own. Seeing her so radiant lifted every anxiety he'd harbored rushing over from the judge's house. Just seeing her so marvelously transformed told him he'd done the right thing.

"Thank you," she said. "This is quite light. Rina, dear, see if you can find Oscar to help you load the carriage. He ought to be somewhere near the kitchen."

"He's in the woodhouse," Mrs. Ingram murmured darkly from her place on the stairway. "He was sleeping. I roused him."

"Thank you, Harriet. But, dear, you're not dressed to go. Please hurry."

"I'm not going."

"But why not?"

"I'm not letting any man chase me out of this house. And if you had any sense, you wouldn't either."

Carrie's glow dimmed a little.

"Please, Harriet. You know it isn't just that. Please come along. It will be ever so much better."

"Who'll watch the house?"

"We'll lock up the house until we return."

"How do we know someone won't burgle it? No. I was hired as housekeeper. I swore to your late husband I would remain here as housekeeper as long as I could stand up. I stay now."

"Won't you even come to be company for me?" Carrie asked.

Mrs. Ingram folded her arms over her chest, but did not say a word.

"I'm afraid for you if you stay," Carrie tried.

"I can take care of myself, thank you."

"I'm not so sure. I wish you would change your mind, Harriet. We both could use a vacation. A change of air. It will be so much fun in the country."

Mrs. Ingram kept her posture and her silence.

"If you please," Ransom said, taking Carrie Lane aside. "I

have nothing particularly pressing for the day. I'd be happy to accompany you on your little journey."

"Thank you, you are kind," she said, looking past his shoulder at her housekeeper a minute. "Yes, I think I would like that very much. Lavinia will be joining me tomorrow," she added in an undertone as they moved down to the hallway, and from there to the formal parlor with its Grand Rapids furnishings. "I still wish I could persuade Harriet to come. I'm so afraid for her. Can't you do anything?"

"Perhaps once you're gone, she'll change her mind. I'll come by tomorrow if you wish, to try again."

"You're too generous with your offers of aid. Look where it's gotten you. Into a carriage stuffed to the roof with hatboxes bound for the next county."

He was pleased by her easy return to high spirits. "You deserve everything good I know of to offer."

"You almost make me believe that. Bless you for it."

Rina had found Oscar, the gardener, and together with the coachman they were moving the trunks out the door.

"You'll be safe there, you know. He can't leave the county."

"I'm afraid I'll be safe from everything but ennui. I've packed a dozen three-decker novels Henry got for me years ago I've never even looked into."

"Perhaps you'll accept a visitor from Center City every now and again. We'll have to meet, anyway, before the trial."

She didn't say anything but looked at him with that curious mixture of fear and relief he'd seen in her so often.

"I think I might enjoy this vacation," she said firmly. "And, of course, you'll be welcome."

Rina came into the parlor to say that the carriage was packed and ready. She would return to the judge's house and join Mrs. Lane with her mistress.

Carrie Lane thanked her with a kiss on the delighted girl's cheek. Rina ran off, and Ransom accompanied Mrs. Lane into the foyer. Mrs. Ingram stood by, her arms still crossed, her attitude still icily offended.

"I do wish you'd come," Carrie repeated.

"You have company enough, I dare say. Though if you're running away from one man, I'd say you're not being terribly clever by running to another one so soon."

The color rose to her mistress's face instantly, and Mrs. Lane's hand rose, as though to strike her housekeeper. But it fell to her side again, as she quietly said:

"Take especial care of the palms in the conservatory. They were Henry's favorites, you know. They'll die if it's too cold or too wet." Then she glided out the door and down the stone steps.

Mrs. Ingram's arms came unfolded, and for a moment she looked as though she would follow and apologize. Then she became aware of Ransom again.

"Please feel free to call on me for any assistance if you need it, Mrs. Ingram," he said. "Any time at all."

Her eyes still looked at Mrs. Lane, getting into the carriage. Then Harriet Ingram shut the door in his face.

———————•———————

RINA HAD BROUGHT DOWN A QUILT to cover their legs inside the carriage, already so packed full of small bags and boxes they could hardly spread it.

The driver had not been told to avoid the center of town, and as High Street went right past the Lane Hotel on its way south and out of town, that was the route he selected.

At this moment, Mrs. Lane completed rearranging the extra baggage and sat back to look outside. Suddenly, she gasped, averted her face from the window, and fumbled to drop the jet veils on her hat.

"What . . . ?" Ransom started to ask.

"Nothing," she replied in a small, frightened voice. Then: "I thought he saw me."

"From the hotel?" Ransom asked, turning around to try to peer through the small, opaque back window. But they had already clattered blocks past the Lane Hotel. "He would never recognize this carriage," Ransom said. "That's why we're using this one instead of your own."

"I know," she said. "It probably wasn't him at all. Probably only the light striking in a certain way."

And, although her words were brave, she couldn't help shuddering.

Ransom reached under the quilt to hold her hand. When he did, she let him take it, but became strangely quiet, even pensive, and although she had lifted her veils again, Ransom thought her eyes seemed even more enshrouding with their tawny brown and gold flecking, and the vague distances within them.

He was exultant. Not only to be sitting next to her, but because he had saved her, and now he would make absolutely certain those forces that would enslave and destroy her would never again be able to even touch her. Dinsmore could have the support of the whole town, the whole state; Mrs. Ingram could fret and fume and be mule-headed; but Carrie Lane would be free. Free for him. Without being conscious of it, he pressed her hand more closely.

"Yes?" she turned from her view of the carriage window. "What is it, James?"

She had called him by his name. The first time she had ever done that. He held her arm now, and pointed outside.

"Look. It's snowing."

It had begun flurrying only minutes before, but it was already coming down in fat, wet, spiraling flakes that seemed to grow by accretion as they fell, and in growing to cause more of them to join in the stately, slow, silent dance of descent. Together, Ransom and she looked at the rimed window as the snow became heavier and thicker, until they could hardly see the gray of sky for all the white of it.

"How beautiful," she said.

"Beautiful," he agreed. And already the carriage wheels and horse hooves were muffled to nothing by the heavy snowfall.

BOOK THREE

The Trial—
Early Spring, 1900

WILL YOU THINK ME VERY sentimental if I say I will very much miss being here at Plum Creek?"

"Not at all," Ransom answered. "I've become equally attached to the place. I think that Lavinia might let you come here later on in the spring, after the trial. It will be lovely then too."

Carrie Lane closed the book of Tennyson's poems from which she had been reading aloud, interrupted by the sudden outcries of children outside, around a small but crackling bonfire at the edge of the creek, the whole wintry scene wonderfully visible from where they sat facing the window.

"Ah, yes. The trial. That has been the only blot on my total contentment here. Knowing it must happen sooner or later."

"And be over soon too," Ransom said. "That ought to allay your anxieties."

"How soon?" she asked.

"We begin voir dire tomorrow. The selection of jurors. I foresee only another week at most. We may begin at any time after they have been selected. It will all be over soon."

"So you persist in believing."

"Don't you believe it?"

"I don't know. I believe in you," she said intensely. "That's all I do believe in any more."

"Then that is enough. The trial will soon be over. You have my word for it."

"Then I will think no further upon it," she said, as though reprimanding herself. "Shall I continue reading? Some of these are quite lovely."

Ransom nodded assent, and settled back in his chair. Within minutes though, he no longer heard the words she was reading, but merely the steady, dark liquid tones of her voice, and the rhythmic stanzas, soothing him as they had served to soothe him over these past three months.

He wished he could completely quash her fears. He supposed he had no right to do it. Who knew as well as he how complicated the upcoming trial had become, and how crucial, not only to those directly involved but to everyone else in Center City? It was as though every enmity, every disagreement, every antagonism between the townspeople that had been hidden until now had suddenly come to the surface in a boiling, seething mass.

The small farmers and shop owners who constituted much of the citizenry now understood that this was not only a criminal trial but also a test of their strength against the wealthy landowners, the bankers, the politicians who had surrounded Dinsmore with their support. The usually quiet winter months had been filled with contests between these newly polarized groups.

It had begun with Dinsmore's announcement that the Lane properties would sow all their fields next year using mechanical plows purchased in Indianapolis, and in the fall use mechanical combines for reaping and threshing. A half dozen of the machines had been unloaded at the railroad station just after New Year's Day with great panoply. Their cost, the Lane manager said, through an editorial in Joseph Jeffries' newspaper, would be quickly absorbed by their increased efficiency. What he didn't say, and what the small farmers knew from other towns farther east where the machinery had already appeared, was that the rye and sorghum would not only be planted earlier with the machines but also harvested and shipped off to Chicago several weeks before theirs. And if there was a good crop—and *The Farmer's Almanac* predicted a whopper—he could lower his prices to force them to lower their own prices so drastically there would scarcely be a margin for profit.

Less than a week after the harvesters had come, the Lane Feed and Grain announced price rises on all of its products. This unexpected move, when stored grains in the small farmers' barns were dwindling, was met with great ire. Finally, in protest, two dozen men had decided to purchase their feed outside the town. With shipping costs added on, they ended up spending as much as though they had bought from Dinsmore, but at least they had some satisfaction.

Then Dinsmore had built a conveyor belt directly above Emerson Street, going from the Lane Warehouse to the railroad loading station. It seemed to be a rickety, wooden thing, couldn't last but a few years, and was susceptible to all sorts of mechanical failures, but it worked, and everyone saw that its use would eliminate paying a half dozen day laborers who would otherwise be employed loading the freight cars.

Dinsmore rode everywhere in Henry Lane's big glittering Reo. And he'd convinced Mason to purchase a horseless too— a plush, maroon-colored Oldsmobile. In yet another supportive editorial, Jeffries declared that within fifty years horses would no longer be used except for sport. Public, personal, and freight transportation would all be accomplished by motorcars, motor trucks and motor buses: the age of the internal combustion engine was upon them. Many of his readers scoffed, especially when they saw the motorcars chugging slowly along the town's streets. But the fear of Dinsmore's innovations surged.

Less than a month before, the small farmers had convened the first Grange meeting in twenty years. This time the enemy was not the cattlemen, but Dinsmore and his cronies. Speeches had been made, complaints aired, suggestions for overcoming the common enemy broached, calls for unity stressed—and, as usual, nothing at all accomplished.

But shortly after that meeting, at the annual Chamber of Commerce election meeting, Cal Applegate had nominated Dinsmore for president. The meeting had soon turned into a scramble. Insults were offered, brawls narrowly avoided. Dinsmore had finally been defeated in his bid for office, but only by the thinnest of margins. And only after considerable panic had arisen. Naturally, the following day, Jeffries editorialized at great length about the "medieval and retrogressive elements" that had brought off the defeat. But many people—Ransom included— had been astounded by how much general support Dinsmore had received. After all, the man was known to be under indictment for murder.

The worst of it, from Ransom's point of view, was that all Dinsmore's innovations were being made to increase the Lane holdings—a fact not easily glossed over. It would certainly affect how Mrs. Lane would be received by the jury, which would consist mostly of these very farmers whose livelihoods were being threatened.

Once his indictment had been accepted, Ransom had tried, unsuccessfully, to wrest control of the various Lane businesses from Dinsmore. Judge Dietz had been adamant on this point. So long as Carrie Lane's signature was required for any business transaction, and so long as the court could not find Dinsmore negligent or otherwise detrimental to her financial interests, he might remain as general manager. Dietz did grant one concession to Ransom: from the day of the indictment, the county clerk was empowered to review the Lane accounts every week, to make certain all remained above board. So far, the accounts had been scrupulously correct, and there had been no other reason for Judge Dietz to alter his ruling.

Ransom suspected this had been done as a shrewd political courtesy to Dinsmore, and through him to those powerful men in Center City who supported the newcomer. Since the decision, Joseph Jeffries had substantially toned down his editorial venom whenever he wrote about Dietz or the judiciary.

Trying to get Carrie Lane to accept this was more difficult for Ransom. Like almost everything they discussed, he believed she only partly accepted it. Still, the new situation had its obvious advantages, as it provided another reason for Ransom to visit her in her comfortably self-imposed exile, for Dietz had granted them yet another favor—he had appointed Ransom court courier between Center City and Plum Creek for all Lane business matters. Whenever a document had to be signed, Dinsmore would furnish a copy to the judge, who—after the county clerk had read and assessed it—would give it to Ransom to bring to Carrie Lane for her signature.

He had other reasons to visit her too: she was one of the most important witnesses for the upcoming trial, and they had to rehearse her testimony over and over. But the hours they devoted to this and to her business were small compared to the time he spent at Plum Creek.

Three or four days a week, he would ride the twenty miles or so, usually late in the afternoon, when all his other work was completed. After such a long trip, it was expected that he would remain for dinner. Old Mrs. Traverse, a half-deaf woman, cooked, and a girl from one of the nearby families stayed on as day servant and to keep Carrie Lane company now that Rina had returned to town and only came out with Lavinia Dietz. Naturally, after dinner, Ransom would be obliged to remain some time—to converse, to be read to aloud from Tennyson or Keats, or the novels of Mrs. Gaskell and George Eliot, sets of which covered the top rows of shelves in the big central sitting room.

Other times, he would accompany Carrie Lane on walks and visits to the other inhabitants of the community. Winter sports abounded in the little colony, and though it was too level for skiing, it was perfect for sledding down the sides of the small hills that abutted the creek, and even better for ice skating.

Then, too, some nights, once dinner was over, would be far too inclement for him to ride the distance back to Center City, and he would have to remain. There were a half dozen bedrooms in the large, rambling, one-story edifice set so snugly into the land that it almost seemed an outgrowth of the small rise of earth that protected its north side from the wind. The walls were constructed of large chunks of feldstone Judge Dietz had had quarried in nearby Colorado, and had sent over wagonload after wagonload. The slightly slanted roof was made of logs, planed smooth but unpainted, bonded with the ubiquitous Nebraska dried mud. The lodge was so warm and cosy, Ransom could hardly believe it was equally cool—with all the windows open—in the heat of the plains summer, as the judge and his wife insisted.

They used the place a great deal, driving out from town every Friday afternoon and remaining until Sunday or even Monday morning. This provided further company for Carrie, and for Ransom, who would be asked to make a fourth for the weekend.

Three idyllic months had passed this way; an idyll which he knew would soon be gone. When the trial began, Dinsmore would once more be put under house arrest in the Lane Hotel, and Carrie Lane would once more return to Center City and her house on the Hill. There it would be more difficult for Ransom to see her as often, or as informally, as here, until the trial was over.

He would see her once it was over—neither of them doubted it. Ransom did nothing to disguise the fact that while he was preparing her for a trial, he was also romancing her. Not with gifts and compliments, protestations of his affection or any of the other, more obvious forms of lovemaking, as he might have done, as he had done twenty years before with Florence Poindexter. But instead, with his company, his quiet support, his repeated assurance that all would turn out well. A delicate, yet a mature sort of courtship, Ransom told himself by way of argument, whenever he found himself too frustrated by the limits so clearly imposed upon them.

Limitations he sometimes found so restricting that after an evening with Carrie Lane, he would have to swerve off the road to Center City, to go to the Widow Rogers' house, often hours after she and her children had been asleep. She never protested. She never denied him. She would throw a robe over her shift, and sleepily open the door, then wordlessly lead him into her room, close the door, watch him hurriedly undress and allow him to take her with his fury of displaced passion. Nor did she ever demand an explanation for his behavior or his comings or goings. She was a large, gaunt woman, as silent and hard as the land she and her growing sons broke and farmed for their subsistence. Often, she astonished Ransom by bringing a passion to equal his own, leaving him to wonder—riding away from the Rogers' farm an hour or so later in the still dark morning—what frustrations she had, and if she ever thought of him when he wasn't there.

After these sessions, Ransom felt satisfied, but sobered, sometimes even chastened and humiliated by the excess lust he had displayed. But what else was he to do? The most he could demand of Carrie Lane was to hold her hand. She had revealed such shame at what had passed between her and Dinsmore that to even beg a kiss of her—he knew—would be to make her believe he thought her as depraved as she herself thought. He would wait. He had to wait until after the trial. Until the time he could ask her to be his own, and then as his marital right possess her as ardently, as completely as he wished.

Did she ever suspect that he thought about such matters while they sat in the big fire-lit room, she reading to him as she was now? Who could say. She must know how desirable she was. Especially now that she had put on some weight—"gotten plump as a hen," she had recently declared, passing a mirror. To which he had replied a courtesy which suggested only a whit of his pleasure at the change in her. She was hardly plump, but her bodices were more deliciously full, her face softer, all of her ripe and desirable.

And this change seemed to have carried over. These days she was seldom anxious, seldom meditative as she had been in the beginning. She was ready to laugh, to sit down at the small upright piano and play and sing as she declared she hadn't done since she was a girl. She took particular delight in a stereopticon device the Dietzes had—whereby two postcards placed in a holder would coalesce through the viewer into one picture of three dimensions so startlingly rendered it looked as real as life. She became friendly with Mrs. Traverse and had gotten the older woman to show her how to bake—and she took pride in her pies and cakes of great lusciousness. She was easily persuaded to join with the neighbors' children in leading their indoor and even some of their outdoor games. Often Ransom would arrive at the lodge, and find her in the middle of a circle of children, reading aloud to them. Then, too, she had her own books to read—especially the long novels of Ouida. "I know you men don't approve of such romances, but I love them," she would say, and Ransom would order yet another half dozen from Omaha for her.

Ransom found himself wishing they had met years before, before this terrible Dinsmore business had happened, so that

perhaps it wouldn't have happened at all. He knew her life
would be marred until the ordeal of the trial had passed. He
wished he could protect her from that, in some way mesmerize
her so that she wouldn't even know it was happening until it was
over.

"Isn't that lovely," she was saying, interrupting his thoughts.

"Yes. Please read those few lines again."

"Here," she said, handing over the book, and brushing his
hand with her own. "You read them."

He began:

> " '. . . *wherefore let thy voice*
> *Rise like a fountain for me night and day.*
> *For what are men better than sheep or goats*
> *That nourish a blind life within the brain,*
> *If, knowing God, they lift not hands of prayer*
> *Both for themselves and those who call them friend?' "*

Sheep or goats indeed, Ransom thought. He would certainly
lift his voice for her, like a fountain, night and day, if necessary.
He itched to do so, to begin the trial, to expose her plight, to
see Dinsmore and his cronies blanch with shame. He longed to
see the looks of disgust on the faces of the spectators and jurors
as they learned of his methods, as they heard all of his monstrous-
ness.

"I wish," Carrie started to say, then stopped herself.

"What do you wish?"

"I almost wish we didn't have to go back there. You or I. I'd
be willing to let him have everything. Everything."

"I thought we'd agreed you weren't to worry," Ransom said.

"You're right, of course. I'm being foolish."

———————————●———————————

"IF YOU GENTLEMEN ARE READY, I'll allow the jury into the
courtroom," Alvin Barker, the court clerk, said.

Ransom said he was more than ready. Cal Applegate, sitting

stony-faced at the defense table, nodded. The clerk disappeared through the left-hand door behind the bench where the jury chamber was.

It was some time before the twelve men selected to try Dinsmore walked into the courtroom, and looked around at the huge crowd that hadn't stopped murmuring since they packed into the rows of seats behind the two attorneys' desks, and in the U -shaped balcony overhead. There were greetings between the jurymen and the spectators, but if the crowd was in an excited, anticipatory mood, the twelve men who filed into their own double-level box at the left of the room were more somber.

As they ought to be, Ransom thought, after how much they'd already witnessed in their selection earlier this week. By now they knew this wasn't going to be a "horsing around" trial where they might catnap and converse among themselves as evidence was presented—a not uncommon type of behavior among jury members in less serious trials.

Ransom's own enthusiasm had been muted by the events of the voir dire that he had first thought might last at the longest an entire morning, but which instead had stretched on four mornings and three afternoons.

He had expected to walk into the impaneling room, see a dozen men already selected from a revolving hopper where the court clerk had placed the names of all twenty-five, ask them their names and whether they felt unable for any prejudicial reason to sit on the jury, have Applegate in turn ask a cursory question or two, then have all twelve brought into the judge's chambers to be sworn in.

That illusion had been shredded the minute Ransom had passed as acceptable the first juror—Helmut Lucas, a prosperous sorghum farmer. Cal Applegate had immediately challenged Lucas on the grounds that he had been one of the speakers at the Grange meeting held several months ago, and one of the dozen farmers who'd boycotted Lane's Grain and Feed to purchase feed out of town when Dinsmore had raised his prices.

Ransom had let Lucas go, and a new name had been selected from the hopper for jury foreman: James Bowman, a habitué of

Bent's Saloon, who'd been unemployed since Dinsmore had installed the conveyor belt at the Lane warehouse, eliminating Bowman's job.

Once more, Applegate challenged, and he didn't stop challenging jurors until five had come and gone from the seat, and they still hadn't settled on a juror. By then it was time for lunch, and Barker had adjourned the panel until the afternoon session, with Ransom suddenly aware that Applegate was out to win this case, and was beginning to do it right now.

Well, Ransom thought, if that was what he wanted, that was what he'd get: it would be blood for blood. And his first act upon returning from lunch was to challenge the next man—Andrew Jefferson, a black waiter at Lane's Hotel; then the next, a porter who worked at the railroad station but who lived in a Lane-owned building on Emerson Street; then a third who had once worked at the Lane Public Stables. Ransom had finally passed as acceptable Abraham Mathis, the town mortician. With an icy smile and no questions Applegate had accepted Mathis as jury foreman.

Each attorney had as many prejudicial challenges as he could convince the court clerk was necessary. In addition, they each had two pre-emptive challenges—often based on nothing more than a feeling that a specific juror would not do for them. The four days of selection had used thirty-nine prejudicial challenges and all four pre-emptive ones. Three groups of panels—twenty-five men in each—had been seated. One seat on the jury—the third place—was changed fifteen times before both attorneys were satisfied.

Ransom had been hotly angered the first day, annoyed the second, and furious toward the end of the voir dire. He'd never heard such insubstantial challenges from Applegate before; he'd never before been forced to be as tenuous himself. Thrown on the defense from the first, he had watched his ordinarily taciturn and reserved opponent lard into each juror with a sharpness he'd never before beheld in the man. He'd dealt with Applegate before—just last year, in fact—and the man had always been unruffled, almost unconcerned. Not that he wasn't a good lawyer; he was. But he also always acted as though any overacuteness were merely court shenanigans he wouldn't bother to soil his hands with. All the more reason for Ransom to be shocked that he now thrust his hands right up to the elegantly sleeved elbows and stirred up the swill he found there.

It soon became clear to both of them that finding twelve unprejudiced men would be difficult, not only in Center City, but anywhere in the county. Dietz rejected a change of venue motion Applegate made on the morning of the third day of selection, and irritated by how long they were taking, the judge came to oversee the voir dire himself. If Dietz hadn't personally rejected half their challenges, it might still be going on.

A jury was supposed to consist of twelve honest and objective men. But after those four days Ransom knew it wasn't so. Neither attorney wanted objective men; each wanted men who would be on his side. In a town as divided over the trial as this one, that wouldn't be hard to find. Finding jurors acceptable to both sides was the problem. So, half the jury came from outside Center City; men who'd scarcely heard of Dinsmore; while the remainder had to be composed of the few men they could find who had no axe to grind for or against him or the Lane businesses.

The twelve men chosen to serve were a fairly balanced sampling of Center City and its surrounding countryside in terms of age, occupation, and national background. But Ransom had to admit—looking at them—that what they might think individually, or as a group, was terra incognita to him, and more than likely to Applegate as well. Each would have to be watched to see how he responded. One might fall asleep during long-winded but necessary speeches; another exult in them. One might want to be treated formally, with sober respect; another prefer to be talked to as an equal. One might have a prejudice against beautiful women; another be secretly enamored of Carrie Lane. One might be easily influenced by his wife, by friends; another not give the case a thought outside of court. They were all potential friends, as equally, all potential enemies.

What to make of any of them, what to make, say, of Abraham

Mathis, the town mortician, the man first selected and thus jury foreman? Ransom had first met Mathis years ago. He'd seen him at numerous wakes and funerals over the years. But what really did he know of him? That he was a hardworking, very private, sometimes forbidding man—married twenty-five years, childless, well-off due to good business, with a house in town and a small ranch close by. But nothing more. Or what of Bernard Soos, the retired barber, a crony of old Floyd's, Ransom knew, as given to chattering as any of the other old men who sat outside the court building on the park bench? Since his selection for the jury, old Soos had taken his oath of secrecy very seriously. According to Floyd, Soos hadn't spoken a word to his pals about the trial, or Dinsmore, or Mrs. Lane, or anything else for that matter, having become "downright taciturn and unsocial," as Floyd put it. And what of young Anthony Pulver, the pharmacist's assistant, a bright, slender, active man just turned twenty-five years old, and more interested in courting every eligible young lady in the county in his search for the perfect wife than in anything so dull as a trial for murder? Or Caldwin Bain, a teller in the Mason Centennial Bank, aged thirty-one, good-looking, carefree, a loose man, given to riding and equestrian matters altogether, whose professed ambition was to own a racing stable and run his own thoroughbreds against the biggest and most famous eastern stables. Did Bain care a pin about Henry Lane or Carrie Lane? Could he be made to care about the future of Center City? Could he find room in his life to care? Those four men along with Ned Taylor—a wagon driver for the town's only commercial bakery, a quiet, married man of about forty with several children and no evident passions or aspirations—were the jurors Ransom at least had met and greeted around the town.

The other seven he'd never seen before. Not Kurt Magoff, a thin, balding, old-before-his-time-looking egg candler up at Schober's poultry farm; nor Everett O'Shea and Cao Chu, both repairmen for the Topeka Line Railroad, who scarcely came into Center City at all, except occasionally for supplies, and who were seated on the jury because of what amounted to accidental occupational residence in the county. Nor did Ransom know Dan

Harrow, the large, strong, but surprisingly gentle-spoken black-smith from Platte City, or any of the three farmers who had been selected: not Gus Tibbels, who had been a cattle rancher until a few years back when he had sold all but fifty head, and turned his spread up west of town into wheat-growing farmland; not Bo Lindquist or Theo Vollsen, both independent farmers of middle age, immigrants who'd become naturalized citizens up at Swede-ville, and whose obvious resentment at being pulled off their land for the time of the trial was matched only by their grim-faced pride in being the first members of their community to be asked to serve on a jury trial.

Not a very imaginative or inspiring dozen men, Ransom had to conclude. He'd have to be extra persuasive with them, make everything clear as spring water to them, not so much by irrefuta-ble logic as by repetition, by a call to their values and morality, and more than likely by a series of assaults on their emotions.

As for Applegate's transformation, that was far more disturb-ing. Was it because the attorney saw himself allied to Dinsmore's future? Or—a sinister thought which once it had entered Ran-som's mind never completely disappeared—had Dinsmore mesmerized Applegate too? Mesmerized him and in some way effected the change in the lawyer by threats, fears, or some combination of the two? If so, Applegate would be a formidable rival, especially with Dinsmore sitting next to him, right there at the defense table, reinforcing his grip over the man.

The jury had settled into its seats, and Alvin Barker was rap-ping with the judge's gavel for the courtroom to quiet. Slowly, the murmuring ceased; the verbal speculation became silent wonder. Word of the difficult voir dire had leaked out of the courthouse from the first day. By the end of that week it had become a sensation. No such thing had ever occurred in town. It portended an equally sensational trial, and attracted men, women, and even children in great numbers—drawn to the courtroom as though by some traveling circus or county fair. It disgusted Ransom, looking at the eager faces and bobbing heads; it cheapened the whole process of the law. But he promised himself he'd give them something to talk about today.

Barker announced the judge, and everyone shuffled to his feet.
The right-hand door behind the bench opened, Dietz stepped
out in his robes, went to the bench, looked disapprovingly at the
crowd, and, bidding them to sit down, declared the court in
session, and immediately issued a general warning to the spectators, followed by a more specific one to the two attorneys: he had
no intention that his courtroom would be treated other than with
the utmost respect to the law. This said, the court clerk began
reading rules of the court.

Ransom gathered his papers, preparing for his opening
speech, already recited into his shaving mirror twice last night,
but open to inspiration and spontaneous improvement.

He could see Dinsmore's handsome bored face, as the man
leaned back in his seat just beyond Applegate, resting the back
of his chair on the carved wooden railing that separated the
spectators. The defendant hardly looked the scoundrel Ransom
would soon declare him to be. Scrubbed, shaven, and manicured,
his dark hair and mustache clipped and brushed illustration-
perfect, his clothing rich, and elegant—Dinsmore looked the
wealthy industrialist, or at least the important landowner. Clever
of him to think his appearance would matter so much in court:
clever and accurate.

"Mr. Prosecutor. May we hear your charges against the defendant and the prosecution's opening remarks."

As Ransom stood, he noticed Applegate lean over to listen to
something Dinsmore said. Then the sparkling blue eyes flashed
across at Ransom, as the defendant nodded a greeting. Without
returning the greeting, Ransom took the floor.

"Your honor, gentlemen of the jury, ladies and gentlemen of
the court," he began. "It is my duty as representative of the
Sovereign State of Nebraska, appointed prosecutor of Kearney
County, and citizen of Center City, to present evidence that the
defendant, Frederick L. Dinsmore, did willfully and nefariously
bring about the death of Henry Lane of Eighteen High Street,
on April seventeenth, 1899, and prior to and since that date, did
willfully and nefariously utilize a species of mental manipulation

to control the actions and will of Mrs. Carrie Lane, widow of the deceased, in order to secure his current position as manager of the deceased's various business enterprises."

He halted, testing the silence of the room. Then went on:

"This prosecution will present evidence both by witnesses who have been mesmerized by the defendant, and by authorities from all over the world who have investigated this curious mental technique and have proved its effectiveness, in order to show how the defendant, by cruel and cunning use of his extraordinary powers, has caused misery and anguish not only to the deceased and his widow, but to the defendant's own deceased wife, and to his former mentor and assistant, in a carefully engineered plot to gain control of a financial empire."

Now the silence broke, as gasps issued from various throats around the room. Ransom faced the jury. They weren't so much shocked, it seemed, as pained. Only Bain, the horseman, looked as blank and supercilious as ever. Fine. He'd continue strongly.

"During the course of this trial, gentleman, you will sometimes hear testimony from reliable witnesses which might tax your imagination or belief. I beg you to keep an open mind until you have heard all. Many of you have witnessed examples of mesmerism before—as an entertainment. I too have witnessed it and always believed it a fraud, prepared beforehand by collusion. Now I must ask you to believe it is not a fraud, but instead a strange and insidious force. I will present incontrovertible evidence of its great power in the hands of those who know best how to use it. Many distinguished physicians and scientists have utilized mesmerism and shown it to be an effective remedy in the relief of pain, of neurasthenic and other nervous disorders—in short of inestimable benefit to medicine. Through the testimony of the defendant's own mentor, one of the great experimental scientists of Great Britain in this technique—I refer to Mr. Simon Carr—" he paused and let the crowd buzz with the name, "I will show how the defendant learned and perfected the art of mental control through mesmerism in order to make of both Mr. Carr and the defendant's own wife lifetime slaves; how the defendant attempted to coerce young women to leave their families in other cities of this nation, how he seduced them through its use . . ."

Another pause, another longer buzz from the crowd.

". . . seduced them with false promises of marriage while his own poor wife had been abandoned."

"Objection! Your honor," Applegate called out. "Point of argument. Immaterial and inflammatory."

"Sustained," Dietz said.

"How," Ransom went on, undaunted, "the defendant used his mesmeric powers to continue his notorious life of crime which had already swept across the nation."

"Objection!" Applegate shouted, standing now.

"Sustained," Dietz said. "To the present, Mr. Ransom."

"Which I will prove with reports from police agencies from three states," Ransom said, "including warrants for the arrest of the defendant still outstanding in Illinois." He paused, waiting for Applegate to object. He didn't. "And, how posing as a dental surgeon . . ."

"Objection, your honor. Libelous and prejudicial."

"Reword, Mr. Ransom," the judge said.

"How, as a dental surgeon, the defendant mesmerized the deceased, Mr. Henry Lane, on numerous occasions, and in so doing learned from the deceased many personal and business secrets which he then utilized to cause the deceased to believe he was a ruined and bankrupt man . . ."

More than a buzz; a murmur now from the spectators.

". . . How the deceased did indeed come to believe this, although it was clearly not the case, and how the deceased then hanged himself until death, and wrote one final message to his dearly loved wife giving in his final moments the reason for his suicide."

"Objection. No evidence," Applegate said.

"I have a copy of the note in my hand, your honor," Ransom declared.

The court clerk was directed to show the note to the defense, who read it as Ransom continued.

"How, gentleman of the jury, the defendant also mesmerized Mrs. Carrie Lane of Eighteen High Street, in a supposed attempt to cure her of the insomnia she had suffered for many years . . ."

A more feminine murmur now.

"How instead of curing the insomnia, the defendant then took control of this poor woman's life through his mesmeric power so that—bereft of her only support—she was like a marionette in his hands."

Murmurs breaking out all over the courtroom. Of all the jurors, only one reacted: O'Shea, the railroad man. Mark him down as the misogynist of the group, Ransom thought.

"To this last, Mrs. Lane herself will testify in this room, in a manner that I assure you will be heartbreaking."

"Objection," Applegate said, up in his seat again. "Seeking to sway the jury in favor of a witness."

"Sustained," Dietz said. "Go on, Mr. Ransom."

"And, in conclusion," Ransom continued now, letting the murmurs cascade around him like cooling ocean wavelets at his feet, "how the defendant thus gained managerial control of the largest single holding in Kearney County.

"The prosecution will show all this, and more, and will then ask you, gentlemen of the jury, to find this defendant guilty of a multiplicity of charges, to find him a scoundrel, and a monster in man's and God's eyes—and to request that he be deprived of his life, in this Sovereign State of Nebraska."

The murmuring, which had never ceased, built to a dull roar as Ransom asked for the death penalty. Dietz began gaveling, and the court clerk stood up demanding in a loud, whining voice that there be order in the court. One juryman, Pulver, the finicky wife-seeker, looked deeply pained now, as though angry with himself for having to sit there. Otherwise, the room was a seat of motion: heads, mouths, arms, hands, everything in motion. Only the defendant's desk was still. Applegate's long torso was huddled over, scribbling. Dinsmore still leaned back in his chair, a vaguely amused smile on his lips, but his bright eyes were flashing like sunlight reflecting off the edges of icy stilettos.

"That is all, your honor," Ransom concluded.

"Order in the courtroom," Dietz called out gruffly, still gavel-ing. Then, when it didn't come: "This court is adjourned until two P.M."

Dietz stood up and was gone from the room before a quarter of the crowd had risen to their feet.

———————————●———————————

AS USUAL, WHENEVER HE'D WORKED himself up into a state of such excitement, Ransom felt doubly sobered once the court had reconvened for the afternoon. It was the defense's turn to pre-sent the outlines of its case, and this proved a depressing affair, not only for Ransom, who had read it all before in Joseph Jeffries' many editorials, but also for the spectators, who had expected some sort of climactic rebuttal and instead got a somewhat dis-torted history lesson.

Why Applegate had chosen this method of defense, only he— and possibly Jeffries—could say. It certainly had none of the cleverness, none of the smart elegance that Ransom associated with Dinsmore.

The defendant seemed as bored as anyone else in the room, as Applegate stood at the jurybox railing, tall and lean, reiterat-ing his charge that his client was being framed in a conspiracy engineered by certain conservative elements in the county. He then read off a list of the innovations planned or already carried out by Dinsmore, and how they would revitalize the town and the county. He defended a man's right to seek to better himself through hard work, pointing out recent and not so recent exam-ples of the American success story—as though his word were doubted. When he depicted Dinsmore's childhood deprivation in the slums of New York's Lower East Side and compared the defendant to the young Abe Lincoln he drew more than a few guffaws, and even Dinsmore had to smile. Unabashed, Apple-gate went on to say he would show evidence of a conspiracy against his client; he would show how discreditable most of the prosecution's witnesses would be. He named no names, made no startling statements, brought not a gasp or murmur to the court-room.

Ransom listened with only half his attention—and that only to be able to raise an objection in the unlikely case that Applegate would make an objectionable allegation.

With the rest of his attention free, Ransom inspected the spectators, slowly thinning out as people realized nothing half so thrilling as this morning would happen and remembered they had chores or appointments they ought keep. From them, he turned to the jury, bored or inscrutable in their still sobriety, then to Dinsmore, bored, picking his clean white teeth with what appeared to be a silver toothpick, and finally, as Applegate repeated and reiterated his charges, droning on and on, to the courthouse itself.

It had been spruced up for the trial, Ransom now noticed. The ceiling and lower walls had been freshly whitewashed. The jury-box, the witness stand, and the judge's bench—all of heavy mahogany, carved with bas-reliefs depicting Biblical and mythological scenes somehow connected with agriculture—had all been polished to a fine gleam. His own desk, the defense desk, the spectators' pews and all of the railings—made of a fine, blond tiger oak—had been sanded and polished too. The hard-tiled floor glittered beneath Applegate's patent-leather shoes. Everything but the large painted murals on each upper wall—similar in style and content to the bas-reliefs—seemed clean and new.

When it had been built some ten years before, the courthouse had been the finest and most costly public building in the state outside of the capitol. It still was. With its fine Palladian proportions, its gleaming craftsmanship in every interior and exterior detail, and the evident care and technical skill that had been lavished upon it, the courthouse had come to stand as a symbol of Center City's pride in itself, and its nickname "the second capitol of Nebraska."

Henry Lane had been instrumental in its construction. So had Carl Dietz. It was ironic, Ransom found himself thinking, that one of the two men had already been destroyed by Dinsmore, while right here in the center of his own courthouse, the other was being maligned and insulted. Not that Dietz seemed to care. He was too adept at keeping his professional mask in place to show the anger he must be feeling as Applegate droned on about reactionary forces and how they wanted to drag Center City down from its fine eminence in the state.

How much and how often would good and virtuous men have to keep quiet rather than defend themselves from the likes of such as Dinsmore? Ransom wondered. Always? Too often? And was that any kind of explanation for Dr. Murcott's sudden reluctance to testify as Ransom wanted him to?

The evening before the trial had begun, Amasa Murcott had come to Ransom's room. They had taken an after-dinner cordial, and the older man had unburdened himself of his troubled spirits.

He could not testify to declare under oath that mesmerism was as effective a method of mental control as Ransom said it was. He simply could not. Not without having himself used the method. Just as he could not testify that any other medical or surgical technique was effective unless he had attempted it. He had a professional ethic to stand by, he said. His decision on the matter was final.

That was a real blow, but Ransom tried to soften it. He reminded Murcott that he would be called anyway to testify as county coroner, that he would then be asked in detail to repeat his earlier comments regarding Henry Lane's state of health, and mind, and to repeat for the courtroom the comments he had made to Ransom regarding the similarity of Lane's and Margaret Dinsmore's features in death. Murcott said he would testify to all that. But nothing more.

Then Ransom led Murcott, just as he planned to do on the witness stand, to the subject of mesmerism as presented in the various medical journals he'd read, and in the letters he had received from various physicians. Murcott hesitated, explicated a bit, allowed facts to come out, qualified each one, until Ransom saw that he would have to tread as carefully with his best friend on the witness stand as with the most hostile and unsympathetic defense witness.

In a sense, however, he felt gratified by this. The doctor was known in Center City as an irascible, independent man with a staunch sense of integrity, and Ransom felt that even one or two concessions from such a witness would be worth more than a half dozen fully supportive pieces of testimony.

He had just reaffirmed this important point in his mind, when he realized that Cal Applegate had finally ended his opening monologue, and Judge Dietz, thanking the defense attorney in a half-sarcastic tone, was adjourning the court for the day. The courtroom was suddenly astir, with spectators and jurymen alike rising. Once the room was half-empty, and Dinsmore had been led by the bailiff back to his suite in the Lane Hotel, Ransom gathered his papers and turned to Applegate.

"That was a mighty American speech, Mr. Applegate. Reminded me of a schoolmarm on Independence Day."

"Thank you," Applegate said, unstung by his words. "As for your own speech this morning, why I think you ought to write for Mr. William Jennings Bryan. I'm certain you might teach him some of the finer points of rhetoric. He's been hammering away at that same old 'Cross of Gold' far too long."

Their opposition stated, they both chuckled and promised to make the going rougher for each other as the trial progressed.

Later that evening, at the Center City Board and Hotel, Ransom got some other opinions on his opening address. Isabelle Page said it had been "terrifying and terribly exciting." Everyone at the dinner table had agreed—an unusual, almost unprecedented situation for them—and some even suggested that he had assured Dinsmore's conviction already.

"Whoa now," Ransom said. "I haven't produced any evidence or testimony yet."

"If you produce a tenth of what you say, you'll have that Dinsmore lynched on the nearest telegraph pole," old Floyd declared. He had recently taken up residence at the Page Board and Hotel, bringing public opinion right to Ransom's front door. "That's what everyone was saying after today." Floyd went on. "Imagine, will you"—he turned to Isabelle now—"having such kind of terrible powers as Mr. Prosecutor said he has?"

"I can imagine only too well," she said with a shudder. "Poor Mrs. Lane. I wonder, Mama, if we oughtn't pay a call on her."

"I suspect that after today half the women in town will be doing that very thing. If only to apologize to her," Mrs. Page said. "Nate, what's wrong with that succotash?"

"Nothing, ma'am."

"Then eat it all. As for Mr. Ransom's business, I'm certain he'll produce more evidence and with great care to its accuracy and truth and relevance. I have known him these nine years as boarder and friend, and he is neither a slapdash nor a bloodthirsty man."

"Hear. Hear. I'll drink to that," Floyd said.

"Not in this house you won't. Otherwise out you go," his landlady warned.

"And if Floyd's smart," Murcott put in, "he won't do any drinking out of the house either. It's hard enough climbing up to the top floor when you're sober. Am I right, Floyd?"

Floyd just mumbled under his breath and swept up his plate with a chunk of sourdough bread.

Ransom excused himself from the table.

"Do you want coffee upstairs tonight?" Mrs. Page asked. "If you do, I'll make a pot special for you."

"I'll pass it up for tonight. I think I'll take a ride."

"Not to Plum Creek?" she asked.

"No. Just a ride. I've found it helps me think."

———————————•———————————

THE GERMAN COOK RECOGNIZED RANSOM and let him inside with a wide smile and an explosion of incomprehensible speech. For the first time since he'd been coming to the Lane ranch, there were ranch hands inside, playing cards at the kitchen table. But Ransom was not able to more than glimpse them in passing. Long enough to see that Simon Carr was not among them. And from the manner in which the cook shook her head and grimaced as she led Ransom to the old man's room, it seemed likely that Carr had taken to his bed again.

"He's been here," Carr said, sitting up in bed, the second Ransom entered the bedroom.

"Dinsmore? Today?"

"Not today. Last week."

"Did he threaten you?"

"I'm not entirely certain what he did or didn't do."

Ransom closed the door so they wouldn't be overheard. "Did he mesmerize you?"

"No. Or at least I don't think so. I was a bit dizzy all that morning. I can't recollect anything too clearly."

"Surely you'd remember if he'd mesmerized you?" Ransom argued.

"I said I don't recollect."

That struck a curious, an uncomfortable note. But Ransom decided to let it pass for the moment.

"What's this all about? Not feeling so well?" he asked.

"I had a relapse. Right after he left last week. I suppose with all the excitement . . ."

Ransom pulled up the rocking chair. The old man looked as bad as—no, worse than—when Ransom had first met him. Even in the dim candlelight his face seemed more drawn, his eyes more sunken, his nose and chin and cheekbones thrown into higher, more bony relief. His appearance worried Ransom.

"Did he say anything about the trial?" Ransom asked.

"He talked a great deal of nonsense. I didn't pay much mind to any of it."

"You didn't argue, did you?"

"I'll testify," Carr said fiercely. "More than ever before I want to testify against him."

"Can we be sure you're well enough to?"

"I'll be well enough. Don't think I won't be."

"Oughtn't you see a doctor first and let him decide?"

"You forget I'm a doctor myself. This was only a minor stroke. Not half so bad as the first. Believe me, I can tell the difference. I'll testify all right."

Ransom wanted that too, he needed the old man's Oxford-educated voice filling the courtroom, telling all that had occurred between Dinsmore and him, between Dinsmore and his wife. He wanted Carr's anger and indignation to be heard by those jurors and spectators. Not for a few days yet, but soon. Perhaps he ought be in Center City, closer by. Close to another medical opinion too, just to be certain he could take the stand.

So Ransom quickly outlined an impromptu plan to Carr. He'd drive out tomorrow after the trial session, with Murcott and a shay. They'd bring Carr into town, move him into the Center City Board and Hotel.

"I'll be delighted to go anywhere you want," Carr said. "At least anywhere that's warmer than this place. It's like a cold-storage cellar here. I can't seem to get warm enough."

That stirred up Ransom's fears for the old man's precarious health again. He and Dinsmore must have argued. Dinsmore must have threatened Carr, and that had led to some sort of confrontation. Now that Dinsmore was under arrest at the Lane Hotel, he couldn't come out and bother the old man anymore. But he could send others to harass him, which would be as bad.

"We'll be here tomorrow by sundown. Make sure you're alone. Tell the cook you're to see no one, absolutely no one but me tomorrow."

"Why?" the old man asked. Then he seemed to understand why. "Don't you worry. I can take care of myself."

He reached under one of the pillows and flashed a tiny, glittering, ivory-handled Derringer.

"I assure you no one will annoy me. If the devil himself stepped inside this doorway, I'd handle him. And I'm not so certain that nasty character hasn't been here recently."

He laughed, and his grim humor relieved Ransom until he had said good-bye. But not for long. As he rode back to Center City, Ransom couldn't help but wonder why the old man wouldn't speak of Dinsmore's visit. Especially after having been so open with him before. Whatever had happened between them had been responsible—Ransom was certain—for the old man's relapse; and also for his increased anger and determination to testify. Ransom wanted to keep that anger fanned to a white-hot intensity. It would make an effective counterpart to Mrs. Lane's own reticence on the witness stand. But he did not want it at the expense of Carr's health. Carr had looked as fragile as fallen leaves under the quilted covers. There was too great a risk of his collapsing before he could testify. Or worse.

When Ransom arrived back at the Center City Board and Hotel, Amasa Murcott was waiting for him. He immediately thrust a newspaper into Ransom's hands.

"Look at this!"

Ransom opened to the front page. Across the top, in red print, it said: "Special Evening Edition."

Underneath that, a huge headline proclaimed: "Dinsmore Trial Begins. Widespread Anti-Progress Party Denounced."

Half of the front page was devoted to Applegate's tedious opening speech that day. Barely a paragraph was given to Ransom's own opening remarks.

"Yellow journalism of the worst kind," Murcott said scornfully. "Not even Hearst has stooped so low. And that's not all." He took the newspaper, opened it to the editorial page, and gave it back.

Halfway down the column, Ransom laughed.

"What did you expect? Encomiums heaped on my head?"

"It's libelous," Murcott fumed. "Look. He calls you a fraud and a liar."

"He implies it. He's not a fool. Jeffries knows exactly how much he can get away with."

"Look here," Murcott said, and taking the paper again, read: " 'The good people of Center City must raise their voices against the hypocritical, ambitious party-seekers who would besmirch the name and life of one of our most prominent citizens with allegations of hocus-pocus even a Cherokee Indian would scoff at.' That's patently ridiculous. Most prominent citizen my foot!"

"Write in and tell him," Ransom suggested.

"I'll do a deal more than that," Murcott said. "I was about to go over to that so-called newspaper in person, when I heard you come in."

"It's after nine o'clock."

"He must still be there. This rag was tossed onto the porch less than an hour ago."

"Wait a minute," Ransom said, an idea forming in his mind. "I'll go with you."

"To the newspaper office? Will you take him on?"

"No," Ransom laughed at the doctor's suggestion of violence. "To the telegraph office. I agree with you this is yellow journalism, and I think I know how to stop it, or at least how to tone it down a bit. I'm going to telegraph William K. Reese at the capitol and have him send reporters down from Lincoln. I'm sure people all over the state would like to know what's going on here in Center City. You wait, after Jeffries gets a look at what the Lincoln *Journal* writes, he'll be forced to be less one-sided."

The two men strode rapidly toward Center Street, and parted at the telegraph office on the corner.

"By the way," Ransom said. "You'd better cancel any appointments you have tomorrow. I'm putting you on the witness stand first thing in the morning."

The doctor stopped and his face got very sour. But he didn't say a word.

———————●———————

"THE PROSECUTION CALLS DR. AMASA MURCOTT to the stand."

Murcott got up from the second-row seat in the spectators' gallery—where he'd been sitting, dourly, for the last half hour, dully listening to the county clerk's recital of the court business from the previous day—went to the witness stand, and was sworn in. He looked as somber as the twelve men of the jury he now directly faced. Ransom knew he wasn't happy about being called to testify. Murcott hadn't said a word to anyone at breakfast.

"Dr. Murcott," Ransom began, "you performed the service of coroner for Henry Lane last April, did you not?"

"I did."

"Would you tell the court what your findings were."

"Mr. Lane had been hanged by the neck. Death by strangulation."

"How long had Mr. Lane been dead?"

"Couldn't say for certain. Only partial rigor mortis had set in. I'd say two, three hours at the most."

"And you appeared on the scene at eight o'clock in the evening?"

"About then."

"In her deposition to the sheriff, Mrs. Ingram stated that she found Mr. Lane's body at six thirty in the evening, when she went in search of him to call him to dinner. He would have been dead approximately an hour or two when she found him. Is that right?"

"Approximately," Murcott said. So far, Ransom was asking him only the most common, technical questions a coroner would have to answer. But the doctor remained wary.

"Could you tell the court, Doctor, if there was anything unusual about the corpse when you examined it? Anything, specifically about the limbs of the corpse."

"Yes. The right hand of the corpse was inside the knot of the noose that had hanged him."

"You mentioned before that rigor mortis had only partially set in. Could Mr. Lane's hand have gone into this position during the spasms associated with such a method of death?"

"Not likely."

"Could the hand have been placed there, for whatever reason, after Mr. Lane had died?"

"No. It was put there before death. The thumb was stuck in the knot. The knot had been pulled tight during the act of hanging. All the blood vessels of the thumb had hemorrhaged. This suggests the thumb was also strangled."

"Is this unusual in victims of hanging, Doctor?"

"Quite unusual," Murcott replied. "Usually their hands are tied behind their backs."

Laughter greeted the doctor's sardonic remark. Of all the men in the jurybox, only Mathis didn't even crack a smile. He must have seen his share of hanged men with their hands still bound in death. Would his experience put him for or against Dinsmore? For or against Ransom?

"Is this usual when the victim's hands are free?"

"Most unusual."

"Could you tell the courtroom what conclusions you reached as to why Mr. Lane's hand was stuck in the knot."

"I concluded at the time that Mr. Lane had possibly thrust his hand into the noose to keep himself from strangling."

"In other words, Doctor, while in the act of hanging himself, Mr. Lane changed his mind?"

"Possibly."

"Can you offer any other reason for his hand being up there in the knot?"

"No, I can't."

A small ripple of talk passed over the spectators.

"You were physician to Mr. Lane before his death. Is that so?"

"Yes. It is."

"How recently had you examined Mr. Lane?"

"Two months before his demise."

"And what was Mr. Lane's physical condition at that time?"

"Excellent."

"Thus, you would say it was highly unlikely that Mr. Lane hanged himself because he discovered he was terminally ill?"

"That's correct."

"Would you tell the court, Doctor, of Mr. Lane's mental condition at the time of your examination."

"It was poor. He was melancholy, anxious, depressed."

"Did he specify any reasons for this?"

"He refused to speak of it. Refused to even admit it."

"Was this a common mental condition for Mr. Lane?"

"Most unusual."

"Would you then speculate for the court that this anxious and depressed condition might be in some way connected to his suicide?"

"Objection," Applegate called out, before Ransom had even

completed his question. "Prosecution is requesting speculation rather than facts."

"There can be no facts until they are established," Ransom argued. "Besides, speculation on the part of the county coroner is tantamount to a fact."

"Objection overruled," Dietz said. "Go on, Mr. Ransom."

"Dr. Murcott, what else struck you as unusual or out of place about the corpse of Mr. Henry Lane?"

"Nothing else."

"Doctor, may I refresh your memory? Did you not say to me at the time of Mr. Lane's autopsy that he lacked a feature usually found in victims of hangings?"

"Yes, I did. He lacked protruding eyes."

"What was the condition of Mr. Lane's eyes?"

"Normal. Except that they had already been closed by the time I arrived."

"By another hand, Doctor?"

"Well, no one admitted to it."

"So they may have been closed at the time of Mr. Lane's death?" and, as the doctor said this was possible, Ransom asked another question. "This general condition of Mr. Lane's eyes, contradicted in your own mind your speculation about the cause for his hand being in the knot, did it not? One aspect said he was trying to save his life; while the other said otherwise. Is this correct?"

"Yes. His face ought to have been more strained. Especially around the eyes."

"Have you, Dr. Murcott, ever encountered another example of an extraordinary lack of tension in the corpse of a person who had suffered a violent death?"

"Yes, I have."

"In Center City?"

"Yes."

"Recently?"

"Several months ago."

"Who was that person?"

"Mrs. Margaret Dinsmore."

A murmur passed over the room. Ned Taylor, the bakery driver, who had been slowly slumping during the testimony, sat up in his jury seat. Ransom looked to see if Applegate had any objection. He didn't.

"Am I correct in believing that Mrs. Dinsmore had died by drowning in the town reservoir?"

"That was the general belief, yes."

"Thank you, Dr. Murcott, you've been most helpful," Ransom said, turning to his desk. "No. Don't step down yet, Doctor, I have a few more questions." He returned to the witness stand holding a large pamphlet. "Are you familiar with this periodical, Doctor?"

"Yes. I receive it eight times a year."

"This is the *New England Journal of Medicine and Surgery.* Founded in 1825, it says here. Tell me, Doctor, is this a prominent periodical?"

"It's considered the best in the country of its type."

"I assume that in the interest of your own professional knowledge and skills you read this journal quite thoroughly? Even articles with no direct bearing on your cases. Is that so?"

"I'm a general practitioner. All of the articles pertain to my cases. I read it from cover to cover."

"Then you must have read this article, by a Dr. Hubert Larkin. On the uses of hypnothesia in surgery?"

"Yes. I have."

"And this one by Dr. Rawlings . . . and this one? and this . . . ?" Ransom went on reading off the names of a dozen articles by a dozen physicians. Murcott had read them all.

"Is it not true, Doctor, that what is called hypnothesia is more commonly known as mesmerism?"

"It is."

"In the past two years you have perused over a dozen articles then on the subject of mesmerism in this journal. What can you tell this court of the subject?"

Murcott was silent. In a small voice he said, "Only what the articles say. I've never used the technique."

"Isn't it true though, Doctor, that all these articles claim great success for the technique? Both for the relief of physical suffering and for mental disturbances?"

"I suppose so."

"Are you familiar, Doctor, with a physician named Sir James Braid of London, England?"

"Not personally. I've heard of him."

"Dr. Braid was a distinguished physician?"

"I believe he was knighted by the Queen."

"A very distinguished physician then. Were you aware of Dr. Braid's experimentation using the techniques of mesmerism?"

"Only what I read."

"He was known to have experimented a great deal in it, though?"

"He's considered the founder of hypnothesia in surgery."

"Thank you, Doctor. Are you aware that Simon Carr was not only a student of Dr. Braid's, but later on an associate of his, and even later, that he continued Dr. Braid's experiments in that distinguished man's own office?"

"No, I wasn't," Murcott said, clearly impressed by the fact. So, audibly, were others in the courtroom. In the jurybox, O'Shea whispered to his Chinese co-worker, who didn't appear to respond, but kept staring ahead. Ransom suddenly wondered how much of what was being said in the court Chu could even understand. His answers at the voir dire had been succinct, heavily accented. Mightn't his traditional values be totally different to those Westerners held? Wouldn't that make a real difference in how he would vote when the jury went into chambers?

"Are you further aware, Doctor," Ransom went on, "that Simon Carr was not only a licensed and accredited physician but also a licensed dental surgeon?"

"Objection," Applegate rapped on his desk with a ringed finger. "The prosecution is asking information beyond the admitted knowledge of the witness."

"Objection sustained," Dietz declared. "Mr. Ransom?"

Even so, Ransom had made his point. Simon Carr had now been given professional credentials at the trial that he otherwise might never have had. Murcott saw how he had been used to accredit the other man, and squinted one eye, trying to appear even more wary than before.

Ransom next asked if the doctor knew of a half dozen physicians whom Murcott had earlier recommended to Ransom for information on the subject of mesmerism. He said he did know them, as was only natural. When asked, he gave each of them a high, professional rating, then sat, irritated, as Ransom read from the letters they had returned to Murcott, discussing their use of mesmerism. When he was done, Ransom said:

"Based on these statements, Doctor, and on the articles before mentioned, could you now say that under the controlled guidance of an expert practitioner the technique known as mesmerism or hypnothesia is useful not only in the elimination of pain during surgery, but for other complaints as well?"

"So it would appear."

"Could you also say that this method works or can work to effectively alter the mood of a patient, as has been suggested and stated in these various testimonials?"

"I suppose so."

"Not merely the mood, but also the attitude? I have here Dr. Rawlings' statement that one man was completely cured through this technique of a great fear of cows—"much laughter at that, "and that several women were successfully treated with it for melancholy and insomnia."

"Well," Murcott said. "I guess."

"May we then conclude, Doctor, that a mental technique which elevates a person's mood may also be utilized to drive his spirits into the opposite direction?"

"I could only assume it," Murcott suddenly said, with some anger. "I have not used the method, as I said before."

"But Dr. Rawlings has and he says it works. And so does Dr. Josiah Held of Paoli County, Pennsylvania. And Dr. Joseph Breuer of Vienna further declares, Doctor, that his experiments using hypnothesia have shown that it may be utilized to alter mood, beliefs, or attitudes from one extreme to another in a matter of seconds. Given all this, couldn't we then conclude, even without ourselves having used the technique, that in the hands of an expert practitioner such as Dr. Breuer or, for that matter, Simon Carr, anyone in this courtroom could be altered by it?"

"I assume," Murcott said, disgusted.

"Is it not so that the purpose of this periodical, Doctor, is to disseminate new medical discoveries where they have proven to be efficacious?"

"That's one purpose."

"Therefore, we may safely conclude that, based on its proven effectiveness and its frequency of appearance as a subject in this journal, mesmerism is in fact deemed to be useful in the medical profession. Is that not so?"

"Only with a proviso," Murcott said.

"What proviso?"

"That the practitioner know and uphold the Aesculapian code."

Ransom had hardly expected this. He knew Murcott was angered, but he had to draw him out. He had to.

"Would you tell the court, Doctor, what that code is."

"It's an oath taken by every physician in the world."

"And what does it say?"

"That no method or technique will be used except to relieve suffering, to curtail pain, or to keep a patient from death."

"In other words, Doctor, such a technique as mesmerism is a highly dangerous one?"

"I think that is evident!" Murcott said.

Bonanza! Ransom thought.

———————————●———————————

AMANDA BENT WAS THE NEXT WITNESS to be called. She'd been subpoenaed only the day before, and was sitting pale and indignant in the spectators' section when the bailiff called her name and swore her in. She had dressed in her Sunday best for her day in court, and looked more like a prim schoolmarm than the harridan barkeep she was, Ransom thought. But that impression would alter the minute she began to speak. Her strident little voice would say what her still surprised face couldn't.

"Good morning, Mrs. Bent," Ransom said.

"Morning," she responded in a tiny voice; as if unwilling to be more than civil. She even looked past him at Dinsmore, who was leaning back in his chair against the railing, diffidently inspecting his perfectly manicured nails.

"May I ask you, Mrs. Bent, if you know the defendant? And if so, under what circumstances?"

"He was our tenant."

"He lived in the Bent Saloon?" Ransom asked, hoping to annoy her into being more garrulous.

"No. He rented the rooms upstairs."

"For what purpose?"

"Business."

She was being far too succinct. It was unlike her. Ransom wanted her to open up much more, as she had done with him before.

"What kind of business, Mrs. Bent?"

"Dental surgery."

"How long ago did he first rent the rooms?"

"Three and a half years ago. A little more."

"Could you describe those rooms to the court?"

"It used to be a family flat. But it's changed now. There's a waiting room, a dental surgery room, and a smaller room, more like a large closet than anything else. The office has indoor plumbing." She still spoke as though unwilling to let the words out. She continually looked past Ransom at Dinsmore.

"What other connection did you have with the defendant?"

"Connection? No other kind."

"Did you not also work for him?"

"I cleaned up the surgery office. That is after his wife had passed on. Is that what you mean?"

"Yes. But weren't you also a patient of the defendant's?"

"Yes."

"For how long were you a patient?"

"On and off. I wasn't a regular patient, you see. Whenever he had no other business and I was free, he'd work on my teeth. He never once charged me for it," she quickly added.

"That was very kind of him."

"Right kind of him," she agreed.

"And how much, Mrs. Bent, did you charge him for cleaning?"

She was silent. Then, tight-lipped, she answered: "I didn't."

"Well! That was right kind of you, Mrs. Bent. Right kind. Now please tell the court how much dental work Mr. Dinsmore did for you."

"He extracted two bad teeth. And he drilled and filled three others."

"Over what period of time?"

"I don't know. He did it whenever we were both free."

"A week? Six weeks? A year?"

"A few months, I guess."

"That must have been a painful time for you, Mrs. Bent?"

As she didn't reply, he asked again.

"I say, Mrs. Bent, that must have been a painful time. What with all that drilling and extracting?"

"It wasn't so painful. Mr. Dinsmore is a fine dentist."

"No one doubts it. But as anyone in this courtroom will assent, the extraction of a tooth is a painful affair at best."

"He never once hurt me."

"Well, I find that hard to believe."

"He performs painless dentistry," she went on to say, a bit more glibly now. "He never caused pain to anyone if he could at all help it."

"Would you tell the court why that was, Mrs. Bent?"

She hesitated. So Ransom decided to help her out.

"Did the defendant give you pain-killing drugs beforehand?"

"Oh, no."

"Then did he administer Nitrous Oxide? Laughing gas?"

"No. Not at all."

"Then how in the world did he manage to eliminate pain?"

"Well, I don't exactly know how. He sort of talked to me. Reassured me it wouldn't hurt."

"And after he reassured you, he extracted the tooth. And it didn't hurt?"

"That's right."

"Well! I'm astonished, Mrs. Bent. Half the dentists in the country assure their patients it won't hurt. But it always seems to hurt like tarnation."

There was a nervous titter in the courtroom.

"He advertised painless surgery," she said. "And it *was* painless."

"I'm willing to believe you, Mrs. Bent. But I'm afraid you're going to have to persuade this jury. I'm certain more than one of them has had a tooth extracted. With or without reassurances, they could testify to how painless their own experiences were."

Again nervous tittering from the spectators. Several jury members stared at Mrs. Bent with obvious disbelief.

"Well, it was painless," she declared. "He never once hurt me."

"Do you mean to say, the defendant simply sat you in the dental chair, reassured you there would be no pain, then reached into your mouth with the dental clamps, tugged and pulled, and there was no pain at all?"

"I never saw him use any clamps on me."

"Or some other instrument?"

"He never used any instrument on me."

"Well, he must have used some sort of tool to extract teeth? Surely he didn't reassure the tooth too, and have it come out all by itself?"

"I don't remember any tools in my mouth."

"Surely when you were cleaning up the office, you noticed clamps, and other instruments?"

"Yes. I had to boil them afterwards. He is Anti-Septic."

"Well, then it stands to reason that such instruments must have been used in the extraction? Doesn't it?"

"I guess." She sounded dubious.

"But you don't remember?" he prodded.

"No. I don't."

"Perhaps you were asleep when it happened?"

"Objection," Applegate called. "Leading questions."

"Overruled," Dietz said. "Please go on, Mr. Ransom."

"Were you sleeping during the extractions? Is that why you don't remember the instruments being used?"

"Not sleeping, but . . ."

"Yes. Go on."

"I don't know. He would talk to me really nice, reassuring me it wouldn't hurt and all. And I really don't recall what else happened, until I was out in the waiting room again."

"And the tooth had been extracted?"

"Yes."

"Or filled?"

"Yes."

"Could you describe how the defendant talked to you at these times? Did he repeat words over and over again? Did he tell you you were feeling restful? Over and over again?"

"Yes. That's right. That's exactly what he did."

"And although you were anxious about the extraction, you did become restful? So restful that you fell into a state much like sleep?"

"I guess."

"Mrs. Bent, do you know what mesmerism is?"

"Only what was said here earlier."

"Mrs. Bent, are you aware of the fact that the reason you felt no pain during these many occasions, which ought to have been extremely painful, is because the defendant, Mr. Dinsmore, had mesmerized you?"

"Objection!" Applegate shouted. "Prosecution is forcing the witness to infer."

"Deposition number five, your honor," Ransom said. The bailiff took the sheaf of papers from him and gave it to the judge.

"Mrs. Bent," Ransom went on, "have you ever seen me in Mr. Dinsmore's office? And if so, when?"

"Last fall. You had a tooth extracted."

"What were you doing there?"

"I brought in the boiling water for the instruments."

"Did I see you at that time?"

"No. You couldn't see me."

"Mrs. Bent, I did have a tooth extracted that day. Painlessly, Mrs. Bent. By the same method that was used for you. Your honor, gentlemen of the jury, as is stated in deposition number five, I had a lower right molar extracted by the defendant just after noon, on October fifteenth, 1899. The method used to eliminate pain was mesmerism. Thank you, Mrs. Bent."

"Can I go?" she asked, bewildered.

"Mr. Applegate?" Dietz asked. "Have you any questions."

"No questions."

"Then court is recessed until after lunch."

———————●———————

"YESSIR," MILLARD SAID. "I remember that afternoon very well. As I ought to. Me and Yolanda's Billy was up in the threshing shed. We rent us a piece of rye field up near Swedeville, but we does all our threshing back of the house, next to the mule stable. So there I was, putting sheafs of rye inside the machines, when all of a sudden the boards I was standing on jes' gave way. Next thing I knew, my right leg had just gone into it too, like it was wheat. 'Lord Jesus,' I shouted, and grabbed to stop that contraption. Billy shut off the engine real fast too. When I pulled my leg out it was all covered with blood. 'Lord Jesus,' Yolanda's Billy says and runs off. Well, I just fell down on that threshing floor, watching the blood pour out of that leg, and screaming my fool head off for the pain which was c'nsiderable, and out of being so afraid.

"Then Yolanda's Billy comes back and with him is Mr. Dinsmore. He sent Yolanda's Billy back into the house for the doctor bag old Carr kept in his room. And I'm thinking, Oh, Lord Jesus, it hurts so much I know I'm gonna die. Look at all that blood! Oh, Jesus, I'm gonna die. 'Cause it was bleeding right up to here."

Millard marked off the spot with a finger on his upper thigh. The courtroom was perfectly still. Millard made a fine witness,

Ransom thought, if only for this unforgettable incident in his life.

"Then what did Mr. Dinsmore do?" Ransom asked.

"Why he jes' took me by the throat"—he illustrated by holding his own throat, and gurgling through it—"like as he was to strangle me. I thought, what's this? First my leg is all threshed up, and now this man wants to strangle me. You see, I thought for sure that was my day for dying, no matter what."

"But you didn't die."

"Nossir. As you can see. Mr. Dinsmore he jes' started talking into my ear then, saying that I was going to be all right, did I understand? That my leg would be all fixed up, did I understand? He said that more than a dozen times. 'Coursen I couldn't say to him whether or not I did understand, even if I did, which I didn't, on account of being took like that by the throat. I was scared too."

"But you stopped being afraid?"

"Tha's right. I jes' stopped being scared. And then Yolanda's Billy came back with the doctorin' bag, and Mr. Dinsmore he let go of my throat, and he started in cuttin' away at my trousers and shaking his head. And I wasn't scared no more, even though oncet my trousers were cut away on both sides it was a terrible thing to see all that blood right down to my foot just bubblin' up and all. Why, it done soaked the threshing floor all around till it was all brown a man's length in every d'rection. And Mr. Dinsmore, he said to hisself, 'All this blood is bad.' And he reached over and took my throat again and said to me I would have to stop bleeding, did I understand. Over and over again. Like as I could do something about it bleeding so much."

"But the bleeding did stop?"

"Well, it sort of stopped somewhat. It still had to be soaked up a little while he was stitching it. But it didn't jes' pour out like a waterfall in the springtime."

"Did this surprise you?"

"No, sir."

"Why not?"

"Well, I jes' don't know. All of a sudden I felt all calm. He told me he'd fix me up and I believed him."

"Had you ever seen or even heard of Mr. Dinsmore's performing surgery before?"

"No, sir. I hadn't."

"But you were calm anyway?"

"Tha's right. I saw everything he did. How he washed it all with the 'bolic fluid, and then how he threaded this long needle with the catgut and held the skin together and jes' sewed it up."

"You watched this entire process?"

"Yessir."

"How long did it take?"

"Well, I don't rightly know. By then Yolanda and Nancy and all t'others were there too watching. We didn't go on back inside the house for another hour or so."

"Would you know how many sutures were put in your leg?"

"Well, Yolanda's Billy counted a hundred and five," Millard said proudly.

"That amount," Ransom said, turning to the jury, "would take any surgeon at least an hour. Probably an hour and a half. I would like to read to this courtroom two accounts from the *New England Journal of Medicine and Surgery.* This first is by a Dr. Abel Clark of Rochester, New York. Dr. Clark writes: 'In our experiments utilizing the deepest of all mesmeric trances, one subject's hand was cut quite deeply. He did not feel any pain, and watched the cut being made quite calmly, and the flow of blood too, as though it were happening not to him, but to someone else. When told the blood would no longer flow so rapidly, he said that he understood. Seconds later, the outpour of blood turned into only a trickle. Without any surgical or medicinal interference at all. The subject continued to watch calmly as his hand was cauterized and surgically sutured. This experiment was used only with a voluntary subject who had proven time and again to be able to enter the deepest of possible trances while remaining awake, and with a control Mesmerist who had been in contact with the subject over a period of a year of experiments. Thus, conditions were at their optimum for this extraordinary incident.'"

Ransom passed the particle to the court bailiff, and said:

"I have another piece from the same journal by a Dr. Charles Causable of Magdalen College, England. 'In cases of emergency, when hypnothesia must be accomplished instantly, it can be so done by an experienced control over any subject known to be suggestible, by several methods.' I'll pass over the first two," Ransom said, "as only the third interests us. 'Lastly, by manual depression of the upper thoracic cavity, and great pressure by finger and thumb to the carotid artery, the subject will appear to be strangling, but will be instead thrust into a state characterized by total trance and complete suggestibility. This may be accomplished only in one out of a thousand cases.'

"Gentlemen," Ransom said, "this last method was applied to Millard Bowles. Millard"—he now turned back to the witness—"tell this court, before this incident, were you ever mesmerized by the defendant?"

"No, sir. Not that I know of."

"In other words, gentlemen, your honor, in this emergency situation, the defendant utilized a rare and little-known method of inducing the mesmeric trance on a subject who had never before been shown to be subject to it. And furthermore, he performed an extraordinary, hour-and-a-half-long surgical suturing in which he added on the further unusual stipulation of causing the naturally copious flow of blood from such a mishap to cease almost completely. All this done instantly, and by mere suggestion."

"Objection!" Applegate said, standing now to make himself heard. "Prosecution is attempting to summarize before all the witnesses have been called."

"Point of law, Mr. Ransom," Dietz said.

Undeterred, Ransom turned to Applegate, even as he said, "Your honor, the prosecution was not summarizing. The prosecution was merely attempting to show that not only is the defendant by the sworn testimony of this and other witnesses a Mesmerist, but that he has utilized the most daring, the most hazardous of mesmeric methods with a skill and casualness which suggests that he has done it before, many times, with great success. I am trying to show, your honor, that the defendant, Mr. Frederick Dinsmore is not merely a circus illusionist, but that he is a master Mesmerist, perhaps the greatest Mesmerist now alive!"

By then Ransom's voice was high and strident, shouting over Applegate's vociferous objections, and over the sudden vocal release of the courtroom spectators, Judge Dietz's unceasing gavel, and the bailiff's calls for order in the courtroom.

When all had quieted somewhat, Ransom said, "I have no further questions for the witness."

"No questions," Applegate seconded him.

———————————●———————————

"REVEREND SYDNEY, ARE YOU FAMILIAR with the defendant?"

The black pastor looked at Dinsmore for a longer time than necessary, as though he could not believe his eyes.

"Yes, sir," he said sadly to Ransom.

"Could you tell the courtroom how you know the defendant?"

"Well, sir, my congregation, the First Baptist Church, meets right underneath Mr. Dinsmore's offices."

"Was the defendant a member of the congregation?"

"No, sir. Though the late Missus Dinsmore did attend our meetings when she could."

"But the defendant never did attend?"

"Sometimes. Once or twice."

"So you know the defendant mostly through proximity and through his wife?"

"Not exactly, sir," Sydney replied.

He was being as cautious as Murcott had been, though for other reasons. Earlier that day, he had taken Ransom aside to say he would do nothing to incriminate Dinsmore nor any other man he thought innocent. Ransom had quickly calmed the nervous minister. All he needed answered were a few questions. Nothing the Reverend could say would incriminate Dinsmore. He needn't worry. But that had occurred before Mrs. Bent had testified. Sydney had seen how her innocent enough words had been turned against the defendant. And too, Sydney had been much impressed by the swearing-in on the Bible—the word of which directed Sydney's life. He affirmed in a loud clear voice he would tell the truth to the best of his ability, and now he quaked, hoping those words would not harm Dinsmore.

"You see, sir," Sydney began to explain, "Mr. Dinsmore was made aware through our congregation of the brotherhood of man, no matter their color or their denomination. So's when I asked if he would help some of the congregation who couldn't afford his services, why he did the dental surgery without charge."

"And it was mostly through these recipients of the defendant's generosity," Ransom asked, "that you knew of the defendant?"

"Yes, sir."

"How many members of your congregation would you say the defendant treated free of charge?"

"'Bout a dozen."

"Over what period of time, Reverend?"

"Well, I'd say from the winter of ninety-eight to just about the present time."

"Would you name those members of your congregation to the court?"

Sydney did so, the court clerk copying the names at Ransom's request. Ransom looked them over quickly, then asked:

"Isn't Alonzo Johns the manager of the Lane Public Stables?"

"Yes, sir."

"For how long?"

"Since the summer, I believe."

"What kind of work did Mr. Johns do before that?"

"He was a field hand."

"That's quite a promotion," Ransom said. "And Althea Robbins. What kind of work does she do?"

"Well, sir, she's the woman in charge of cleaning the rooms and replacing the linens at the Lane Hotel."

"Since when?"

"Since about June of this year."

"Had Mrs. Robbins done this kind of work before?"

"Not that I know of. She was a housekeeper once, a long time before. For a white family in Ohio somewhere."

"And Junius P. Brown. He's now the foreman at the Lane Warehouse on Emerson Street, isn't he? What did he do before that?"

"He was a sometime mechanic."

Ransom read down the entire list one by one, asking Sydney the past and current occupations of all the people the pastor had named. They all held fairly important positions under Dinsmore's managership, and had all been taken on since Dinsmore had assumed that role, often displacing people who had held their jobs for a decade or more under Henry Lane.

"Reverend Sydney, you say all of these people underwent 'painless' surgery under the defendant, free of charge?"

"Yes, sir. Every one of them declared to me there had been no pain at all."

"And no charge either?"

"That's right, sir."

"We may therefore conclude," Ransom said, not to the witness but across the room to the jury, "that all of these people named by Reverend Sydney were mesmerized during the course of their dental surgery by the defendant. As a matter of fact, gentlemen, depositions of oral or written testimony by seven of the twelve the witness has named are available for your inspection, corroborating the fact. What is also clear is that these eleven men and one woman were quickly placed under the defendant's authority as soon as he assumed control of the various Lane enterprises, despite their lack of experience or skill at their new occupations."

"Mr. Ransom," Judge Dietz said wearily, "not everyone is able to follow your reasoning. Would you be so kind as to get to the point?"

"The point is, your honor, that the defense in its opening remarks declared a conspiracy against the defendant. The prosecution is now declaring that the defendant himself conspired to wrest control of the Lane empire, and to that end mesmerized until they were under his complete control all of these people we have named to the court, to be placed in key roles when that takeover was accomplished."

Cal Applegate was on his feet, his face livid. "That's an absurd allegation."

"Mr. Applegate!" Dietz said sharply, "if you have an objection to make, please utilize the proper channel for it. Otherwise you will be held out of order in this courtroom."

"The defense objects to an unsubstantiated allegation," Applegate now said.

"Mr. Ransom," Dietz said, "continue if you will."

"The prosecution contends that the defendant's care in insuring he would have dependable underlings was planned at about the same time that Henry Lane first began going to the defendant for dental treatment. Thus, the defendant had as early as two years prior to the deceased's so-called suicide planned for a takeover of his business."

"Can you substantiate that?" Applegate cried.

"Can you otherwise explain," Ransom shot back, "why those people and only those people who were by their own admission mesmerized by your client now hold the positions they enjoy? I for one cannot see why a man who has been a field hand all his life is suddenly elevated to the position of stable manager. Unless he is a trusted, no, a devoted and furthermore easily manipulated man. Reverend Sydney, I have no further questions. Your witness, Mr. Applegate."

Applegate had no questions for the witness, and the now appalled Reverend Sydney stepped down from the witness stand and slowly found his seat.

At the same time, the court bailiff called Yolanda Bowles to the stand. Like all the other witnesses today, she was dressed in her best, in this case a floor-to-neck maroon serge dress with froglet buttons down the front, which made her appear even more immense than Ransom remembered. She was sworn in, and her bulk helped into the witness box, which she filled to overflowing. Her bright eyes flicked around the room, as if intent on taking in every detail from her new perspective.

Ransom knew she was on his side; he needn't urge her or circle around her with questions.

"Mrs. Bowles, the defendant rented an apartment of four rooms from you in your house on Winter Lane from March of 1897 until early June of this past year. Can you tell the court how the defendant came to rent from you?"

"He'd been recommended by Mr. Bent, from the saloon."

"Could you tell the court what kind of contacts you had with the defendant and your other tenants?"

"Little enough with Mr. Dinsmore. Or Mr. Carr either, for that matter. They kept to themselves considerably."

"And with Mrs. Dinsmore?"

"We talked jes' about every day."

"Please tell the jury, Mrs. Bowles, your initial impression of the defendant."

"Well, to tell the truth, I wondered why such a well-dressed man like that, so clean and neat, would want to come live among nigrahs."

"What conclusion did you arrive at?"

"I concluded the man had done somethin' wrong in another town and sort of wanted to stay in hidin' a bit. No one would think to look for a white man in a yardful of pickaninnies."

Her honesty delighted the spectators. She kept a serious face, however, adamantly uninterested in their reactions.

"But you had no proof of this?" Ransom asked.

"No, sir. But as I said afore, I had no business with him, nor with Mr. Carr either. The missus always paid the rent. Except for one occasion, the d'fendant didn't talk to me at all."

Evidently, she had remembered something since their talk on the front porch. Ransom wondered if it were important.

"Would you tell the courtroom of this one occasion."

"When they first moved into the room, he comes to me and says they couldn't use the same outhouse as we nigrahs used." She disregarded the laughter from the gallery. "So I told him,

'Well sir, that's the onliest one we got here, and this ain't Chicago with indoor plumbin' and all.' So then he tells me he wants a privy on the other side of the ice house. So I said, 'Go right ahead, if that's what you want.' But he said he wasn't going to do it, and that my Billy and Millard ought to do it. Well, it was sowing time then, and both of them was out in the field all day long, planting. They couldn't be spared to do it. And that's what I told him."

"What happened, Mrs. Bowles?"

She looked down into her lap. "Well, sir. He caught that Billy one evening after dinner and he somehow persuaded him to dig the hole for the privy and put up the shed. Billy didn't go out to sow the next day, but stayed at home, working at it until that privy was built and ready to be used. 'Course I hollered and even beat on Billy when I found out what he'd done. But he said he didn't mean no harm by it, and he didn't even know he'd been doing it until it was all done and working. So it couldn't be helped. After that time, I kept all the other nigrahs away from the d'fendant."

"He had mesmerized Billy to do it?"

"I spoze, sir. He could get his way by talking to anyone in the house, 'cept myself. I wouldn't listen to him at all. But the rest of them, why if he wanted something, they'd just cease whatever they was doing and wait on him. And that's the Lord's own truth, Mr. Ransom. I swore on the Good Book."

"I believe you, Mrs. Bowles," Ransom said. This had been an unexpected windfall. One that seemed to count strongly with the spectators, who murmured loudly until Judge Dietz gaveled and called for order.

"Now, Mrs. Bowles, you said that you talked with the defendant's late wife every day or so. Could you tell the court what you talked about?"

"Mostly 'bout how unhappy and sickly she was."

"Unhappy about what?"

"Well, she had come from a fine family, she said. Ran off against their wishes to marry the d'fendant many years before.

Well, he sometimes took her in, but oftener than not he would jes' go off and leave her again. She had hauled herself clear across this country, following after him."

"But at the time he lived in your house, and until her death, Mr. Dinsmore was living with her. What could have caused her misery?"

"She believed he went to other women, sir. She was lovesick over him. But he wouldn't have none to do with her, she said. He treated her worse than a house nigger. Making her clean up the rooms, then up at the offices too, above the saloon. Then never being no proper husband to her. Not speaking to her sometimes a week at a time, though she served him hand and foot and worshiped the ground he trod upon."

Her last words trailed away quietly. Every eye in the room seemed to shift from Yolanda to Dinsmore, sitting as indifferent as ever, and as nattily clad as the day before, at the defense desk.

"You said, Mrs. Bowles, that the defendant's wife was sickly at this time?"

"She said she was sick with the consumption. Though I had reason to doubt that, sir. I 'tributed it all to her unhappiness."

"Objection," Applegate called out. "Witness has no medical knowledge."

"I does too!" Yolanda said, flaring up. "And especially of the consumption. Why when I was the mammy at the Cabot plantation back before the 'mancipation, I nursed my little mistress of the consumption for over two years, till the poor thing died of it. You can't tell me I don't have no medical knowledge. Leastways of the consumption. And I tell you that poor Mrs. Dinsmore, whatever she did suffer from, didn't have the consumption. She never once spit no phlegm more than an ordinary person, not to mention no blood at all. She never ran no high fevers. She never had the pockets and the pustules on her chest that I ever noticed. As the Lord God is my witness, when you sit watching a beloved child die you sure enough sees what a particular disease looks like."

"What symptoms did Mrs. Dinsmore have?" Ransom asked.

"Well, she done lost her appetite. Didn't never eat enough for a baby. And she didn't sleep much at night. And she worked so hard and sorrowed so much she jes' began wasting away. Almost as though she actually had the consumption."

"She might have been suffering from another, an undetected disease," Ransom offered, to stop a further objection from the defense.

"That she might have. But she declared it was the consumption. Wouldn't disbelieve nohow. She was certain she'd die of it."

"From such close contact with the lady, would you say she would commit suicide because of her beliefs of illness?"

"That I can't say. All I know is I never met such an unhappy creature, nor do I hope to again in this life."

"Mrs. Bowles, did you ever hear the defendant and his wife arguing?"

"Objection!" Applegate said. "The prosecution's line of questioning as to the personal affairs of the defendant and his wife seem to have little bearing on the case before us."

"I'm afraid they do," Ransom said. "Your honor, gentlemen of the jury, tomorrow morning, the prosecution will present a witness who will repeat before you what he has already testified to in writing—to wit, that the defendant wished to rid himself for once and all of this unfortunate woman whom he saw as plaguing his life since their marriage, whom he abandoned time and again, but who went through great hardships to search and find her legal husband, only to be once more abandoned by him. This witness will declare how on one of these occasions the defendant's wife found her husband in Chicago, Illinois, just as the defendant was preparing to marry a young woman of considerable wealth, and how Mrs. Dinsmore thwarted this bigamous action. The witness will declare under oath how the defendant's control over his wife included the constant mesmeric suggestion and reinforcement that she was suffering from severe tuberculosis and that her condition was worsening to the point where she would never recover. My purpose in calling Mrs. Bowles to the stand today was to confirm that the defendant's wife did in fact believe this illusion, even when no symptoms of this terrible affliction were in evidence."

"If neither attorney has questions for the witness . . ." Dietz began, then paused. "Fine. Court is adjourned until tomorrow morning." He disappeared into his private chambers in the midst of a thunderous outburst of shocked courtroom conversation, as the spectators began to comment on what they'd heard.

A half hour later, as Ransom was leaving his small office in the court building, Dietz passed him going out.

"You're doing well, James. But keep it coming. Make it stick!"

"It will stick. Especially after Carr takes the stand."

———————————●———————————

DESPITE THE STILL WINTRY WEATHER, Simon Carr was sitting outside, in the light of the declining sun, when Ransom and Murcott drove up to the Lane ranch later that afternoon. Next to him was a large, battered traveling case he must have used for the last half century. The old man was dressed for traveling, bundled up in a shabby gray Ulster, gloves and scarf. But his head was bare. Thin wisps of long white hair floated around his face in the wind. Amid all the material that surrounded it, his face looked more gaunt, more birdlike than ever. How ghastly, Ransom found himself thinking, that in illness and old age, when we so much need others, nature had arranged to make us seem most grotesque and repulsive, as though to frighten off those much needed companions.

As Murcott was getting down from the driver's box, he said to Ransom in an undertone:

"That man is very ill. I don't know that he ought to be moved at all."

The doctor went over to the seated Carr, but before Ransom could make introductions, Murcott had taken the old man's bony wrist and was feeling for a pulse.

"Pleased to meet you, Mr. Carr," Murcott said drily. "What are you doing sitting out here without a hat on?"

"Getting the benefit of the sun. I can't feel it on my head with a hat on, now can I?"

"We'll have to keep him on the first floor," Murcott said to Ransom. "Can you walk, Mr. Carr?"

"My left side is fine. The right is a bit off. That will mend soon enough." He reached down and picked up a gnarled old cane. "I have my old ashplant. I'll walk with it."

Ransom sat with Carr, and Murcott drove. Covered with blankets, the old man looked curiously around as though seeing the landscape for the first time. He resisted all of Ransom's attempts at conversation. They would have had to shout to be heard for much of the ride anyway, the carriage rattled so much.

As soon as Carr hobbled into the entry of the Center City Board and Hotel, Mrs. Page understood the need for a first-floor room.

"We'll put the Murphy bed in the small back parlor. He'll be near the kitchen and to the office in case Amasa is needed. I can do with some help, James."

Ransom watched her convert the small dark room into a sickroom, then waited in Murcott's outer office until the examination was over.

"You're to rest awhile now, Simon," the doctor said, leading Carr into the waiting room. "Mrs. Page will show you to your room. It's only a step away from the dining room, you lucky dog. We'll be having dinner soon."

They bantered another few minutes, long enough for Ransom to see that in the short interval of the medical examination they'd become friendly. Once Carr was out of hearing, Murcott frowned, and turned on his friend.

"We were insane to bring that man here."

"But why? He's walking about. He seems well enough."

"For how long? An hour? He could have another stroke any minute. I'm surprised he didn't have convulsions after that ride. I thought all my teeth had shaken loose. He can't testify, James. He's too ill."

"I'll only keep him on the stand an hour."

"It will take an hour to get him out of bed, dressed, and down to the courthouse. He's too ill to testify."

"But I need him," Ransom said. "You know that."

"I know it all right. But I also know what condition Carr's in. I can't let you do it. I can't let you kill an old man just for your precious case."

"Damn," Ransom said out loud. "It was all going so well." It was building so well. Tomorrow Carr would testify, then after him, Carrie Lane. His case would be built solidly, like a Roman road. "He's really that bad, Amasa?"

"Bad? His pulse sounded like Marian's telegraphic receiver. You ever hear it. Dot. Dash. Dot. Dash. Dot. You'll simply have to read his deposition. That'll have to do."

"It won't do at all. I want the jury to hear Carr's words from his own mouth. You must see how important that is. No deposition could come close to having the same impact as a direct, face-to-face accusation."

"He's too ill," Murcott persisted.

"Wait a moment, though," Ransom said. "What if I were to set all the other witnesses first—Carrie, Isabelle, whoever. Carr can remain here. Under your constant care he's certain to be better soon. Say in a week or so. Then I'll take him for an hour at a time. I'll read part, and have him speak the rest of the deposition. Explaining all the while how ill he is."

Murcott was silent.

"I promise you I won't cause him any strain or overexcitement."

"Of course you won't. But what if he's cross-examined?"

"For only an hour a day? In a week's time?"

"Well . . . perhaps. We'll have to see."

"He wants to testify. He's expecting to do it. He'll be disappointed not to be able to do it. I know he'll improve here, Amasa. I'm certain of it. He was always so cold out at the ranch. He told me so himself."

"I said perhaps, James."

But that was as good as a yes for Ransom, well as he knew the doctor. It buoyed him up through the noisy dinner that followed, and prepared him for the visit he would now have to pay Carrie Lane tonight, giving her the news that she and not Carr would take the witness stand tomorrow. It still might work this way. Carrie was certain to be an intriguing and, he thought, a popular witness. And her words might have a greater impact at this point than Carr's.

The old man did not join the other boarders at the table. Isabelle Page was so taken with the fact that he was British, she declared she wanted to have him all to herself. She brought his meal into him, and sat by him as he ate, and long afterward, being her fresh, curious young self. And evidently delighting old Carr, whose cracked laughter could be heard now and again from the dining room during the infrequent pauses in conversation at the general table.

"Well," Carr said, when Ransom went in to see him before leaving the house, "I'm certainly pleased with myself for coming back to Center City. The food is far better than that Fraulein's eternal sauerkraut, and the company is far, far more attractive."

Isabelle smiled at the compliment, but caught Ransom's signal to leave the two men alone. "I'll be back," she promised.

"Charming girl, Mr. Government Man. I wondered why you were living here all this time. Now I think I know."

"Bosh. She's like a little sister to me," Ransom protested. "I've watched her grow up." Then he changed the topic. "You won't be testifying for another few days, so I would like you to take a bit of time to think about what you'll say."

"I thought I was to begin tomorrow? I'm ready, you know. I need no practice for it. I know what I'll say all right. Or is it that Murcott said I'm too ill?"

"It has nothing to do with that," Ransom lied. "I'd decided yesterday to have Mrs. Lane testify before you. There's a reason for it—but it pertains to the presentation of the case and has nothing to do with your health."

"I'm glad to hear it. You're the only sensible one about. Save myself, of course. I'm a physician myself, you know. I ought to know if I'm well or not. No matter what everyone else says."

"Who else thinks you're not well?"

"That slimy bastard you and I are going to hang."

"Dinsmore? When did you see him?"

"Not for a while. Not since I last saw you."

"But he said something about your health when he last saw you?"

"He said, Mr. Government Man, that if I dared to testify, that I'd never have the opportunity."

"What exactly did he say?"

"That's all."

"He threatened you then."

"Not in so many words. Of course he didn't know then how much I'd helped you to jail him. He thought it was all Mrs. Lane. Blimey, he had harsh enough words for her. He'd come to gloat over me, as usual, and to tell me how his important new friends would take care of him, trial or not. Oh, he was full of himself that day. It made me sick to my gullet to listen to him strutting and boasting so. That was when he said it."

"That if you chose to testify, you never would?"

"Something like that. Oh, he's a bad one, the devil. No, wait, I recall his words now. 'Naturally no one will listen to you, you old liar. But even if they did, you'd never get past the first word of your blather.' And I asked why not. And he said to me, 'You old idiot, you'll keel over from that bag of dung you call your heart. It's no better than a sack of beans as you well know.' "

Ransom was disappointed. He'd hoped for a more definite threat.

"Ah, he's too sharp to catch himself in anything definite," Carr said. "But I tell you I will personally see to it the noose is placed about his neck."

"Were you mesmerized that day?" Ransom asked.

"No. He didn't even try. He'd tried to once before, and had been unable to."

"What do you mean?"

"Well, it's rather difficult to explain. But when I was aware that he was trying to do it again, I decided I would not let it happen. Then I began concentrating very intensely upon some lines of poetry that had come into my head that day. I recalled the entire poem. An ode of Livy, I believe it was. One I'd learned by heart years ago when I was a schoolboy. And I found that if I concentrated on the poem hard enough, I scarcely heard him. I suppose he thought that being as ill as I was that I couldn't concentrate at all, and that I wasn't subject to his influence any more. But I was, I tell you. All the while I repeated 'Nos omnia deceptit' I could feel his words insinuating into my consciousness. It was a battle of his will through his words and my own. And I won it. I don't know if I could do it again. I would certainly try. I don't ever want him mesmerizing me again. Not ever."

Shortly after this conversation, Ransom was climbing against a sudden blustery March wind up High Street to Mrs. Lane's door. All the way there, he'd been reviewing how his presentation would be shaped by the change of witnesses. It really was too bad Carr couldn't speak tomorrow. That would have been such a fine way to prepare the court for Carrie's testimony. Like a Roman road, he'd told Murcott. But it would be more like a Roman arch now, with everyone else's words building a strong, secure foundation for the sweeping accusations she would make. To be followed by Carr, and afterward, minor, corroborative testimony by others who had seen or known Henry Lane in his last months. The case against Dinsmore wouldn't merely stick, as Dietz so often repeated it must. It would soar, arch, then come crashing down on the heads of the jury with an inevitability, a force of truth despite the many questions they still might harbor, that could not be denied. What Ransom himself could not say, except in summary, a dozen witnesses would say for him. Through their words he would show the potential and already realized horror that Dinsmore was capable of. Hearing it like that, from so many—an ensemble, a chorus, not just one voice —the jury would have no choice but to believe, and to convict Dinsmore.

The long walk had become rote with all this thinking; so had his slapping of the big knocker on the front door. He had to break off a thought in surprise as Mrs. Ingram suddenly opened the door.

"Oh," she said: annoyed, disappointed. "It's you."

She stepped aside for him to enter, but did not offer to take his hat and coat. She seemed as angry with him today as when he'd last seen her—the day he and Carrie Lane had driven off to Plum Creek.

"She's upstairs. In the reading room," she said sharply, then turned to leave the foyer.

Ransom stood a minute watching her thin, high shoulders and her tightly wound hair recede. Then he took off his outerwear, and hurried upstairs. It crossed his mind that he ought to call Mrs. Ingram after Carrie and Carr. She'd been in the courtroom every day so far. Was she disappointed he hadn't called her to testify already? Then again, if she didn't want that, but remained as unexplainably resentful of him as she was now, it might be worth a half hour's amusement to annoy her in public. No. It wouldn't be worth it. She'd be far more trouble than the value she'd give, if her past performances were any indicator.

Carrie was expecting him, her hand outstretched to take his as she led him into the gaslit room. She was wearing an ivory-colored gown, which became her wonderfully. She was radiant, so beautifully precious he wanted to hold her closely, to pull her to his breast and keep her there, to feel and smell and touch her. But that wouldn't do. Not yet. So he contented himself with taking her hand, and still holding it, leading her to one window with parted curtains.

"It's been three days since I've seen you," he complained.

"You look tired, James. Have you been getting enough sleep?"

"Even at night the view is beautiful from here. How the courthouse is lighted up."

"I watched you walking up High Street. You looked so stern, I thought, perhaps . . ."

"Plunged in thought," he said. "Look. You can see my windows from here. There. Just through the bare trees."

"There?" she asked, leaning her face close to his. The pane of glass was icy in front of them. It misted over with their conjoined breaths.

"No. To the left. Two windows are lighted."

"The orange ones?"

"That's my shades. They're really yellow. I suppose the distance or something else distorts the color."

"Now that I know, I promise to blow you a kiss every night," she said.

"Carrie?"

She turned her face to his, and now he kissed her. She didn't draw back, but neither did she give herself to him as completely as he'd hoped she would.

"Are you disappointed in me?" he asked.

Her eyes questioned him. "No."

"I'm not being very professional wanting this, am I?"

She drew away from him. "You know how much you've done for me. Why, tonight's the first time in days the parlor hasn't been filled with ladies who wouldn't walk next to me a few months ago."

"Does that please you?"

"A little. But they can be tiring. And Lord, how they can talk! And eat while talking. We haven't a thing left in the larder. Mrs. Ingram's up in arms about it. But then she seems to be up in arms about everything these days."

Her mood changed so completely that Ransom sat her down. He had to know more.

"Since I've returned," she began, "we've done nothing but argue. I don't know why. Perhaps I was away so long she now considers herself mistress of the house and I merely a guest. I soon enough disabused her of that notion. She got so bad with that nonsense she insisted on calling advice that I had to remind her she was still only an employee and could be replaced. That happened today. She hasn't spoken a word to me since. For which I must say I'm grateful."

Ransom admired her spirit, even in sadness, over the tiff with her housekeeper. He hoped that same spirit would show up at the trial. It would impress others too, he thought.

"It always struck me that Mrs. Ingram presumed a great deal," he said.

"She keeps on talking about the trial. She says I oughtn't

testify. That I'll bring ruin on the Lane name. If she only knew," Carrie sadly said, "if she only knew. I don't know when she decided she was the guardian of my reputation, though. It's most irksome."

"Carrie, one of the reasons I'm here tonight is to tell you you'll have to testify tomorrow instead of next week as we'd planned." As she looked blank at his statement, he went on quickly to explain how ill Murcott said Carr was, and how he could not take the stand. Their case was going too well to jeopardize it now. It had to continue strongly. He needed her for that. He then explained that Applegate wouldn't be much of a problem. He was putting on only the minimum defense these days, obviously knowing his was a lost cause. She oughtn't worry about his cross-examining her. "And besides," he added, as further encouragement, "you have half of Center City on your side already. After tomorrow you'll have every man, woman, and child for you."

"Then Mrs. Ingram will really complain," Carrie joked. But she couldn't hide her anxiety.

"I'll be right there," he said. "Not a foot away. You need not be in the courtroom until you have to take the stand. There are waiting chambers. And afterwards you can stay in the chamber in case you're needed again."

"I'm not afraid. Or at least I don't think I will be, James, with you there. I do want to testify. Oh, so badly. I don't care what anyone says or thinks of me anymore. I want to do it."

"Good. Nine thirty at the courthouse. Go right to Alvin Barker. He'll show you to a waiting room. I'll find my way downstairs and out. Get some rest now."

Downstairs in the foyer, as he was buttoning his coat, Ransom thought he saw a shadow under the stairway. He opened the street door and quietly said:

"I was thinking of serving a subpoena upon you to testify also, Mrs. Ingram. How would you like that?"

Her only answer was the rustle of skirts and the muffled closing of an inner door.

Crossing Lincoln Avenue on his way home, Ransom noticed

a crowd of more than a score of men milling about on the sidewalk in front of the Center City *Star* office. Had Jeffries veered even further from the truth in his absurd reportage of the trial?

But when he neared the corner, Ransom saw the crowd was not in front of Jeffries' office, as he had supposed, but a few yards away, gathered about an open-backed canvas-roofed wagon parked alongside the curb. Within the wagon, someone was selling newspapers. At closer range, Ransom recognized many faces in the crowd. Among them old Floyd, who spotted his co-boarder, held up the newspaper and chuckled.

"Well, that easterner'll be drinking printing ink from now on," Floyd said.

"Stop wagging that thing and let me have a look at it."

"It's the Lincoln *Journal.* Tomorrow's edition. Sent down on the Missouri Express. That reporter feller telegraphs his reports, they print them up, and in a few hours we can read it. Who— ee! This is what I call living in the twenti—uth century!"

Ransom ignored him. A largish headline read: "Evidence Accumulates Against Hypnotist." A subheading said: "Prosecutor shows Dinsmore planned Commercial Takeover. Questions thrown on Suicide of Hypnotist's Wife." Below that, in smaller print, another heading: "Witnesses testify to widespread mental control over a period of three years. Defendant offers no rebuttals."

Therewith followed an extensive story on what had transpired that day in the courtroom, with references to earlier testimony. At the end of the article—continued on the following two pages —a separate box had been inserted into the body of the story. It contained a note which read: "Because of the strongly partisan reportage on this trial at its source, the Lincoln *Journal* will print and deliver full transactions of the court proceedings for residents of Kearney County." A sly and quite strong dig at Joseph Jeffries.

"Well," Floyd asked, impatiently. "What do you think of it?"

"Looks good to me."

"They're going to deliver them every evening at nine P.M. is

what Goff, the barber, says. He'll keep copies of them in the shop
the following day for anyone who missed them. That Easterner
sure got hisself a spur placed square on his rear end."

"Are all these people buying the *Journal?*"

"You bet they are. We've all had a bellyful of lies. That
reporter feller, Merrifield, why he says that they'll be printing
the trial all over the country now. 'Cause the *Journal* is syndicated. As far as New York and San Francisco."

"Well, that pleases me a great deal," Ransom said. He must
make certain to thank this Merrifield personally. Who knew but
after Carrie Lane's testimony tomorrow the coverage on the trial
might be even larger. Then the reporter would thank Ransom.
The revelations still to come would surely sell more copies of the
newspaper.

"Here, now," Floyd called out. "You're walking off with my
paper. Git your own if you want one."

"When did you learn how to read?" Ransom retorted.

"Well," Floyd was suddenly sheepish. "I still want it. As a
memento and all."

———————————————●———————————————

RANSOM BREAKFASTED IN HIS ROOM the next morning, reviewing his notes for the questions he would be asking Carrie
Lane. He became so involved in these, when he looked up to the
clock on the bureau it read almost nine thirty.

He arrived in court, still breathless, and was opening his folio
onto the desk, when Barker called the trial to session, and Judge
Dietz stepped out into the courtroom. A minute later, Ransom
was addressing the jury.

"Yesterday when this session was adjourned, I promised to
place on the witness stand the man who had worked with and for
the defendant for the last several years. I said then that you
would hear from this man how the defendant had abused his
extraordinary powers of mesmerism to manipulate and enslave
not only those names which Reverend Sydney gave to the court

yesterday, but also the defendant's closest relations—his wife, and Mr. Simon Carr."

"Mr. Carr is now in Center City. But he has suffered a series of severe strokes in recent months, and I have been given the strongest medical advice against Mr. Carr's testifying at this time."

A murmur swept the room, and the usually somber jurymen looked disappointed, except for old Soos, Floyd's friend, who wore a smug look as though he'd suspected all the while that Carr would not testify. Ransom had always thought Soos was on his side. Maybe he'd been wrong.

"I have been assured that Mr. Carr ought to be sufficiently recovered to testify in a short while. And although I could read Mr. Carr's deposition of testimony to you, the witness is eager to directly face the accused. Ill as he is, and as ill-used as he has been, this courageous old man insists upon this right, and I am certain he will provide shocking evidence."

"Thank you, Mr. Ransom," Dietz said drily. "Have you another witness to take Mr. Carr's place?"

"I do, your honor. Carrie Lane."

A sudden hubbub from the spectators. They too had been disappointed that Carr would not testify. Having Carrie Lane on the witness stand was even better. Give them bread and circuses the emperor Domitian had said, and that will satisfy the mob. How right he had been, Ransom thought now.

"Mrs. Henry Lane of Eighteen High Street is called to the stand," the court bailiff called out.

Even Dinsmore sat up in his seat. No indifferent slouching and half-closed eyes for him today. Ransom could feel expectation crackling in the air.

"The prosecution calls Mrs. Henry Lane of Eighteen High Street," the bailiff repeated shrilly.

Still, she didn't appear.

"Mr. Ransom," the judge suddenly said, "would you kindly produce your witness. Perhaps she is in one of the waiting rooms."

Ransom was about to go look for her, when the door on the right side of the courtroom opened. Carrie Lane looked out.

"The prosecution calls Mrs. Henry Lane of Eighteen High Street," the bailiff called yet again.

"I'm here," she said, then swept her trailing skirts into the room. She was dressed as though she were a fashion plate from *Peterson's Catalogue* in the most elegant mourning costume Ransom had ever seen, yards of black silks and satins, trimmed with jet lace. Her bearing, her entire entrance left no room for questions or doubts: she was a wealthy woman, an important woman.

Ransom took her arm and directed her to the witness box. Her swearing in could scarcely be heard for the sudden feminine chatter that erupted in the spectators' gallery. Ransom looked for, and finally made out, Mrs. Ingram among them. But the housekeeper wasn't talking or even looking at Carrie Lane. Her gaze was upon Dinsmore, who sat stonily at attention for the first time so far in the trial, staring at the witness, almost as though he did not hear Applegate whispering hurriedly into his ear.

In the jurybox, all twelve men were staring at Carrie Lane, not merely the seven who didn't know her, but also the five who might have seen her any day, looking at her now as though inspecting a stranger. Pulver, the courting man, looked most intrigued, as though suddenly aware of another possibility in his conjugal search.

Dietz gaveled the room to order. It was slow in coming, but as soon as he felt he had their attention, Ransom turned to the witness box. He'd done well to call her now. And she'd done beautifully well by her choice of apparel.

"Mrs. Lane, are you familiar with the defendant?"

"I know him. Yes."

"Would you explain to the court what your relationship is to the defendant?"

"I'm afraid that would be rather difficult. It's all rather complicated."

Good answers, Ransom thought. "The defendant works for you, does he not?"

"I suppose you might say that."

"The defendant is employed as manager of the Lane Public Stables, the Lane Hotel, the Lane Dry Goods Company, the Lane Feed and Grain Company, *et cetera,* is he not?"

"He manages them, yes."

"All of which, since the death of your husband, Henry Lane, on April seventeenth, 1899, have been under your ownership, have they not?"

"Yes."

"Yet you say he does not work for you?"

"He works for himself," she said with a trace of bitterness.

"Yet is it not true that whatever profits derive from these various companies go to you?"

"Yes, that is so."

"Did you not then hire the defendant to manage these businesses?"

"He hired himself."

"And you did not hinder him from doing so?"

"I did not."

"Why not, Mrs. Lane?"

She was silent, looking at him, uncertain of what answer to give him.

"You cannot say why you did not hinder him from hiring himself, Mrs. Lane?"

"I can, yes. But no one would believe me."

"Mrs. Lane, may I remind you that you are in a court of law. That you are under oath to tell the truth. Now, Mrs. Lane, please tell the jury why you did nothing to hinder the defendant from hiring himself into these lucrative and powerful positions that he assumed in the early summer of last year."

"Because," she said, letting it out slowly, uncertainly, "because I was under his complete domination at that time."

"What kind of domination, Mrs. Lane?"

"I was under mesmeric control."

"Please speak up, Mrs. Lane."

She repeated herself in a loud clear voice. One could hear a pin drop in the held-breath silence. "I was under mesmeric control."

"How long had you been under such control?"

"For a year or so."

"And because of the nature of this control, you could do nothing to hinder the defendant from taking those positions?"

"I could not hinder him from doing anything he wished to do."

She was wonderful, Ransom thought. Better than he had hoped. He gave her a half smile now, by way of encouragement. Then, needing a minute or two for what she had already said to enter into everyone's mind, he went over to his desk and pretended to be looking for some notes. A low murmur gathered in the spectators' section. When he walked back to the witness stand, Carrie looked troubled for the first time today. He smiled again.

"Mrs. Lane, would you please tell the court how long you have known the defendant?"

"Since the late fall of 1898."

Ransom asked her to speak louder again. Not for greater effect, as he had done before, but because she was suddenly so quiet.

"Under what circumstances did you meet the defendant?"

"My husband . . . my late husband invited him home to dinner."

"Mr. Lane was friendly with the defendant?"

"I would not say friendly."

"How then would you characterize their connection at that time?"

"I did not know for certain until later on. At that time I thought Henry was merely associating with Mr. Dinsmore out of gratitude for the fine dental work he had done for Henry. I thought they were merely acquainted."

"What did you think of their connection later?"

"Later I knew that Henry had been under mesmeric control."

"How did you know that, Mrs. Lane?"

"He told me."

"Your late husband told you?"

"*He* told me," she said, and pointed to Dinsmore, then looked away immediately.

"Why did the defendant tell you such a thing, Mrs. Lane?"

"I don't know for certain. To torment me, I suppose. He was very fond of doing such things to make me suffer."

Ransom let that too sink into everyone's mind. He circled the open area between the witness box and the jurors' box, as though in thought. When he approached her again, Mrs. Lane had her hand up to the left side of her face.

"Mrs. Lane, would you tell the court how long your husband had himself known the defendant?"

"Since earlier that year. He first went to the dental office in January of that year, I believe." She looked pained now.

"Your late husband had a great many visits to the defendant in his dental capacity?"

"Yes." She looked distinctly frightened now. What was wrong with her? She'd been doing so well.

"Could you be a bit more precise, Mrs. Lane?"

"I believe he visited the defendant's office once a week for many months. He had extensive dental surgery done. I would say more than half of the teeth in his mouth were worked on."

"Mrs. Lane, is something bothering you?"

"No," she said hesitantly.

"Then why do you keep putting your hand up to your face? Is the light bothering your eyes?"

Even more hesitantly, "No."

"Then please take down your hand, so everyone can see you."

She did as he said. But immediately raised her left hand to her face again.

"I can't," she said in a timorous voice.

"Why not, Mrs. Lane?"

She looked as though she were about to burst into tears. What ever was wrong with her?

"Mrs. Lane?"

"I can't," she repeated in a half cry. "I can't. He's looking at me so. I can't."

Ransom spun around. Dinsmore sat like a statue. His face was hard as marble. But his eyes blazed like tiny kerosene flames. Damn it! He was trying to mesmerize her. Right here in the court. In front of everyone. Ransom had been standing between the judge's bench and the witness stand, as with all the other witnesses, so they could be seen by both jurors and spectators. Remembering how he had broken the spell at the pre-election dinner, he now blocked her view of Dinsmore.

"Is this better?" he asked.

"A little. Yes." She could hardly be heard.

"Mrs. Lane, please tell the court what the problem is."

"I . . . I . . . I can't," she stammered.

The man's daring amazed him. Right here in court. Well, he could be as daring too. He moved out of the way so that Dinsmore could see her clearly again.

"Mrs. Lane, I want you to look at the defendant and to tell the court precisely what is happening at this moment."

Her hand shot up to cover both eyes now.

"I can't. I can't look at him."

"Tell the courtroom what is happening."

"No. Please. Please don't make me. Stop him. Stop him!" she cried and jumped up from her seat, trying to get away. Ransom grabbed her and held her there.

"Tell them what is happening, Mrs. Lane. Tell them!" he demanded. "Tell them why you cannot look at the defendant." She was shaking in his grip now. He pulled her hand away from her eyes and held it, fixing his gaze at her only inches away. "Tell them."

She stared at him, dazed, lost, frightened.

"Tell them. Go on."

"He's . . . he's mesmerizing me."

"From where he sits?"

"Yes."

"Without doing anything? Just by looking?"

"Yes. Yes. God, yes!"

"Has he done this before? Mrs. Lane, has he?" Ransom had to shake her to get a response.

"Yes. He's done it before. He's done it a hundred times."

The words had scarcely escaped her, when she began to sway. Her trembling ceased, her eyelids fluttered, and she crumpled forward into Ransom's arms. She had fainted. In the complete and total pandemonium that ensued, he lifted her out of the witness box and carried her to the jurybox.

"Gentleman, you have just seen incontrovertible proof of this man's powers."

"Objection!" Applegate shouted, on his feet now, pounding the defense desk with his fist. "Objection, your honor. The witness could not look at my client because she was lying and she knew it. Because she was slandering him under oath. I demand that her testimony be stricken from the record and the witness be held in contempt of this court."

Dietz was gaveling like mad. The court clerk was shouting for order in the court.

Ransom ignored them all. Still holding Carrie Lane, he went to the same door she had used to enter the courtroom.

"I have smelling salts," someone said, opening the door for him. It was Isabelle Page, her face flushed to the hairline with color.

———————————•———————————

ONCE CARRIE LANE HAD BEEN CARRIED into a waiting room, set down on a divan and revived, Ransom felt angry with himself for having let the whole business go so far, even if it had seemed necessary at the time; even though it had been successful.

"How are you feeling?" he asked her.

"A bit light-headed."

"You were wonderful, spectacular," he told her, pressing her hand. "I'm really dreadfully sorry I did all that. But I had to, you must understand. You showed in a few minutes what a year's testimony by a hundred witnesses could never have shown. Please forgive me."

As she didn't respond, Isabelle said:

"He's right. Everyone was so shocked and frightened for you."

"Will I have to continue?" Carrie said. "I can't. I just can't. Not with him sitting there. Oh, James, you don't know what it was like. I could scarcely see you, scarcely hear you speak. There was a noise like a dozen locomotives. And my eyes hurt so much. Please don't ask me to continue."

"Don't think about it," he said. "Just rest. I have to talk to Judge Dietz for a minute. You'll be all right. Don't worry. You were the best witness so far. Really excellent." And truly effective, he thought, recalling how half the jurymen had shot up from their seats when Carrie Lane had fainted, how even dull-witted little Magoff had been shocked by the incident into evident concern, and Gus Tibbels had offered to help Ransom with her. That might have won him the case already.

She stared at him for a second, then sighed.

"Stay with her," Ransom instructed Isabelle. "And don't let anyone in here but me."

Mrs. Ingram was standing outside the door in the long hallway between the courtroom and the waiting chamber. Ransom blocked her way.

"I have to go in," Mrs. Ingram said, her eyes fairly bulging out of her head.

"Someone's in there already."

"I told you she oughn't have testified. I told her not to."

"She has testified. And she will continue to do so."

"After this? You're heartless."

"Not as heartless as Dinsmore. What about you, Mrs. Ingram? How would you like to tell the court about some of the amusements you provided for him?"

"I don't know what you're talking about."

"Amusements like cutting open your arm while he watched. Or becoming lost and hysterical not forty feet from your own home."

"Leave me be," she said.

"Then stop interfering. And keep away from Mrs. Lane. Here, and at home. Do you understand? Otherwise I'll have you up on that witness stand so fast your head will spin worse than Dinsmore made it do."

"You're as bad as he is," she said. "You're all heartless animals."

But she turned around and went into the courtroom again, and he followed. Court had been recessed in his absence. Dozens of people still milled about, standing and stretching by their seats, unwilling to wander away in case the session should be reconvened.

"Judge Dietz is in his chambers," Alvin Barker directed Ransom. "Applegate's in there too."

Standing outside of Dietz's door was a tall stranger with a shock of red hair and a freckled face. As Ransom approached, the stranger took his hand.

"Will Merrifield. Lincoln *Journal.* How is the lady?"

"Fine. Fine. She's much better now."

"Will she be able to continue testimony?"

"Don't know yet, Will. I'll let you know what happens. By the way, keep up the good work."

"This will be front page, Mr. Ransom. Center of the page."

"Fine. Fine."

Inside the judge's chambers, Applegate was leaning over Dietz's desk, white-faced with anger.

". . . worse than a carnival," Ransom heard as he entered. "Is this the kind of trial that's supportable?"

"Well, James," Dietz said, relieved to see him. "Come in. Take a seat. Why don't you take a seat too, Cal?"

Applegate sat down in a high-backed chair and sulked.

Ransom reported Mrs. Lane's recovery.

"She doesn't want to testify anymore. But I'm afraid I have more questions for her."

"I want no more swooning and fainting," Dietz said.

"Worse than a third-rate theatrical," Applegate put in.

"It's *your* client's fault!" Ransom replied.

"Bosh! She's a hysterical female."

"Well, James," Dietz interrupted. "Can you keep such things from happening again?"

"How?"

"You'd better find out how. Cal is right. It is a bit too theatrical."

"If Dinsmore weren't in the room while she testified . . ."

"Objection!" Applegate interrupted. "The accused has a right to be present during all testimony given. English Common Law."

"He's right, James."

"Can't he be faced away from her?"

"My client has a right to face all witnesses. He is not the problem, Mr. Ransom. It's your client who is."

"What about veils?" Dietz suggested.

"Perhaps. If they were thick enough."

"She doesn't have to see anything at all," Dietz said. "If an exhibit is to be identified by her, the veils can be lifted."

"Can we find thick enough veils?" Ransom asked.

"Ask Mrs. Brennan. She's out there somewhere. I saw her up in the balcony, keeping a running commentary on the proceedings with some other old hens."

Mrs. Brennan was found and called, and she was so pleased to be of help that she offered half her shop for Mrs. Lane's use.

"Those are my designs she's wearing today, you know," she added proudly. Evidently, much of her balcony conversation had been sartorial in nature.

As her shop was directly across the side-door street from the courthouse, it was only five minutes or so before she returned. Isabelle and Carrie seemed to be in intimate conversation when Ransom returned with the dressmaker. They looked up in surprise as Mrs. Brennan came in, went directly to her customer, and began pinning the veils upon the broad brim of the hat Carrie Lane wore.

"James? What is this?"

"Veils. Can you see anything?"

"Vaguely."

"Can you see me?"

"Only as a blur. James, am I going to have to testify again?" She lifted the veils from her face to look at him.

"I am going to, aren't I?"

"Just for a little while. We still haven't established your late husband's attitude and mental condition before his death. That has to be made absolutely clear, very strong. Others will support your testimony. Isabelle will, won't you?"

"Why, yes. Of course."

"You see, Carrie. The testimony has to continue. If only to establish that. It's most important."

She took it with doubt. "You think these veils will keep him away from me?"

"I don't know for sure. I think so. The minute you are certain they are not protecting you, I want you to say so. We'll stop the testimony immediately."

"What if they don't work?" she asked. "What then?"

"We'll worry about it when it happens. We'll figure out something. Carr might know, if anyone does."

The veils were tested again and again and found to be fairly vision-proof. Ransom instructed the bailiff that the witness was now ready, and the trial was put into session again.

When the spectators and jurors returned to their seats they were treated to the curious sight of a black-veiled lady in the witness box. Dietz had to gavel a great deal before the courtroom conversation died down.

"The witness," Dietz said, "has asked for visual protection. The decision of the court on this matter is that we will provide whatever means are rational and available and within the law to enable testimony to be given."

In the front row of the spectators' gallery, next to Will Merrifield, was a small bearded man whose head bobbed up from his lap to look at Mrs. Lane: the Lincoln *Journal*'s illustrator.

"You are still under oath, Mrs. Lane," Ransom began. "Are you comfortable."

"Yes." Her hands held on to the arms of the seat.

"Then we shall continue. Mrs. Lane, would you tell the jury when you were first mesmerized by the defendant, and under what conditions?"

"My late husband knew that I had been suffering from insomnia for some time. In the summer of 1897 it began to seriously affect my health. I soon began using a tincture of opium to bring on sleep. It was an effective remedy, but a dangerous one too. Henry noticed my growing distraction and absent-mindedness. In his concern for me, he mentioned the problem to the defendant. It was decided that I might be able to sleep without use of the drugs if I were mesmerized."

"When did this take place?"

"That first night that I met the defendant."

"Could you tell the court exactly what occurred that night?"

"After dinner I was placed in a large comfortable chair in the smaller parlor. The defendant sat close by on an ottoman. Henry sat to one side of me. The defendant then told me to rest, and he suggested that each limb of my body was feeling increasingly relaxed. He talked only for a short while, suggesting that I relax even more. I recall closing my eyes for an instant, and then opening them again upon his command. At that point, I suppose I was in the mesmeric trance, for he then began to test it. He said that although I was extremely relaxed, that I could still stand up and walk around. And I did so. Then he suggested that my right arm alone was so relaxed that I could not lift it. He then asked me to lift it. I tried to very hard, but did not succeed in getting it a half inch off the armrest."

"Did this frighten you, Mrs. Lane?"

"No. Not at all. Then he said I could lift the arm, and I found that I could again lift it very easily."

"You were completely awake and aware during this?"

"That time, yes. I later discovered that was only one type of trance state. That there are other, deeper trance states in which I seemed to sleep deeply, not being able to recall anything at all of the time that had passed. He used those deeper trances for questioning me and for finding out secret matters and for inducing suggestions I would not remember."

"Why did he do that, Mrs. Lane?"

"Because of the nature of the suggestions."

"What was the nature of the suggestions?"

"Things I would not ordinarily do."

"And you did those things?"

"Yes."

"Despite your wishes?"

"My wishes were as nothing to his will."

"What else do you recall of this first instance of mesmerism?"

"He said that I would be able to sleep very well that night without using the drug."

"And did you?"

"Yes. Very well. But only that night. Not the following one." She paused then went on again. "I asked Henry to have the defendant mesmerize me again."

"For what purpose, Mrs. Lane?"

"I thought that if the cure worked, I wanted it to be a more lasting cure; permanent, if possible."

"And was it permanent?"

"The defendant agreed to mesmerize me again, but he also said he did not know if the cure could ever be made permanent. He then mesmerized me and induced the sleep suggestion to last for a week. Later on, it was extended to a month. And then to three months."

"So you had to see him again, and to again submit yourself to mesmerism?"

"Yes. I did. I believe he told me a falsehood then. Especially from what I understand of cures that have been effected by this method. Usually the cures are life-lasting. The defendant was doing it gradually so that he would have to continue to mesmerize me."

"To complete his control over you?"

"Yes. As he had done with Henry."

"When did you become aware of his control over your late husband, Mrs. Lane? When the defendant told you?"

"No. Before that I had already gotten some intimations of it. It was about four months after we had met. It was at another dinner at which only Henry and I and the defendant were present. It was an ordinary enough meal, until I stepped out of the dining room into the kitchen. I believe I wanted to inspect the dessert—specially prepared for the occasion. When I returned with the dessert, Mr. Dinsmore began flirting with me. Naturally, I was mortified. But his speech became more outrageous, more daring every minute. When I lifted my face to see how Henry was dealing with this incivility, to make him stop it . . . well, it was very curious indeed. Henry seemed to not be hearing a word of it. He went on eating his cake and seemed content. I said his name, and he didn't hear me. It was at that point that the defendant became . . . well, I could no longer listen to him. I went over to Henry and shook him and said something to him to show how upset I was. He looked at me and smiled as though everything were fine. I became very frightened then and began to call for the servants. Mr. Dinsmore stopped me. He said nothing was amiss. He snapped his fingers twice, and suddenly Henry was as he had been before I had come back into the room. He asked me what I was doing standing by him, and why I looked so upset. I was completely bewildered, naturally, and I left the dining room."

"You were not mesmerized that evening?"

"Yes. I was. Shortly after I had gone to my room, Henry came to demand I rejoin his guest. We argued. Finally I did rejoin them. I was then forced by Henry to allow myself to be mesmerized again."

"By this time you were very frightened?"

"I don't know what I was. Angry. Confused."

"Did you ever discuss this occurrence with your late husband?"

"I attempted to several times. He seemed to not understand what I was talking about. We argued again. I said I did not wish to see the defendant ever again. Henry accused me of preferring the addiction of the drug to a cure by mesmerism. It was a horrible scene. The worst we ever had."

"I take it, Mrs. Lane, you and your late husband did not have a great many differences?"

"Until then, hardly any. After Mr. Dinsmore entered our lives, it happened all the time."

"In other words, Mrs. Lane, because of the direct intervention of the defendant your marriage suffered?"

"Yes. Oh, yes," she said sadly. "But I wouldn't have even minded that, if Henry hadn't died so horribly. We had already had a much finer marriage than most people. I was prepared to suffer some difficulties."

Out of respect for her grief, Ransom did not continue immediately, but instead went back to his desk, once more using the ruse of gathering and checking some notes. When he did return he said:

"Mrs. Lane, the court recognizes the tragic nature of your situation. But I'm afraid there are more questions we must ask regarding the last months of your husband's life. Do you think you can answer them?"

"Yes. I think so."

"Then I'll continue. You said that after the defendant had entered your life there were many differences between Mr. Lane and yourself. I take it not all of these centered upon Mr. Dinsmore. What did these other questions concern?"

"Most of them were because of his changed attitude toward business."

"Please elaborate."

"Until then we never discussed Henry's business. My advice had never been sought, and I'd always assumed he knew best. Then he became morose, which was very unusual. And when I naturally sought to discover the causes of his troubles, he began speaking for the first time of his concern for the businesses."

"When did this begin?"

"In the early fall of 1898. It worsened quickly, however. Henry became suspicious of his employees, then of his business associates, and later of everyone else, his friends, here and at Lincoln, the gardener, Mrs. Ingram, sometimes complete strangers. He was becoming persuaded that everyone was trying to steal from him, and to bring about his downfall."

She went on in great detail, with only small prods from Ransom. It was far quieter testimony than what had been given earlier in the day, not a quarter as sensational. But stronger, and more necessary, Ransom felt, if the case against Dinsmore were to come crashing down upon his head. Ransom stole a look at the defendant every now and again. Foiled in his attempt to mesmerize the witness, he sat back indifferently again, his chair propped against the spectators' gallery fence, a smile on his cupid's-bow lips, one knee over the other, inspecting his hands —those fine, white, well-kept hands. Ransom was about to turn back to the witness box, and Carrie Lane, when a sudden tiny glitter caught his eyes. Then another. What was it? Another one. From somewhere in the spectators' gallery downstairs? Or where. And yet another gleam. Tiny. Almost imperceptible. Must be the sunlight reflecting in off some object. But from where? From . . . and there it was again. It was refracting off Dinsmore's cuff. What the . . . ?

Carrie was speaking in a lower voice now, almost mumbling.

"Please speak up, Mrs. Lane," Ransom said.

But she continued murmuring. Now Ransom saw a flash of light pass across the veils over her face, directly at eye level. Then it happened again. Turning to catch it, he saw it came from Dinsmore. From his wrist. His cuffs.

"Mrs. Lane," Ransom said loudly. Then repeated himself.

"Yes," she answered slowly.

"Mrs. Lane, is there a light flashing in your eyes?"

Behind him, Ransom could hear the murmur of the spectators asking each other what was happening.

When Carrie did not answer, Ransom leaned across the witness-box railing and lifted the veils. She looked dazed. He grabbed her by the shoulders and shook her repeatedly, calling her name. She came to her senses a bit.

"Mrs. Lane, are you feeling well?"

Her eyes slowly focused. The dazed look disappeared, and was instantly changed by a fright so intense it scared even him. She gripped his arm so hard he felt her fingernails bite through his jacket cloth.

"It's happening again, James," she breathed out the words. "He's doing it again."

Spectators were getting to their feet now to get a better look. Carrie held on to him like a frightened child, whimpering.

"What's the matter, Mr. Ransom?" Dietz asked.

Ransom tried to get her off him. When he couldn't, he turned and shouted, "Bailiff! Seize the defendant!"

Now she did let go of him and fell back in the seat. Before the bailiff could move, Ransom shot forward and grabbed Dinsmore's hands.

"Your honor, gentlemen of the jury, look! A practical demonstration of mesmerism through a half dozen of the thickest of veils we could find." He twisted Dinsmore's wrist until the light from the window was caught, then said, "Now watch!" and he flashed the caught light by turning Dinsmore's wrist. Carrie Lane put her hand up to her eyes that second. Ransom did it once more, grappling with the defendant and ignoring Applegate's shouts that he let go.

"Even through the veils, your honor, the regular flashing was beginning to mesmerize the witness."

"Objection!" Applegate shouted now.

"You're loco," Dinsmore said, pulling his hand out of the grip.

"I demand to have this defendant manacled."

"And I object," Applegate put in.

Before either of them could go on, Dietz gaveled for order in the courtroom, and called both attorneys into conference at the bench. "Order in the court!" the bailiff shouted. Merrifield was scribbling on his pad. His illustrator was leaning over the court railing, sketching Dinsmore in his usual pose at the defense desk.

"My client will not be manacled," Applegate said. "Not only because he is a gentleman. But because there is no proof that he is in any respect dangerous. He's just sitting quietly."

"He's mesmerizing the witness. I showed you how."

"Quiet! Both of you. Now, listen carefully. I'm willing to go along with you, Mr. Ransom, but only so far. Mr. Applegate has reason when he says his client is not violent and ought not be bound or in any way restrained."

"If he is manacled, I'll go to the Supreme Court and ask for a mistrial," Applegate said, made bold by Dietz's words.

"I'll have no threats from you either, Mr. Applegate. One more such statement from you and I'll find you in contempt of this court. Now, Mr. Ransom. It is obvious that the veils are insufficient visual protection for your witness. I will adjourn this court. Get better protection for the lady by tomorrow."

Before either man could reply, Dietz turned away and gaveled.

"This session is adjourned until tomorrow at ten o'clock."

———————————●———————————

"SPECTACLES?" DIETZ ASKED.

"Tinted spectacles. Like those for people with cataracts on their eyes," Ransom replied. "You know, made of smoked glass. And if that isn't effective, then a screen made of it."

"That's what Carr said?"

"That's exactly what he said."

"And he's certain it will be effective?"

"No. Not certain. But it would shield her eyes. Even from any nonsense like flashing reflections off cuff links."

"It seems a great trouble to go to for one witness."

"It won't be only for one witness. We'll need it when Carr testifies too. He was under Dinsmore's control as deeply and longer than she was." Ransom pulled a sheet of paper out of his portfolio. "Here's the design for the shield. It would be built to clamp right onto two sides of the wooden bar of the witness box. A simple wooden frame, with the smoked glass inside. Note that you and I can see the witness clearly. But no one in front or to the left can."

"It looks awfully elaborate."

"Carr said isinglass could replace the smoked glass—so long as it's a very textured sheet. It would be far less costly, and less clear, but effective. As soon as I have your word, I'll go to the glazier."

"You believe all this mesmerism business, don't you, James?"

"Don't you? You've seen an example of it yourself."

"I know. But that was only one instance. A shocking one, I admit, but to lead a man to suicide . . . ?"

"You'll hear more about it in court tomorrow."

"Doubtless. All I can say is I'm damned happy there is a jury to decide. I don't know what I would conclude."

"But the man's a criminal! You've seen his record."

"I know. I know. But why does he just sit there? Why aren't they offering a defense? Applegate hasn't cross-examined a single witness. That's not like him."

"Applegate hasn't been his usual self since the case began. He's like a jack-in-the-box with his objections."

"And you think that's their only defense? I wouldn't underestimate Applegate, James. I've tried dozens of his cases. I've seen him at work. He's usually right out there. Whenever he's as quiet as this, I suspect he has something up his sleeve."

"What? A surprise witness? Dinsmore's mother, perhaps, to say what a good boy her son always was? No, your honor, I don't think Applegate has any case, which is why he's been so quiet. And why Dinsmore has suddenly begun to exercise control over witnesses. He knows I've got him. He's afraid."

The judge had no answer for that. Out in the hallway, a clock began to strike.

"Ten o'clock," Ransom counted. "Well?"

"Go ahead with your glass screen. Get the isinglass one. That way the taxpayers can't complain as badly. It'll be a sight. I know how much you like to entertain the gallery, James."

When he left the Dietz house, Ransom did not go to Henley, the glazier. Certain of getting the judge's approval, he had already ordered the isinglass screen. He ambled now to the corner of Lincoln Avenue, where he could already make out the *Journal*'s horse-drawn wagon, and people gathered to buy the special night edition. It was an unusually mild night for so early in

March. Spring already, he thought. How lovely spring would be
this year at Plum Creek. What a true spring it would be for him,
after so many years: a real rebirth, with new ambitions, new
goals. With Carrie.

How marvelous she was. Spirited too. And she trusted him.
Even after the second attempt at mesmerization she had agreed
to continue to testify. Especially after he had told her of Carr's
idea of the tinted glasses and the screen.

He knew she wanted to testify not only as a civic duty, but also
as a sort of public confession and expiation; an unburdening of
the sordid past so their future would be scrubbed clean of its
insidious influence.

To Ransom this was a crude, even a primitive gesture. Like
Oedipus putting out his own eyes with Jocasta's brooch. But it
was strangely fitting for Carrie Lane. Alongside her undeniable
refinement ran that darker current of the primitive. Look with
what gusto she had described those scenes with Dinsmore. How
detailed had been the baseness, the perversity of it all. As though
she had enjoyed it. Almost. Because she hadn't really enjoyed it:
she'd made that clear. Yet it spoke of a hidden passion in her that
might be easily enough unleashed once legal ties had been made,
and his own appetite had been realized. Ransom tried to think
what that would be like. All he could do was to recall the Widow
Rogers' hard, muscled thighs raised up for him. Carrie's would
be soft, downy, and smooth as a satin sheet. Ah, he would
. . . well, as soon as the trial was over, he'd ask her to marry him.
She expected it. Waiting, like him, for all this to be settled. He
stretched to see the lighted windows of her reading room on the
second floor. She must be still awake. Pity it was so late.

"Evening, Mr. Goff," Ransom said to the local barber, who
was purchasing a newspaper. Ransom did likewise, and was
pleased at once.

Merrifield said he would give it a large spread. He had. "Witness Veiled Against Mesmerist's Power," the headline marched
across the page. Directly beneath, in the center of the page, an
illustrator at Lincoln had caught the scene from the reporter's
words as a spectator might have seen it. Underneath that was a

smaller sketch of the defendant leaning back against the railing, one knee crossed. The face wasn't Dinsmore's, naturally, although tomorrow's edition and the syndicated editions that reached the bigger cities would show the original illustrations done in court, not yet delivered to the Lincoln printer. But it worked well. Especially the halo of light around the cuff links on each wrist.

Ransom waited until he'd gotten back to the Page Board and Hotel before reading the article. Merrifield fancied himself a prose stylist in the fashion of Howells, really quite readable. Besides which, it was logical. The most important aspects were clearly drawn, and the damage of the testimony against Dinsmore irrefutable. Naturally the article devoted a great deal of space to the various collapses and dramatic moments, but it was accurate—and quite strong.

Before turning down the gas lamp, he looked at the front-page illustrations again. They were effective. But compared to the tinted glasses and the isinglass screen that would be seen tomorrow, they weren't much at all.

It was remarkable, Ransom thought, how every obstacle he'd encountered so far, once overcome, proved an even greater asset. He was not building the case as he had planned it, but it was taking shape nevertheless, even if the form it was taking seemed a curious one. He had a split second of uncertainty, wondering if he did not know its ultimate form because it was completely out of his hands, and he only an aid to it, as everything else seemed to be. That was frightening. Like being part of some expanding historical event one found oneself in for no clear reason. The War Between the States had been that way: all noise and crisis and chaos and change with no explanations given that could be satisfactory. No. That was a foolish comparison. Yet Dinsmore was more than a man. Through his business decisions he affected many. Through his compelling personal influence he affected many more. Yes, more than a man, a sinister force. Who could say how large or small his influence might not turn out if he were not checked? He already had allies in the state house. They had not spoken up for him yet, and if Dinsmore were convicted, they never would. But their influence was felt everywhere: in Applegate's appointment as attorney for the defense, in Mason's protection, in Jeffries' editorials. For all Ransom knew, the outcome of this case might be part of a power struggle between two factions at the capitol itself. The lines of interest ran deeply on both sides. Dietz knew that, and was being extra cautious because he knew how closely they were all being watched by people up in Lincoln. Especially now that they could follow the case daily in their own newspaper.

It was too much to think of. It made his head swim to do so. He would have to make the best possible case, detailing carefully, overriding every obstacle, and ensure the conviction. That's what mattered. Nothing else.

———————————•———————————

THE ISINGLASS SCREEN was an even greater sensation than Carrie Lane's veils.

When Ransom arrived in the courtroom the next morning, he found the screen already in place. Mr. Henley, the glazier, was answering questions and trying to keep the crowd of onlookers from touching it. They parted to let Ransom through for his own inspection, but gathered even more tightly around it when he sat down in the witness chair to make certain it would obscure vision. Through the mica faults and marbelized surface, all the faces outside looked quite grotesque, like performers in a freak show. He would make certain to stand on the open side at all times, so Carrie could see him undistorted.

"Is this another protection against mesmeric powers, Mr. Ransom?" Will Merrifield asked, pen in hand, his Huck Finn hair as disordered as ever.

Outside the booth, the court bailiff was sending the onlookers to their seats. "Give me a minute more," someone said querulously. Ransom peeked over the screen and made out the bearded visage of the newspaper illustrator. Then only the reporter remained.

Merrifield repeated his question. Country-boy looks with city-slicker sharpness. Ransom decided he liked this young man.

"It is. The witness will also be wearing tinted spectacles."

"Is it true that on two occasions yesterday Mrs. Lane was mesmerized by the defendant?"

"Almost mesmerized," Ransom corrected. "We didn't want to let it happen, naturally." And as he went on, he found himself being interviewed by the reporter. He wondered whether Merrifield knew the reactions to the case in the capitol.

"It's sensational," the reporter said. "We've sold out every edition of yesterday's paper. Tomorrow's will do as well, because of the illustrations of this alone."

"But are people talking of it at Lincoln?"

"I suppose. I can't say. I'm here in Center City all the time."

"Yes, of course. But surely you're in contact by telegraph every day. Don't you get any reaction at all?"

Before Merrifield could answer, the bailiff was calling the session to order. Ransom and he agreed to talk again, during the recess.

Carrie Lane was called to the stand to continue her testimony. Her black garb had been changed to a plush brown velvet, but she wore the tinted spectacles as she entered the room and was led to the witness box, and this elicited much comment from the spectators' gallery. Once seated behind the screen, she reluctantly agreed the hindrance seemed complete, and gave him a brave smile.

Ransom explained the aids to the courtroom, looking to the defense table and the jurybox for their reactions. Applegate didn't hide his disgust; he faced away from the center of the room, looking out the high windows above the jurors. Dinsmore held his usual position, indifferent, slouching. He still appeared to be playing with his cuff links, but their reflections would never threaten the witness today. Gus Tibbels, the rancher turned farmer, seemed most fascinated with the screen, and declared audibly enough for Ransom to hear how he believed such protections was necessary. Ned Taylor, Tibbels' neighbor in the jurybox, nodded in agreement and glared at Dinsmore. Two jurors on his side, Ransom calculated.

Once Ransom was satisfied with the effectiveness of the screen, he continued the line of questioning from the day before. Carrie Lane gained confidence as she too recognized she was in no danger of being mesmerized, and she answered his questions succinctly and fully. By the time Dietz called for a lunch recess, Ransom had covered so much ground, so thoroughly and repetitively, he was certain the testimony could stand as it was.

After lunch, with the court back in session, Ransom found he only had a question or two more for her. Then he turned to the defense desk:

"Your witness, Mr. Applegate."

The other attorney did not hesitate for a moment. It was only when Ransom was seated at his own desk that he noticed a juror's seat was empty: he motioned over the bailiff and whispered to him.

"I know, sir. It's O'Shea. He was taken ill at lunchtime. He's expected back tomorrow morning. He'll be able to read the testimony he missed. That's what the scribe is for."

Ransom was about to complain, but he had to hush; the defense attorney was speaking.

"Mrs. Lane, I know you've had a trying day and a half upon this witness stand," Applegate began. "I'm afraid I must ask a few questions more. It is the right of the defendant that his counsel be able to go over any questions that might remain in the jurors' minds. You understand this, don't you?"

"I understand, yes."

"Good. One question that I myself found indistinctly explained was the nature of your connection to my client. Would you be so kind as to tell this court what the nature of the connection was?"

She was silent. Then: "I was completely dominated by the defendant."

"From the very beginning?"

"No. Only once he had secured control over me."

"I see. And this domination, as you call it, or control, how did it manifest itself?"

"I don't understand."

"Let me put it this way: did the defendant exercise this control, as you called it, while your husband was still alive?"

"Yes."

"And you say it was a complete control. Does this mean that you deferred to my client in all matters—dress, manners—or what exactly does it mean?"

"No. None of that. But I had to see him whenever he wanted. And when I was under his control he manipulated me to whatever end he chose."

"This all very well, my dear lady, but still quite indistinct. Can you give us an example?"

Before she could, Ransom caught Judge Dietz's eye: the old jurist was staring very hard at him, as though to say, "There! I told you Applegate would start in when he chose to."

"I can give you an example," Carrie finally said. "Henry's funeral services. I didn't wish to attend these at all. The defendant forced me to attend."

"By appealing to your sense of duty?"

She was silent.

"Well, that hardly seems a very terrible thing to do. Can you give us a further example, perhaps?"

"Yes. The pre-election dinner. Again, I did not wish to attend it, but Mr. Dinsmore forced me to."

"I must say again, Mrs. Lane, that hardly seems to be such a terrible thing to do. Isn't it possible that all the defendant wished was to attempt to divert you from your grief? There are enough people in this town who would desire very much to attend such grand affairs as his honor's dinners."

Laughter greeted this sally. Ransom wondered how long Applegate would play the fool. He seemed to hover over the witness box with his slim height, like a rattler about to strike.

"Well, mayn't that be so?" the attorney asked her.

"No," she replied. "Mr. Dinsmore knew as well as anyone

that if I attended that dinner, I would be snubbed. He specifically wished me to suffer from it."

"Snubbed? At one of Judge Dietz's dinners? But why?"

"There was talk about me. Scandal."

"I see," he said. "Talk of your connection with the defendant?"

"Yes."

"Would you tell the court the nature of this talk?"

"That Mr. Dinsmore and I were . . . well, that our relation was personal though not legal. So soon after Henry's death, and given Mr. Dinsmore's employment, this talk was fanned up, and was believed by a great many people. Including, Mr. Applegate, your own wife, who was one of the people who snubbed me that night."

The spectators enjoyed that dig; even the jurors laughed. But Applegate went on, unembarrassed.

"Wasn't my client living in your house at the time?"

"At which time?"

"At the time of the funeral?"

"No."

"Well, then, at the time of the political dinner?"

"Yes, he was."

"As a result of your invitation to do so, I take it? To be on hand in case you were needed for business matters?"

"That was exactly how he explained the move to me," she said. "Nevertheless, it was not at all by my invitation. Nor did I ever approve of it. Mr. Dinsmore arrived with his baggage one day and moved in. I was powerless to stop him. I may add we seldom, if ever, discussed business matters, before or after he moved into the house."

"Yet isn't it true that your signature was required for every contract or legal paper that passed through his hands?"

"That is true. I signed them when they were presented."

"What you are saying then, Mrs. Lane, is that my client was merely a boarder in your house?"

"More or less. Naturally, he did not pay rent. But he lived in his own rooms downstairs: a bedroom, the office."

"And it was this quite sensible arrangement that gave rise to such scandal?"

"Yes."

"And you never had a personal relation with my client?"

"I don't know what you mean by that."

"I mean that there was no personal affection between my client and yourself?"

"I had none for him, certainly. I despised him. I still do."

"But did my client feel affection for you, Mrs. Lane?"

"I cannot say what he felt."

"Did he ever express his affection."

"He said something about it, yes."

There was a murmur in the gallery. Ransom couldn't puzzle out what Applegate was up to—unless . . . just let him try, he'd see how quickly an attorney could object.

"As a matter of fact, Mrs. Lane," Applegate went on, "my client told you several times of his affection, and even expressed how deeply enamored he was of you, did he not?"

"He said that, yes. He said a great deal, however."

"And you rejected his advances?"

"I disbelieved his words."

"You find my client repulsive? Physically grotesque?"

"No."

"I'm glad to hear you admit that, Mrs. Lane. My own wife, who claims to have much taste in these matters, assures me Mr. Dinsmore is not unattractive to most women. She was incorrect, however, I take it, Mrs. Lane, in envying you for having such an attractive man for a lover?"

"She was incorrect if she thought us so, yes. I never loved him. For his own part, he never understood that love must be given and received freely, not wrested by force or controlled by cunning."

Bravo! Ransom wanted to shout out. Carrie was doing excellently well. Not only countering Applegate's insinuations, but at the same time damning his client better than she ever had before. Behind him, Ransom could hear approving words in snatches of conversation. Young Pulver was beaming. Evidently he shared

Mrs. Lane's ideas about love and marriage. Another likely juror for the prosecution, Ransom thought. Dinsmore was looking darkly down at his fine hands.

Applegate decided to change tactics. He then asked how often she had seen the defendant before her husband's death.

"A dozen times. Perhaps more," she answered.

"Always at your own home?"

"No. Not always."

"Where else did you meet?"

"At his office on Van Buren Avenue."

"Were you ever accompanied on these visits?"

"No."

"Was any other party present at these visits?"

"No."

"I suppose these comings and goings to Van Buren Avenue were noted?"

"I suppose so."

"You didn't by any chance have dental work done during these visits, did you, Mrs. Lane?"

She ignored the laughter. "No."

"What did occur there at those visits, Mrs. Lane?"

"I cannot say with any accuracy. I was usually mesmerized directly after my arrival. I cannot recall much of what occurred."

"Mesmerized, so you could not recall?"

"Yes."

"So anything at all might have occurred?"

And now Ransom did call out.

"Objection, your honor. The defense attorney is harassing the witness. She has already declared she does not remember what occurred during these visits."

"Objection sustained. Mr. Applegate, another line of inquiry, if you please."

"Very well," Applegate said. But his next line of questioning arrived right back at the same point. Once again Ransom objected. Once again Applegate was warned. Once again he led the witness by devious means back to his one and only question. Once again Ransom objected. It was annoying, irritating. But she was holding up wonderfully, not answering the question, always throwing something new in Applegate's way to not answer it, until Ransom objected at great length, pointing out the defense attorney's tactic, and demanding he be held out of order. Whereupon, Dietz began to reprove Applegate.

"Your honor," the attorney said, "I must insist on getting a clear answer on this matter."

"Why, Mr. Applegate?"

"Because I believe the indictment has been fabricated against my client, and that the witness is merely a pawn in the hands of the prosecution. Because, your honor, if the relations between my client and the witness were closer than we have so far been able to establish, and as I believe and hope to show this court, then my client's sudden employment as head of the various Lane businesses and his position in the Lane house will be understood not as a result of any hocus-pocus, as the prosecution claims, but merely as those of a man who naturally enough took deep and considerable interest in the affairs of the woman he loved."

"Objection!" Ransom shouted.

"Hold on, Mr. Ransom," Dietz said. "Mr. Applegate, you realize, don't you, that you are making a rather large and unsavory claim against the witness?"

"I'm claiming only what is so."

"Are you prepared to back this up, Mr. Applegate?"

"I am."

"By sworn testimony?"

"Yes. I have another witness."

"Then the present witness will leave the stand. Call in your witness, Mr. Applegate."

The courtroom had been seething during this last exchange of dialogue. Now it bubbled over in loud comment. People were standing and leaning over the edge of the upstairs gallery to get a better look as the court bailiff read the note Applegate handed him:

"The defense calls Mrs. Harriet Ingram."

Carrie left the stand, and had found a seat just behind Ransom when Mrs. Ingram strode forward and was sworn in.

"I do not require any visual protection," she said scornfully, when motioned over to the witness box. A chair was found for her nearby, and in full view of the judge, jury, and courtroom.

Was that Dinsmore humming to himself? He had a slight smile. The judge gaveled for order in the courtroom. Ransom leaned forward to be careful to catch every word. So this was the surprise witness. Damn! He ought to have called her first. But what was she going to say? What could she say?

Applegate all but swaggered as he approached the witness box. He asked if she were comfortable then dove right in:

"Mrs. Ingram, I believe you've been with the Lanes for some time, is that so?"

"Since 1890. Henry Lane hired me to be housekeeper right after my Alfred passed on."

"I suspect that in all this time you've become more than just an employee. More like a member of the family?"

"You might say that."

"And in such a position, Mrs. Ingram, I suppose you would be subject to knowledge that others might not know. Confidences and the like?"

"Mr. Lane always had great confidence in me." She was nervous, Ransom noted. She looked only at Applegate, and when he wasn't in view, at the baseboards of the jurybox.

"And Mrs. Lane too? Did she also have confidence in you?"

"Well . . . up to a point, yes."

"Could you tell the court, then, what the relations between Mr. and Mrs. Lane were like?"

"They were fine, I suppose. Up until about five years ago. It was then that Mrs. Lane got this idea that she wanted to have children."

"Yes. Go on, Mrs. Ingram."

"They'd been married awhile without having children, and Mrs. Lane thought it was about time. She began to fret about it and all. Thought she was to blame. She began to see doctors about it. Not here in Center City, but up at Lincoln, where she accompanied Mr. Lane several times a year."

"What were the results of these medical visits?"

"She was fine. She could conceive and bear dozens of children. Mr. Lane was the problem. One of the doctors she saw said he had treated Mr. Lane for some sort of infection years before. It was this doctor who told her Mr. Lane could not sire."

"How did Mrs. Lane receive this news?"

"She was disappointed, naturally. But she came to accept it as her part of life's misfortunes. Lord knows, she had everything else a woman could want."

"You said, Mrs. Ingram, that this changed their relations. Could you explain how?"

"I suppose he got wind of what she'd found out. It didn't change matters all that much. They were always kind and affectionate to each other, as far as I could see. But about that time, he kept complaining about how old he was getting. It was then that he had his sleeping quarters moved to the first floor."

"Before that he had shared a bedroom with Mrs. Lane?"

"No. He'd had his own room. They were connected, however."

"And this sudden change of sleeping places, what did that suggest to you, Mrs. Ingram?"

"It suggested that they weren't . . . well, you know, acting like man and wife any more."

"Did you notice any changes in either of them as a result?"

"No. Not for a while. But then Mrs. Lane began suffering from sleeplessness. Naturally, I'd heard old wives' tales on the subject and attributed it accordingly."

"To the cessation of personal relations?"

"Yes."

That was enough, Ransom decided. "Objection! your honor. The prosecution fails to see how this detailing of the witness's private life has relevance to the defendant or to the crimes charged against him."

"Mr. Applegate?" Dietz asked. "What is the purpose of this line of inquiry?"

Applegate went right to the judge's bench and spoke quietly so that no one else could hear. The courtroom was clearly titillated by these new revelations: whispers formed a concert behind

Ransom. He turned to see how Carrie was taking it. She had left the room. Thank God for that.

Dietz frowned, but said, "Objection denied, Mr. Ransom. Go on, Mr. Applegate."

What was Dietz doing? Ransom wondered.

"Mrs. Ingram, from the time that Mr. Lane moved his sleeping quarters on, were you aware that Mrs. Lane had personal relations with any other man."

"Objection!" Ransom shouted, standing; furious.

"Denied. Sit down, Mr. Ransom. The prosecution will have the opportunity to cross-examine the witness."

"But, your honor, what is the point of this questioning?"

"I'm afraid you'll have to find that out with the rest of us," Dietz said, ignoring Ransom's obvious anger.

"Thank you, your honor," Applegate said. "Now, Mrs. Ingram, do you recall my last question? Or shall I repeat it? During the last five years or so . . ."

"I remember," she cut in. "I would have to answer yes."

A great deal of murmuring now. Merrifield was scribbling furiously. The illustrator was sketching the new witness.

"While Mr. Lane was still alive?"

"Of that I'm not certain. But afterward, yes."

"Please explain."

"Well, naturally, I could only be sure of what I heard."

"*Inferred,* your honor," Ransom shouted. "If not actually witnessed, she could only have inferred. There's only so much that can be gotten from peeping and listening at keyholes."

Dietz gaveled, and reproved Ransom, telling him to sit down.

He sat down again; he had made his point. He'd maligned Mrs. Ingram. Something had to be done to keep her from completely ruining Carrie. What was she doing up there anyway? Defending Dinsmore? After all he had done to her? It was insane.

"Go on, Mrs. Ingram," Dietz said.

She was more than a little flustered now. "As I said, I only knew about her and him once he'd moved into the house. So I can't say what happened except for that."

"Her and him? Who, Mrs. Ingram?"

"Mrs. Lane and Mr. Dinsmore, of course."

Hubbub. Much gaveling. Order restored.

"The defendant, Mrs. Ingram?" Applegate asked. "Please point out the man to the court."

"He's right there," she said, pointing to Dinsmore.

That, Ransom knew, was done for maximum effect. It received all the talk and commotion it deserved. Why was Mrs. Ingram doing this? Because she hated Ransom so much? He couldn't believe it. She didn't seem to be mesmerized either. Or was she?

"In effect, your honor," Applegate was saying, "what this witness has declared completely contradicts what Mrs. Lane testified to this court under oath. I move that she be held in contempt of this court, and her testimony stricken from the record."

He ended in a flourish, but Ransom was already on his feet.

"Objection! The attorney for the defense is in error. The previous witness claimed she had never had a personal relation of affection with the defendant. She claimed nothing else."

"I don't see what affection has to do with this?" Applegate said.

"Check the scribe's records. It's all down in black and white."

"May I repeat my question to the counsel for the prosecution?" Applegate said. "What is the difference? Personal relations with or without affection are still the same thing."

"Nonsense, Mr. Applegate. The previous witness has testified under oath that she was completely dominated by the defendant. The prosecution was aware of this. And that the personal relations that you are so adamant in showing did exist—and in fact, that your client, the defendant, Mr. Frederick Dinsmore, did, on more than one occasion while Mr. Henry Lane was still alive, force Mrs. Lane into such relations by use of his mesmeric powers, the strength of which we have conclusively proven to this jury yesterday. That the prosecution has not charged your client with forcible rape as well as the other crimes he committed was done only from consideration of the previous witness's reputation. We will now add that charge."

Ransom was holding on to the edge of his desk, shaking with fury as he screamed out his last words. The noise from behind him was incredible. The judge was gaveling once more.

"Mr. Applegate," Dietz finally said. "Here is the record of Mrs. Lane's testimony. We find the counsel for the prosecution is correct. There is no contradiction in her testimony. Your motion to hold her in contempt is denied. Have you any further questions for this witness?"

"Only one more, your honor. Mrs. Ingram, the prosecution has brought up the question that Mrs. Lane was under the defendant's mesmeric control. Was there anything you overheard on those occasions of lovemaking that suggested such was the case?"

"Not at all. Both of them seemed quite involved."

"Did you ever have ocular proof of these allegations?" Applegate asked.

"Yes!" she said. "I did. It was ridiculous and perverse. Her all dressed up like an Emerson Street floozy, taking lewd poses. They were both laughing and drinking alcoholic beverages."

"I have no further questions, your honor."

"I do," Ransom said. He would wipe that smirk off her face.

"Mrs. Ingram, you have made many accusations on this witness stand today. But you don't seem to realize the nature of what you witnessed. My client contends she was under mesmeric control on all of these occasions, that she was forced to perform humiliating acts by the defendant because she refused to succumb to his desires of her own free will. You have said you witnessed or overheard one or more of these occasions. Given your position in the Lane house, almost one of the family, as Mr. Applegate pointed out, why did you never attempt to stop or interfere with these occasions which so offended you?"

"I . . . I . . . it was none of my business what they did."

"But it is now, Mrs. Ingram. All of a sudden. Why?"

She had no answer for that. Her eyes dropped.

"Isn't it true, Mrs. Ingram, that since your employer's return to Center City you two have argued considerably? And isn't it also true that at one point in these arguments she threatened to replace you?"

She still didn't answer.

"Isn't that true?"

"Yes."

"Isn't it also true that these arguments came about because you insisted on advising Mrs. Lane to not testify at this trial?"

"Yes."

"Are you aware, Mrs. Ingram, that attempting to influence a witness who has been subpoenaed is considered a felony in this state? A crime, Mrs. Ingram. You have just admitted to this crime."

She was frightened now. "I didn't know that. I just didn't want to see her all torn apart here in court. That was all. I wanted to save her name."

"To save her name, Mrs. Ingram? But you have just sat here for the last fifteen minutes and slandered her, ruined her name. How dare you say you were trying to save her name?"

Applegate objected to harassment now.

Mrs. Ingram was pale, her huge eyes beginning to brim over with tears, her large hands twisting about each other in her lap.

The judge reprimanded Ransom, who no longer cared about such matters. He had Harriet Ingram, now he would sweep the whole business clear.

"Mrs. Ingram, please tell the court if you ever knew of Mrs. Lane's being mesmerized by the defendant? Remember," he warned, "you are under oath, and don't want to add perjury to your other problems."

"Yes."

"On more than one occasion?"

"Yes."

"Even after Mr. Lane was dead?"

"Yes."

"So it is possible—I say, more than likely—that Mrs. Lane *was* mesmerized on those occasions you have just reported?"

"I don't know."

"Tell the court, Mrs. Ingram. Have *you* ever been mesmerized by the defendant?"

A long silence, then, "Yes. I think so."

"Think so? It is not such a vague matter, Mrs. Ingram. Were you mesmerized or weren't you?"

"Yes."

Good. Now for the clincher. "And, Mrs. Ingram, did you ever discover after you had been mesmerized by the defendant that you had performed actions you ordinarily would not have done?"

"Nothing like what she did. I'd never do anything so awful."

"Why, Mrs. Ingram. I do believe you are jealous you were never asked by the defendant to do such things. Is this true?"

She glared at him, tight-lipped, as though she would like to strike him dead.

"But you nevertheless did some extraordinary things, Mrs. Ingram, didn't you? Tell the court what these were?"

"I don't remember."

"Perhaps I might be able to refresh your memory, Mrs. Ingram. There was an incident one day in the kitchen, wasn't there . . . ?"

Before he could finish his words, the back doors of the courtroom were flung open with a great noise, and Nate Page was running down the center of the aisle, shouting Ransom's name.

The bailiff jumped to his feet, but Nate ran to the edge of the court railing, and Ransom got to him faster.

"Go home, boy," he said. "Can't you see I'm in the middle of a trial?"

"Ma sent for you. You have to come quick. Simon Carr's been shot."

———————————————— ● ————————————————

AMASA MURCOTT RAN OUT OF THE COURTROOM as soon as he heard Nate. It was another minute or two before Ransom could leave. The session was recessed; then adjourned, due to the late hour.

By the time Ransom reached the Page Board and Hotel there were people standing about in front of the house, on the lawn, up the steps, and crowding the overhung front porch. As he picked his way to get inside, he was stopped by someone: Floyd.

"We got the varmint," Floyd said. "Here he is."

"Who?"

"The varmint what shot old Carr."

A half dozen men pushed forward. Between two of them—twisted half down to his knees by the rope that bound his hands—was Millard.

"Him?"

"Yep. And we got the gun too." Floyd pulled out an object wrapped in his old checkered bandanna. "Didn't want to get no more fingerprints on it," he said. "Just in case."

Ransom looked on as Floyd opened the cloth. A six-shooter. Where the hell had Millard gotten it? And why had he shot Carr?

"James! James, are you out there," Mrs. Page called from the doorway.

"Right here."

"Well, come in, then. All you others get now. I said it, get!"

"Floyd, you and two other men bring Millard into the parlor. I want to talk to him. You others," he raised his voice, "go on home. You'll all find out soon enough."

Mrs. Page was taking a broom to them. Ransom, Millard, and the others managed to get inside before she locked the door.

The waiting-room door was shut. "Can I go in?" Ransom asked.

She didn't know. Ransom opened the door and saw Carr, with the doctor leaning over him.

"Amasa," he whispered.

The doctor turned, then shook his head.

"Is it bad?"

"Shoulder and arm. I got one out. But he's had a seizure. Another one will do him in."

Carr's sunken eyes fluttered open, then closed again.

"I'll call you in a minute, James," Murcott said. "Let me try to get this other shot out first."

Ransom closed the door and looked at his landlady.

"What happened, Mrs. Page?"

"I don't really know. There was a knock at the front door. I was in the kitchen. Mr. Carr was in the foyer. He said he'd see who it was. The next thing I knew, I heard two shots. I dropped my pastry and came out here." She pointed to the entry floor, where a brown blotch was still partially liquid on the parquet floor. "Carr was there and Millard was in the doorway, holding that gun. I must have cried out or something. It nearly took my breath away, seeing that right at my front door. Millard looked up. He threw the gun on the floor, then ran. I must have screamed then, 'cause people started running from across the street. Floyd stopped him. Knocked him half over. Then all the others came."

"But why would Millard shoot Simon Carr?" Ransom asked. "Never mind. I'll ask him myself. If he did do it."

"James, will he live?"

"Who knows? I don't understand any of it. This whole day has been one insanity after another. First Applegate, then Mrs. Ingram, now this. I just can't make heads or tails of any of it. I think I must be going mad."

"Calm down, James," she said with sudden concern. "I've never seen you like this before. Come with me to the larder. I have some brandy there. A bit of that will do you good."

Ransom let her lead him away from the foyer. He drank a tumblerful as she directed, but he felt no less perplexed or upset. He couldn't believe what had happened. It made no sense to him. But he had to be calmer to talk to Millard. So he had another tumbler of the liquor and sat down until he felt more composed.

"I won't need you, gentlemen," he told the men who were guarding the prisoner in the parlor. "Wait at the door. I'll call if I need you."

They left grumbling. Ransom closed the door behind them. Millard was on his knees murmuring half under his breath.

"Come on, Millard, get up. No one's going to hurt you."

The frightened face looked up.

"I didn't mean to do it, honest. Oh, Lord Jesus, wha' am I going to do now."

"Come on, Millard, stand up."

He lifted the cowering man. Sweat had broken out on the dark face.

"That's better," Ransom said.

"I didn't mean to do it."

"Where did you get that six-shooter?"

"Don' know, Mr. Ransom. Swear to the Lord."

"What were you doing here today?"

"Lord. Oh, Lord, help me now. I swear's I don' know. Honest. All I know I was down in the kitchen of the Lane Hotel visiting with Althea Robbins, when Mr. Dinsmore came in from the court, all laughing and suchlike. He called me over and told me to visit with him up in his room, while he was having his dinner. Well, up there he done complimented me for all what I said about him on the witness stand. How he fixed my leg up and all. He thanked me, real nice. Then I went away from there, down to the dry goods store, where I was to pick up some feed for the mule we got. Afore I got there, though, I was all of a sudden standing in the doorway here, with Miz Page yellin' fit to be tied. I looked down on the old Professor layin' on the floor all shot up and then that there six-shooter I never before seen in my life, I swear to Lord Jesus. Then I got so scared I jes' threw it away and ran for my life. What ain't worth nothin' now. You won't let them men hang me up on the telegraph pole, like they said they'd do, will you, Mr. Ransom? I didn't mean no harm to the old Professor. I swear it. He never done me no wrong."

Ransom quieted Millard, and went over what the man said, two and then three times. It always held up. He had been on his way to the grain store and had suddenly found himself in the doorway here, having shot Simon Carr. That had to have taken a half an hour at the least. A half hour he did not recall. A half hour gone from his life. By mesmeric trance?

Ransom made Millard repeat everything that had happened in the Lane Hotel. None of it meant anything, suggested anything at all until Millard, more desperate than ever, said, "You don't b'lieve me, I can see. But here's the silver dollar, Mr. Dinsmore gave me.''

He pulled a glittering, new Eagle out of his pants pocket.

Ransom took it from him, and inspected it.

"Did he give it to you right off?" Ransom asked. "Or did he hold it in his hand first?"

"He held it in his hand. And he sort of flipped it over, back and forth, to show me it was a real one. You know the way gam'lers does it."

"Like this?"

"Tha's right."

"And after you had inspected it, he gave it to you?"

Millard looked bewildered. "I don' rightly remember. I b'lieve he jes' put it in my pocket when I left."

Ransom flipped the coin back and forth in his hand, tilting it to catch the sunlight. No doubt about it, its regular, reflecting light was even stronger than the cuff links in the courtroom. He'd mesmerized Millard, given him the gun, and sent him to kill Simon Carr. A pretty way to thank a man for his testimony: a distant, effective way to kill a man.

There was a knock on the parlor door. Floyd looked in.

"Sorry to bother you. The sheriff is here."

"What's all this?" Eliot Timbs said, his high, whining voice preceding his great bulk into the room.

"Oh, Lord Jesus!" Millard said, and fell back on his knees.

Ransom took Timbs into the hallway and sketched in what had happened. From the uncomprehending look on the sheriff's face, he suspected very little of what he was saying was making an impression.

"What the hell did that nigger want to shoot Carr for?" Timbs finally said, confirming the impression: about half of what Ransom had said had sunk in. He tried to explain again.

"Where's the gun?" Timbs asked.

Ransom got it from the hall drawer and unwrapped it.

Timbs whistled. "That's a beauty!"

"Don't touch it. We'll have to dust it for fingerprints."

"That nigger must have stolen it to come shoot Carr."

"Nonsense! Dinsmore gave it to him."

"It belongs to Dinsmore? No, it don't. Look! There, in the wood are some initials. C. D. That's not Dinsmore. His name is Frederick. But it sure is a beauty. Look! Got four chambers still filled. Weren't taking no chances was he?"

What it came down to was that no matter what the reasons surrounding the shooting, Timbs insisted on having his prisoner and the revolver. Ransom argued this and even sent Nate with an explanatory note to Judge Dietz, but in the end he had to see Millard dragged back out of the parlor, still whimpering and praying; with Timbs acting self-important as he took his captive through the crowd still gathered around the house.

He'd just stepped back from the window, awaiting Nate's return and the judge's answer, when someone called his name. It was Isabelle Page, still dressed for outdoors.

"Mrs. Lane is here," she said. "Upstairs. In my room. After she heard about what Mrs. Ingram said in court, she didn't want to go home."

Ransom expected to see Carrie in tears. Instead, when she descended, she was very concerned about Simon Carr.

The three of them held a vigil in the downstairs parlor, directly across the foyer from Murcott's office. Augusta Page brought tea and joined them. No one spoke for a long time. Then a clock chimed five o'clock, and Mrs. Page said she had supper to see to. Isabelle joined her, and Carrie and Ransom were alone. He took her hand across the small table, but neither of them spoke.

Finally the doctor's door opened. Murcott came out, wiping his forehead. "Miss Page. Could you bring some fresh towels?"

"Can I see him?" Ransom asked, getting up.

"Might as well now as never," Murcott answered crossly.

"What do you mean?"

"The man's dying, James. Dying. Go on, Mrs. Lane. He's asked for you."

"James?" she asked.

"Go on. I'll be with you in a second."

She went inside and knelt beside the bed.

"Well, are you satisfied?" Murcott said. "I knew this trial business would be the death of Carr. I told you so."

"But not like this, you didn't."

"No. This was a surprise."

Ransom tried filling the doctor in on what had happened, but he was interrupted.

"He's still a dying man, James. No matter who did it, or how cleverly it was done. Don't you realize that?"

"Stop this arguing right now," Mrs. Page said, coming between them. "Amasa! Look at you! Your hands need washing."

Murcott glared at Ransom, then walked into the kitchen.

Carr was stretched out on the waiting-room sofa, his head propped up on a bolster, his tan vest and white shirt completely blotched with drying blood. His eyes were open, blood-shot, watery, but unafraid. His cheekbones and nose ridge stood out so far from the shrunken flesh of his face he looked like a dead man already. His lips moved slightly, and from this, Ransom gathered he was talking in a very weak voice to Carrie Lane who leaned over him.

Ransom went closer, kneeling beside her.

". . . need to thank me, my lady," Carr was saying. "We're free of him now, aren't we? Soon enough I'll be free of all of you."

She did not contradict him. But feeling Ransom at her back, she said, "Mr. Ransom is here. He would like to say something." Then she withdrew to sit on a nearby chair.

Ransom moved into her place.

"So that's your name, Ransom? I never did know that before," Carr said, almost cheerful now. "I used to know some other Ransoms once. Irish they were, I believe, though they lived in London."

"I was always told we came from Roscommon, near Galway Bay," Ransom said.

"Same family. They were from Roscommon too. Isn't that odd? The girl I courted was probably your cousin. May Ransom was her name. What beautiful red hair she had. Like her head was on fire." He stopped himself. "I've ruined my good suit, you see. The one I was going to wear to court. Ah, boy, you should have called me there before. I was well enough then, compared to now."

"Are you feeling so poorly?"

"No pain. It's all just ebbing out of me. The strangest sensation. Like a million tiny pinpricks, and after each one, nothing at all. That's what life is, isn't it? All these little irritations and annoyances you've grown so accustomed to, you only notice they were there when they no longer are there."

Ransom didn't know what to say to this, but he did want to somehow console or calm Carr. "Don't worry about the testimony. I'll read it to the court for you."

"Just so long as they hear it," Carr said. Then he was silent. His eyes fluttered closed, and Ransom had difficulty making out his breathing. Was he . . . ? Ransom put his ear to Carr's chest. Breathing. Perhaps he was sleeping. Then he spoke.

"Promise me this, Mr. Ransom. That you will read it as though you were I."

"I'll sure try to."

"Do more than try. Make certain he is convicted. You see, don't you, that he will not be stopped except if he dies. If he goes free, he will spread his malignancy throughout the land. He's young, he's still discovering his powers, still testing them out. He has a genius for the insidious. His power of invention when it comes to doing ill is unlimited. You must be very careful of him in the courtroom and out of it. I do not doubt that he has control of the minds of his very jailers and comes and goes as he wishes. He once told me his real wish was to control not just a single man or woman here and there, but an entire group, the larger the better. You understand, don't you, that his power would be boundless."

Carr stopped long enough for a rattling cough, then went on:

"You must never underestimate him. He seems to take advantage of everything that goes against him. He may not seem like much to you, but he uses that as a mask to cover his real ambitions. He has no value whatever for another's life—none at all. You know that already. Never forget it. He is not intelligent as you and I are, but he has the cunning of an animal of prey. He enters crevices in you that you never knew existed, and he opens them out into abysses. He hides in there like an animal. And like an animal he jumps for the throat. And he will be worse the more he thinks he is caught. I would never have been hurt if you hadn't cornered him. You have, you know. That's why he did this. When he's certain he can't escape, he'll stop at nothing. I've seen him trapped before. He's like an animal, vicious. Be careful. Do you hear?"

"I hear."

"Yes? Well that's all I want to say to you. Now I want to see my pretty Anglophile."

"Miss Page?" Ransom asked. "Isabelle!" he called out.

"Belle," Carr said. "There's our sweetheart."

"I'll get her," Ransom said.

"Mr. Ransom, one more thing."

He leaned over Carr again.

"Remember, Mr. Ransom, read my words not as you heard me say them to you out in the backyard in the rocking chair, but as I would say them in court. There is a power in truthful words that will never be denied. Read them as I would."

---------------●---------------

SIMON CARR DIED while everyone but Isabelle was at the dinner table. She stepped out of his room just as dessert was being served and motioned for Dr. Murcott to come. It was clear to all why.

In the interim, messages had arrived. Nate had returned from Judge Dietz, who wrote that he was going to the Williams Street Jail to talk to Millard. Carrie Lane's letter was from Mrs. Ingram, delivered by Oscar the gardener. The housekeeper apologized for all she had said in court and begged her mistress's forgiveness. Whether or not this was forthcoming, it was decided that Mrs. Lane would return home, accompanied by Isabelle, who would remain there for the night. Both women were upset about Simon Carr's passing; but quietly so. After dinner, Mrs. Page asked the rest of the boarders to go to the second-floor parlor, away from Carr's room. Ransom went up to his own office, and continued to work on notes connected with the case. Every moment, he expected Amasa Murcott to knock on his door, either to apologize or to continue their disagreement. But his friend never did, and late in the evening, Ransom heard Murcott's exhausted tread ascending the stairs, passing the door, and going into his own bedroom. The doctor was already out of the house the following morning when Ransom went down to breakfast: it was the day of his visit to Swedeville. Ransom couldn't help feeling irritated at his friend's disaffection coming on top of everything else.

Once court was in session, he had other matters to think of. He still had to interrogate Isabelle Page, Mrs. Brennan, the former manager of the Lane Hotel, and Noah Mason about Henry Lane's last months; his suspicions, his fears of bankruptcy, and his obviously changed attitudes toward life. These examinations passed without incident. Even Applegate kept some decorum: he only objected twice during this minor corroborative testimony.

Everyone had heard of Carr's death, and Ransom's announcement that he would read the old man's deposition was greeted by a churchlike quiet not common in the courtroom all that week. The late-morning sunlight streaked the tiled floors in a manner suggesting a cathedral window, the room was silent but for the infrequent scratches of the court scribe's pen nub. In this somber mood, he read Carr's deposition in as moving a fashion as though it were a funeral oration.

Only when he was done, and court recessed for the afternoon, did Ransom realize what a crowning indictment Carr's words had been—more effective now that he was dead than if he had faced Dinsmore. "Testimony from the Grave," the newspapers would probably call it in tomorrow's edition. It was that, but more too. It was also the last piece of evidence the prosecution would offer, and the most damaging to Dinsmore—sitting in the court as usual, indifferent, leaning against the back railing, as though he weren't even there.

Ransom found himself surprised, but by no means displeased by the final shape the case had found for itself. It now had all the crushing impact he had hoped for it. He could sense it in the haggard faces of the jurors, the curiously somber expressions in the spectators' gallery, even in Applegate, the defense attorney. So it was with complete confidence that Ransom answered Judge Dietz, that, yes, he was done; no, he had no more testimony to offer: yes, the prosecution rested.

That sense of confidence was not fully restored when he returned from the lunch recess to take his place at the prosecution desk. Several troubling elements had arisen since: matters he was not certain would work for or against Dinsmore's conviction.

The most troubling concerned the certain identification of the six-shooter Millard had used to shoot Carr. Dietz called Ransom into his chambers to show him the gun and to point out the initials engraved in the wooden handle, just as Timbs had done. Then he had shocked Ransom by telling him that C.D. stood for Carl Dietz, and that it was the judge's own gun, always kept oiled, cleaned, loaded, and ready to use in the bottom desk drawer of the judge's library. Millard must have gotten it there. It seemed obvious why this particular weapon had been selected by Dinsmore for the deed—to add insult to injury. But how Dinsmore had found out the gun's existence or its hiding place, the judge could not say—unless during the pre-election dinner, which seemed unlikely.

A second matter concerned the time elapsed between Millard's departure from the hotel and the shooting—an hour and a half. That much time made sense, if the man had to come steal the gun, then get over to the Page Board and Hotel and wait until Carr was within range. But it also gave rise to a frightening thought: Ransom had never thought a mesmeric trance could last so long.

Dietz still declared the shooting inadmissible evidence in the trial, and would not allow Ransom to even mention it when it came time for closing remarks. He did hint, however, that if Ransom chose to let the story somehow get to the reporter of the

Lincoln *Journal,* that he, the judge, would disapprove in his official capacity, but would be otherwise powerless.

That was only a minor consolation. No sooner had court been called into session when another disturbing matter arose. Ned Taylor, the bakery wagon driver, and one of the eleven remaining jurors, began to complain of severe stomach cramps as soon as he was seated. He nearly collapsed on his way out of the jurybox, and for the next half hour the court was aflutter with speculation until the bailiff returned to say the man had been sent home as he was in no condition to sit in court. That left only ten men on the jury, not all of them by any means convinced of Dinsmore's guilt. Taylor, like the railroad repairman, had been a strong juror for the prosecution, Ransom thought. If he did not return to sit, it would be difficult to impanel a juror who had both his belief and his knowledge of the case.

With this matter still unsettled, the court clerk called the court to order again, and Dietz returned to the bench, frowning at the newly depleted jury.

"Will the counsel for the defense begin?" the judge said.

Cal Applegate stood up at his desk, leaned over to say a word to Dinsmore, who then flashed a blue-eyed look at Ransom, but made no other response. Then the lawyer took his place at the witness stand, facing the jury.

Ransom had wondered before if Applegate were under Dinsmore's mesmeric control. It wasn't unlikely, given the defendant's reckless use of his powers. But if so, then Applegate was a special case. Instead of being numbed, deadened to what was going on about him, the counsel for the defense had from the first been intensely awake, aware, and attentive. Ransom had grumbled over the jury selection and over the many objections Applegate had made, but he had to admit that if he were sitting at the defense desk instead, he would have done the same for his client. No, instead of being dulled, Applegate seemed sharper than ever: subtle, scheming, cunning: more the way the dying Carr had said Dinsmore would be. Had the Mesmerist somehow transferred this entire part of himself onto the attorney? After all,

Dinsmore hadn't said more than two words so far in court. Was his attorney completely his tool? Or—more sinister still—had Dinsmore merely perceived this untapped streak in Applegate, and so badly needing it, tapped it? Mesmerism might not even have been necessary then. Especially given the obvious benefits to the attorney should he win his case for Dinsmore.

Whatever the cause, Applegate was to continue to amaze Ransom in the following two days of the trial by his extraordinary presentation of a defense case.

It began that afternoon with the attorney's speech to the court and the remaining ten jurors.

"Your honor, gentlemen of the jury, ladies and gentlemen. I don't pretend to be as good at speech-making as my colleague for the prosecution. I know my manner is rough and ready, not at all oratorical. For this, I beg your forgiveness in advance. I'm a Nebraska man. I didn't have the benefit of an eastern college education. I didn't study Cicero and Demosthenes and the other classical authors I'm certain my colleague knows pretty well by heart. So this isn't going to be a speech at all. More like a little heart-to-heart talk.

"Now, I've been here in the courtroom like all of you, and I've seen the prosecution talking to a lot of different people, and they answered questions and said a great many varied and confusing things in this witness box. Now, I don't want to say anything about these witnesses and how reliable their word is— or even imply it isn't reliable. I concede there were more than a goodly share of the fair sex up here this past week. So we even had us a sort of fashion show—most of the ladies being quite fair, even if we couldn't always see their faces. We know this from our colleague for the prosecution's refined taste in women. He's a bachelor, you must know. And so we've had a lot of fair ladies.

"Now, you men that are married and have ladies for mothers and daughters too, I don't want my colleague's using so much feminine testimony to be held against him. You know that the ladies are sometimes moody and given to different sorts of pets. They even sometimes embroider on the real facts a bit. I want you to forget all that. On this stand, these ladies were sworn in to be truthful and so we must presume they all were."

"As for the witnesses of the male gender, well, they were a little more varied. We had Dr. Murcott here, of course: a respected man in this town. But we also had a frightened minister from Van Buren Avenue, and a few more nigrahs, including one that's sitting in jail this minute. He's the man that shot the prosecutor's most elusive witness at this trial—I refer to the unfortunate Mr. Simon Carr, whom my colleague continued to promise us, but who managed to escape our acquaintance to, I sincerely hope, a better place than this.

"The testimony all these people gave over the past few days as I said before was voluminous. For myself I found it consistently interesting. Almost like one of those three-volume romantic novels my wife is always recommending I read, but which I never get around to. We heard stories of great courage, of superhuman powers over the mind and the body. We were treated to the spectacle of a bereaved widow in full panoply, who nevertheless was unable to face the man she was accusing. We made some interesting medical discoveries and a few salacious ones too. A couple of rumors were confirmed. Several others displaced. But for all this, I have to admit I simply could never come to grips with what my colleague for the prosecution was saying. Hocus-pocus it always came down to. A strange and powerful influence over other people. Mesmerism. Hypnothesia. Trances. Suicides. Suicide letters. Insomnia. Curious drugs. I don't know about you, but I found it all a little hard to take; just a little bit like one of those novels Mrs. Applegate tells me about at the breakfast table. Not a bit like a reason for convicting a perfectly dependable and hardworking man as Mr. Dinsmore is.

"So I'm not going to waste all of your time by calling folks to come up here and answer a lot of questions that no one can make sense out of anyway. No. I'm just going to talk to you about my client, the defendant, Mr. Frederick Dinsmore. About his life, his struggles, his work at progress already evident in Center City, and why it is he's been selected out by certain people to be on trial today in this courtroom.

"Mr. Dinsmore was born in 1859, the eleventh child of a family of fifteen children. Both parents had emigrated to this country during the potato famine in Ireland. They came looking for a better way of life. Instead, they found poverty, squalor, crime, and enforced labor. They lived in a few cheap and crumbling rooms off East Broadway in New York City. The elder Mr. Dinsmore labored on a farm in Brooklyn all day. The mother and her two eldest daughters were factory seamstresses. We've all read about the East Side of New York City in Frank Leslie's *Illustrated,* and we have all seen this terrible blight on the face of a great city graphically portrayed. But even illustrations cannot give a true sense of how it would be for a child who knew no other world than that of overcrowding, lawlessness, near starvation, and lewd commerce—even children were impressed into prostitution, you know. Not to mention gambling, disease, alcoholism, theft, street brawling, and dissolute behavior as a way of life.

"Of all the children, Frederick alone wished to know a better life. He'd somehow or other come by books that taught him a better one existed. He decided he would find that better life. The boy studied hard and won a scholarship to an uptown academy where the boys lived and boarded. And, although he was an excellent and diligent student there, he discovered that his poverty, his background, continually told against him. He could not realize his ambition of becoming a physician and returning to help those more afflicted than he. For after the academy, where was the money to be found that would pay for the extra schooling he needed? No scholarships were found to cover that. Imagine, if you can, this boy's disappointment when, after having come to see what he wished in life, he realized he could not have it. After the academy, he was forced to return to the slums of the East Side, forced to labor for his bread, crushed by the return to the squalor he'd hoped so desperately to escape."

That afternoon, Applegate went on to tell how the boy had managed to retain his high ethics and sense of aspiration during the many setbacks that had marked his early life. His words were very stirring, even gripping; Ransom was surprised both by his eloquence and, especially, by how subtly he twisted the facts to support his client. It was true that the boy had come from poverty and that he'd gone to a fine school afterward. But, as Ransom knew, he'd never completed his schooling: he'd been booted out in his thirteenth year for being an immoral influence on the other boys. The labor he'd returned to hadn't lasted long either. By the age of fifteen, he'd become a pimp for two of his own sisters. By seventeen a respected member of the Black Squad, a notorious Bowery gang that was hired by Tammany Hall to break up the opposition's political rallies. And that was only the least they did: beatings, burglaries, paid assassinations; name the crime, Dinsmore had been connected with it. But his defense counsel passed over this active period to the young Dinsmore's connection with Cornelius Van Wycke, one of the wealthiest and most socially prominent men in New York. The young man had been Van Wycke's protégé for several years—a fact that had astounded Ransom when he'd first encountered it in the police files he'd received. What had Dinsmore to offer a man like Van Wycke? Still, he'd ended up by robbing the old man of considerable valuables and had not been "forced out of his protector's grace and affection by nefarious enemies among Van Wycke's relatives" as Applegate assured the courtroom.

Ransom copied each misstatement as it was made, prepared to refute it by documented proof once the defense was done. Meanwhile, he had to sit quietly listening to Applegate's utter nonsense and absurd distortions. What did he hope to gain by it? Didn't he suspect that Ransom knew the facts and would release them soon enough, dispelling all he wished to achieve?

Applegate had said he wasn't going to make a speech. But what else could one call it? He'd begun shortly after two o'clock; it was four o'clock now, and he'd just gotten to Dinsmore's marriage, "an impulsive act of generosity on my client's part toward a love-stricken young girl who'd been coldly thrust from her paternal domicile," as Applegate put it. There hadn't been a sound from anyone in the room in an hour but the defense

counsel, who seemed to gain voice and rhetoric as he went on
with his verbal biography. Yet no one seemed bored. Well,
everyone liked a good yarn, as Dietz had said, and Applegate was
surely spinning them a tall one. He must know it himself. He was
no fool. But perhaps there was nothing else he could do? The
conspiracy theory with which he'd opened the trial was so much
cow manure. Perhaps this was a last-ditch maneuver by Applegate, who didn't have any more witnesses to call, who had no
case to build? The man had to be desperate. How else could one
account for the voluble lying he was engaged in at this very
moment?

Judge Dietz finally had had enough too: he called for an ad-
journment at four thirty, and wearily said that the defense would
continue, and hopefully complete its case, at the next session.

Neither Applegate nor Dinsmore seemed put off by this sarcasm. And the following morning at ten o'clock, Applegate took
up where he'd left off;

"It was at this crisis in my client's life," Applegate said, after
refreshing the court of his tale of woes from the previous afternoon, "that my client met Dr. Carr, whose deposition was read
to this court yesterday. The nature of Dr. Carr's words were both
shocking and offensive to my client, as he had nothing but the
greatest esteem for the man who did so much to help him in his
lifelong ambition to be of medical service to the world. We
cannot doubt that Carr's words were his own. To do so would
be to impugn the counsel for the prosecution, and we have no
intention of doing that. Yet my client and I feel strongly that
those words read to the court were the eccentric wanderings of
an unfulfilled, bitter, and invalid old man. We do not doubt that,
face to face with the defendant, Mr. Carr's words would have
been quite different."

Applegate followed this attack with a fanciful description of
how Carr had been begged by the eager Dinsmore to teach him
dental surgery. How successful a student and later a practitioner
of the dental arts Dinsmore had become. How his concern for
his patients' welfare had led him to adopt the newest methods in
his work: vulcanite settings for dentures, machine drilling, use of

silver amalgam alloy to fill the caried teeth. Then he went on to say how Dinsmore had shown his gratitude to Carr by keeping the old man on as an aide and mentor when Carr could no longer work, and how he had later unstintingly supported the older man when he could no longer do even menial chores. Other manifest works of his magnanimity were mentioned, and the "ungrudging nursing of the increasingly mentally deranged Mrs. Dinsmore" was painted in glowing words. Dinsmore's many beneficences were pointed out. The love of his neighbors and former patients evoked. The defendant's concern for Mrs. Lane—once her husband, "the defendant's close friend who had so tragically passed on"—was limned. As was Dinsmore's "sacrifice of a lucrative profession" to aid the woman, by "taking the burden of so much labor and thought from her onto himself."

This hypocrisy was astounding to Ransom. He was glad Mrs. Lane was not present to hear how well cared for she'd been. It was enough to make one ill. Even Dietz must have become disgusted by it—he interrupted Applegate in mid-sentence in order to call for an early recess.

An hour later Ransom was removing his outerwear, getting ready for the afternoon session, when Barker, the court clerk, called him into the judge's chambers.

"We lost another juror," Dietz said bluntly.

"What? Who? When?"

"You're beginning to sound like one of those damned reporters. All they know is questions. Well, it's Gus Tibbels, one of the farmers from out of town. He went out of the jury room for a breath of fresh air and he never came back."

Taylor had returned that morning. "That means we're back down to ten jurors. This is ridiculous, Carl," Ransom protested, remembering Tibbels' solicitude when Carrie had collapsed. "I've never seen a trial where so many jurors have become sick. Is someone out looking for Tibbels?"

"Well, Mrs. Brennan saw him riding out of town after the morning session. She said he was riding westward, in the direction of his farm. If he isn't there, I can't go scouring the county looking for him, you know."

"I can't understand it. This trial has been nothing but a series of catastrophes so far."

"And Taylor was complaining of dizziness all morning," Dietz said. "We may not have him back tomorrow."

"Dizziness?"

"That's what he said. Spots in front of his eyes. A ringing in his ears. The doctor who examined him could find no cause for it. But he doesn't feel very well."

The word dizziness hit Ransom like a rock in the chest. He asked Dietz to repeat the symptoms Taylor had complained of. Then he said:

"It's Dinsmore. He's doing it. That's exactly how Carrie Lane said she felt when he was trying to mesmerize her. The spots. The noise in her ears."

"Could be," Dietz said, unconvinced.

"He's trying to mesmerize the jury! That's what all this bosh is about that Applegate is doing. He needs time to do it—and Applegate is giving him time. He'll stay up there lying through his teeth until Dinsmore has mesmerized the whole lot of them!"

"Careful now, James. Jury-tampering is a serious offense. Especially since neither Dinsmore nor Applegate has admitted he used it, or even knew how to use it. You heard them."

"I heard a lot of rubbish. And so did you. It's all lies and distortions. I'm prepared to set it straight with the facts when I begin my summary. Don't worry about proving he mesmerized anyone. *I* was mesmerized by him. If you want evidence, I'll get up on the witness stand and testify to it."

"I don't think that will be required."

"All three of those jurors were for the prosecution. I would swear to it," Ransom said. "It's tampering, all right."

"You're going to need more than three jurors to convict him. And no one will know for certain until they decide who's for or who's against it. No, James. I can't accept your charge."

"You're going to let him get away with it?"

"No. I'm going to impanel more jurors. From men who have been in court so far. There's enough of them. Before this afternoon's session meets, I'm going to hold a voir dire, impaneling

directly out of the spectators' seats. I'll impanel two reserve
jurors too. Now get Applegate in here. I'll need both of you.
And call in Barker again."

"That won't stop Dinsmore."

"What do you want? To put him behind that glass contraption?"

"That's the only way I can be certain he isn't tampering."

"Applegate will raise hell about it. No, James. Not yet. Let me
do this. It will make him rethink it all, knowing that for every
juror lost two will be found. And when the session begins, if you
see him doing anything in the least bit suspicious, or if I do—
for I'll be looking as hard as you—I'll slap him right behind it.
But not until then."

The afternoon session was spent repeating the voir dire for
four new jurors. For Ransom it was a return to the first days of
the trial, and more than dispiriting. It was after five o'clock
before they were done.

Ransom was able to watch Dinsmore closely during the next
morning's session. But if he was doing something, it couldn't be
seen. Applegate went on talking, this time coming closer to date,
telling of his client's steps toward progress, his scrupulous business
dealings, and the respect and admiration he had gained in
the town and county through them.

Dinsmore did look at the jury from time to time. But not
regularly, and with only a mild sort of interest. He didn't flash
his cuff links or buttons or do anything else that might be taken
as a manner of seeking to mesmerize them. He did hum in a low
voice every once in a while, for minutes at a time. No, it wasn't
so much humming as the purring of a large cat when it is content:
an almost mechanical half-heard sound to Ransom, and more
than likely impossible to hear at the distance the jury was from
the defense desk.

Despite this, they had lost another juror that morning, a piece
of bad luck unbelievable to Ransom—Caldwin Bain, the teller at
the Mason Centennial Bank, the youngest of the twelve, and,
Ransom was certain, a prosecution-influenced juror. Bain had
been thrown from his horse the evening before and was in bed,

only slightly injured, but not well enough to get up. So a reserve juror was already in use.

Applegate finally began to wind up his case. He did so by rehashing his opening statement of a week and more before, going back to the still unidentified conspiracy against his client, and adding to it a great deal of blather he'd lifted verbatim from Joseph Jeffries' editorials about the "need for progress and the inexorable drive toward modernity by those farsighted enough to feel there is still room for the pioneering spirit in this country."

Judge Dietz thanked the defense counsel for what he termed "a lucidly obtuse and inspirational talk," an irony that was not lost on Applegate—or many spectators, who derived much mirth from it. Then recess was called.

In the afternoon session, it was Ransom's turn to summarize. He did so by rebutting Applegate's "fantastic account" of Dinsmore's life. Every distortion was repeated, rebutted, and the appertaining document of proof given to the jury and judge to see for themselves. This accomplished, Ransom moved into the real summary of the case. He methodically reviewed what had been said by each witness, and then proved by simple equation how Dinsmore had done what they had said he'd done. And how two people—and possibly three now, he hinted—were dead as a result of the defendant's ruthless rise to power.

When he sat down, Ransom knew he had done well. For the last two hours he had held the jurors in the grip of his words: he had seen their attention, almost felt it. He had done what Simon Carr had advised him to do—spoken the truth as clearly, as forcefully as he knew how, putting his trust in the fact that the words themselves would have the power he so much wanted for them.

He was pleased with himself, but quite exhausted, still relaxing before going home in the small side chamber given him as an office during the course of the trial, when Barker, the court clerk, came in with a sealed envelope. Ransom's name was written on the outside in a hand not known to him. Nor was the sender's name evident. But before he could ask Barker about it, the clerk was gone.

Ransom tore it open and read:

> *The better man has won, it seems. Come to Suite 100 at the Lane Hotel tonight after 8 P.M. and I will personally concede to you.*

The stationery was that of the Lane Hotel. The message was signed FREDERICK L. DINSMORE.

———————•———————

RANSOM'S FIRST SURPRISE was that Applegate was not present.

From the moment he had gotten Dinsmore's note, he'd been filled with excitement. He had conquered, triumphed. The defendant was in his hands, this farce of a trial over—and with it the new life Ransom wished for begun. With this case successfully prosecuted, his future might go almost anywhere—to a judgeship, to Lincoln, possibly to the State House or even the halls of Congress in the District of Columbia. Yes, it might go that far. With Carrie Lane beside him it would almost have to. He would return to his place of humiliation and defeat some twenty years later with wealth, position, and a drive to be a respected and well-known lawmaker. An astounding return in a city where such comebacks were uncommon.

By the time he sat down to dinner at the Page Board and Hotel, however, all these hopes had been put aside. In their place were fears and suspicions. What if this weren't a concession, but a trap instead? Ransom's rebuttal of Applegate's spurious defense narration had been completely effective. Dinsmore knew it. Applegate knew it. They were running scared now, stampeding. And Dinsmore was going to make one last attempt to save himself. But how? By attempting to take Ransom's life? He wouldn't dare. By trying to mesmerize him? To what end? To make him stop the trial? It was too late for that now: the prosecution had rested; after tomorrow morning's defense summary the case would go to the jury—that ill-starred group of men—who would then decide all.

That was all the more reason for not going to accept the concession. Why not just let it go—not take up Dinsmore's invitation, and tomorrow morning watch him squirm as the jurors marched somberly back into the courtroom, their deliberations quickly done, their verdict visible on their faces?

By the end of the meal, Ransom had decided not to go to the Lane Hotel. His sulky mood changed to one of high spirits as he joked with his landlady and the other boarders and even tried to draw out the doctor, who also seemed to be in a serious mood.

But right after dinner, he found himself upstairs in his rooms, changing into the same suit he had worn in the courtroom—his professional garb, almost his insignia of business to be done.

He would go to see Dinsmore after all, he said to himself, fitting on the starched new collar. See him. Accept his concession. And furthermore convince Dinsmore's attorney to have the defendant change his plea. It would be a difficult thing for Dinsmore to do, but worth it in the end. For Ransom had decided to barter the man's life for an admission of guilt. If Dinsmore confessed, Ransom would lessen the charges, eliminating the death penalty. He would show the quality of mercy; he'd let Dinsmore see how civilized men punished. A wild animal he might be, but he would nevertheless see how a man triumphed: with generosity as well as firmness. And above all, with respect for the value of human life.

Buoyed up by these thoughts, Ransom left the house without disclosing his destination to anyone. He felt proud, like a missionary on his way to some great conversion.

This fine feeling remained with him until he reached the desk in the lobby of the Lane Hotel. A man he'd never seen before was behind the carved marble. He looked up at Ransom with black little eyes and a small black mustache cut as evenly as a whiskbrush.

"I'm expected by Mr. Applegate."

The whiskbrush moved as though the man were talking, but Ransom didn't hear a word.

"I beg your pardon."

"I said we have no Applegate in the hotel that I know of."

"I'm to see him after eight. It says so here," and Ransom showed the letterhead. "Room One hundred."

"Mr. Dinsmore, you must mean," the clerk said, with some annoyance. "I'll take you to his suite."

He came from behind the counter and led Ransom to a large pneumatic lift, half hidden from view by a glass door, with a protecting bronze gate. Neither the opaquely milky glass nor the gate seemed functional, they were so ornamentally conceived of twisting, curving lines approximating vines, flowers, and pieces of fruit—a pattern repeated elsewhere in the lobby. The lift— one of three—was yet another innovation in Center City, and part of Dinsmore's revamping of the Lane Hotel.

The ascent to the second floor was swift and silent. Once there, the clerk opened the glass door and outer gate, remained where he was—but gestured for Ransom to get out.

"The last doorway to your left," he directed.

The gates clanged shut, the opaque glass door closed, and the lift disappeared from sight.

Someone was sleeping in a chair outside the door to Suite 100: a guard, one of Timbs' deputies. Carr hadn't been so wrong, after all. Dinsmore probably did come and go at will.

Ransom shook the man awake and gruffly warned him to stay awake. The frightened deputy jumped up and knocked at the door. Ransom wondered meanwhile how many other doors led from the suite out onto the hall, and whether they were kept locked or guarded.

Before he could ask, a voice within called for him to enter. The guard closed the door behind him but did not lock it.

Ransom's second surprise was Dinsmore himself. He certainly didn't look or act like a man who had in effect put his life into the hands of his executioner.

Dinsmore sat half across a ruby-colored love seat, wiping his cupid's-bow lips with an expensive-looking embroidered napkin. The jacket to his pin-striped gray suit was open, his shot silk vest shimmering in the gaslight of the chandeliers. One elegantly booted foot rested on a matching ruby red ottoman. Before him, a table was littered with a vast array of china, stemware, and crockery. Sitting in a stuffed chair pulled up to one side of the table was a long-legged young lady Ransom did not know. Her golden hair was twisted into a small bun with a long fall behind.

"Ah, Mr. Ransom!" Dinsmore said cheerily. "How clever of you to arrive in time for dessert. I've been told there's pecan pie tonight. That ought to please a Georgia-bred man like yourself."

"Where's Applegate?" Ransom asked, not moving from the spot.

"Why, at home, I suppose. I don't keep tabs on him. Tillie, clear up all this," he said to the woman, "and bring up coffee, dessert, and some Armagnac. You will join me in an after-dinner cordial, Mr. Ransom?"

"I thought Applegate would be here," Ransom said. "What's all this about, then?"

"Exactly what I wrote to you. But surely you couldn't expect Applegate to be here too. The man would have a conniption if he knew what I'd written to you."

"You mean he doesn't know?"

"Of course not. This is between you and me. He'd never approve. Be reasonable, now. Come and sit down." He stood up, and gestured for Ransom to sit down in the chair Tillie had vacated.

Ransom didn't like any of this, especially not Dinsmore's attitude—that of a magnanimous host. None of this was how he had pictured their meeting. He'd seen it somewhat more formal, with documents and great reserve on all sides—somewhat like a painting he'd once seen of Lee's surrender to Grant at Appomattox. Not as a social engagement with dessert, cordials, and a prostitute on each side.

"Come now," Dinsmore insisted. "You're not going away, are you, because Applegate isn't here?"

"I came here because of this," Ransom said, showing the note.

"In good time. In good time. I don't see why we can't take advantage of some comforts, do you? Let's do this in as congenial a manner as possible. After all, you want to deprive me of all this soon enough, don't you? That's it. Let me take your hat and coat. We'll think of this as the sugar coating put on a bitter pill to make it easier to take."

Ransom sat down and looked about him. This suite had been done wonderfully, like one of the best homes in town: fine furnishings, mirrors, paintings, *objets d'art,* everything very rich, very fine-looking.

"It's the Senatorial Suite," Dinsmore explained. "It has a dining room too. But I prefer not to use it except for larger affairs."

Tillie returned with a smaller but equally laden table on wheels, like a tea caddy. She served them and was about to take a seat next to Dinsmore on the love seat, but he asked her to leave them alone.

Then he lifted a finely cut glass she'd filled for each of them.

"To you, Mr. Ransom. Your speech this afternoon was utterly persuasive. Your entire handling of this trial pretty near perfect. Your investigation thorough, your presentation a model of logic and symmetry."

Ransom was bewildered. He hadn't come here to be praised. He did not touch the drink.

"Come now. All you need do is take a sip to show you don't decline my admiration."

Ransom took a sip, then turned to the coffee. He would need it to remain sharp and alert.

"I really do admire your professional skill. Right from the beginning of our acquaintance I've wanted you on my side. I knew then you were the best of them all. A shoddy lot in my opinion. But not you. It's been a great disappointment to me that you've been so misguided as to be against me instead of with me."

Ransom let this pass unremarked. But he did say, "It's known that I'm here tonight, you know."

"I'm certain it's known. You're a clever, cautious fellow. I don't doubt that it's known."

"Not the reason, however," Ransom quickly added.

"Naturally not. Your high professional ethics would forbid that. Yes, that's what I admire in you, Ransom, your holding to the line even when it's most difficult. Watching you these past weeks has been like watching a wire-walker in the circus. Will he fall? Won't he? But you cling on through one thing after another. Tenacious. I admire that." He lifted his glass and drank again.

"You did your best to make me fall."

"Without the risk, where's the sense of accomplishment? I couldn't let you by so easily, could I? I had to make your feat all the more glorious for overcoming such obstacles."

"Then you admit you tried to mesmerize the jurors?"

"Admit? I admit nothing."

"Then we have no reason to talk," Ransom said, putting his cup down and rising.

"Yes. We do. Do sit down. Try for a moment not to be an attorney with me. I'll deny to the hilt all your questions and statements. You know I will. Allow me to do this thing my way."

Ransom sat down again, but didn't touch his cup.

"Aren't you going to try the pie?" Dinsmore asked. When Ransom didn't answer, he went on. "You know, while I do truly admire you, there are some things you don't know about me. Wouldn't you like to have some of those questions answered? There must be some areas your so careful documentation couldn't fill in? Haven't you ever wanted to be certain about them? I thought I knew you well enough to be certain you would not rest until every shred of evidence was explained. I felt an aesthetic sense in you, a need for completeness. I'm not wrong, am I?"

"What areas?" Ransom asked.

"So! I'm not wrong. Good. Even though you will not have everything exactly your way, still I will be useful to you."

"What areas?"

"In time. In time. Another little matter first. Since you are so open to criticism—an admirable trait, by the way, in my opinion —there is another minor matter."

What sort of nonsense was this? Ransom thought. Like play-acting. Dinsmore totally at home in some comedy of manners, where people gossiped at the tea table.

"It concerns your philosophy," Dinsmore said.

"My philosophy?"

"Yes. That's what I would call it. The way you think of life. I've had ample opportunity to watch you all these days. You're a consistent man, and obviously your philosophy is the underpinning of that consistency. But I'm afraid it's really rather an immature sort. Perhaps even distorted. The philosophy of a far younger man. Untouched, so to speak, by life and its unfortunate realities."

"What are you talking about?" Ransom said. This was the last thing he had had in mind for this evening.

"When we are children," Dinsmore said, eager to explain, "we think of this as good, and that as bad. What we mean, of course, is that this is pleasant and that is not. To be given a chocolate is pleasant, thus good. To be given a spanking is considerably unpleasant, and so bad. Later on, as we grow and develop, we learn that life is not quite so simple. The chocolate may be the last of two dozen, and may cause an upset stomach. So is the good turned to bad. And, as schoolmasters are quick enough to point out, a spanking in youth may instill virtue that appears only in manhood. Thus the bad becomes good."

"Go on," Ransom said.

"These are simple analogies, of course. But as we go on in life we discover further subtleties. The spanking may after all be bad. It may, besides instilling a taste for virtue in a man, also instill a taste for chastisement of the flesh for pleasure. The British have discovered this curious phenomenon. I trust you've heard of such methods of gratification?"

"Yes."

"Well, now, is it good, or bad? Or neither? You see, Ransom, there are subtleties to such things. Contradictions that cannot be settled once and for all to be truth. Most matters in life are a balance—now better, now worse, now neither of the two."

"If this is meant to be a philosophical defense of the way you've used people . . . ?"

"Wait! Let me continue. As are matters not so easily claimed to be either good or bad, neither are people. They are generally a mixture of the two."

"But they incline," Ransom interrupted. "And ought to incline to the good."

"Whatever good is," Dinsmore said delightedly, holding his hands aloft as though they held the answer. "You see, Ransom, that is where you disappoint me. You sound to me like that foolish Sydney of the Baptists. He goes to the Bible for an answer to what ought to be and what ought not to be. It's foolish. But I wonder if it isn't better than your way. In your thoughts, only *you* have the final word. You're like the child repeating over and over that the spanking is bad and the chocolate good. It's absurd, it's ridiculous. You're a grown man. You ought to know better."

Ransom laughed. "That's my problem, if it is one. Don't concern yourself about it."

"Then you do think that way? For example, you think of me as all bad. Bad through and through. Come on, admit it."

"The evidence doesn't look terribly good."

"Your evidence doesn't. But there's other evidence. What about all of this as evidence?" He waved his hand about the room. "The hotel. The businesses. Henry Lane was never able to come close to as much as I have done. He couldn't have in ten lives. He didn't know how. He didn't know how a hotel ought to look, or what services it ought to supply. He scarcely looked into mechanical improvements for his enterprises. At the rate I'm going, in five years Lane Industries will be a force to reckon with. It will be a real empire. People will speak of it in the same breath with Riis and Morgan and Rockefeller. And it will revitalize Center City in ways no one could suspect. The way Pittsburgh became a city because of the steel industry—or Buffalo, once the Erie Canal got going. This will become the agricultural center of the country. Right now it's claptrap to call this town 'the second capital of Nebraska.' But in a few years' time it will surpass Lincoln and Omaha and probably even St. Louis. Now, is that good or bad?"

Ransom didn't answer.

"You see, that isn't so easy a question, is it? If I were already considered the town's benefactor, with a monument under construction, you would think differently of me, wouldn't you?"

"It was Henry Lane's business. Not yours. You had no right to take it the way you did. Small or large, it was his."

"There you go again. Even the hundredth-and-first chocolate is good, even though you'll vomit from it in a minute."

Dinsmore looked sullen. He lighted a cigar and sipped his brandy.

After a minute, Ransom said, "I didn't come here to discuss ethics with you, Dinsmore."

Still pouting, Dinsmore said, "Well, then. Ask your questions."

"What questions?"

"Those areas you so much needed filled in."

"I thought you were going to confess."

"I never said that. I said I would concede to you. There. I've already done that. Now, what is it you wanted to know?"

"How did you mesmerize the jury?"

"There's that word again. It's really quite out of date, you know, Ransom. Carr and his ilk might have called it mesmerism. I speak of it as hypnotism."

"What's the difference?"

"You know mesmerism has such awful connotations. Like a snake enthralling its prey by sheer eye power or something equally absurd. Hypnotism's not at all like that. Not at all. I'm surprised at you for thinking it. If you understood what it meant, you'd know I had nothing to do with any of the jurors."

"But you did with Mrs. Lane."

"Nonsense. I was merely trying to distract her attention. Lord knows that's a difficult enough task when a woman scorned is bent upon telling her side of the story."

"But I saw you do it to her before, too. At the pre-election dinner. Now don't deny that she glanced at you every two minutes that evening."

"I don't at all deny it. It was a horrible night for me. She wouldn't look away, she was so jealous."

"Jealous?"

"Of course. As soon as I saw we were to be seated apart, I drew a deep sigh of relief. Finally, for an evening, I was to be free of her. She was incredibly jealous of any woman who came anywhere near me. That evening it was Mrs. Mason. Imagine! That old bag of bones. And yet Carrie's jealousy wouldn't allow me a moment's peace. And then, afterwards, she would sulk because of our situation, saying how much people talked about us. What did she expect? With her hanging onto me wherever we went, like that night. And it was as bad during the day. She would follow me from the house to here, to the warehouse, to the office. Half my time was spent trying to persuade her to let go of me so I might get some work done."

As Dinsmore talked, Ransom's face began to burn. He was intensely ashamed to be sitting here listening to the man's utter lies. He longed to shut Dinsmore up, to smash into that smug, pretty face to stop him. But he didn't. Nor did he say a word. He felt almost paralyzed by the man's hideousness—yet unwilling, too, not to let him go on.

"That was when I knew I had been mistaken about Carrie. She wanted us to marry. But how could we, so soon after her husband's death? It would have been unthinkable. That was when she turned on me. Hell hath no fury, as they say. Why, she was even jealous of Mrs. Ingram. Can you believe it? Even at her worst, Margaret had more sense than that."

It was a second or two before Ransom realized that Dinsmore meant his wife.

"They were two of a kind, Carrie and Margaret. I ought to have seen that from the beginning. But no, my head was turned. I was thrown into that pleasant confusion of infatuation the first time I saw Carrie. That was only a month or two after I'd come to Center City. I recall it so vividly. It was a rainy, misty day in the summertime. She was wearing the palest green, from hat to shoes. She passed by me out a doorway and into a waiting carriage. But she stopped at the lintel first and held out a hand to check how bad the downpour was. It was only a trickle. Then she turned and smiled at me. It was girlish, mischievous. Her hair looked as though it were lighted from within. It just glowed.

Then, without bothering to open the parasol she had with her, she ran the dozen or so steps to the open carriage door. Someone standing next to me told me who she was. I'll never forget how much promise that smile held for me." Dinsmore sighed again, sipped his drink, and then relit his cigar. "And you see where it has brought me? I always suspected a woman would be my undoing. My Aunt Angeline always said so. 'They'll be the death of you, Freddy,' she used to say."

This reflective mood alarmed Ransom more than anything before. To be cruel, he said, "And you the death of them."

"I? Of whom?"

"Your wife."

"Margaret? Poor dear, no, I didn't kill Margaret. She slipped on the muddy bank of the reservoir. She was dead drunk, I suppose. As usual. Wandering about in the fields and bemoaning her lot to an unlistening heaven. Again, as usual. What, you didn't know that? Margaret was, Lord rest her, a sot. One of the several terrible discoveries I made only after marrying her. Another was what a liar she was. She worked as a downstairs maid in a house we would meet at. She told me she was the daughter of the house. They had no daughter. She lied about being with child so I would marry her. No, Margaret—old Meg with the legs as they called her—wasn't with child. She was a drudge, a harlot, an ill-tempered, possessive, overdependent sot. But she was no worse than I. And if I left her a great deal, it was what any sane man would do. I knew she'd always find her way back. I never would have harmed her. I was sort of relieved when she died, I have to admit. But now I wish she hadn't—at least her being alive would have kept me away from the inestimable Lady Lane.

"Ah, but you're frowning, Mr. Ransom. Why is that? Because you were certain in your infantile view of the universe that these women were so good, so angel-pure? Hardly. Although which of the two was the worse I couldn't say now. At least Margaret had the candor to own up to what she was and not hide her harlotry under ninety-dollar silk crinolines. Yes, you're surprised. As I was too, although I must say quite pleasantly. Before

Carrie, I'd never met a woman with such abandon, such a loosening of restraints, and I'd been around a bit too. Naturally, I was madly in love with her at the time of these discoveries; just to be near her was enough for me. Imagine my delight then when she proved to be such a devoted and such an inventive mistress of the amatory arts! What is it, Mr. Ransom? Are you looking for the water closet?"

Only half aware of it, Ransom had jumped to his feet.

"Surely you're not going yet. I've not answered half of your questions, I believe."

"If you expect me to sit here while you so malign people . . ." He couldn't finish it.

"Ah, I see you're sensitive to criticism about Mrs. Lane. I half suspected so."

"Really Dinsmore, surely you don't expect me . . ."

"Naturally she's told you otherwise. How I mesmerized her and forced her into all those madnesses I'd never heard of before. Or did she ever tell of them? Well, sit down. I'll not say another word about her. I promise you."

Once seated again, Ransom said, "Don't deny you used it or knew about it. Simon Carr told me about his experiments. You can't deny your part in them."

"A tiny part, I grant. Far less than he would have liked. I knew Carr had filled your head with all this business. Once you'd read his deposition I was sure of it. What you don't know about Carr, Mr. Ransom, is that he was obsessed by hypnotism from the moment he met that Braid fellow to the very end. He bankrupted himself because of it, he threw over a woman he loved and who loved him because of it, he was forced to leave one place after another because of it. If you are still looking for your master mesmerist—as you were so inaccurate as to style myself —Carr's the one. And it was worse once he realized how little hypnotism could really accomplish. What a failure his life had been, because the tool he claimed so much for was merely a halfway tool. Then he tried to persuade me to devote my life to it as he had done, and Braid before him. Absurd, as I then realized. I at least got him to teach me dental surgery so I could be of some use to myself and others. What a tragedy his life was, poor Carr. Wasted talents, wasted intellect. He could have been a great physician, a savior of mankind. But he was only a quack. And in his realization of such a wasted life, he blamed me."

Ransom felt that everything was topsy-turvy. The man's ability to lie—if that was all it was—was phenomenal.

"And Henry Lane too?" Ransom asked. "Was he too disappointed? Is that why he hanged himself?"

"Henry Lane is a rather special case," Dinsmore admitted. "Here, have a cigar." Ransom didn't take it, but he continued to sip the now cool coffee. "Do you recall those five years I lived with Cornelius Van Wycke? Haven't you ever wondered how I ever met such a man, coming from the slums as I had?"

"I thought perhaps through someone you knew at the academy."

"The academy? Don't believe it. I met Van Wycke through prostitution."

That made sense to Ransom. "And you pandered to him?"

"I see you still don't understand yet. I was the one being bought and sold. I'd gotten into trouble with the head of the Black Squad once. Fellow by the name of Kelly. A rough character, I assure you. Even the police didn't tangle with him. Well, I was in debt to him for a considerable sum—and just then down on my luck. Kelly and some of his goons wanted to rough me up. But then he had a better idea. He'd make back the money I owed him and still have a laugh at my discomfort. Van Wycke was only one of a half dozen notables who sent down to the Bowery looking for young men."

Ransom must have looked astonished, because Dinsmore said, "Surely you know of the existence of such men. Why, the newspapers were full of it a few years back when that Oscar Wilde fellow was on trial."

Ransom admitted to reading a bit about it.

"Well, that was only scratching the surface of it. There's big business in pandering to such men. Inverts or urnings or whatever you would call them. It's not so terrible as you might think for the boys either. Not for me, leastaways. Old Corny was taken with me. I let him know soon enough how matters stood between me and Kelly, and Van Wycke paid off the whole kit and caboodle I owed at once. An all-right situation for me, then, in the lap of luxury, living uptown in a mansion off Fifth Avenue. I was growing plump and sassy with so much good living."

"Until you robbed him?"

"I never robbed him. He gave me all that stuff. Wanted to give me more too—horses, carriages, houses—instead of just clothing and a little jewelry. Love-struck old fool that he was. But after not so long I was beginning to grow a little tired of it all. So I just up and left. He was heartbroken, poor old Corny. That was what all the fuss was about. You'll notice the charges against me were dropped later on, once Corny realized he couldn't get me back. I still have some of the fine things he was good enough to give me."

The charges *had* been dropped, Ransom knew. Could this be the real explanation? Or merely another distortion?

"Well," Dinsmore said, "Henry Lane was just like old Corny. Not that he ever admitted to it and carried on the way Van Wycke did. But then, that's the difference between being a millionaire living in a big Eastern city and a prosperous farmer in a small town like this. I doubt that Henry Lane ever did much about it, either. Oh, several indiscretions in his youth. But nothing besides that. He succeeded in hiding it a bit better than anyone suspected. Got himself married to a beautiful younger woman and all. But it was bound to catch up with him sooner or later. When it did—well, Henry just couldn't face up to his true nature. Then, too, he was calf-eyed about me. I doubt he would have had so much work done on his teeth if that hadn't been the case. Naturally I'd had enough of that sort of business in my own youth, and so he stayed pretty much unfulfilled."

"Are you trying to tell me that's why he committed suicide?"

"As close as I've been able to figure out."

"Because you were going to expose him? Is that it?"

"I had no intention of exposing him. All I wanted was for him to remain quiet while I made love to his wife. As far as that went, it was hunky-dory. That fool even said he didn't mind if I did.

It would make us all the closer, he said. Not for long, though.''

"He said nothing about that in his suicide letter."

"That was just a smoke screen. He knew as well as anyone how solid his business was. He certainly never hid it from anyone."

"But his wife said . . ."

"He wouldn't tell her the truth. How could he? Admit that he'd married her only for the show of it? Then he became jealous of us. I suppose that's what led him to hang himself."

And, strangely enough, it all seemed to fit together. The lack of interest Henry had shown in her; his sleeping alone all those years; even his inability—or was it unwillingness—to sire children.

"Why haven't you said any of this before?" Ransom asked. "In court?"

"And dishonor the dead?"

"You've done worse. No, Dinsmore. I just don't believe you. I don't believe you haven't used mesmerism on all these people."

"Hypnotism," Dinsmore corrected. "And I didn't say I didn't use it on some of them. On Henry Lane, for example, for dental work. On Mrs. Lane too, to try to cure her insomnia. Beyond that . . . it's all rather mythical."

"What about Millard? Are you going to deny he was up in this room just before he went to shoot Carr?"

"Not at all. I thanked him for his good words of testimony."

"You mesmerized him!"

"Not at all. I merely pointed out how all Millard's gratitude would be worthless once Carr got on the witness stand to slander me. You have made such claims for Carr, that even Millard understood the old man's words would hang me."

"So he just went out and shot Carr out of gratitude to you?"

"For saving his life, yes. Why not?"

"I find that difficult to believe."

"That's because you have a distorted understanding of what hypnotism can and can't make a person do. Surely you've read all these journals you brought into the courtroom? You ought to know far better. For example, did you ever read in any of them that someone was hypnotized against his will? No, of course you

didn't. All the evidence you presented dealt with voluntary subjects. I tell you it can't be induced without one's wish to have it
induced. Or, at the very most, not against one's will. You ought
to know that. Despite whatever Carr ranted on about."

That was a sore point: one that Murcott had pointed out early
on in the investigation; and the reason the doctor had not borne
witness to medically support the prosecution.

"Second," Dinsmore went on, "not everyone can be hypnotized. Somehow or other some people are easier subjects than
others. But I've encountered enough difficulties using it as an
anesthesia in dentistry. More than a few times I've had to resort
to using Nitrous Oxide, which I've never quite trusted, because
the patient's hypnotic trance wasn't strong enough. I even had
to use it on you when you came to see me with that infected
molar."

"You put me out in a minute," Ransom said.

"In a light trance, yes. I needed the Nitrous Oxide for the
greater part of the time. That's why you slept so long. I'd wager
that without your wanting it, I couldn't even put you into the
lightest trance."

"You were able to easily enough that time."

"Ah, but you *wanted* me to. And you were weakened by a day
or so of pain and illness. You all but begged me to stop the pain.
It's completely different now. You're unwilling. Come on. Let
me try."

He said it in a light, mocking manner. But that didn't fool
Ransom. So it was as he had suspected. Dinsmore did want to
mesmerize him again. But to what end? Then all that about
Henry Lane and Van Wycke and Mrs. Dinsmore and Carrie Lane
was lies. Or were they? So much of what Dinsmore had said
sounded true. So much of it neatly filled in spaces that had badly
needed filling in. But which ones? And how much of it? That
Ransom couldn't determine.

"No thanks, Dinsmore."

"Suit yourself. I thought you had a more inquiring nature than
you evidently do have. All I wanted to do was to show you how
wrong you are. How your case is based on a false premise. Won't

you feel even a little bit guilty if I am convicted and hanged and you discover hypnotism can't do all you claimed it could do? No? I suppose I misjudged you. I thought you were more ethical than that. Well, then, do it for the sake of truth. As an experiment, in the great scientific tradition. Don't you want to know the truth, Ransom? 'Truth is beauty, beauty truth,' as Keats said. You see, I'm not completely uneducated. Old Corny saw to that."

Even as he spoke, Ransom had to admit he very much wanted Dinsmore to try. Not for the reasons Dinsmore was busily giving, although he had struck a raw nerve with one of them. And not perversely either. He felt certain he could will the mesmerism to not occur, or fight against it if it did begin to occur. Carr had done it: a sick, a dying old man. Why couldn't he too? He had the experience of it already; and with it the experience of a dozen other people who'd had it happen. Most of all, he had Carr's advice about how to prevent it from happening—by concentrating intensely on something else. The old man had used lines of poetry, hadn't he? Saying them over and over, he had told Ransom.

Dinsmore was seated as he had been when Ransom had first come into the room—so comfortable, so smug, and so attached to the sleaziest aspects of human nature, almost taking pleasure in the vices and follies that had surrounded him. It made Ransom want to take up the challenge, if only to show him that his seaminess and filth could never prevail. It was the same feeling of a mission Ransom had had leaving the Page Board and Hotel, but concentrated now, honed to a hard, cutting edge.

"What if you don't succeed?" Ransom asked. "Am I supposed then to accept your word about it, and drop the case for lack of proof?"

"Naturally I hope you will do some such thing. Although knowing your view of me, I doubt that you will."

"You're right. I won't. And if you don't succeed it will only prove one thing, Dinsmore—that my will is stronger than yours."

Dinsmore laughed. "Does that mean you'll chance it?"

"I'll chance it. Yes."

"Well! There's the sporting interest."

Dinsmore stood up and had Ransom turn his chair away from the small table. He pulled another chair up to his. Then went and turned down the gas in the chandelier until the room was far less brightly lighted. "Shall we begin?"

Ransom had been searching for a line of verse to concentrate on. For a while none came. But as soon as Dinsmore asked if he were ready, a line did suddenly appear. Only a fragment, and he didn't know where from, but he had it.

"Go ahead," he said.

"Are you relaxed? You needn't answer. Just nod your head. . . .

"No. I can see you're not relaxed enough. I want you to rest every limb of your body."

Ransom did as he was told, but he slowly recited his line of verse to himself. *"Then save me, or the passed day will shine/ Upon my pillow, breeding many woes—"*

"Your arms feel heavy. Your hands are like lead in your lap."

"Save me from curious conscience"—wasn't that how it went?— *"that still lords/ Its strength for darkness . . ."*

"Your head is especially heavy. Like an overgrown sunflower on a thin stalk. How it shudders and falls to one side. So heavy. So heavy on your neck . . ."

". . . lords its strength for darkness, burrowing like a mole." Yes! That's how it went. But was that all? No. There was more.

"Your legs are heavy now. Heavy as fallen tree trunks on a dark canyon floor. Rotting. Dead. Lifeless. Heavy and lifeless. No feeling at all. Heavy. So heavy."

There were two more lines to it. What were they? He'd have to start again. *"Then save me, or the passed day will shine/ Upon my pillow, breeding many woes . . ."*

"You're rested now. Completely rested. Totally at rest."

. . . *Save me from curious conscience* . . .

"Your head is heavy. Your eyelids are heavy."

. . . *curious conscience that still lords its strength for darkness* . . .

"So heavy. Your eyelids are heavy. They're closing. Closing."

. . . burrowing like a mole . . . burrowing like a mole . . . burrowing like a mole . . . Then what?

"Relaxed now. Completely relaxed. Relaxed now."

. . . darkness burrowing like a mole . . . dark now too *. . . curious conscience that still lords it strength for darkness . . . darkness . . . darkness . . . burrowing like a mole . . .* His voice like that *. . . burrowing like a mole . . . darkness . . .*

"So relaxed that you cannot move. Cannot move. Cannot move."

. . . darkness . . . no! not darkness but light! sunlight *. . .* sunshine *. . .* not darkness *. . .* yes! *the passed day will shine upon my pillow . . .* Now how did it end? *. . .* that wasn't the end *. . . burrowing like a mole . . . like a mole . . .*

"Relaxed. Heavy. Relaxed. Heavy."

. . . save me from curious conscience, it went *. . .* and *save me from curious conscience . . . burrowing like a mole . . . a mole . . . a mole . . .* But then what? save me from the passed day? from the pillow? *. . .* why didn't the last lines come? why? *. . .*

"Mr. Ransom!"

The words were like a thunderclap.

Ransom opened his eyes. Dinsmore's own eyes, cut and faceted like blue gemstones, were only a few inches away.

"Are you awake, Mr. Ransom?"

"Yes," he answered. "Yes. I'm awake," he repeated, only now realizing he'd been awake all the while, hearing everything Dinsmore had been saying, his incantatory words.

"You're awake?" Dinsmore asked again.

"I said I am. I've been awake all the time."

"You closed your eyes."

"I know. But I've still been awake. Are you disappointed?"

Dinsmore drew back a pace or two. "If you are awake, then stand up and walk around this chair."

Ransom laughed. It had worked just as Carr had said it would. Just by concentrating. He stood up and walked around the chair, then remained standing by it. "I told you I'm awake."

"But your arms and legs were completely relaxed."

"Perhaps. But my mind was completely awake. I was trying to remember the end lines of a poem all the while you talked."

"What poem?"

"I'm not sure. It went . . . oh, wait! I have it all now:

> *'Then save me, or the passed day will shine*
> *Upon my pillow, breeding many woes—*
> *Save me from curious Conscience, that still lords*
> *Its strength for darkness, burrowing like a mole;*
> *Turn the key deftly in the oiled wards,*
> *And seal the hushed Casket of my Soul.' "*

"That's it! All of the sestet," Ransom said with great relief. "And I even know what it is too: Keats' sonnet 'To Sleep.' Your mention of Keats before must have prompted me to think of it. I had a hell of a time trying to put it together."

Dinsmore had walked away during Ransom's little recitation. He filled the crystal goblet with Armagnac and took several sips.

"You're disappointed, I can see," Ransom said. "For all your talk you wanted me to be mesmerized, didn't you?"

Dinsmore looked at the glass, then at Ransom. "I admit to it."

"What would you have done if you had succeeded?"

"I don't know. Something mischievous. Make you go down on all fours and meow like a cat, perhaps. It's late. My powers of invention wane as the day grows long." He raised a leg upon the cushion of the love seat.

"I think I will have some of that brandy," Ransom said.

Dinsmore waved for him to help himself. He was silent, staring down at his glittering glass.

"You seem very satisfied with yourself," he finally said.

"I'll be more satisfied if you take the witness stand tomorrow."

"What for?"

"To confess."

"To what? To being used as an amatory toy by all and sundry?"

"If you do, I'll change the penalty."

"You mean I won't have the benefit of a public execution? Pity. I always hoped to make the front page of a newspaper. How will you change it?"

"Plead guilty to the new charges."

"What charges?"

"We'll work them out."

"It can't be in any way related to manslaughter or homicide. According to Applegate all of them carry the death penalty in this lovely state."

"We'll change it to fraud, misrepresentation, mishandling of funds—business-connected things. You'll still get a prison sentence."

"I think I'd rather hang than have umpteen years of hard labor."

But he and Ransom bargained over it for another ten minutes. Finally Dinsmore said, "All right. All right. Do whatever you want."

"You'll take the witness stand, then?"

"If you insist."

Ransom wanted to shake hands on it.

Dinsmore laughed as they did. "This is ridiculous. I'm supposed to confess to things I've never done. Things I haven't even been accused of doing."

"It's your only chance of survival."

"You think I don't know that? Why else would I do it?" Without waiting for an answer, he handed Ransom his street clothing. "You'd better go now. I'll have to rehearse my little scene for the witness stand tomorrow. This is going to require the acting skill of an Edwin Booth."

"Just tell the truth, then," Ransom said.

"Oh, the truth!" Dinsmore said scornfully, closing the door.

Ransom waited until he was out of the hotel and onto the street before clapping his hands.

"I've won!" he said aloud. "I've won!"

AS SOON AS HE ARRIVED in the courtroom the following morning, Ransom looked for Carrie Lane. The spectators' seats were filled, and there she was, in the last row on the right side, almost hidden in veils, alongside Lavinia Dietz. Mrs. Ingram was nowhere to be seen. But in front of the two ladies, others were turning around to look at Carrie, who carefully ignored them. She saw Ransom, though, and signaled a quick greeting to him.

He'd asked her to come last night. Much as she disliked attending the trial, she had agreed. She'd agreed to other matters too. . . .

Ransom had been halfway home from the Lane Hotel after his meeting with Dinsmore when he'd just spun on one heel and walked back up High Street. Once at her house, and encouraged by the lights still on upstairs despite the late hour, he'd knocked at her door. After a short while, Carrie herself had thrust open one front bedroom window.

"Is that you, James?"

He'd told her he had to see her.

"What's happened?" she'd asked.

He'd repeated that he had to see her. . . .

She disappeared then, and a few minutes later opened the front door for him, shushing him as he entered the foyer. Her hair was down. It covered her shoulders, as much a covering as the shawl she had thrown over her satiny nightdress.

"Harriet must be sleeping," she said. Then: *"What* has happened?"

Without answering, Ransom reached for her shoulders, and despite her surprise took her into his arms and kissed her until both of them were so breathless with it that they had begun rocking on their feet.

When she pulled away to look quizzically at him, Ransom took her hand and kissed it. "Marry me," he murmured into the smooth, scented skin. "Marry me, Carrie. Be my wife. Say you will."

"But I thought we'd agreed to wait until all this was over?"

"It will be over. Tomorrow. Give me your word now."

Her face was flickering with emotions, just like the candlelight in the drafty entry. *"What* has happened?" she asked again.

He wouldn't answer, but pressed her to him again and asked her again if she would have him. Quickly, and he was certain of it, disjointedly, he told her the trial would be over very soon, tomorrow. But he wanted her consent now.

"But it's not over yet," she said.

"I see you and I must bargain too. Then give me your consent on condition that he will be convicted. That's good enough for me. More than enough."

"You're so certain?" she asked, bewildered.

That was when Ransom asked her to come to the courtroom the next morning to see for herself. All that she'd undergone would be nothing, he said, in the face of her vindication. She would see.

He went on in that vein for some time, excited, persuasive as never before, until she consented to both the request and to the proposal—with the condition.

Then Ransom thanked her and embraced her again, at such length and with such responsive passion from her that he no longer hesitated. In one motion he bent down and swept her into his arms and began up the stairs. She let out a tiny cry and held onto his shoulders tightly, as though afraid of falling. At the top of the stairs she heard a noise, or claimed to hear one. He waited a few seconds, still holding her tightly to him, nuzzling her. Then he whispered that it was nothing, hearing his own throaty, drawling voice as though it came from a stranger. Before she could protest, he had carried her through the reading room and lightly kicked open her bedroom door. A cornucopia of unseen scents and perfumes assailed him all at once, reminding him of another place he'd been with her, although where or when it had been he couldn't say. Only when he had put her down on her feet and had closed the bedroom door did he kiss her again, deftly slipping off first her shawl, then her nightdress. This time she didn't merely yield to him but helped him, fumbling to undo his buttons, as breathlessly, quiveringly, he took his conqueror's due of her.

Hours later he was kissed and sent out the door. Despite the stiff March breeze, her warmth and scent lingered on his clothing, in the air he breathed, until he was home and finally asleep.

Even the next morning he could still smell her; smell her and remember how she had felt under his fingertips, under the length of his body; smell her still and recall so clearly how she had met him with an eagerness that had seemed to match his own, uttering half-cries, half-words, as he had slaked what seemed to be an unending thirst for her. . . .

She would be vindicated. Despite her fears. Despite Judge Dietz's apprehensions about the reduced plea.

That had almost proved to be a major obstacle. Ransom had gone to the judge's house before breakfast that morning to lay out his scheme. Lavinia had served the men, then had quickly abandoned the breakfast room to them. Dietz had frowned at the interruption, and had been incredulous at Ransom's suggestion.

"What's wrong?" Dietz had asked. "Don't you think they'll convict him?"

"Of course I do."

"Then why all this namby-pambying? Prosecute him to the furthest extent of the law, and let him worry about the rest."

"It's not necessary. It's excessive," Ransom had said. But he knew Dietz was too hard-headed a man to listen to his own reasons for doing it. He'd have to offer convincing practical reasons. "All we want, your honor, is Dinsmore out of the Lane businesses and in jail. That's all that is needed to break the back of the opposition in Center City. They'll be like a headless chicken without him. You know that."

Even so, Dietz had argued over it on a half dozen grounds. The upshot was that he'd remained unconvinced of Ransom's plan, but had agreed to it if Dinsmore testified accordingly. He didn't trust the man one bit, and neither should Ransom, he said. He understood the implications for both of them if a lesser charge were given to the jury: it would be most favorable for them. But he still didn't like it. So he would wait until Dinsmore had taken the stand, until the defense had rested; only then would Dietz charge the jury and, in so doing, would set up the lessened charges Ransom asked for. Dietz made it clear he found it an unsavory business. He did agree, however.

It would be over soon, Ransom thought, opening out his portfolio of case notes, pen stubs, ink, and note pad on the desk after greeting Carrie and Lavinia in the courtroom. He did this last only for effect. He wouldn't have any need for them today. All he had to do today was sit back and listen. He'd done all the work he or anyone else could be expected to do already. If he didn't feel that same keen elation he'd felt last night, it was because he considered his work over, like a piece of music with only the obbligato coda remaining to be played. This contented exhaustion did not leave him even when the bailiff led Dinsmore into the courtroom.

The defendant was more spiffily dressed than ever—his vanity always told on him—in a charcoal brown pin-striped suit with ivory-tinted vest and necktie. Dinsmore seemed to be in a serious mood, almost contrite. He did not acknowledge Ransom or anyone else while the clerk read off a precis of the previous day's events to the judge and a thankfully undiminished jury.

That accomplished, Dietz said: "Yesterday, the prosecution rested its case. Today, Mr. Applegate, it is your turn to follow suit. I sincerely hope it will be succinct."

"Before I do summarize, your honor," Applegate said, standing now, long-legged and stiff as a stork, "my client, the defendant, would like to take the witness stand briefly."

"This is a most irregular proceeding," Dietz said, playing the game by the rules, as though he didn't know what was supposed to occur next. "Unless I misapprehend you. Did you wish to have the defendant answer questions relating to testimony already given in this court?"

"That would be most irregular, your honor. I realize the prosecution has already moved to rest its case. My client has merely asked that he may address the jury on his own. I cannot say precisely why. Perhaps he feels his own counsel has failed to adequately present his case . . ." Applegate made a deprecating motion with one hand. "I do not know, your honor. I do know, however, that there is more than ample precedent for such a thing. May I refer your honor to the case of Christian versus the State of Virginia, 1874, or Lebenhook versus Anthony, a civil case in Philadelphia, just last year."

Dietz waved aside the attorney's offer to show the precedents he had cited.

"You may call the defendant to the witness stand."

Dinsmore stood up as his name was called, and was sworn in and brought to the stand. Once there, however, he refused to enter unless the isinglass screen were removed.

Ransom found that only mildly annoying. He supposed that Dinsmore would be sticking on such minor details, having to give way on so much else.

Dinsmore also declined the offer of another chair. He would stand, he said, to face the judge and jury. He did so, waiting until Applegate had retreated to his desk seat. The room was filled with half-uttered questions and speculations.

"I don't know," Dinsmore began informally to the jury, "if any of you gentlemen have been on trial for your life. If you have not, allow me to assure you it is a most fascinating process to observe and to experience."

The room had hushed to a crackling silence.

"I do not for those reasons, however, recommend the experience. It is most annoying and frustrating. Especially in a case of this nature: as evidently fabricated as this one has been. Where the evidence is of such an ambiguous and fantastical nature. And where the witnesses called to testify are either hysterical women, old mammys, or dead men—whom we've been assured never lie."

What was he doing? Ransom wondered.

"All of you men know of my business dealings here in Center City. I've been a respectable professional for years. And only recently, you know how much I've been involved in the growth and welfare of this town. Whatever else you may have been told about me, you've never been told to doubt my professional abilities or my faithful and ethical management of an unwieldy and difficult business. Have you? Any of you?"

The jurors looked at each other. None had a response.

Ransom felt as though he'd been thrown back in his chair. What in the hell was Dinsmore doing? How would this lead to a confession?

"So that much is certain," Dinsmore said with the finality of a mathematician proving an axiom. "Yet last night, that man—" and he pointed out Ransom—"that man, I say, came to my hotel room unbidden and declared to me that he would drop all of the ridiculous charges he has been trying all these weeks to prove against me if I would agree to plead guilty to fraud and mismanagement in my business dealings. I'm telling the truth, by God!" Dinsmore asserted. "I've been sworn to on the Bible, and I am. Ask him to deny it. Go on. Ask him!" he said.

People were beginning to stir behind him, Ransom felt it. The jurors were astir in their seats too. He felt paralyzed.

"Ask him also why he came to me! Because his case is a farce, that's why. A fabrication. A ridiculous tissue of hocus-pocus and lies! Ask him. Go on. And because he wants a conviction no matter what the price, or what the charges."

"He's lying!" Ransom shouted, just finding his voice. "I object, your honor."

But at that moment there was a general noise and confusion from the spectators.

"Let him speak," someone behind Ransom shouted out. "We want to hear what Dinsmore has to say," someone else said, and the anonymous shouts were taken up by others.

Why didn't Dietz stop Dinsmore?

"Why does Mr. Ransom want this conviction so very badly?" Dinsmore went on, in a louder voice. "Ask him. Because he wants to be the next state senator and his pals up in Lincoln said to him last summer, 'Bring us the head of Frederick Dinsmore, and by gum you'll be the next candidate.' It's simple for them. It's that easy. Ask him. And, ask *him!*" Dinsmore now pointed to the judge's bench. "He's the one who makes congressmen in

this county. Not you or I. Not the people. And it's these two men
who want my conviction on this trumpery of a case."

Dietz began gaveling now. The court bailiff stood up and
called for order in the court.

Dinsmore went on unheeding, addressing himself strictly to
the jurybox now. "And do you know how trumped up this case
really is? I'll tell you. That fancy witness of his, Mrs. Lane, is the
other stake in his game. Ask anyone in her house how often Mr.
Ransom visits there. And for how long he stays!"

"Restrain that man!" Dietz called out. "Bailiff!"

Both the bailiff and the court clerk jumped to grasp Dinsmore's arms. During the struggle with them, he went on
shouting.

"It's she who is the cause of all this! The harlot! Because I
scorned to marry her. The whore! Would you marry such a
trollop? She puts to shame the most experienced courtesans of
Paris. Take my word for it, men. Mr. Ransom will tell you. Ask
him what he was doing there after midnight!"

"Get him out of this courtroom," Dietz shouted, white-faced,
standing at his desk. "Out of here!"

"He'll tell you what he was doing there after midnight. He
and his fancy whore! Tell them, Ransom. Tell them how good
she is at the French arts. Tell them . . ."

His last words were stifled as he was finally maneuvered out
the courtroom's side door.

Ransom was still on his feet, gripping the edge of his desk,
numb with the shock of the betrayal.

"Order in the court!" Dietz said, gaveling. "Everyone take
your seats. Everyone!"

Someone grabbed Ransom from behind, forcing him to sit
down.

When the court clerk returned to the room, there were a few
more murmurs from the spectators. Then silence ensued.

"Mr. Applegate," the judge began. "I find your client in contempt of this court with an appropriate fine to be levied against
him. If I suspected any complicity on your part in his outrageous
behavior, I assure you of an equal finding and fine. I've never

encountered such blatant disregard for a court of law. I will not have this courtroom used as a platform for personal or for political vilification. Not by the defense, not by any party. Is that perfectly clear to all?"

Applegate had risen when his name was called. Evidently he was as surprised and humiliated as anyone else by his client's outburst. He merely hung his head.

"Now, Mr. Applegate, is the defense prepared to rest its case?"

"The defense rests," Applegate said.

"Fine! This court will recess, then, until three P.M., at which time it will reconvene for the jury to be charged. I want all parties to be here at that time."

He banged the gavel three times, then quickly left the room amid the general rising of spectators and the sudden explosion of their conversation, repressed for the last few minutes.

"Would you comment on Mr. Dinsmore's allegation?" someone said close to Ransom's ear. It was Will Merrifield, blocking Ransom's way out. "Will you deny his allegations? What is the exact nature of your relations with Mrs. Lane? Is it true you visited her last night at midnight?"

Ransom had slumped into his seat as the session ended. Now he came alive in every nerve and limb and blood vessel. Alive with anger. Without answering, he began gathering his gear.

"Is it true that you will be announcing your candidacy for the state senate?" Merrifield went on, not an ally now, but a demon, with his country-bumpkin face and his fire-red hair. "Would you care to reveal the name of your sponsor for the candidacy?"

Merrifield was still blocking his way.

Ransom pushed past the reporter toward the back doors. But the crowd lingered thickly there, still curious. He searched for another way out. And the reporter was asking him yet another question. Ransom looked for Carrie among all the bobbing heads. But of course she was gone. And to think he had specifically asked her to come here today. For this!

The reporter was grabbing at Ransom's sleeve, trying to get his attention while he asked another question. And now others were coming down from the upstairs gallery and crowding around him and the reporter. Ransom's anger subsided in the need to escape.

"Look," he suddenly said. "Dinsmore's back!"

When everyone turned to look, Ransom shoved his way through the crowd to the side door. Once out, he found his way to his small court office and locked the door. They had followed him. They were knocking on the door, calling out his name, pounding on the door.

He stood by the window with his portfolio lifted as though to defend himself if they managed to get in. But in a few minutes the knocking, the calling ceased. He turned around and looked out the window, and was quiet for a long time.

———————————•———————————

IT WAS A RESTLESSNESS AT FIRST, undefined but peculiarly present. Then it was like a constant, annoying itch. Not a physical one that could be located and scratched, but a mental one—like having a word at the tip of one's tongue and not being able to remember it. Its last manifestation was a desperate, almost primitive urge to do something: although what he did not know.

He'd been in the side office for only fifteen minutes or so when it first began. After he thought the others had gone, he peeked out the door to make certain no one waited outside. Then he went to the window again. That's when it began.

At first he thought it was only due to what had happened. Dietz had been right. He had been a gullible fool to trust Dinsmore. The result had been as awful a spectacle as he might have dreamed up in his most pessimistic nightmares. The repercussions were unfathomable: but somehow Ransom felt they would wane soon enough.

What had Dinsmore hoped to gain by such wanton destructiveness? Certainly not the support of the jury. They'd been as horrified as anyone else in the room. It must have been an impulsive act. An impulsive rebellion against doing the right thing, even if it meant Dinsmore's conviction. How else could it be explained? Or had he somehow noticed Carrie Lane among the spectators—had that set him off? Who knew. It could only harm Dinsmore. Why bother about this restlessness, this itch, this need to do something—what?—when the defendant had all but thrust his head into the hangman's noose already? But something remained undone, an action uncompleted, and Ransom could not for the life of him think what it was or how to correct it.

He'd have to face a dressing-down from Dietz. It was unavoidable, but it could be postponed for now. He would also have to see Carrie to explain to her what Dinsmore was supposed to have done, so she would understand why he had asked her to come to court today. He admitted now that it had been a cheap enough motivation—the need to show off, to display his powers over someone she had once felt so enthralled by. Ransom would own up to that. He'd visit her right after this afternoon's session. Doubtless the jury wouldn't take too long to convict Dinsmore now. At least that would be some good news to mix with his confession to her, a balm to help her injured sensibility.

So that was accounted for too. Yet the gnawing sense remained, increasing instead of lessening; and with the restlessness Ransom got up from his desk and began pacing his office. He shifted his case papers around, putting them back into some order. He gazed almost absent-mindedly out the window at the bright spring day with the old bark of the trees contrasting to the red-edged tiny leaves just beginning to burst out of bud into growth. He even stepped out into the hallway again as though expecting someone to appear and tell him what it was that remained undone.

This was foolish, he finally decided. He'd been in here almost an hour already. He wouldn't have enough time to go back to the Page Board and Hotel for lunch if he continued to linger.

Hastily he put together his papers, locked them in a drawer, and dressed for the street. He stepped out of his door into the hallway and immediately recognized Eliot Timbs a pace or two ahead of him. The sheriff turned, hearing Ransom's step behind him. My, wasn't he getting broader every year, now that he had such a soft job as sheriff. He'd soon have to add another leather extension to that ridiculous Wyatt Earp–style holster he insisted on wearing.

"It's you, Mr. Ransom."

"Who did you expect, Timbs? Jesse James?"

"No. They'll be bringing him out soon. I'm supposed to keep an eye on him, in case he gets violent."

"Dinsmore? He's still in the building?"

"Down the hall. In the defense office," Timbs said. "A minute ago you could have heard him and Applegate from here, they were yelling like a pair of cats in heat."

"Arguing?"

"Sure sounded like it."

Timbs walked alongside Ransom to the end of the hallway, where it turned before opening out into the large, wood-paneled lobby.

"Those were pretty hard words he used," Timbs said, shaking his head sadly. "Pretty hard indeed. Makes a man wonder what to think. I sort of felt sorry for him until he began saying all that filth about Miz Lane and you. Hard words."

Ransom merely shrugged as though to say he paid no attention to such slander. He was pleased to hear Timbs say it, though. It corroborated what he'd thought before. If Timbs, who was more or less a Dinsmore supporter, even a henchman, thought this way, so would the jurors.

There were still a dozen or so people milling about the lobby in front of the courtroom doors. Ransom had time to exchange a glance with Amasa Murcott, who then started across the room toward him, before Timbs pushed Ransom back.

"Stand aside, everyone!" the sheriff called out, even though no one but Ransom was anywhere near him. "Stand back! The prisoner is coming through!"

Everyone in the room formed a group and came to take a better look, giving Timbs an excuse to repeat his words and to act as though he were doing something official and important. Through it all, Ransom could just make out the sounds of men's feet advancing. And, with the sound of their tread, the restlessness he thought had vanished returned to him with renewed force.

It became so all-pervading in the next few seconds that he felt as though he were dizzy, spinning, losing his balance, even his consciousness.

He saw three men turn the hallway corner and walk into the lobby. Dinsmore led, his hands manacled in front of him, an overcoat thrown over his shoulders. Beside him, holding onto his upper arm, was the court bailiff. Just behind them was Applegate, looking irritated and tight-lipped.

Now the itch was unbearable—the need for action, for completion, totally pervading.

The trio passed through the lobby, approaching Timbs and Ransom. Dinsmore stopped and spoke to someone hidden from Ransom's view. The others went on ahead of him a few steps toward the lobby exit. Then Dinsmore stopped talking in midsentence, turned, and simply looked past the sheriff at Ransom.

Every light in the place seemed to intensify. All else in the lobby—people, voices, noise, motion—seemed to flow away as though to a great distance. There were nothing but lights now, lights sparkling, refracting, reflecting. They emanated from one point—the sparkling, refracting, reflecting center of Dinsmore's eyes. Blinding glitter. And along with it the answer Ransom was looking for, the action that must now be accomplished, the completion he could not live without.

Dinsmore turned aside again and spoke, but no one else was there to be spoken to. Ransom darted forward immediately, and in an instant seized the pistol from Timbs' holster, cocked it, and with his outstretched arm held steady, aimed, and fired.

A shout. The metal of the gun reflected, refracted, sparkled, wavered, then was knocked from his hand. Dinsmore fell forward slowly, a halo of light around him. As slowly he reached for one arm with the other and began to twist around. Slowly a dark liquid erupted from his upper arm, flew out into the air, and stopped, splattered. Slowly other limbs and materials came between Dinsmore and his shining shield of light and Ransom's eyes, moving ah so slowly, like waves colliding.

Then it all snapped like a taut telegraph wire. Movement and noise and faces suddenly rushed in on him so fast and with such confusion that he was dizzy unto swooning again. Timbs rushed forward, then spun around and shouted. Someone grabbed Ransom from behind. A woman screamed. There were many shouting now. Dinsmore was hidden from view by others. Everything seemed as though viewed through one end of a stereopticon—three-dimensional, but unembodied, present but somehow very distant.

". . . the hell is wrong with you," someone said next to him. Murcott. It was Murcott talking. ". . . have killed him for sure . . . hadn't hit your arm away in time . . . fool thing to . . . ever possessed you, James?" Then his voice was gone, and others rushed in to take its place, even less comprehensible, as Murcott pushed through the group of bodies to get to the wounded man.

All the lights flashed and glittered again briefly, then died out, and everything was as it had been before. Ransom was back in the lobby, being held from behind. In front of him, only a few yards away, the bodies were dividing slowly, until he could see that Dinsmore was on his feet. The manacles had been removed from his hands. A handkerchief had been wrapped around his forearm to stanch the blood. It was almost completely brown. Blood streaked his waistcoat and even his trousers. His face was pale. He half supported himself by leaning against the court bailiff. Everyone stood still.

At first Ransom thought he would come over and say something, do something—he didn't know what. But no. Dinsmore just stood and stared at him. His eyes their usual sparkling blue again, as though nothing had happened.

Then Ransom saw the cupid's-bow lips form a smile, and the smile made him sick to his stomach. Dinsmore wasn't angry, he was pleased, delighted. Somewhere inside of Ransom a crevice opened up, deep, splitting apart. Then Dinsmore's smile broke into a white-toothed laugh, and Ransom understood that this was precisely what Dinsmore had wanted to happen. One sparkling blue eye closed in a luxurious, long-lashed wink, and the crevice within Ransom became a chasm, an abyss of incredible depth, and he was falling, falling, falling into it, unable to stop his ears from the truth that rang through and through in the foul, whizzing air as he continued to plummet so endlessly down, the truth that when he had thought he had won, he had really lost, lost all, the truth that this entire last hour of his life, this restlessness, this itch, this need for completion had been implanted the night before, despite his will and awareness, despite his thinking he was awake, despite his wish or his consent, implanted for a reason, a very specific and necessary reason: he'd been mesmerized without his knowing it had happened, mesmerized to become another tool for Dinsmore—the worst, the deadliest of tools.

"WHAT DOES HE SAY IN THE LETTER?" Amasa Murcott asked.

"He wants me to resign from the case. Here. Read for yourself," Ransom said, showing him the two sheets of paper.

"What's that other one?"

"That's the resignation. Dietz drew it up. All I have to do is sign it." He bent over the table to do so.

"As easy as that?"

"I don't see what else I can do. Dietz thinks that if he reads it to the jury before they retire to deliberate it might help."

"Help get a conviction? Do you think so too?"

"I suppose. I don't know what to think anymore," he said, but without any expression of the gloom his words contained. He folded the resignation, slipped it into an envelope, and called Nate to deliver it to the judge.

"What will you do now?" Murcott asked.

He'd been asking questions of Ransom from the moment he'd come back to the side office in the court building where Ransom had been brought until the seriousness of Dinsmore's wound could be determined. Ransom had listened without comment as Murcott had reported that Dinsmore had been hit in the arm, the bullet striking an artery, but that the bullet had been removed and hadn't struck a bone. Luckily, for both of them. Shortly thereafter, Timbs too had come into the office to remove the manacles he'd put on Ransom in the lobby, and to inform them that no charges were being pressed. He seemed only half relieved about this. Murcott was pleased, but Ransom showed no reaction to the news.

Then Murcott and he had walked home to the Page Board and Hotel, with the doctor keeping up an interminable barrage of questions, repeating his incredulity at what had occurred. By then, Ransom had already ceased to answer his friend.

Walking along the familiar street past well-known shops and housefronts proved to be an astonishing experience for Ransom. Never before had these familiar places and objects appeared to him so clearly, so individually defined and differentiated. The trees, bushes, and grass too looked strange—fresh and young, as though they'd just shot forth out of the earth. The very air about him seemed as brand-new as if it had only in the last minute been created. Ransom had never seen so much or in such detail, heard so many sounds about him—birds, leaves rustling, snatches of conversation through open windows; never had he felt so awake or alive.

It was as though, in waking out of the posthypnotic trance in which he had accomplished the preordained deed, he had only just fully and completely awakened in his life. Not to a life of security, of the known and the accepted. But to one wherein all was possible, everything uncertain and changing, transforming, growing, developing about him—and he could see, almost *hear,* the birth and decay. A bright, hard life, wherein all was sharp-edged, fearful. Not a comforting softness where he could sit back and relax. No, absolute alertness was required to catch the changing of things in the very act of change. Not a comfortable world at all, with so much vigilance required. Rather exhausting, in fact, Ransom concluded. So he answered Murcott's last question—what he would now do—with the most truthful and practical answer:

"I think I'll rest a while in my room. Make certain I'm called for dinner."

He fell into a deep and dreamless slumber, and only awakened when Nate knocked on his door. It was much later—he could tell that from the darkness outside and in the room. Instead of fussing with the gas lamp, Ransom lighted a candle and by its poor light cleaned himself up at the washstand.

The new sharpness of his senses had not vanished with the nap, nor had the curious, analytical calm that accompanied it.

As he descended to the first floor, he saw a folded newspaper lying on the seat of a front parlor chair. Two newspapers, on closer inspection: the Center City *Star* and the Lincoln *Journal.* And, for the first time thus far, they had the same headline— "Attorney Shot to Kill Hypnotist!"—blazoned across their front pages. Ransom scanned each one. They might have been written by the same hand, they were so similar. Neither gave motives for the shooting, although both reported the "offensive remarks offered earlier that day by the defendant," and both gave the judge's unofficial dictum that the prosecuting attorney had been suffering from "severe overwork and exhaustion." Ransom dropped the newspapers back onto the chair, marveling that he felt no strong emotions; then he went into the dining room.

Everyone quieted as he entered. Without a word of greeting, he took his seat and began eating. Slowly, conversation began around him again in bits and fragments. All over town, everyone would be talking of only one thing tonight, and the boarders felt restrained.

He had a good appetite, and the food gave plenty of play to his new sensitivity. He became so engrossed in the tastes and textures set before him that he didn't look up until only Isabelle, Murcott, and Mrs. Page were left at the table.

"Will you be going now?" Isabelle asked him. Then she blushed. "I meant . . ." She stopped in total befuddlement.

"Say it, Isabelle," her mother prompted. But she had to say it herself. "We both thought you'd be wanting to see Mrs. Lane, James. Both of us would be happy to accompany you."

"Naturally we know there is nothing at all to what was said in court today," her daughter continued.

"But we've been meaning to pay Harriet Ingram a visit these many months anyway," Augusta took it up, "so why don't we all go together."

"Mrs. Lane," he said slowly. Then, "Yes. Thank you. Of course I'll go. Whenever you two are ready, I'll get the shay."

Carrie Lane. Of course. He hadn't thought of her all afternoon. Not thought of her until he'd been reminded just now. Of course he had to go to her. But for what? What could he say to explain? And why should he have to explain at all? He hadn't to Murcott, who still threw glances at Ransom as though he were a patient very much in need of watching; and he was still obviously waiting for an explanation. Everyone thought he ought to see Carrie Lane. He supposed he ought to too. For what reason he could not exactly say.

Nor was he any the wiser after they'd driven to High Street and were standing on the top step of the stone stairway, waiting for their knock to be answered. The two ladies were busy expostulating on the view, which they must have noticed twenty times before. He did hope that Carrie wouldn't answer the door herself, to give him one more minute to try and figure out what he ought to say to her. But when the door was opened and Harriet Ingram looked at them with her large, startled eyes, Ransom felt even more flustered.

Not the Page ladies. With one voice they explained their visit, almost completely shielding Ransom with gestures, parasols and enthusiasm. Before Mrs. Ingram, or for that matter Ransom, knew it, they were all inside the house, with the ladies hustling the still bewildered housekeeper into the back parlor. He was left alone at the carpeted stairs. Once more he stood indecisively.

He knew why. He did not know how she would act, or he in turn react. Though he had awakened sometime earlier this afternoon into a new sharpness, she alone remained as mysterious to him as ever. He couldn't quite believe Dinsmore's estimate of her, close though it actually came to what she'd more than once said of herself. Just as he couldn't completely accept Dinsmore's account of Simon Carr, or Henry Lane, or Cornelius Van Wycke. But neither could he believe his own blinded assessments of these people. The truth was somewhere between the two extreme views, he suspected. And the worst of it was that Dinsmore had known him, Ransom, better than he had known himself. It was that—not mesmerism—that had been the real cause of his defeat today.

Augusta Page appeared in a doorway.

"She's in the reading room," she whispered. "Go on up!"

The reading room was so dimly lighted that it took him a minute to pick out Carrie's still figure at the window. She was looking out toward the great, empty parkland in front of the house. She hadn't heard him. She did not move, and as his eyes became accustomed to the dimness, he saw her too with his newly sharpened sight.

A figure in a painting lost in meditation, rendered in the somber tones and hues of an old master. Her hair pulled back and bound behind, exposing her face in three-quarter profile. Her cheeks hollow, her eyes pools of shadows, her temples indented and remarkably shiny, as though they were made of some material bearing none of the qualities of mere skin and flesh. Hardly a person at all: she was so distant, so unreachable, although only a few feet away. Not pensive or even melancholy, but clearly set apart, as much by some inner necessity as by some unknown fated hand.

He was awed by her. This was the way he had pictured that she would look long ago, months ago, when he and Murcott had gone to call on her following her husband's suicide. Only she was more so now than he had expected then, a hundred, a thousand times more than he could have expected. Awed, he sought to withdraw.

She heard him move and turned with a start.

Ransom said something: his name, or hers. He wasn't certain which.

Her surprise wavered; her gaze dropped.

"I'll go if you'd like," he said, not knowing what else to say.

She didn't answer but glanced out the window again; then she backed into a chair. She still didn't look at him.

"Do you want me to go?" he asked.

She waved her hand vaguely. He took it as an invitation to stay, to sit. He did so, finding a place near the spot where he'd stood. They faced each other now in the dimness, in the silence,

Ransom growing more uncomfortable in her presence every minute. As though he didn't belong there, had no further business with her. He wished he could say something that would have weight, meaning, consolation. He could think of nothing.

She saved him, finally by saying: "So. It's over now."

He didn't understand that at all. "The jury went into deliberation this afternoon. They haven't come out yet."

"They knew?"

He searched his mind for a way to say it, but settled for, "Yes, they knew. I resigned the case. They knew that too. Dietz thought that might help."

"Yes . . . yes, it might," she answered absently. Then, in a different tone and manner, "But who will help you now?"

"I need no help. No charges have been pressed against me. It was his last gambit. The risk of a desperate man. It had to be. All day he was desperate. You knew that."

She stared at him, then stood up. For a moment he thought she was stumbling, but instead she dropped onto the floor at his knees, grasping them and looking up at him.

"I know you will never forgive me, James. How can you? I don't expect it. But for God's sake don't despise me. Promise me that, if nothing else. Promise me."

"Despise you? You don't think I paid heed to any of his ravings, do you?"

"That's of no account anymore. Now something far worse has happened, James. He has done it. Through me he has struck at you, making you dishonor yourself, ah, so much, my head aches thinking about it. And through that, through you, he has struck back at me."

Ransom must have looked blank at what she said, because she went on, still gripping him hard and talking rapidly.

"Don't you see how much harm he's done you? You're ruined here, James. Ruined more deeply and completely than Henry ever thought he was. Your future, your ambitions, they're nothing now, smoke rings. Because of him, because of what he made you do today. You understand that, don't you? And how I am responsible for it? I knew then it would be perilous for you to interfere. I warned you, James. I did. But you wouldn't listen. And I thought perhaps this suffering would pass because I hadn't deserved it. And I believed you, James, believed you were the stronger because you were a good man. Don't you see how he has betrayed you through your very virtue? Betrayed you so utterly? Dear God, don't tell me you have not yet understood!" she said, and clapping a hand to her mouth she stood up, tottered, and shrank away from him.

He rose and took the hand that covered her lips.

"None of it matters. Not ambitions or any fantasy future or anything else. So long as we are one, Carrie. However much you may think differently, I am not ruined at all. He has not succeeded in sundering us. That remains. I don't care about any of the rest of it, so long as we are together. Last night . . ."

She shook her head, not wanting to hear.

"Not now, perhaps," she said, "nor even next week, but soon enough you will come to despise me because of this. I know that, James. I know. It will be like a poison entering you slowly, turning you against me. A month from now, or a year, you will look at me and you will think, 'But for this woman, I would still have a good name, a profession. Now I have nothing but what is hers. Nothing at all. I am a woman's man now.' Believe me, James. I know you, and I know this for certain. I do."

"You're upset." He tried to reason with her. "We'll think about it later on. Not tonight. I'll come by tomorrow morning and then we'll talk. You'll feel differently after you've had some sleep. Please, listen to me."

"You're wrong, James. Tomorrow morning after you've pondered my words, you will understand me better."

"I tell you I don't give a damn about my future or my reputation, Carrie! I just want you. I've always wanted you."

"No. No. It must not be," she said, pulling out of his grip and turning to the window again. "It will not be now. I couldn't stand having you hate me too. I couldn't."

His feelings were so jumbled that they could only be released as anger. "Then you're playing right into Dinsmore's hand! You see that, don't you? This is exactly what he wants."

"It's already accomplished."

"Then it must be what you want too. Is it? There can be no other reason. Admit it. You won't have me because I fell into his trap. Because he proved the more powerful. Isn't that why?"

"The poison has already begun its work, James," she said quietly. "Do you see?"

He turned away from her in disgust. "I'll come by tomorrow. We'll talk it over then."

"No. Don't come tomorrow," she said softly.

"Why not? Why do you want to do this to me? To hurt me even more? If you believe what you are saying, then can you bear to have me lose everything and then you too? Can you?"

She didn't answer for a long while; then she said quietly, "You have lost much. But you still have a chance. I am altogether lost now. In this life and in the next one."

He was so staggered that he let her pass him, cross the room, and go to her bedroom door. At the lintel she stopped and, without turning to face him again, said, "Don't come back, James. Not tomorrow morning. Not ever again."

She closed the bedroom door and he heard the click of its lock.

———————————●———————————

FOR A MOMENT HE THOUGHT to go after her, force open the door, kick it if necessary, and demand that she listen to him. But all the fight was gone from him. He was totally exhausted. He dropped into the nearest chair and sat for a long time, mad schemes and plans filling his mind, until the gas lamp, already dim, began to flicker and finally went out.

He got up instinctively to shut off the gas-supply valve. Then he slowly went downstairs. No one was in the darkened foyer. He heard no voices in the house. The women must have left already.

He let himself out the front door and spotted the ladies in the shay waiting for him at the bottom of the steps. As he descended, he promised himself he would come back here tomorrow to try once again, even if she had forbidden it.

When he had untethered the horse and gotten into the driver's seat, Mrs. Page mumbled something. He didn't answer. He didn't want to talk. Not now. He took up the reins and had just turned the shay around in the street, heading south, when he heard a horseman galloping toward them. Even at night the shock of red hair was like a beacon.

"Whoa!" Ransom said, slowly his horse to a stop. "Will? Is that you, Will Merrifield?"

Merrifield reined his mount suddenly, then trotted up to the shay.

"Mr. Ransom?" he asked, peering in. "Evening, ladies."

"It's I. What's the big hurry?"

"Got to get up to Lincoln. They just telegraphed. They want me up there now that the case is over and the verdict delivered."

An embarrassed silence then. Ransom would not ask, yet he had to know. Merrifield's horse kept tugging to get going again, primed for a run. Why didn't the reporter say something? He was always fast-mouthed enough when he had questions.

"What was the verdict?" Augusta Page asked for Ransom.

"Not guilty." Then the reporter reined to one side and horse and rider shot off into the night.

"I'm so sorry, James," his landlady said, putting a hand on his shoulder. "So very sorry."

He turned around to look at her, but instead saw the Lane house looming above them. Every light was out but one, and as he looked, that flickered, and all was dark.

BOOK FOUR

Return from the Dead— Summer 1901

SUNDAYS WERE THE EMPTIEST days now. Church bells from all over lower Manhattan would toll throughout the morning, calling their much depleted congregations in sorrowful, reproachful tones, as though aware of their desertion. Wall Street and Pearl Street were desolate. The crowds of bankers, financiers, clerks, and investors who thronged it, jostling each other in hurry each Monday through Saturday, were gone this day of Sabbath. Torn newspapers and shredded legal documents spiraled down the littered stone-faced canyons, driven by eddies of wind from the Hudson River until they arrived where the East River set up its own current, and everything would rise and whirl like a tiny paper tornado. Every once in a while, some minor functionary—a building janitor or lamplighter—would trudge alone through the streets on an errand. One could walk up Broadway for blocks without seeing another soul.

At night it was much the same. True, Chambers Street was a bit livelier around dinner time, when court clerks, lawyers, and other courthouse personnel left their lodgings to fill the small restaurants of a half dozen ethnic varieties. But this was not a high-spirited or jocular group by any means, and though the diners were often packed shoulder to shoulder, the dining rooms tended to be somber, silent but for the scrape of flatware on china and the frequent, hollow-sounding calls of roving aproned waiters with orders for the kitchen. And after dinner hour, the streets were solitary as mausoleums.

One would have to go further uptown, to Fourteenth Street where the Ladies' Mile began, and where shoppers were found in abundance all days of the week, or further east, where—their own Sabbath having occurred the day before—for many of the resident immigrants it was a day of business as usual, and the tiny, pushcart-littered alleys and lanes were always bustling with activity.

Sometimes he would stay in his lodgings all day on Sunday, gazing down from his grimy sixth-story windows at the desolate street until the sun set hazily over the river and the Jersey shore. Other times, he would leave his tiny two rooms early in the day and descend, going around the corner to Walker and Jerome's, letting himself in and out with a key that Hugh Jerome, the younger partner and his direct superior, had given him. There, in the small copying alcove, he hardly noticed the passing of the day: except, of course, for the darkened and abandoned offices all around his own lighted corner.

Too often, there wasn't any extra copying to do. Then he would sometimes be drawn out of doors by the deceptively beautiful weather, and he'd walk past the empty courthouses and municipal buildings to where East Broadway stretched with its colorful immigrant life. He never went up to the Ladies' Mile anymore. One Sunday he had, and, stepping into the door of a large, glass-windowed clothing emporium, he had had to stop and blink and almost hold his fluttering heart until the woman he'd glimpsed indoors had come out onto the street and had not after all been Carrie Lane. No. Not Carrie at all; as she passed close by he saw that the nose was snub instead of small and straight, the cheeks too full, the eyes a dull and not at all tawny gold-flecked brown. But it had given him a start, a shock, and he had immediately turned around and boarded a passing trolley to retreat downtown to his quiet lodgings.

He spoke to none of the other lodgers except to greet them as they passed each other in the shabbily papered, narrow hallways. His landlady was hardly to be compared to Augusta Page. This woman was short and sallow, dry as an old stick, and given to no dealings with her boarders save to receive her weekly or monthly rent. Nor did he socialize at all with the other clerks or copyists at Walker and Jerome's, Inc. From the first day he had entered the law firm's offices and had been shown to his alcove desk on one side of a large room filled with a dozen or more just like it, the others had looked at him with an unfeigned recognition: yet another despondent failure had joined their already funereal, despairing ranks.

Ransom didn't mind. In fact, he more than shared their evaluation of himself, and he took his place as one more outcast among outcasts with equanimity, believing it only just. Just, and more than obvious if he had to place himself alongside any of the smart young attorneys-at-law who would shove into the copying room with a fistful of documents to be done, all in a great hurry, all bursting with energy and responsibility and self-importance— and most of all with the certainty that the future belonged to them as clearly as it *didn't* belong to any of the aged scriveners who toiled under the green linoleum lampshades to abet that very future they themselves had soundly renounced.

Only Hugh Jerome could know how much of a failure he really was—and that would primarily be supposition—and he would certainly never deign to get into such conversation with any mere copyist: he had too many other matters to attend to. Nor, after their first talk in the plush upstairs office, did Jerome ever talk to Ransom except when it referred to a piece of copying. During that interview, the partner had shown Ransom the recommendation received from William K. Reese of Lincoln, and had tried to convince him he might have an important post with the company. He'd been solemnly refused, and had never again mentioned the matter. Ransom would never practice law again as long as he lived. That was his decision: he hadn't been forced to it; and after a year of living in New York City and working as a copyist, that decision had not altered.

He could explain what lay behind the decision—oh, easily enough could he say how little faith he had in the jury system, in the trial system, in English Common Law that ruled the system, in the federal, state, and county law that modified it. But he could never adequately explain how great a loss he'd sustained one day in the spring of 1900 when he'd realized with an intensity that had paralyzed him and had made him sick to the stomach that justice was a meaningless word, that virtue was equally useless, that the universe was a demonically constructed trap for anyone who thought otherwise.

To think of it, even now, made his legs shake and brought a bitter taste, like rotten walnuts, to his mouth. He did think of it, and of the past and of Center City and all that had occurred there. It seemed so long ago, and as distant as the background of a city in a landscape seen through a stereopticon device. But at least once a month he would have to adjust his mind to think of it, for there would invariably be a letter for him on the foyer table in his lodging house from someone at the Page Board and Hotel; and though, often enough, he let it sit unopened a week or more, ultimately he would open it, and read it, and despite the writer's tact and fear of offending, be reminded again.

When the first letters had reached him, Augusta Page and Amasa Murcott had alternated as correspondents. She still did write, but not the doctor any more, not after the time when Ransom had written angrily back to his old friend, rebutting all his arguments for returning to Center City, declaring he would remain where he was and desired no further interference.

Murcott's place was taken by Isabelle Page, the most faithful and informative of correspondents. She too reiterated how much Ransom was missed in every letter she wrote, but of all the three only Isabelle seemed to understand that Ransom had had no other option at the time he'd left—and still hadn't one. So she closed every letter with the hope that he would return if and when he saw fit: his office remained unrented, waiting for him.

In between greeting and closing, she wrote of the many changes that almost daily occurred in Center City. Not so much among the boarders, who remained a stable enough lot, but in the town itself.

Carl Dietz had finally retired from the bench, and had not been succeeded by any handpicked Mason-Dinsmore-Applegate crony, but instead by Thomas Dalger Jackson, a man from Omaha with dull enough credentials but strong ties to Dietz's supporters in Lincoln. Nor had Joseph Jeffries gained much ground. Following the trial many townspeople who'd read the Lincoln *Journal* had asked that it continue to be delivered. Instead, the *Journal* had opened an office and printing press right on Emerson Street and now competed quite openly with the Center City *Star*.

To balance these positive changes was the news that Dinsmore had succeeded in having himself elected president of the Chamber of Commerce, and that the Lane businesses—under his continued control—were growing at an unprecedented rate. His failed attempt the year before to raise and fix feed prices had this past winter succeeded. The Lane Hotel was now a major attraction for anyone traveling west of the Mississippi—completely revamped to reflect rich living. He had purchased a plot of land on one side of the railroad siding and had erected two large cylindrical grain elevators with the most up-to-date machinery, so that freight cars could be loaded right there, a hundred yards from the station. Dozens of other machines—harvesters, motor-trucks, and motorized scythes—carried the Lane name on their sides. Profits were expected to treble this year, and again next year, with all the improvements. A library had been donated to the town by Lane Industries. It was already under construction on the block of McKinley Avenue that fronted the plaza and the courthouse, and would soon be joined by a rebuilt town hall and post office, also to be constructed on the plaza; they were to share the Greek Revival style of the courthouse, and were to be co-financed by Lane Industries and the Mason Centennial Bank. Motorcars had proliferated in town—and were all the rage on the Hill, where stables had been converted to garages and coachmen transformed into chauffeurs. Dinsmore rented out motorcars with drivers from a large private garage in back of the railroad station, off Taylor Avenue. Plans for asphalting a dozen streets and laying concrete sidewalks all over town had been approved by the town council. As had trolleys on Center and Dakota Streets. Naturally enough, as the council itself was merely an inkstamp for Dinsmore and his friends.

Some other townspeople who had undergone changes, according to Ransom's correspondents, included Abraham Mathis, Millard Bowles, and Anthony Pulver. Mathis had finally retired from the mortician business and had moved to his property outside of town. After three or four months a successor had been found to take over the onerous responsibilities: a nephew of Mrs. Brennan's who had come from Kansas City, Missouri, to live in Center City. Another juror from the Dinsmore trial, young Pulver, had suddenly gone amok less than a month ago, proposing marriage to a half dozen young ladies in the space of three days, all of whom had accepted—to Pulver's and everyone else's consternation and confusion.

On the darker side, Millard Bowles had somehow escaped custody and fled town. He'd been taken on as gardener and general handyman by Judge Dietz, who had promised to help him win his case. Millard's escape had naturally proved embarrassing to the judge, and old Yolanda had taken it very hard, especially when—less than a week later—posters fixing a price on her son's head had been put up at the post office. It was believed by most townspeople that Millard had gone down to St. Louis, where he was probably working under an assumed name. If so, Yolanda never admitted it and never stopped grieving for Millard. Should her son ever be returned to Nebraska he would be held without bail until tried. No one in Center City doubted that he would be found guilty.

Carrie Lane, of course, was now the second Mrs. Dinsmore. That had happened last September, to no one's surprise after all. She was not much seen these days, although the wedding had been a large one with a lavish dinner and reception held in the Lane Hotel's newly expanded restaurant–dining room: a third of the town had been invited and attended. Not, curiously enough, Harriet Ingram, who nevertheless remained as housekeeper in the big house on High Street. Nor did Carrie ever appear at any of the town's social functions without her husband, and then only briefly, so briefly as to cause comment. Neither Isabelle nor her mother had been able to again gain entrance to her house: their visits were ignored, their letters returned unopened. This was especially saddening to Isabelle, who had hoped to remain friendly with Carrie, she wrote, if only for Ransom's sake.

When the letter containing this last news had come, Ransom had felt caged in his small rooms on Pearl Street, and had left the lodging to go where he could breathe more easily. Walking over to the East River, he had found a stone balcony that had been built to jut out over the rough waters. He had remained there for more than two hours, hatless, insufficiently clothed against the wet, gusty weather, staring blankly across the torrents to the gray farms of Long Island on the other side. Not thinking of anything in particular, he'd had to admit—only feeling slightly, if bitterly, pleased that he had been right to leave, to come here. Hadn't he known, that last night he'd seen Carrie in the reading room, that this would happen? Seen it so clearly that that fact alone had finally impelled him to leave Center City? . . .

Without that fact, with Carrie, he could have undergone all the other humiliations and anxieties as though they were nothing. Dinsmore's change of mind after the shooting and his attempt to have Ransom tried for murder and for influencing witnesses; the three weeks of waiting to hear that the state grand jury had rejected all motions against Ransom; the withdrawal of one after another of his clients; the looks without greeting he got from so many townspeople he'd previously thought friends; and finally the realization that while his life and liberty had been protected by allies at the capitol, he was now considered of little value and would never figure in any of their future plans—all this—his ruin, as Carrie had so succinctly, so heartlessly termed it—all this Ransom could have survived. But not with her rejection the evening of the acquittal, nor later when he'd tried to see her, to write her, and—like the Page women—hadn't succeeded.

Whenever he meditated now, it was not on these matters, nor even on the curious pattern this failure had made after one so like it, twenty years before, but on how foolish he'd been for so long to think that life held any good at all.

That was the legacy he'd inherited upon awakening that dreadful day not only from a mesmeric trance, but from a far more insidious delusion—that of optimism, faith in an ethical system that was in truth chaotic, and belief in himself as someone who could in some way help others when in fact he had been an absurd, sleeping fool all the while and had probably done more harm than good.

His face would set hard whenever he thought like this, his lips would draw right down into the graying whiskers of his mustaches, wrinkles would furrow his forehead, and he would look and feel not merely forty-four years old, but sixty-four, eighty-four, a hundred and four.

And it always seemed to happen on a Sunday, when there was no copying or routine to occupy him, when the streets of lower Manhattan were abandoned by all but souls as lost as himself, when church bells would toll endless reproaches through the urban canyons, and he would feel empty again with longing.

———————————•———————————

THE AUGUST AFTERNOON THAT the letter from Center City was delivered to Walker and Jerome, Inc., and subsequently laid upon his copying desk, was also the birthday of Hugh Jerome, partner of the company, and so a half-holiday for the office.

After Ransom had joined the others in raising his glass of sherry to toast his employer, he grabbed the big envelope and, stuffing it into his waistcoat pocket, walked outside and down to the Battery Park, where he found a bench and sat staring for a while at the water traffic of New York Harbor and its environs. Once he decided he had enjoyed as much sun as he wished, he moved to another, shadier bench and there weighed the bulky packet from Isabelle in one hand, wondering what had compelled her to send it to the office, instead of to his lodgings as she usually did.

The minute the letter had been placed before his eyes he had seen that it contained something, and he had copied page after page of his work, unable to stop speculating on what it contained. He decided finally that whatever was inside was either trivial or terribly important: and the possibilities immediately made his stomach flutter. Thus the trip to the water's edge, thus the need for placidity, utter calm, and even a little thought before looking inside.

He carefully tore one end of the envelope and the packet slipped into his palm. Another envelope was within the familiar sheets of Isabelle's stationery. The inner envelope was familiar to him also—seen before and well remembered. But when he shook it loose and inspected it, the handwriting was not what he expected, the scent he had anticipated was not present, the sender not her, but her housekeeper. What had Mrs. Ingram to say to him now? was his first thought. Then disappointment flooded in: the letter hadn't been important after all.

So he balanced it on one knee and read Isabelle's letter. Only at the end, in a postscript, did she mention the enclosure. It had been received a day before her own had been written and so she had included it.

Ransom reread Isabelle's letter, and once more gave himself to his now habitual meditation on the past and what it meant. That rite completed, he once more moved out into the sunlight, and opened Mrs. Ingram's letter only as an afterthought.

It was dated August 8th, and was quite startling:

Dear Mr. Ransom,

I have wronged you. I have betrayed you, and Carrie, and myself—most of all, myself.

I wish to right these wrongs before it is too late. Not for myself, not even really for you, though I owe it to you. But so much for her—from whom I can never hope to be forgiven for all the ill I have brought.

I am willing to give testimony that will not only prove the crimes HE has been acquitted of, but also will indict myself along with HIM in a plot to have her murdered and to thereby gain all her possessions.

To do this I must have your assistance. I can turn to no one else. They are all his tools and co-conspirators. Only you never were, never could be.

I know you have left Center City and have gone to live somewhere east. I am sending this to you at the Page Board and Hotel, knowing that the good Augusta Page will forward it. I sincerely hope this letter reaches you. For with it, I believe, you will return here and save her, and save all of us—God willing—from this Lucifer who has been unleashed upon us.

I will meet with you at whatever date and time you wish, but only in Dr. Murcott's office, as I fear that my movements are closely watched.

I beg you do not delay. Her life is still in danger. I beg you do not deny me the opportunity to atone, nor she the opportunity to live.

Harriet Ingram

Was it a joke? A monstrous joke perpetrated by Dinsmore or one of his cronies?

Ransom reread it. As his eyes scanned the lines, he pictured the tall, rawboned woman with her plaits of ash-blond hair, her huge goggling eyes—pictured her not as she'd been at the house on High Street, or even on the witness stand, but as she'd looked when she'd come up from Dr. Murcott's office on that surprising visit so long ago, armed with her enigmas and bizarre behavior. Sitting bolt upright in the chair, her porkpie hat perched atop her hair, her eyes wandering to the door, her whispering intense voice. She had led him into the madness of the past once before. Wasn't it like her to try to lead him into it again! The contrary spinster, the reeling, revolting, back-stabbing bitch! She'd hated him from the beginning. Now that she could see what a fool he was, she'd try it again. No thank you, ma'am.

At a third reading his anger dissolved. He reread the lines about the plot to murder Carrie. Imagine! Mrs. Ingram and Dinsmore. And it hadn't come off. Why? Had she demurred at the last moment? And had Dinsmore not been able to do it without her help? She wrote that Carrie's life was still in danger. How? Why? And why was she begging him—she, one of the potential killers—to come save the intended victim? What kind of nonsense was that?

Not nonsense at all, a chill up his spine told him—the same kind of chill one might feel despite the blazing hot weather, and of which superstitious people would say, "Someone's treading on your graveplot this very minute."

Now he was angry again at Mrs. Ingram. For, if it weren't a

joke, why drag him—half the continent distant—into it? There were others who would help her. She said there weren't, but there were. It wasn't his business any longer: he lived here, not there. Carrie Lane was Dinsmore's woman, not his: she never really had been his, except as a tantalization. It was Dinsmore's problem. Or Dietz's, or this new Judge Jackson's, even Murcott's: not Ransom's anymore. He would send her letter to one of them, to that new judge, and let him worry about it. Let him decide if it were worthwhile testimony. Ransom didn't even practice law anymore, never mind have prosecuting powers. Jackson did. Let him worry about it.

That decided, that was the course he took, returning home and immediately writing a short note to the new county judge to explain her letter, then quickly posting it, the thick envelope so much resembling the one he had received that morning, but its disturbing contents at least out of his hands.

But not far from his thoughts. Much as he tried in the following days to forget it, he could not. Sometimes he thought it must be the work of an overwrought, a hysterical woman—none of it true. But too often he found himself wishing Mrs. Ingram had given more details. How she had wronged him and Carrie was evident, but how had she betrayed herself? What of this murder plot? Was it real or imagined? Fabricated because she thought it would draw him back?

Then came his second surprise: a long, pale brown envelope that appeared on his copying desk during midmorning, the telegraph company's name emblazoned across its front. Everyone in the room stopped work, as though on signal, their pen nubs silenced, and all around Ransom a hush of expectation loomed. But he worked on as though oblivious to the telegram's presence until the other copyists slowly returned to their work. A minute later, he heard one of them, an ancient, pale-eyed, blank-faced man named Barnaby, pronounce in a loud voice, "Someone's dead." That was all Ransom needed. He immediately tore it open.

It had been sent that morning from Lincoln. It was from Judge Jackson and was remarkable for both its tersity and content:

THE WOMAN WILL TALK TO NONE BUT YOU STOP YOU
ARE EMPOWERED TO RETURN STOP YOU ARE REAP-
POINTED STOP WIRE IF TRAIN FARE REQUIRED.

Ransom held onto the desk and reread the telegram. Then he
turned to face the room. They had all once more stopped their
work, and were eagerly awaiting the news. Even Hugh Jerome
had noticed the stoppage from behind the glass panel through
which he kept an eye on his copyists. He strode into the room
and said, "Well, what is it? Will it be stop and go all day?"

Jerome threw a particularly suspicious glance at the old scrivener as the possible ringleader of the copyists' mutiny, but then
caught sight of the brown block of telegram in Ransom's hand.

The others bent over their work once again, but Ransom just
held out the telegram until Jerome came over to read it. The
partner snorted once, then harumphed loudly and returned the
paper to Ransom, reminding him to finish his day's work. Then
he went back into his office.

Later that evening, as the employees were all leaving, the old
scrivener who'd spoken up before came to Ransom's desk and
once more hollowly asked:

"Someone's dead?"

"No," Ransom replied. "I am called back."

———————— ● ————————

HE HAD WIRED TO AUGUSTA PAGE, saying he had been given
a holiday and would be visiting for a short while.

Even so, he was not met at the railroad station, and he preferred it that way, wanting to attract no attention. A trolley line
now met the trains, and as it went right past the Page Board and
Hotel, Ransom got onto it with his single bag. He stayed away
from the windows and the other passengers—two young women,
not of his acquaintance, who were preoccupied anyway in flirting
at the front of the car with the open-faced young driver.

The changes on the face of Center City since his departure
were evident everywhere. The new sidewalks, this trolley car,

the half dozen motorcars of all shapes and sizes he had already seen. But more than all of it had been the unmistakable sign of change in the two huge, black-painted Lane Grain and Feed Co. grain elevators just north of the railroad station. The track had turned east coming into town, passing them on one side, but from the railway platform they looked as though they framed the Hill, guarding the way into the town with the same ebony indifference as the gates of hell.

Ransom's welcome was a quiet one. It was midafternoon: Mrs. Page was out shopping, Dr. Murcott seeing a patient, and none of the other boarders present. Isabelle—no longer at Mrs. Brennan's shop full-time, she explained—answered his ring and half jumped up to kiss Ransom's cheek, unashamedly glad to see him. She sobered up immediately after in response to his own seriousness, and led him to his old room on the second floor. He protested, not wanting to displace any other boarder, but she said the rooms still hadn't been let out: he was displacing no one. She would fix him tea or coffee downstairs in the kitchen, or bring it up here if he wished. He must be hungry.

He wasn't, but he ate an obligatory home-baked cookie or two as they had their tea. Isabelle did not ask how long he would be in town, or why. But she did emit an unmistakable aura of pleasure, even though he did look pale and tired to her, as though he didn't get enough sleep and fresh air, as though he worried too much.

Ransom was grateful for both her concern and her tact: and, as she got up from the table and went to work in the kitchen, half turning to talk to him as she cleaned vegetables, he found himself thinking that if he had had any sense at all two years ago, he would have realized what a prize of young womanhood Isabelle Page really was. Old Carr had known that: and said as much in his dying words. If Ransom had only not gotten involved with Carrie Lane, not listened to Mrs. Ingram that sweltering day— if he had remained as he had always been, Isabelle might have remained within his reach, and not become—as she was now— only another possibility he'd missed by not seeing it in time.

Nate was the next family member he encountered. He had just

returned from school—half a head taller, much more gangling than before, with his mother's fleshy nose and wide cheeks, and with a shock of hair that was almost blue it was so black. Nate recalled Ransom, naturally, but he was shy with him until their old relations were reestablished. This was accomplished when Ransom asked the boy if he would run an errand for him, or if he no longer did such things.

"Bringing a letter somewhere?"

"There's a tip in it for you," Ransom tempted him.

"Aw! I don't want any tip. I'll bring it for you. Where to?"

"High Street. You've been there before. Mrs. Ingram."

The brother and sister exchanged glances; then Nate said: "They don't take our letters anymore at High Street."

"She'll take this one," Ransom declared, and, leaving it an enigma, he went upstairs to write to her. Meeting in the doctor's office would not be necessary, he wrote: his own office would be available. He set the meeting for the following afternoon, when ostensibly her domestic duties would be the lightest. Then he gave the note to the boy and sat at the desk, looking out his window toward the Hill, until his reverie was broken by the call to dinner.

That proved to be far easier than he'd feared. Only the immediate family and old Floyd and Dr. Murcott were present. The other boarders had been sent to the Lane Hotel restaurant this evening. There were only two of them anyway, the boarding-house having become associated with Ransom's name; like Ransom himself, still somewhat shunned.

Everyone was on his best behavior at the table. Ransom and Murcott were reconciled immediately, and old Floyd edited his gossip or had it limited by Mrs. Page with various throat-clearings and stern looks. The older man and the boy went out for a walk after dinner, and the others went upstairs to the second-floor parlor, where a card table was set up and whist dealt out. Ransom became exhausted quite early on and retired to his room, feeling not so much at home in it as he'd thought he would.

The following day was passed rather aimlessly until after

lunch. Amasa and he talked: his friend confirming each of the details of the news one of the correspondents had mentioned. Ransom did not tell his friend the cause of his return: as far as he was concerned it was still only a visit. He would hear what Harriet Ingram had to tell; he'd bring her testimony to this new judge, Jackson, and make certain the case would be reopened if need be and someone reliable at Lincoln found to do the prosecuting. Then he would return to New York, to Walker and Jerome, Inc., to the empty Sundays and his by now consoling meditations on the past. Seeing the housekeeper would be nothing more then tying the last knot in the last loose thread. He owed it to himself to see it well tied. He owed nothing further to anyone else.

Only when Harriet Ingram arrived and was sitting in his office did Ransom acknowledge to himself that he had once more mis-anticipated. He'd expected a woman on the brink of madness, her suspiciousness and intent whispering of that previous meeting worse than before, and decorated by other quirks of growing illness.

Instead she was reserved and quite calm—with the same calm that he knew so well in himself: the calm of having known utter despair. She was dressed in dark clothing, her face covered by beige-brown veils hung from a large hat that all but hid her features except at close range. But at close range he could make out easily enough her drawn cheeks, her eyes red-rimmed as though from too much rubbing.

"You are very kind to have come this great distance," she said as he asked her to sit down.

"I had a few other matters to attend to in Center City," he lied.

Humbled, she replied then that he was kind to have agreed to see her. Ransom let that pass without comment and bade her speak when she wished. They remained quiet for several moments.

"I know you must think me deranged," she began again, hesitantly. "But I assure you I am not. There have been times when I have been. Yes. Or so close to it that it makes little difference. But not now."

She still looked to him. He still held back.

"I did not lie upon the witness stand," she said suddenly. "I mean it about he and she."

"I know."

"I thought if I said it that you would stop the trial. That you would somehow or other end it all. I couldn't have it go on. Not with the possibility that . . . that Frederick would die," she finally blurted out.

"I was jealous," she went on more glibly. "I admit that now. Jealousy was not something I'd ever felt before I met Frederick. Before he came to the house, I adored her. You can't imagine how much I adored her. If Henry Lane was like a father to her, I tried to be a mother, a sister, an older friend to her. But he came and all that changed. The moment I noticed Frederick he was looking at her in that unmistakable manner you men all have. And then I began to hate her. To envy her. Not only for all she had, but because in addition she would have Frederick too."

Ransom listened, feeling the past suddenly sweep into the office like a large bird of prey, its pinions fluttering in the too confined space. Why did he have to hear all this? Again. And still again. But he listened, and when she paused, he said:

"Is that when you plotted against her life?"

"No. Later."

"Go on then," he prompted, not wanting to hear another word.

"What will you do with all this?"

"That depends. If it is adequate testimony to reopen the case . . ."

"It is," she interrupted. "I know it is."

"If it is, then Judge Jackson will order a retrial."

"Do you know him? Do you trust him?"

"He's trustworthy. Don't worry."

"And you will re-try him. And this time I'll tell the truth," she said.

"Judge Jackson will decide all that. I will not personally re-try the case."

"Why not? You must!"

"I'm no longer an official of this county. I can't."

"Then how will you gain back your name, your reputation?"

"Mrs. Ingram, that's not the problem we're dealing with. Let that be my concern, if it is one. If you please, just tell me what it is you have to say, and I assure you a prosecutor from the capitol will be appointed. I will brief him. I will make certain he is not known to Dinsmore."

"You despise me, don't you?" she suddenly asked.

"Not at all. I do wish you'd tell me . . ."

"You haven't even asked about her. I thought that would be the first thing you would want to know. Is it that you don't care for her anymore?"

The woman still hadn't lost her ability to exasperate him.

"If you wish to tell me, go ahead."

"Awful. Terrible. Horrible," she spat out the words. "He has sent her out to the ranch. Forbidden me to see her. I've been once despite him. I wish I hadn't. She's using the drops again. Too many of them, I believe. She is quite distracted-looking. I don't know what he told that German woman—that Carrie is mad and must be watched closely, I suppose. It makes no difference. Carrie is hardly aware of anyone else, even in the same room."

Now Ransom truly wished Mrs. Ingram would leave. The past swirled slowly about the office, enfolding him, smothering him.

"I am very sorry to hear that," he said.

"Will you see her?"

"I think not."

"Ah! It's my fault. Mine, that she refused you. Mine, that all this has come to pass. But you see I loved Frederick so, and I was so afraid you would hang him."

"Mrs. Ingram, understand this: if you give testimony, in all probability he still might be hanged. You know that, don't you?"

She was silent. In a small voice she said, "I know, yes."

"As that is understood, I suggest you begin."

The tale she proceeded to tell over the next hour and a half was not a very pretty one, and she did nothing to make it any more palatable. She was so intent that the blame be laid at her door, that her faults and errors be known, that she never once hesitated. She did not look directly at Ransom as she talked, but at some spot on his desk blotter. This made it easier for him to turn away, too—to gaze at her, at the wall, out the window, anywhere so as to not have to see the past everywhere about him.

Why must she feel that she had to confess to him? Why must everyone, anyone, feel that he was the sole repository for their vices, their secrets, their pondered guilt? It irritated him to sit listening to her. What did he care of her or her ridiculous passions?

Or rather passion—because as she talked, he realized why he was to be the listener. Because, like her, he too had been drawn into affection and then spurned once and for all. And, in both their cases, what was so pathetic was that such mature people had let themselves be trapped in all-consuming passions usually associated with the youthfully ignorant.

Harriet Ingram hadn't been present when Frederick Dinsmore had been brought to dinner on High Street by Henry Lane. She had not served the meal, nor had she attended at the table. But housekeepers were seldom noticed, although *they* seemed to notice everything and everyone. She had seen the dental surgeon that night and had been taken with him that very instant. She had also seen his immediate attraction to Carrie Lane. She had thought, however, that she knew her employer well enough to fear no reciprocation of affection. In this she had been sorely mistaken.

She went on to relate minuscule but acutely embarrassing incidents by means of which she had finally communicated her interest and secured Dinsmore's attention to herself. His reaction was both mocking and gallant, she said. He was clearly intrigued. On his fourth visit to the Lane house, a later meeting was arranged between them. He left the house by the front door and returned by the kitchen door, and in the course of that night sealed his connection with her.

Mrs. Ingram was more reticent about the extent of their sexual activities, but evidently Dinsmore believed he had her sufficiently under control by her passion alone, and did not mesmerize her for many months. He did—slowly and bit by bit

—reveal to her his plan to take over the Lane enterprises, eliminating first Mr. Lane, then Mrs. Lane. The task would be a difficult and time-consuming one: Mrs. Ingram would have to be patient. Reluctantly, she agreed. In her growing odium of her mistress, she could think of no finer plan than to displace her and reign over the High Street house and its social affairs.

This would be accomplished in a manner that would raise few suspicions. Henry Lane would commit suicide, and after Carrie Lane had married Dinsmore, she would either do likewise or somehow be manipulated into having a carefully planned accident.

Mrs. Ingram's account of her delusion and her ensuing fears and anxieties was detailed to a point that annoyed Ransom. She seemed to take special pleasure now in declaring her foolishness, her blindness to what was so evident. But—and even without being mesmerized—she had agreed to the plan, she said.

Her first shock was the accomplishment of its first step—Henry Lane's suicide. That frightened her terribly. She had no dislike of the man, but no exceptional love for him either—kind as he always was to his wife all the years she'd kept house for him, Lane had been nothing more than businesslike with Mrs. Ingram. Then, too, in those final six months he had gone at her mercilessly in her weekly accounting, making unreasonable demands for savings, even accusing her of theft. Still, she had never expected to see him hanging like that—so Godawful—from the stable rafter.

But at that time she also realized their plan would go on from here. Along with her increased guilt and fear came the pleasure at the idea of her eventual triumph and elevation.

When Frederick moved into the house, she already knew that he held Carrie Lane by a mesmeric bond. Mrs. Ingram decided to play her role of underling as long it was neccessary for the whole scheme to be worked out. But she grew suspicious of her lover. He slept downstairs, close to her bedroom, where he spent many nights, but often enough he would put her off with excuses —lies, she knew. One day she discovered him and Carrie "sporting," as she called it, in broad daylight upstairs. When she confronted him with what she'd seen, Dinsmore told her it had been necessary to insure their marriage. When Mrs. Ingram also discovered them together at night, she threatened to reveal the plan.

The result of that threat was her first taste of the posthypnotic effect. One moment she was on her way to the larder to get something, the next she was outside at the well, a hundred yards away, not knowing where she was or why. Only when she was told by the Masons' gardener that she'd run screaming onto Grant Street and had only with great difficulty been returned did she realize how complete and nefarious his control over her was.

She continued to rebel, however. When Dinsmore was tired of her nagging, tired of explaining his plans to her, he would become angry with her, and she never knew what to expect then: for he would always cause her to harm herself in some dangerous manner. Then his carnal connection with Mrs. Lane appeared to end, and he and Mrs. Ingram were at peace again for a while.

It had been the first of these posthypnotic trances that had frightened Mrs. Ingram into coming to see Ransom that overheated day two years ago. She had been so afraid, and so guilty and unwilling to go along with their plan then, that she had led Ransom right to her lover's door. She had regretted that later. But at least Dinsmore had never learned of her visit—for he hardly ever mesmerized her except to teach her to remain obedient.

Once Carrie Lane had agreed to testify, Mrs. Ingram was certain both she and Dinsmore were lost. The evening her mistress had not come home from the Dietzes' house had been one of extraordinary conflict for her. But not as bad as Carrie's arrival the next morning, and her declaration that she was leaving Center City. That had been ghastly. Mrs. Ingram had sent a messenger to Dinsmore, but he had been nowhere to be found, and had not received the message until after Ransom and Carrie had driven off into the snowstorm.

When the trial began, Mrs. Ingram's fears had not been so much for herself as for him. Her attempts to persuade her employer against standing witness led to a break between them that had never healed. And she had certainly feared what would happen if she herself should be called to testify by Ransom. She knew she would be unable to lie under oath, but she also knew she could not tell the truth with Dinsmore in the room.

Fortunately Ransom had not called her. When she had appeared in court with her damaging evidence against Carrie it had been from desperation, thinking of the noose already around Frederick's throat.

He—and she too—had been saved by the shooting, and later by the acquittal.

Once Ransom was gone, Mrs. Lane had become a doomed woman—one eager for her doom. She had married Dinsmore with no resistance, but she still could not abide having him near her.

It had been just last winter, when Mrs. Ingram had thought she would have only a short wait until the plan was completed, that she had realized how deeply she had been betrayed. . . .

Dinsmore no longer lived downstairs, and his own upstairs room was unoccupied most nights, as he cavorted with waitresses and dance-hall girls at the Lane Hotel. When he did spend his nights at home, his door was locked to the housekeeper. He scarcely talked to her, treated her as much like a servant as Henry Lane had done. When she complained, he bade her be patient: he could not marry and immediately kill off his wife.

Harriet Ingram remembered well the day she became aware that the plan would never go off as he had said: that he would never harm Carrie. The housekeeper had been upstairs one afternoon and was on her way down when she overheard voices in the reading room. She retreated to Mrs. Dinsmore's room and from there saw a curious sight—Frederick, on his knees before his wife, almost in tears, begging for Carrie's affection. She refused him—once again, from the tenor of her words—saying she would never willingly give her heart to him, worthless as that organ was for its inconstancy anyway. Whatever else he wished of her he might take. He'd taken it often enough before. Dinsmore begged and pleaded. He said he had done it all for her. For her! And that he never would have if she hadn't existed.

Carrie remained adamant. Dinsmore finally left the room, shaking with anger, the color drained from his face. When Mrs. Ingram accosted him two minutes later, he not only did not deny the scene or explain it away, but he cursed Carrie, saying she would never sleep a wink again if she continued to oppose his wishes. As for Mrs. Ingram, she ought to consider herself fortunate she still had her job and her life. He would have Carrie or no one. Certainly not Mrs. Ingram.

By the time the housekeeper had recovered from that shock some days later, she discovered his threat had not been an idle one. The insomnia had returned to her employer. Carrie fought it for weeks; then she went back to the consoling drops. After months, Dinsmore could no longer stand to see his wife's degeneration, and put out the word that she was ill and would go to recuperate at the ranch. He admitted sadly to Mrs. Ingram that he had been unable to mesmerize Carrie again to counteract his dreadful edict. She was now too deeply addicted to the drug, and far too distracted with or without it, to be able to concentrate long enough for his mesmerism to work on her.

So Carrie was safe from Dinsmore. Although not at all safe from a new peril—herself. The German woman kept the drops locked up now and administered them carefully to her charge, for Dinsmore and Mrs. Ingram had been given a too-vivid demonstration of how much of the drug Mrs. Dinsmore could take; they had caught her one day draining it from the bottle at her lips. They feared that if she ever had it in her hands again she would use it to take her own life.

Wouldn't Ransom go see her, try to talk to her, Mrs. Ingram begged him? He had always been able to influence her before.

He didn't answer. Instead he asked if she had any further testimony to give, or if that were all.

That was all—wasn't it enough? she asked. And before she could once more begin her self-reproaches, Ransom saw her down to the front door.

Afterward, he sat and looked out the window for a long time, wishing he too could find oblivion in a drug.

———————————●———————————

IT WAS MORE THAN AN HOUR LATER, and only with great difficulty, that Ransom was able to transfer Harriet Ingram's words onto paper. Writing it down was difficult not so much because of its content but rather because his interest in it was so divided. After a half dozen false starts, he put it aside, interrupted by the call to dinner.

Later on that evening he worked at her testimony again, but lethargically. He told himself that he had come all the way from New York for this—he might as well do it. He had no illusions about its efficacy. He doubted whether her evidence was strong enough to reopen the trial, especially with Dinsmore so entrenched in Center City.

Rereading it the following morning, he concluded that it would have to do. After breakfast, he decided to take it in person to this new county judge, Thomas Jackson.

As he walked past the central plaza to the courthouse, Ransom couldn't shake a feeling he had had since he'd returned to town that there was no longer a place for him here. No one noticed him; or if they did, they pretended to not recognize him. Not that this area was so crowded at ten in the morning: only a few women shopping and several servants intent on their errands. But he felt strangely distant—as though he were already dead, an unseen ghost haunting the streets.

All the more of a shock, then, once he'd rung the bell outside the county clerk's office, that Alvin Barker opened the door and looked on him with surprised recognition written all over his face. He recovered quickly enough and earnestly shook Ransom's hand, taking it in both of his own, asking questions Ransom felt constrained to answer.

That done, Ransom asked after Judge Dietz.

"Retired now," Barker said. "Not even in town much anymore. Out at Plum Creek mostly."

"Perhaps I'll pay him a visit," Ransom said; at the same time deciding he would do no such thing. "This is for Judge Jackson. Is he in?"

"Not today. Up at Lincoln."

"He seems to be up at Lincoln a great deal these days," Ransom commented.

"Yes sir. Something is up, though exactly what I wouldn't venture to say. He'll be back today, though. Tonight at the latest. You can leave that parcel. I'll see he gets it as soon as possible."

Ransom then asked after Barker and his family and took his leave. At the bench where he'd expected to see old Floyd, he was told by another old-timer that Floyd was employed nowadays as a driver for the new Lane Public Garage. It seemed that motorcar driving was one of the old man's many talents.

That piece of information depressed Ransom. It seemed that everyone in Center City was employed by or somehow had made his peace with Dinsmore. No wonder he felt like a stranger. Only he could never bring himself to do such a thing. He, and possibly Carrie too.

Talking of Floyd and the Lane Garage reminded Ransom of Golden, still at the Lane Public Stables, boarded and used by Amasa Murcott since Ransom had gone away. He wanted to see his horse again.

The stable hands were the same as last year. They, and Golden too, remembered Ransom. While they chattered on, asking him questions, the horse bent his head to be stroked, and nuzzled Ransom's hat from behind as he had always done before.

"Looks like he's getting old and fat," Ransom said.

"The doctor don't ride him all that much," one man said. "Not a tenth of the way you did."

Just stroking the horse made Ransom itch to ride. He said so.

"No problem at all. I'll saddle him up."

Coming out of Williams Street, Ransom hesitated. He held a loose rein on Golden and walked the steed toward High Street, which ran north and south. To go as far as Plum Creek—to see Carl and Lavinia Dietz—would be unconscionable. What if Murcott needed Golden for an emergency? Before Ransom could decide, the horse decided for him. Restless to be off, Golden snorted impatiently, then turned left up High Street toward the Hill. That was as quick a way out of town as any, Ransom thought, so he took a firmer hold on the reins and rode north.

As always when they rode together, Ransom let the horse go at his own speed. Today Golden seemed to require a great deal of exercise. Before Ransom knew it, they were so far from Center City that all he could make out was the gabled roofs of the two dark-colored grain elevators: Dinsmore's legacy, the uneffaceable sign of his blot on the town.

A few minutes more and he was at the turnoff to the Lane ranch. His grip on the reins must have been too loose, because Golden immediately turned onto the property and began to descend.

"Whoa! Hold on. We're not going there."

But though he had stopped Golden, he hesitated before turning back onto the old post road again. Maybe this was what he'd been thinking of—just beneath the surface of his consciousness —all the while he'd been at the stables. No. He didn't want to see her. Especially not if she were in the condition Mrs. Ingram had depicted yesterday. So he hesitated, and once more Golden took the lead and slowly walked down to the ranch.

Well, maybe just for a look around. He wouldn't actually go up to the place. He'd stay at a distance and look.

When he'd arrived at the bunkhouse, Ransom stopped. Nothing seemed different. The windows and doors were shut. No one was to be seen. It appeared as deserted as when he'd first come here so many months before. The only sign of the passage of time was the incredible lushness of the cook's tiny garden patch. It had been a coolish, wet summer here, and the little overgrown vegetable plot looked like a minuscule oasis in so much desert.

The German woman must be somewhere. Ought he find her? If only to say hello, and to ask after her patient? He rode up to the ranch, expecting at any moment to have someone come out to meet him. No one did.

Nor did anyone answer his first, tentative knock on the front door. He walked slowly around the building, at the same time wishing to keep his presence unknown and hoping to get someone's attention. Not a window open. Had they deserted the place? Gone somewhere else? The garden gave the lie to that—unless it were a very recent desertion, a day at the most.

When he reached the front of the house again, he knocked once more, then tried the door latch. To his surprise it opened, and he stood teetering for a minute on the lintel, staring at the shadowed interior. Then he stepped down and began to inch forward. What if Carrie had succeeded in getting the drug away from the cook and had taken it all? What if she were there somewhere, dying or already dead? Abandoned by the cook, who had fled in fear? What if . . . ? There was a noise.

Ransom turned toward its source, the kitchen, and as he did, he heard the kitchen door click shut and he just made out the blur of a figure running past the window. He rushed to the door. It had been locked from outside. He tried to see who it was, but couldn't, and had to make his way to the front door.

The daylight blinded him; he had to shade his eyes and adjust to the glare. He looked around. No one. Nothing. Not a sound. All as it had been. Perhaps there had been no one at all? Perhaps his imagination had been playing a trick on him? Yes, that must have been it. He nevertheless walked around the house once more, hearing nothing, seeing no one. Then he mounted Golden again.

He hoped nothing serious had happened to Carrie. They had probably gone into town for some reason. She and the cook. Possibly even to Lincoln, to see a doctor. Perhaps it was better this way. He hadn't really wanted to see her, he thought, cantering out of the ranch yard. As he was about to turn onto the post road something caught his eye. A piece of lace stuck on a branch of blasted berry bush—lace that had once trimmed a woman's collar or sleeve. He stopped and then heard the snapping of a nearby twig. Golden heard it too, and gave a gruff snort. Could this belong to the intruder? Had Ransom caught someone in the act of burglary? That would explain why the front door was open. . . .

He dismounted, hitched Golden to a bough, and crept into the clump of bushes. Only a brief search was needed to convince him that no one was hiding there. He returned to the horse wondering if he was letting his imagination run away with him. Mounted again, Ransom turned to look back at the ranch house so long, so lost in aimless speculation, that Golden snorted, tugged at the reins, and finally began to walk toward the post road again. Ransom let the horse have its way, so unable to shake himself out of the anxious lethargy that suddenly gripped him that it was with a start that he realized that Golden had stopped once more.

A woman stood in the road blocking his way. A gaunt woman, ashen and haggard, her eyes sunk so deeply into the hollows of her face that she looked moribund. Her dress hung from her shoulders as though from a wire hanger. The pattern of the lace trimming on her dress matched the piece he still held in one hand. He looked down at it and up at the woman again, and this time her hair glittered in the sunlight like a sheet of molten copper.

It was her! Carrie!

"Not so long ago, Mr. Ransom, you would have lingered hours waiting for me," she said in a voice so cracked and hoarse that she might have been thirty years older. "Today you do not even bother to call my name."

He was so horrified by how she looked, by the realization that this harridan was her, his own, his Carrie, that Ransom scarcely understood what she had said. But her sense had been carried by the tone of her voice. Feeling unjustly attacked, he nevertheless dismounted and walked toward her.

"Keep your distance, please," she warned, stepping back a pace, until he too stopped.

Her lips were almost blue, her skin blue-white like Chinese porcelain that had aged for centuries. Her bones seemed to poke through the skin, that skin, that flesh that had once—so recently —been so soft, so creamy under his touch. As he stared at her she swayed slightly, but held out a hand to warn him off until she had regained her balance.

"Shouldn't you go back to the house?" he asked. He was sure

now that he had frightened her out of bed. It must have been she who had fled out the back door. Had she thought he was Dinsmore?

"Do I look so ghastly that I should be treated like an infirmary patient?" she asked, imperious now.

He could not answer, and she finally laughed in her hollow, cracked voice and said, "Well then, at least you are no impostor. I'm convinced of that now. Only James Ransom could be so candid with a lady. Yes, I'll go back to the house if you think that right. I was only out for a walk. I walk a great deal now. Not usually out here by the road. Sometimes, though, into the hills." She pointed to a series of mesas that appeared quite distant. "But, yes, I will go back to the house now. I am a bit tired. You may accompany me, Mr. Ransom."

He offered her the mount, but she wouldn't hear of riding such a short distance and started off down the road rapidly, Ransom following on foot.

"I . . . I heard you were out here," he finally was able to stammer when he had caught up with her.

"You live in New York City now, don't you?" she asked, ignoring his words. "Is it much changed since you last were there? It's been a long time since I've been there. Almost a decade now."

"The bridge to Brooklyn has been completed. They have a building twenty-five stories high. It was put up by Woolworth, the five-and-dime stores. Would you please slow down?"

She stopped and looked thoughtful. "Twenty-five stories high? It is changed, then."

He must have stared at her, for she suddenly said, "Do you think me very changed too? Is that why you look so long?"

"Carrie . . ." he began. Then, seeing she must have an answer: "Yes. You are much changed."

"I will tell you a secret, Mr. Ransom. I know that I am much changed. But I am not unhappy about it. Not at all unhappy."

"You can't be serious!"

"Ah, but I am. I'm very serious about it. Before, I had attractions. Now I don't. Before, men came to bother me. Now no one does. Not him. Not you. Not anyone. I'm rid now of all of you. I never wanted any of you, ever. I only wanted Henry, and that was years ago when I didn't know any better. And when that was not to be, well, then I didn't want any of you."

Her words struck him hard; he flushed to the roots of his hair. But then he thought, no, she couldn't mean what she was saying. She was distracted by the opium drops, crazed by the drug. She would say anything in this condition. Do anything.

"Where's Minna?" he asked. "The German woman?"

"You haven't heard one word I've said."

"I've heard all of it. That doesn't mean I believe it. You aren't yourself. You can't be."

"I'm not surprised you don't believe me. How could you?" she said enigmatically. Then, in a lighter tone, "Ah, well, myself or not, what I said I meant. I care nothing for what you or anyone else thinks or does. Nothing at all."

"Not even Dinsmore?"

"Not a bit," she declared.

"You did a few minutes ago," he pointed out. "You cared enough to run away from him when you thought it was he riding up to the house."

"I ran from you," she said. "I could see you. I knew it wasn't him, but you."

Had she found the locked-up drops and taken more than she ought to? Where was Minna? He had to find out.

"Where's the cook?" he asked again.

"I don't know. Off somewhere. Out with her beau!" she said and laughed again. "She has a beau. A very large, very fat man from Swedeville or thereabouts. She's quite enamored. Poor fool, and at her age," she scoffed.

"She just went off and left you?"

"And why not? She's poor enough company when she's here with me."

"But I thought . . ." he stammered.

"You thought what, Mr. Ransom? That she was my nurse? My

guard? Who told you that? Him? Or her? It must have been Harriet. I can't quite see you and him being friendly. Well, good. What else did she say?"

They had entered the yard in front of the ranch house. Ransom marveled to see how undistracted after all Carrie was now that they were talking: how in control she seemed. What was he to make of it?

"She said that you were addicted to the drops again. That you had tried to swallow a bottle of it once. Enough to kill yourself. And that Dinsmore couldn't help you anymore. That he couldn't even put you into a trance."

"And that I had been left out here to die?" she asked.

He hesitated. "That was the implication. Yes."

"Good. Fine," she said, satisfied. "Let them think that. It is just as I planned, just as I had hoped. But do not tell them you've been out here to see me. Do you hear? Don't tell a soul."

Ransom said he wouldn't tell anyone. But he still couldn't understand why. If she were recovered as she seemed . . .

"Do you mean to say you aren't using the drops anymore?" he had to ask.

"Not anymore."

"But . . . why frighten everyone, then?"

"What do I care what they think? Whether they are frightened or not?" she scoffed. "I was using the laudanum. A great deal of it. So much that there were times I thought I would die from it, or at least never be able to live without it. So much that it has turned me from the woman you were so enchanted by into . . . well, into what I am now. But that was a small enough price to pay for my freedom. You still don't understand what I'm saying, do you, Mr. Ransom?"

He was beginning to understand, and he was both fascinated and appalled. She had wanted to get away from Dinsmore so badly, so desperately that she had deliberately become a laudanum addict again, fulling realizing how horrible it would be, fully recognizing that this time she would have to use more of the drops, far more of them, come closer to death, become . . . become this awful, gaunt creature he was looking at in order to convince Dinsmore and Mrs. Ingram that she was beyond help.

"Just to get away from him?" he had to ask.

"From him. From her. From all of you."

He could scarcely believe it. It must have required a strength, a courage that few men possessed, never mind a woman.

"But why was it he couldn't mesmerize you again?"

"He hardly existed for me," she said. "He was merely one of a hundred thousand visions that I encountered every day in the drugged dream world I lived in. And not, by far, the worst of them, I assure you, Mr. Ransom."

"And now you no longer need the drops?"

"No. I am no longer using them. Nine weeks ago Minna buried the remaining few bottles one night somewhere out here. I don't know where. By the time I was brought out here, I was so ill I couldn't much use it. That horrifying experience is over now. Thank God."

"It's incredible," he said, thinking out loud.

"But it's so," she said sadly.

"But you can be mesmerized again. That's why you remain out here, isn't it?"

"No, that's not why I remain here. I remain here to be away from him, from her, from Center City where I have endured such misery. Whether he can mesmerize me ever again, I cannot say. I think not, however. I am free of him now. I never think of him or anyone else but my girlhood friends and companions. I do not think he will ever influence me again."

"But you are not certain?"

"No," she admitted. "I'm not certain."

"What if he should come here and discover the truth?"

"He won't come here. He doesn't think of me anymore. He's given me up for once and for all. Just as you have."

"But I haven't," he said, and was interrupted.

"As you ought to, then. No, he has matters of more importance to keep him occupied now. He cares nothing for me. He no longer exists for me, nor I for him. That's why he will never be able to influence me again. *You* scarcely exist for me, James."

These last words she said not hostilely but sadly, using his given name for the first time so far this day. Now he noticed that her eyes had lost their golden brilliance. They seemed dulled now, like coins that had been passed from hand to hand over a period of decades so that only an old tarnish remained where once there had been glitter.

"I wished I could be as certain he will not harm you as you seem to be," Ransom said. "Nevertheless, I am relieved to find you in better condition than I had feared."

"I thank you for your concern," she said formally, "and for your visit. Now leave me here to my life." She turned to go into the house.

"Carrie . . ." he called out. "Won't you give me another chance?"

"No. Go back to New York. You have seen me. I am well, or at least getting well. You have no further business with me; go now."

"May I at least come back here?"

"Please don't. I'm afraid it will raise suspicions. Remember! Don't say a word to anyone of your visit. Do you hear? Or all this will have been in vain." She hesitated, then said, "How long will you be here before you return to New York?"

"I don't know for sure. A week. Perhaps longer."

"If I want to see you, I shall send you a message. Through the cook's beau. If I don't, make certain not to come here again. Good-bye."

She slipped past the door and closed it firmly on him.

Ransom stood in the front yard a few minutes before riding off.

He was pleased and relieved to know she was no longer in peril from the drops, that she was recovering her health. He was still shocked by what she had gone through in order to escape Dinsmore's influence. But her ordeal hadn't helped Ransom. If anything, it had all the more deeply embedded her rejection of him, her bitterness against him. Before she had been despondent, self-sacrificing; now she was acrimonious, unsparing. And why shouldn't she be? In her eyes he had done as much harm to her as Dinsmore, hadn't he? She hadn't wanted either of them, she had said, lumping them together indiscriminately. She had only wanted Henry Lane. Poor deluded Henry Lane. Now he was dead, and she was alone, living out the rest of her life in this Godforsaken place. Not unhappy, she had told him. Not unhappy, he repeated to himself, spurring Golden on faster and faster as he approached the town. Not unhappy. But still not free of Dinsmore as she thought.

———————————●———————————

THE FOLLOWING MORNING AFTER BREAKFAST, Ransom took a seat on the small back porch of the boardinghouse, still trying to reach a conclusion as to what, if anything, he could or should do about Carrie. He was interrupted by a tap on the kitchen window: Augusta Page trying to get his attention.

"A visitor," she said.

He did not want to be interrupted at this time. "Who is it?" he asked testily.

"Wouldn't give his name. Want me to ask again?"

"No. I'll go myself," Ransom replied. Whoever it was, the matter would be more quickly settled this way.

The visitor was standing in the downstairs parlor. Even with his back turned, Ransom was sure he did not know the man. He was small, and portly, dressed almost completely in black, like an undertaker, but with a pair of fine gray gloves and a tiny matching bowler tipped forward on his head. He held on to a poker-thin, rolled black umbrella with a silver tip with which he was idly flipping over the pages of a newspaper left on the ottoman. He turned around quickly enough when Ransom entered, and Ransom's first impression was of a round face with a tiny black mustache, fat cheeks, and merry eyes behind octagonal spectacles worn low on his tiny nose. The man looked like some minor functionary in a large business from somewhere in the East.

"Mr. James Ransom?" he asked in a sharp, thin, but surprisingly authoritative voice.

"Yes."

"Fine. Fine," the visitor said, striking his leg with the narrow umbrella as though for emphasis. "Shall we go upstairs to your office?"

"To my office?"

"Of course. So we may be able to speak privately."

"There must be a mistake. I no longer have a practice here."

"I know that. I'm Jackson."

What difference did it make what his name was, Ransom thought.

"Thomas Jackson," the little man explained. "We've been in correspondence, Mr. Ransom."

That required another few seconds for comprehension. Then Ransom had it: *"Judge* Jackson?"

"Sh. Not so loud. Yes, the same. Now. Let's get out of here and go somewhere more private."

Ransom made some sort of excuse for not recognizing the name at once and led his visitor upstairs. Once they were settled and the judge had removed his bowler, revealing a head as neatly tonsured as any Franciscan monk's, he began speaking.

"I read over Mrs. Ingram's testimony last night. What did you think of it?"

"I thought it threw some interesting light on past details and on the various personalities involved."

"Spoken without commitment. Like a true lawyer. More precisely, Mr. Ransom, what did you think of its value?"

"Not very much."

"My sentiments exactly," the little man said, his dark eyes twinkling. "Most disappointing, in fact. Not enough to do anything very grand with. I ought to have known from the beginning."

So, Ransom thought, that settled the matter. His trip had been a wasted effort.

"That being the case," Jackson went on, "we'll have to adopt an alternative plan."

"Plan for what?" Ransom asked, wondering if he'd missed something.

"Why, to get rid of Dinsmore," Jackson said with some mirth. "Now, I've thought about it a great deal in the past few months . . . and naturally, I've read all the trial records from last year."

"You did? Why?"

"Why, to get rid of Dinsmore, of course. The man is a great pain in the backside," he added with some indignation. "Now. I have one alternative plan in particular we will discuss. I ought to remain here in Center City. I've been away far too often lately, although in my defense I must say it was absolutely essential. So I'll stay on here and keep an eye on Dinsmore. He does need a sharp pair trained on him at all times. Why, what did I discover after this mere two days' absence? I'll tell you. Dinsmore has been entertaining two out-of-towners. Out-of-staters I ought to say. One from San Francisco, the other from New York. Needless to add, both of them are quite formidably wealthy and powerful businessmen in their own states. You see what he's up to, don't you? A nationwide, transcontinental cartel. Producing, shipping, marketing all in one. We can't have it, simply can't. Can't afford to have him any stronger than he already is, by having such alliances. That's why we must act with all possible haste. First, you'll come to the courthouse; then you'll take the two o'clock local to Lincoln, and change there to the express for Chicago."

The man talked so quickly and so logically, yet so disjointedly, that Ransom kept wondering if he had missed something.

"Why Chicago?" he asked: only one of several questions he had.

"Because that's where the outstanding warrants originate."

"You mean the warrants on Dinsmore?"

"Who else? Now, I've already discussed the matter with the governor here, and it ought to be only a day or so before the extradition order is ready."

"Extradition for Dinsmore?"

"Who else? If we don't feel strong enough to re-try him right off on Mrs. Ingram's evidence, we might as well get him out of Nebraska." He said it all as though it were a great joke.

Ransom was staggered. "What then?"

"Well, we can finagle all sorts of delays once he's in Cook County. He may be stuck there for months. I won't go so far as to say he'll be imprisoned for any length of time. But whether he is or not, once he's let go by the authorities there, we will once again extradite him to Nebraska. Then we'll hit him with a retrial based on Mrs. Ingram's testimony. He ought to be quite dispirited by then. In the meanwhile, his forces here will be leaderless, scattered. The court will have to appoint someone to take guardianship of the Lane Industries, and best of all his direct influence on Center City will have been missed for months, possibly years. He will almost be forgotten here."

"But what if . . . ?" Before he could complete his questions, Jackson interrupted.

"You seem to understand everything but the main thing, Mr. Ransom."

"Well then, what is it?"

"If I had been judge on last year's trial instead of Carl Dietz, this Dinsmore would today be six feet underground. He is completely unprincipled. Totally without scruples. His acquittal came about only because Dietz was too finely principled, too nicely scrupulous to deal with such a man. But in me, Dinsmore has met his match. I'll stoop to anything, Mr. Ransom, in this matter. Especially with so much support behind me: Robertson Sloan, Willy Reese, the governor. Even—" and here he whispered—"even someone in the cabinet of the President of this nation. They don't like Dinsmore, and neither do I. He's forcing progress on this county in a way that's simply not planned for it. Like forcing an annual to bloom all year round in a hothouse. You'll pardon my comparison, but horticulture is my avocation. But now, do you understand? We've only really to set the wheels in motion with the extradition to Chicago. From then on, no matter what we do we'll know he is in other, stronger hands. They'll take care of him from there on."

Ransom had to admit he was astonished. He listened as Jackson gave details of whom he was to see in Lincoln, then in Chicago, and of how he ought to contact the judge in case any problems arose. Jackson insisted Ransom take notes and read back all he'd told him. Then he grabbed his hat and umbrella and began to rise.

"When I've gotten the extradition," Ransom asked, "who will serve it?"

"An Illinois marshal, of course. I doubt if they'll give you more than one."

"Won't Dinsmore be able to escape from him?"

"He'll be handcuffed, of course."

"That's hardly sufficient restraint. You must have read about his powers."

"Then you will choose the marshal you need. I'll assure you carte blanche on that. And you too will accompany them back to Chicago. Select the right man and you'll have no problem. Now. I see it's almost noon. That gives us time for a swearing-in, and then you're off to Lincoln. Let's go. No. On second thought, I'll go ahead and you join me in, say, five minutes."

"I'd rather forego that. I don't need to be sworn in just to be a messenger, do I?"

The little man seemed startled. "You did get my telegram?"

"Yes. You mentioned reappointment. I'll pass it up. I simply want to do this and then return to New York."

"To what? A copying clerkship?"

"That's my concern."

"But I'll need you to reopen the trial! It isn't merely county prosecutor as before. This time it's district attorney. That covers all ten counties south of Lincoln. A large, full-time occupation. Good salary. Benefits. Pension from the state when you retire, which can't be too far off. You couldn't ask for better. And who else can I turn to in the executorship of the Lane businesses? I'm afraid you can't refuse me." He seemed so pleased at his arguments that Ransom did not know how to reply.

"What I really can't understand," he finally did say, "is why you've decided on me to do all this. There must be others who could do it."

"Likely," Jackson admitted. "Very likely. But you know the case. And you know Dinsmore."

"You're counting on my hatred of him?"

"Let's say on your implacability in legal matters."

"But you forget, your honor. The last time Dinsmore and I tangled, I failed. I failed miserably."

Jackson's answer was abrupt:

"Nonsense! If you failed in anything, it was to put a bullet through his black heart when you had the opportunity. No more debating, please. We've got to move fast. At the courthouse in five minutes."

———————————•———————————

LESS THAN AN HOUR LATER, Ransom was walking south on High Street, returning to the Page Board and Hotel, still trying to work out how he would deal with Jackson in the future.

The aggressive little judge had demanded Ransom be sworn in as acting district attorney. Ransom had to admit he'd need some sort of official title to do what was required in Chicago. That much he fully intended to accomplish, but nothing more. He certainly would not remain in Center City after the extradition had been completed. Not to re-try Dinsmore, nor—especially not—to have anything to do with guardianship of the Lane holdings. Not after the way Carrie had received him at the ranch. And, as his appointment would only be temporary, only until the upcoming election, Ransom would be able to quit before that came to pass. Yes. That's what he would do.

He reached this conclusion and crossed High Street from the park side to get a better look at several large, chauffeur-driven automobiles parked in front of the Lane Hotel. One seldom saw this many expensive motorcars all together, even on Park Row in Manhattan. Something important must be going on inside.

He was just about to continue on his way when the large double doors of the hotel lobby were opened by two uniformed employees and several men, evidently the owners of the motorcars, stepped out onto the sidewalk, still conversing. Before he could move aside, Ransom saw Dinsmore among them, and in that instant was himself spotted. The last time they had been as

close as this was in the courthouse lobby over a year ago—and
that time Ransom had held a gun.

"Do my eyes deceive me," Dinsmore said loudly enough to
attract the attention of the company he was in, "or is that Mr.
Ransom?"

Before anyone could answer, he stepped forward and said, "It
is Mr. Ransom, isn't it?"

"You know it is," Ransom said.

"Why, Mr. Ransom!" Dinsmore exclaimed, sounding genu-
inely pleased. "I didn't know you were in Center City."

"I don't think it is generally known," Ransom replied.

"Ah! That would explain it."

The other men—all but Joseph Jeffries and Mason—were
strangers to Ransom, and he supposed some of them were the
coastal tycoons Judge Jackson had mentioned. They kept together in a knot as Dinsmore approached Ransom, allowing the
two opponents to have a better look at each other.

Dinsmore seemed little changed, although his vanity had
found rich soil in which to flourish. He wore the finest, softest-
looking weave of buff-colored suit and vest Ransom had ever
seen over an identically dyed, ruffed silk shirt. Thrown over his
shoulders was a chocolate-colored motoring coat. The only ac-
cents or ornamentation came from a plum cravat and
ruby-studded shirt buttons and cuff links. He was hatless, and his
hair had been allowed to grow into a mass of blue-black curls.
His mustache, too, was grown and elegantly curled. As usual, the
hands were immaculately manicured and white. The electric blue
eyes had lost none of their voltage. Success became him.

"I do hope," Dinsmore said softly, taking in Ransom's own—
he was certain—dilapidated physical condition, "that you will
come to call on me some day."

"I doubt it. I shall be leaving Center City by the next train."

"How unfortunate!"

Sensing that their conversation had come to an impasse, several of the others approached.

"Mr. Horace Wylie," Dinsmore said, referring to one of the

strangers, a small wizened man in charcoal gray with a tall top
hat. "This is Mr. James Ransom. Mr. Ransom is from New York,
like yourself."

Wylie mumbled a sour greeting and did not offer his hand.

"May I be so impolitely inquisitive," Dinsmore said now, "as
to ask what prompted this surprise visit?"

"Just a bit of unfinished business."

"I see. I didn't know you had any business left here." Then,
turning to Mr. Wylie, "Mr. Ransom was once a prominent attorney in Center City. Before he chose to leave us last year."

Wylie murmured some response. Ransom was aware that the
others were all looking at him now. Only Jeffries had been
unable to restrain a snigger at Dinsmore's description, and had
hidden behind the broad back of the banker.

"Actually," Ransom said, "I *was* thinking of returning to Center City. I had thought of trying another profession here."

"Oh, really," Dinsmore said.

"Yes. That of dental surgeon. It seems a good one is sorely
lacking these days in town."

There was a minute of silence as Ransom's impertinence sunk
in. Then Dinsmore threw back his head and let out a rich laugh.

"I ought to tell you, Mr. Wylie, that our Mr. Ransom here is
quite the frontier humorist. Our very own Mark Twain. And, I
might add, also quite a legend-maker too. Why his own work
concerning myself in that area was extremely remarkable a short
while back. I never have adequately thanked you, Mr. Ransom,
for making such a Paul Bunyan of me."

The others—Mason and Jeffries mostly—laughed at this sally.

"But I must also say," Dinsmore went on, "that despite his
humor, Mr. Ransom remains one of the few truly serious men
I've encountered. Really quite remarkably philosophic. I did
hope, Mr. Ransom, that we might once again take up our too
quickly curtailed philosophical discussions. I find I sorely miss
them."

"Perhaps we may yet," Ransom said.

"But you're leaving town by the next train, you said. It's really
too bad. But then I would gladly forego the pleasures of further

disquisition with you to know that you are happily and profitably established elsewhere."

When Ransom didn't comment, Dinsmore went on:

"In fact, I applaud your decision. I believe a town like Center City is really far too limited a field for your particular talents. It strikes me that they require a greater scope, a greater tolerance. In fact, I fear that if you did choose to remain here you would soon enough feel stifled, hindered, or . . . or even worse," he added, his cupid's-bow lips drawn into a smile with the words, but his eyes as hard as the precious stones on his cuffs and shirt front. And, with the veiled threat left hanging, he took Wylie's arm and led the group of men to their automobiles. "Good day, Mr. Ransom. And good-bye. I hope your journey is a fruitful one."

Several of the party turned around to stare at Ransom even when they were seated inside the motorcars. Ransom remained where he was, watching the automobiles as they were cranked up, sputtered to life with a mechanical clangor, and set off in stately cortege up High Street toward the Hill.

———————————•———————————

LEWIS BRADDAUGH HAD MANY QUALIFICATIONS for being a fine Cook County marshal. He was tall, broad, strong, and even in the most dapper of clothing a rough-looking man to have to deal with. He had more than a quarter of a century of experience as a law enforcer, beginning as a deputy sheriff in a notorious rustling hideout town in Utah, including service in Alaska following the first gold strike in Juneau during the '80s and work in San Francisco's Tenderloin District, still a haven for low-life sailors, thieves, pimps, and murderers. He hid a shrewd intelligence and an intuitive understanding of the criminal mind beneath a gruff, almost doltish exterior. He had a knack for finding his man, and a reputation for never accepting failure.

But as far as Ransom was concerned these qualities paled to nothing in the light of two discoveries he made about the marshal: First, that Braddaugh had himself hunted Dinsmore for

more than a year half across the country, before the case was
considered hopeless and he'd reluctantly returned to Illinois.
Second, and more important, that Braddaugh could not be mesmerized.

When Judge Jackson had said all Ransom had to do was to find
the right man to insure Dinsmore's security, that had become the
primary criterion for selection. Once he was in Chicago, with all
the papers signed and nothing remaining but to choose the man
to take Dinsmore, Ransom had sought the aid of one of the
physicians in the city who had answered Amasa Murcott's letter
about mesmerism. This curious practitioner had been so delighted to discover how far his avocation had been taken by
Dinsmore that he had agreed to test every police officer in the
city, the county, and the state, and if necessary to go back to
Nebraska with them to make the arrest.

Braddaugh had been in the first lot of men tested, and even
after another candidate was found, Braddaugh proved far more
impervious to the technique. Whether completely alert or about
to fall asleep, whether irritable or comfortable, hungry or sated,
inebriated or drugged, Braddaugh simply could not be hypnotized. They used flickering candles, twirling objects, flashing
incandescent lights, regulated noises, artificially produced and
reproduced sounds, tones and voices of all timbers and pitches,
and often enough two or three or even all of the methods at
once. Nothing worked. He yawned—not from sleepiness as
much as from ennui. Braddaugh was the rarity, the man in a
hundred, and once he had been told why he was being tested,
once he knew where Dinsmore was, he was eager to leave by the
next train.

It seemed almost too good a combination, Ransom thought.
Almost everything seemed too good: Harriet Ingram's confession, Judge Jackson's plan and how he had never really given
Ransom a chance to decline it, and now Braddaugh, the unmes-
merizable man who was out for Dinsmore's blood.

So good it spooked Ransom all the way down from Lincoln in
the Pullman. Burned once, twice wary, he thought. Naturally, he
could never move ahead with the same blind confidence he'd had

before. Yet he felt as though Dinsmore's rise had ended, and that forces larger than either of them had decided upon his downfall. Ransom moved comfortably enough with these forces; as much an instrument of their will as he had once—so briefly—been an instrument of Dinsmore's rise. Understanding that was both comforting and yet somewhat frightening. It put him in place, put all of them in place within a texture of life, as though everyone—he, Dinsmore, Carrie, Dietz, Carr, Mrs. Ingram, right down to that reporter Will Merrifield, even Millard and that German cook at the Lane ranch—were marionettes themselves, being manipulated by some greater Mesmerist. It was a sobering idea, one he wanted desperately to talk about to someone who might understand too. But to whom? Not Murcott, certainly not Braddaugh, not even Dietz or Jackson. To whom?

But the business of doing got in his way. Here he was, sitting in the dining room of the Lane Hotel at a table with Lewis Braddaugh, waiting for Dinsmore to finish his own dinner before they arrested him.

They had arrived before the hotel manager and his four companions had come down from Dinsmore's suite. Ransom and Braddaugh had taken a small, out-of-the-way table, hidden from most of the other diners by its location and by several large areca palms set in stone buckets all around the plush room, but with an excellent view of Dinsmore's customary table. Both men had then ordered dinner, and the Chicago marshal, unimpressed by what he'd seen so far of Center City, had never once during the meal stopped praising the place, comparing it to the finest hotels in other large cities he'd visited—the Belvedere, the St. Francis, the Waldorf-Astoria. The linen was rich, the decor handsome, the lighting exactly right, the service good, the atmosphere cosmopolitan, and the food delicious.

Ransom too appreciated these amenities, but he also kept his attention trained on the other table. Two women, neither of whom he'd ever seen before, had joined Dinsmore along with his two male guests, Anthony Wheeler, the young scion of the Wheeler fortune, and another man—a wealthy farmer from outside of town whose name Ransom could not recall. All but the host appeared to be in high spirits. Dinsmore too tried to keep up his end of the party, but he would all of a sudden look down at his plate or off into the distance, thoughtfully, a minute or two at a time, before being brought back to the present by a comment from one of the others. Did he intuit impending doom? Ransom wondered. But just then a strawberry frappe arrived before Ransom's eyes, and he lost his speculation in its luciousness.

Once during the meal, Dinsmore got up from his table and left the room. Braddaugh followed cautiously, and returned walking a few steps in front of Dinsmore so as to not arouse any suspicions. Back at the table, the marshal reported that Dinsmore had gone downstairs to the men's lounge, and once there had stared at himself in a mirror above the sinks for some time. Braddaugh described the lavatory fixtures in praise-singing detail.

Not long after he and Ransom had finished their after-dinner cordials, those at the other table did too.

"Let's go," Braddaugh said.

They paid their check, skirted the palms, and walked toward the door as though casually leaving. When they passed Dinsmore's table, Ransom stopped and put a hand on the marshal's arm as though to detain him.

"One moment," Ransom said, stage-loud. "I believe I know this gentleman."

Everyone at the table looked up. Dinsmore was uncomfortably startled. One lapis eye closed as though he were looking through a rifle sight.

"I do know him," Ransom said. "This is the man who owns the hotel."

"Mr. Ransom exaggerates," Dinsmore said. "I'm merely the manager."

"A trifling difference," Ransom replied.

"I thought you'd left Center City by now. Or were you pulling my leg that day?"

"Not at all. I left and returned."

"Really? How irritating. I'm so sorry I can't ask you to join us. We were just getting up."

At this signal the other guests rose too. Ransom stood aside and as Dinsmore came past, he said:

"But I've forgotten my manners. I've forgotten to introduce you to our visitor from out of town. Mr. Frederick Dinsmore, this is Mr. Lewis Braddaugh."

Braddaugh thrust out a large hand, and before Dinsmore could avoid it, began to shake hands with the manager.

"I should mention," Ransom said, "that Mr. Braddaugh is from Chicago, Illinois. In fact, he's a Cook County marshal."

In that second, Braddaugh clamped a handcuff on Dinsmore's held hand attached to one on his own left wrist.

Dinsmore turned to Ransom. "What are you doing?" His voice had a shrill tone Ransom had never heard before.

"Arresting you," Ransom replied calmly. He pulled out a sheaf of papers and read from one of them: "We are empowered by the states of Nebraska and Illinois to take into protective custody one Frederick L. Dinsmore of 18 High Street and the Lane Hotel, Center City, Nebraska."

The other guests thought it was a joke. Young Wheeler, who had imbibed heavily and had his arm around one woman, continued trying to coerce her back upstairs. The others looked on calmly.

"This is an extradition order," Ransom explained, "signed by both governors. Please stand back, folks."

Braddaugh whistled at that moment, and two recently deputized men emerged from the hotel lobby where they had been waiting all evening. Seeing them, Dinsmore's color left his face.

"You're insane, Ransom," he whispered.

"Let's go," Braddaugh said.

"What's going on here?" the farmer asked in an annoyed tone of voice.

"Don't worry about it, Cliffords," Dinsmore said, immediately regaining his composure. "These men seem to have made a mistake. Although they are not yet aware of it."

"Are they arresting you?" one of the paid women asked.

"It's a mistake," Dinsmore said. "Lila, take Mr. Cliffords and

Mr. Wheeler back upstairs. I'm certain I'll be with you in a very short time. Oh, Lila. Get hold of Mr. Applegate, will you, and send him to me."

By now the deputies had taken out their revolvers, and several diners and people from the lobby had gathered. Ransom decided to leave before Dinsmore started something.

"See you later." Dinsmore waved his free hand with mock cheerfulness to Wheeler. Then he all but pulled Braddaugh along with him out of the lobby, bowing and nodding in recognition as he passed various customers as though nothing were wrong.

In minutes, they were out the hotel doors, in a carriage, and had driven the few blocks to the jail without incident. Dinsmore had quieted down in the carriage, but once inside the jail he began to abuse and threaten Eliot Timbs, who apologized abjectly and tried to explain that he had no choice in the face of a state Justice Court order.

"At least get me a proper place to be locked up in," Dinsmore demanded. "You don't expect me to stay in that hellhole, do you?" Within a few minutes, he had ordered chairs, a table, a bed, and liqueurs to be brought posthaste from the Lane Hotel.

The two deputies took up posts outside the jail building, on Williams Street. Ransom and Braddaugh remained in the lockup room, silent along with the sulking Dinsmore, who had been handcuffed to the cell bars until the furniture arrived and was installed. That done, Dinsmore was placed inside. Whether he found consolation in the proximity of his familiar luxuries or within his own thoughts, Ransom could not say, but the prisoner did cheer up considerably and make himself at home.

Cal Applegate arrived more than an hour after the arrest. He explained he had been to see Judge Jackson the minute he had been told the news, and was told the judge could do nothing to contravene a state order. The attorney had then telegraphed the governor. He had received no reply so far. As soon as he did, Dinsmore would hear of it and be released. When asked by his client what would occur if the reply did not arrive by tomorrow, when Braddaugh planned to take him out of Center City by the local train, Applegate said he doubted it would happen, but if so then Dinsmore would have to go with the marshal. That pleased Dinsmore very little, and he threatened his lawyer if he did not get the liberating telegram.

Braddaugh also had made himself at home in the cell room. He remained a few feet distant from his captive, sitting comfortably with both feet up on another chair, reading a *Police Gazette* he'd bought earlier that day in Lincoln. Ransom left the two of them together and went out to Timbs' office. There he explained to the sheriff that no one besides Applegate was to be allowed to see Dinsmore.

Timbs said he understood: he was much impressed by Braddaugh's presence—he had heard of the man through law-officer circles—and by the importance of an arrest involving the names of two governors. When Timbs left the office for his late dinner, Ransom remained at his desk; he wanted to be nearby in case anything did happen.

Nothing did. After three hours or so of catnapping, Ransom awakened to check the cell room. Braddaugh was still reading his magazine. Dinsmore was still awake, dressed, but not pacing or restless, merely sitting in his expensive chair looking at the marshal.

"If you wish to prepare for bed undisturbed," Ransom offered, "Mr. Braddaugh will leave you alone for a few minutes."

"Thank you, but I'm not sleepy yet," Dinsmore said, as though interrupted in a train of thought. "But wait a minute, Ransom. Don't go yet. I may be here another hour or two, if not all night, what with the awful service of telegraph operators in this area. Why don't you keep me company? Your friend here is not a terribly stimulating companion, I must say. Wherever did you find him?"

"On the contrary, Mr. Braddaugh is a most unusual man. Or have you already discovered that?"

"All I discovered was that he is terminally boring. Do come inside for a while. We could continue our little talk from last year."

Ransom calculated that Dinsmore had already tried and failed to mesmerize the marshal; now he wished to try it on Ransom.

"Why not?" Dinsmore asked. "You're not doing anything so very important right now, are you?"

"Nothing at all," Ransom admitted. "But I have two conditions. First, that Mr. Braddaugh remain in the cell room with us. We can talk here on this other side. And second, that I remain outside the cell itself."

"Surely you don't think that I would . . . ?" Dinsmore protested, all innocence.

"I think nothing of the sort," Ransom said. Nevertheless his conditions were accepted. In the swift instant the invitation had been given he'd discovered that Dinsmore knew his own disadvantage. He would talk to Dinsmore all right, but with the rules distorted his way: two might play the same game.

"Now," Dinsmore said, when Ransom had found a chair and was settled out of earshot of the marshal. "Tell me, Ransom, quite candidly, what you hope to gain from this police detective farce you've begun?"

"I? Nothing at all. It's Braddaugh's show. He's been looking for you since '95. I'm just here for the ride."

"You're here just to watch me squirm?"

"Not exactly."

"The more I do squirm, the harder it will be on you later, you know. Things have changed here in Center City. You've been away too long to know it, but they have. I'm the one in power now, and you're the outsider."

"Perhaps so. But Center City isn't the entire world, Dinsmore. Only a little portion of it."

"What's that supposed to mean?"

"You said several weeks ago that I was a philosopher," Ransom said, instead of answering the question. "I wasn't before. But I have to say I may be now. I didn't think matters out before. Since last spring, and thanks to you, I do think them out now. Sometimes I even reach conclusions. I have you to thank for that, Dinsmore. I cannot say I'm a happier person, nor even really a wiser one because of it, but I am a more thoughtful one now—because of what occurred last year."

"I'm delighted to hear it. However, may I point out that if you were even a bit more thoughtful, you would realize soon enough that you cannot deal with me any longer? I'm out of your class. This is an absurd action. One of almost no consequence to me, I know, but to irritate me. But for you it will mean certain destruction."

"I think not. You are out of my class, Dinsmore, I admit that. But you're still outclassed by others. And they're after you, not I. I've just joined in to make sure everything is done quite legally. You've gone far, and fast, too, Dinsmore. But not far enough or fast enough for your own sake. And not all the Wylies and Wheelers and Cliffordses, nor even the Morgans and Rockefellers, are going to be helping you now. You're a marked man. Your party's over, Dinsmore."

Dinsmore looked at him in disbelief, then laughed.

"You're off your head, Ransom. Who? Who's after me? Who are these big guns you're blabbing about? They can't be very much themselves to send one paunchy marshal and a broken-down attorney to do their work, now can they? Getting away from the two of you, the four of you if you count those two idiots outside, will still be snap of the fingers. If it goes that far. Which I doubt."

"It will go that far. Listen, Dinsmore, you may think you're merely a little tired or you haven't found the right way to do it, but that by tomorrow you will have Braddaugh in your power. I tell you, don't even bother. He can't be mesmerized. Not by any one, two, or forty Mesmerists. Not by any kind of technique that's ever been devised. He's been tested a hundred times. He may be paunchy, as you say, but you'll never get him to say boo. That means you'll get to Chicago. He'll see to that. Do you understand that?"

Almost despite himself, Dinsmore looked around at the marshal, still absorbed in his reading.

"So what? So I'll take the trip. What then? A day or two and I'll be back."

"Don't count on it. Once there, you'll be held. It may be a month. It may be six months. You may come to trial. You may be imprisoned. I can't say. I'm not privy to those prosecuting you in Chicago. If you do make it back to Center City, you will be immediately locked up and held here, re-tried. Mrs. Ingram has offered fresh testimony to reopen the trial. I needn't tell you what it is—I think you already know that yourself. It will be enough to not only reopen that trial, but to add a new charge, conspiracy to murder. Again, I have no details, but the case will be handled by people close to certain figures of great power in the state and federal governments. They have left no room for any result but conviction. I've already been told this much."

"Who told you?"

"That's not important. It's so. Neither you nor I count in this matter anymore, Dinsmore. We're like the ball in a scrimmage match. This is your turn to be kicked around as I was. Only this time it won't stop there. They don't just want your power and your businesses. They want your life, Dinsmore, and they're ensuring they'll get it. I'm just a little bit in the big plan, and you're the victim. This isn't just another scrape like so many you've been able to work your way out of in the past. This is for keeps, and neither you nor I can do a damned thing about it. I'm as helpless as that jackass Timbs. Believe me, Dinsmore. So are you. I only realized this today, and it scared the hell out of me. I've been wanting to talk to someone about it all day. I realized a few moments ago that only you would understand it, because you're in it as deeply as I am, even deeper."

Ransom had been looking straight into the faceted, bright blue eyes as he spoke, but he never once felt he had to flinch or withdraw. Rather, the eyes themselves had seemed to cloud over, as though by a thin, almost invisible film. The nictitating membrane of the lizard? Or, more probably, the coming on of fright? Ransom couldn't say for sure. He looked away at the floor as he finished talking. Dinsmore was silent, only two feet away through the metal bars of the cell, silent for a long time, almost as though he were not breathing.

When his words came, they sounded harsh. "You're quite the little Samaritan, aren't you? You talk just like the minister must do before leading a man to the execution chamber. Accept, my son. Accept and repent. But leave all your worldly goods to my denomination."

Ransom stood. Braddaugh looked up and followed him with his eyes until Ransom was at the doorway.

"I made a mistake, Dinsmore. Forget what I said. I thought I could talk to you about it. I made a mistake. You were so correct about me last year—so dead-on correct—that I thought I knew you as well. I thought I could communicate with you. Forget it. Forget everything I said."

But even as he spoke, he could see he hadn't been mistaken. For the first time since he'd met Dinsmore so long ago, the blue eyes weren't veiled or hard, not like a reptile's eyes, nor like chunks of minerals. The curtains had fallen. They peered out of the masklike face with an all-too-human look, and in that human look they revealed not only understanding of what Ransom had said, but, horribly, they screamed out fear.

Ransom couldn't stand them. He had to turn away and grope for the door.

"Ransom! Ransom!" Dinsmore shouted shrilly. "You made a mistake all right! If I'm not back here in Center City in three days your life is worthless! Worthless! Do you hear? Worthless!"

The words were obliterated by the heavy door. Ransom went to Timbs' desk and stared at the grocery-store calendar hung on a wall.

So this was what it felt like to be cruel.

———————————●———————————

RANSOM FELL ASLEEP WITH HIS HEAD in his hands at Timbs' desk, and slept fitfully for several hours.

Timbs came in at eight in the morning. Together, they checked up on the prisoner and his guard. Both were sleeping. Braddaugh with his legs up on the bars of the cell, Dinsmore in the comfort of the bed he'd brought from the Lane Hotel.

Dinsmore, the sheriff told Ransom, was a late sleeper: he wouldn't be up for hours. Especially if he had retired late.

Ransom left the jail in the sheriff's hands with only a moment's hesitation. Eliot Timbs might be a supporter of Dinsmore's, but he had an unflinching regard for the letter of the law that Ransom had come up against often enough before. Unless a remand order was received, Dinsmore would stay put.

That order had not been received at eleven o'clock when Ransom returned from his breakfast at the Page Board and Hotel, carrying his small leather travel bag. Nor at noon when Applegate went into the lockup, was searched, and then given over to his client, who had awakened in a hostile mood. The lawyer fled the inner room shortly afterwards, with Dinsmore still shouting imprecations at him. Braddaugh later reported that they had exchanged words, and the lawyer had been sent to wire the governor again.

A few minutes later Harriet Ingram appeared at the jail door begging to see her former lover. Timbs denied her request and Ransom had to support the sheriff's decision—the housekeeper was still far too susceptible to the Mesmerist's powers to be allowed in: she might cause all sorts of havoc. Mrs. Ingram said she understood the need for precautions, but she still seemed deeply disappointed. Before she left the sheriff's office, however, she mentioned that she had sent word of Dinsmore's arrest to the Lane ranch the minute she had heard the news the night before. The messenger had returned saying that Carrie felt well enough to travel and would probably drive into Center City in the morning to take up residence in her house once again. Mrs. Ingram said she must get back to High Street to welcome her mistress. Ransom wondered if he oughtn't send a note to Carrie via Mrs. Ingram. But hadn't she said she would send for him if she wanted to see him again? She hadn't so far, even after hearing the news about Dinsmore. So he let Mrs. Ingram go without any message.

———————•———————

AFTER A LUXURIOUS BREAKFAST sent over from the hotel restaurant in a steaming silver hot-food cart, Dinsmore felt better. Braddaugh left him to dress, but returned to let in a barber from the hotel, and waited to watch the prisoner's toilette. By then it was one thirty. The local was due in at two. They ought to get moving.

Dinsmore had sent for no luggage, trusting that the remand order would still arrive in time. The deputies got on the outside top of the old coach and Dinsmore was manacled again, protesting his handcuffs indignantly, and was led into the coach along with the marshal. Ransom and the sheriff had to hold back the small but unruly crowd outside the jail before they too could get in.

It was only a half dozen blocks to the railroad station, and from half that distance they could make out the crowd that had gathered on the public-vehicle approach to the platform. At least a hundred men and boys were being harangued by someone who on closer inspection turned out to be Joseph Jeffries, the only person standing up on the railroad platform itself. The minute the familiar coach hove into the newspaperman's view, he pointed it out to the crowd, which turned around to look but otherwise made no move.

"Want me to get out and see what it's all about?" Timbs asked.

"I know what it's all about," Ransom replied. "A going-away party for Mr. Dinsmore."

The two of them stepped down from the coach.

From within, Dinsmore said, "Why aren't we moving? You don't want to miss the train, do you?"

Ransom ignored him and walked over to the edge of the crowd to listen to what Jeffries was saying. He was seen and joined by old Floyd.

"What a heap of malarkey that print-chewer is."

"Why? What's he saying, Floyd?"

"Same old blather he's been saying for two years. Progress. Innovation. Dinsmore. Lane Industries. Center City."

"Are they listening to him?"

"Don't know. About as much as they ever do."

Ransom wanted to thread through the crowd to get a clearer

picture of its mood. But he was soon recognized on several sides, and decided to go back to the others.

"We might as well get back in and wait until the train comes," he said to the sheriff.

The prisoner was—characteristically—trying to strike up a conversation with the taciturn marshal.

"You mean to say you don't play any kind of cards?" Dinsmore asked. "How am I supposed to pass my time on this train ride?"

"Look at the scenery," Braddaugh answered.

"Really, Ransom! Your inventiveness in torturing me is excessive. I protest!"

"Don't worry. I'll be traveling along with you."

"I hope we have a parlor car. Or doesn't the state of Illinois pay for such things? Never mind. I'll pay for it myself."

"I wouldn't try to use Lane checks to pay for it," Ransom warned.

"Why not?"

"You've been let go, Dinsmore. The executorship has gone to the court."

"To whom? You?"

"No. A committee of three: Judge Jackson, Ludwig Baers, and your friend Mr. Mason. You see, they've thought of everything. I told you they weren't playing around."

Dinsmore couldn't hide his initial shock at this. He stared in disbelief until Eliot Timbs corroborated what Ransom had said. Then Dinsmore laughed and sat back in his seat, peering out the coach windows as though expecting someone.

"It's two o'clock," Braddaugh announced. "Let's go."

"The train's always late," Ransom said.

"Don't care. Don't want to miss it."

Ransom was about to stop him, but the marshal had opened the side door and Dinsmore had already pushed his way out. The others had to follow.

The two deputies led, Dinsmore and Braddaugh were directly behind, and Timbs and Ransom brought up the rear. They skirted the crowd and got through easily enough, but they were being watched on all sides. Jeffries went on speechifying; he sounded as though he would have an apoplectic fit any moment. The first four of the group had ascended the stone stairs to the railway platform when someone called out:

"Hey, Dinsmore! Where you going?"

Dinsmore turned to the crowd. "Chicago! Or at least that's what these men tell me."

"What for?" someone else shouted. "To buy more machinery? To put more of us out of business?"

"I haven't taken any bread out of your mouth, Bixby," Dinsmore called back. "What's your complaint?"

Ransom and Timbs got up the stairs. Young Bixby had been the heckler, they could see. He now shrank back into the crowd.

"I don't particularly want to go to Chicago," Dinsmore said in a loud, clear voice. He lifted his hands so the manacles caught the afternoon sunlight. "You see these?" he asked the crowd.

"Serve you right," someone said.

"Where's your luggage?" from another.

"I'm not taking luggage. I'm coming right back here to Center City. Despite what these two men say."

Jeffries came over to them and was pushed by one of the deputies down among the crowd of men. A space was made for him and he went among them sputtering, agitating, tugging them by the sleeves, and talking close to their ears.

Dinsmore continued bantering with the crowd, looking down from his position on the platform and every once in a while scanning the streets—for signs of Applegate and the remand order.

"Where is that train?" Ransom thought out loud.

"You know it's always late," Timbs said.

"Oughtn't we get him away from here, Timbs? Maybe inside the stationmaster's office?"

"It's all right with me. But he's Braddaugh's prisoner, not mine."

Braddaugh was enjoying the exchange between Dinsmore and the crowd. Those men who had earlier surrounded the sheriff's office, making exiting with the prisoner so difficult for the lawmen, had now arrived at the railroad station and swelled the mob to double its size. But the marshal agreed to leave this spot if a place were found inside the building.

Reluctantly Ransom walked the forty paces or so to the station-master's window. Mr. Maxwell was at his desk, his eyes fixed on a switchboard pattern as he received telegraphed instructions from another station about the progress of the local. He had to remove first the black-linoleum eyeshade, then the telegraph earphones before Ransom could make himself heard.

"Five minutes," Maxwell said. "You'll be able to hear it soon. Must be passing the open bend by now."

"We've got a prisoner," Ransom explained. "Can we bring him in here?"

"Who? What prisoner?"

"What's the difference? It's Dinsmore."

"What's he done now?"

"Can we use the office or not? There's a crowd out there, and I'm afraid that if we . . ."

"Who's we?" Maxwell asked.

"Myself, the prisoner, the sheriff, a marshal, and some deputies."

"Not enough room in here," the old man said, shaking his head.

"Well then, just two of us will come in," Ransom said, looking around the office. "The others will stay outside. "Can this office be locked?" he asked, looking at the door. He wished there were another room here—even a closet would do for now. "Or the waiting room? Can that be locked?"

"What for?" the old stationmaster persisted.

"There's a *crowd* out there. I'm afraid it might get unruly."

"What crowd?" Maxwell asked, dropping the earphones to his desk and stepping out of the office onto the platform. "I don't see any crowd. Just a few people standing there. One of them looks sick or something."

Ransom was beginning to lose patience. "Can we come in here?" he asked once more.

"I suppose," Maxwell said doubtfully. "What's wrong with

him? Why, isn't that Dinsmore? Why's he rocking back and forth like that?"

"Like what?" Ransom asked, edging past the stationmaster onto the platform.

Then he saw: Dinsmore was standing at the very edge of the platform above the crowd. The others seemed to have moved back a few paces. Where was Braddaugh?

Ransom started off toward them, then slowed down, sensing something not quite right, and cautiously kept against the wall of the stationhouse as he advanced onto the scene.

Dinsmore was talking—orating, it seemed. As Ransom closed in on him, he could hear words, snatches of phrases ringing in the air, although not enough of any of it to make much sense out of it. Dinsmore was rocking back and forth on the balls of his feet very slowly as he spoke, gesturing with his manacled hands, first holding them in front of him, then lifting them above his head, then bringing them forward and down to his thighs again. Was he trying to incite the mob? Was that why he was gesturing so?

Ransom heard a distant train whistle behind him. It couldn't be far away now. No one else seemed to notice, however. Dinsmore had his hands up in front of him again, still talking.

As Ransom cleared the shelter of the station building, Dinsmore's speech was coming to some kind of climax, as his voice rose up and over everyone. Ransom looked down at the hushed crowd—every face turned up, fixed on the speaker. Even the lawmen, arrayed now behind and to one side of Dinsmore on the platform, seemed to be listening to him.

"Well, is that what you want?" Dinsmore suddenly asked the crowd. "To be under the sway and dominion of the political bosses at Lincoln? Because that's what will happen when I'm gone, you know. Well, is that what you want?"

There was a massed shout from below: "No!"

"I didn't think so," Dinsmore said, lifting his hands up again and going back slightly on his heels. "No. I surely didn't think so."

He was inciting them. And where was Braddaugh? There, just behind Sheriff Timbs. Ransom crossed in back of Dinsmore to where the lawmen and deputies stood, and had to tug at the marshal's sleeve to get his attention.

"Let's go now," Ransom said. "We can use the office."

Timbs and someone from the crowd below shushed him. Braddaugh looked rather blankly at Ransom, then back to Dinsmore, who was putting yet another mostly rhetorical question to the crowd.

"Come on, Braddaugh," Ransom repeated.

"Can't you wait? I want to hear what he's saying," the marshal said, clearly annoyed.

"What he's saying isn't important! He's trying to cause a riot here," Ransom explained. "Let's get him out of here."

"The train will be here in a minute. I heard the whistle a moment ago," Braddaugh said. "We can wait."

". . . strangers coming into your town, *your town,*" Dinsmore was shouting now, the manacled hands held high again, dropping forward slowly, "running your lives, *your lives.* That's what it will be. Strangers from Lincoln saying you can't have trolley cars and automobiles and concrete sidewalks."

He rocked back again as his hands reached his thighs and began their slow ascent.

". . . not merely the second-best city in Nebraska, but the first, *the first.* We're the central link between the East Coast and the West. Between New York and California. We're the center. The breadbox for both of them . . ." And as his hands reached their apogee above his head, the manacles caught a glint of sunlight, then began their slow fall forward again.

". . . will be money in all our pockets, not just the pockets of a few. *In all our pockets . . .*" His hands touched his thighs, just brushing them, then rose in front of him again. ". . . With those cities, we'll have ports to send our wheat and other grains to other countries, all over the world. To Europe from New York, to the Orient from San Francisco." And now the manacles caught the sun and glinted again as Dinsmore went on.

Ransom looked away and down at the crowd of attentive faces, some three hundred of them, listening as though nothing else mattered, while the sun suddenly made a line across their faces, as though it were just coming out from behind a cloud, and swept them from front to back so that every upturned face was touched by it, caressed by it, right to the ragged back edge of the mob.

Ransom looked and saw familiar faces in the mass. Old Floyd there in the middle. His friend, Bernard Soos, next to him. Several blacks at one point in the rear. Was that Yolanda's Billy among them? And the sun slowly crossed their faces again from front to back. Ransom heard the train whistle even closer now. Maybe he oughtn't interfere. This crowd didn't seem unruly; if anything, they looked exceedingly calm, all quietly listening to Dinsmore trying to talk his way out of yet another scrape. And now the sun had finished its course across the crowd and was beginning again from the front. Clouds.

Ransom turned to look at the sky. But there weren't any clouds! The sky was clear, cloudless! Where was it coming from? How was it that the sunlight was crossing in front of the men?

Then he looked at Dinsmore, rocking back on his heels again as his hands were raised to the top of the arc he was making, and the manacles glinted in the sun for a second before the hands dropped again. And sure enough, as that happened, the sunlight went over the crowd of faces again.

Christ! Ransom thought with a jolt. He's using the manacles as he had used the cuff links in the courtroom! He's trying to mesmerize them, all of them!

Ransom grabbed the marshal's sleeve again. "We've got to stop him."

Braddaugh didn't even respond.

"Come on, Braddaugh," Ransom said, pushing the marshal more forcefully now. "We've got to get him into the office right now."

Braddaugh didn't even look at Ransom. No one did. Ransom shook the marshal.

"Braddaugh, what's wrong with you?" Then he saw the man's eyes, his gaze fixed ahead of him, directly on Dinsmore, as though he could see nothing else. "Braddaugh?" he whispered, panicky now. "But you can't be mesmerized," he said, as though to himself, since no one else paid him any attention.

Now the train whistle was right there, tooting merrily as it entered the far end of the station.

Ransom looked at the others on the platform: Timbs, the deputies, all of them looked dazed, frozen. Even Braddaugh. He had to do something fast. There must be someone in the crowd, one man at least who hadn't been mesmerized. Or would he have to do it alone? Ransom looked over the crowd; every face he met had the same glazed eyes, the same stare fixed on Dinsmore.

The whistle blew again, and now Ransom decided he would have to do something. He had stepped away from the others on the platform; now he reached over to Timbs. He'd have to get a gun and grab Dinsmore, force him at gunpoint onto the train, and hope, pray, they would leave the station without the mob attacking them.

He had just put his hand on the revolver when Dinsmore whirled to face him. Ransom froze on the spot.

"Timbs, Braddaugh," Dinsmore said. "Grab Mr. Ransom and hold him."

Arms shot forward and around Ransom so fast he didn't have a chance to get away.

"Braddaugh! Eliot! It's me! Let me go!"

"Take him over there," Dinsmore said, pointing to the wall of the stationhouse. "Tie his hands and gag him with a handkerchief."

Although Ransom struggled with the two, they soon had him at the side of the building. Before he could be gagged, he shouted frantically. Not a man in the assembled crowd did anything to help him. They looked at him and his captors with the bland curiosity of a man looking at a butterfly being pinned to an album leaf. Then they returned their gaze to Dinsmore, who once more continued his speech.

Ransom still wriggled to free himself, but he couldn't even budge the expert knots Braddaugh had tied. The train pulled all the way up into the station and stopped. A minute later, two men got off. One was a salesman for Sears, Roebuck whom Ransom had seen before. The other was a stranger. Both of them looked at Ransom, tied and gagged, between the sheriff and the marshal, as they passed, and although he tried mumbling at them, Timbs said, "Keep moving," in his officious way, and the two newcomers were soon down the platform steps and disappearing into the crowd.

Dinsmore had stopped raising and lowering his hands, evidently persuaded now that he had mesmerized everyone he could, but he still kept orating to the crowd. Ransom tried not to listen to the man's hateful voice, but everyone else gave it total attention. Now they murmured, now they spoke out to support something he said, now they shouted their agreement.

The stopped train blew its whistle.

"All aboard," the conductor shouted, but the call was scarcely heard, and it was ignored by everyone.

Maxwell suddenly appeared around the stationhouse corner, peering anxiously at the mob.

"Isn't anyone going to take the local?" the stationmaster asked. Eliot Timbs hushed him and pulled Maxwell against the stationhouse wall. "What is it?" Maxwell asked. "What's going on? Why, Mr. Ransom, what's happened?"

Ransom mumbled furiously through the handkerchief, but even if he could have been heard, he wondered if the stationmaster would do anything. Timbs was explaining to the man that a very important speech was being made, and everyone had to be very quiet and listen to it.

"Isn't anyone taking the local?" Maxwell asked again.

"All aboard that's coming aboard!" the conductor called again. The locomotive hissed smoke out of a dozen side vents and the train slowly began to chug out of the station in a cloud of white.

Dinsmore kept on orating until the train had left and was whistling in the distance; then brought his speech to a rousing conclusion. The men cheered as he directed them to, and he acknowledged their affection and support, which produced yet another cheer from them.

"Although I will leave you soon," Dinsmore said, "it's only

for a short while. I'll be back in Center City sooner than you'll miss me. Meanwhile, I want you men to all keep the promise we've made together today.''

The crowd cheered once more. Even Braddaugh and Timbs joined in, with Maxwell alone scratching his head above the black visor he had put on again, trying to figure out what was going on.

As the men were roaring, Dinsmore smiled at them, proud, satisfied, victorious; then he slowly descended the platform steps. The crowd parted to let him through as the Red Sea was supposed to have parted for Moses. Dinsmore held his hands up high, the manacles still gleaming a little, until Ransom lost sight of him at the far end of the crowd.

"Where's he going?" Maxwell finally asked. "I thought he was supposed to be on the two o'clock local?"

Both Braddaugh and Timbs had stepped down into the crowd, so Ransom went over to the stationmaster and mumbled to him. Maxwell looked at him quizzically, then took off the handkerchief gag, saying "Whatever you got up like this for?"

"He's escaped," Ransom said. "Help me get untied. I have to go get him."

"Who tied you?"

"The sheriff and Braddaugh."

"Why? What did you do?"

"Nothing. Just untie me, Mr. Maxwell. I'll explain everything later."

"But if the sheriff tied you, he probably had a reason for doing it."

Despite the stationmaster's uncertainty, he had already loosened one of Ransom's hands. Ransom now got the other hand free and the hemp rope off.

"He mesmerized them," Ransom explained. "Mesmerized all of them."

As Maxwell just kept staring at him as though Ransom were speaking a foreign language, Ransom asked: "Where did Dinsmore go? Did you see him?"

"No. I guess he just walked up the street."

The crowd was slowly dispersing now, the men forming chatting groups of two and three. Ransom couldn't see Dinsmore. Even if he were down there he probably wouldn't be able to find Dinsmore among all those men. Were they all still mesmerized? If so, not one of them would be of any help.

The last order Dinsmore had given the sheriff and Braddaugh was to hold Ransom and make sure he didn't get free. There was only one way, then, to find out if the men were still under the mesmeric influence. Spotting his two captors, Ransom called down, "Braddaugh, Timbs, I'm loose."

The two men turned to him as they heard their names called.

"I'm free," Ransom said. "I'm untied."

They looked at him questioningly, shrugging.

"Dinsmore's gone," Ransom shouted.

"No, he's not," Braddaugh said, approaching the platform stairs. "He's right up there . . ." But he stopped himself, seeing no one but Maxwell and Ransom on the platform. "Where did he go?" Mounting the steps to Ransom's side, he asked: "Where is he?"

Evidently the mesmeric influence had worn off already. Probably in order to mesmerize so many people, Dinsmore had had to spread his force, creating a light trance that dissipated once he was no longer present.

"The train's gone too," Ransom said.

"What train? When?" Braddaugh asked. "Where's Dinsmore?"

"He got away. He walked away, through this crowd. You cheered his speech. Don't you remember anything at all?"

"No. Nothing."

"You've been mesmerized, Braddaugh. Even you, whom we were so sure couldn't be mesmerized. How did it feel?"

"Didn't feel like anything," the marshal said, perplexed and very unhappy. "One minute he was talking, and the next you were shouting that you had been untied and he was gone. Who tied you?"

"You did. You and Timbs."

As Braddaugh looked even more upset over this, Ransom decided they were wasting time.

"Maxwell said he walked down the street," Ransom said, pointing directly down Williams Street. "We'd better find him. He said something about leaving town. I'm sure he's going to get away if he can. He's probably at the Lane Hotel right now. That's in the direction he was headed for."

They called Timbs and the two deputies to the platform, and without explaining to them what had happened, agreed that Dinsmore would have to be found. It was decided that the three lawmen would cover the town's main exits—north, south and east—while Braddaugh and Ransom went to the Lane Hotel. They were all to meet back at the Lane Hotel in an hour if there was no sign of their quarry.

Halfway down Williams Street, Ransom suddenly had a thought. What if Dinsmore hadn't gone to the hotel, where he would be seen by many people, but instead gone to the house on High Street? He could make a getaway from there more easily. And Carrie was there, too. Would he try to harm her? Ransom couldn't take a chance on that.

"Go to the hotel," Ransom said to Braddaugh. "There's a slim chance he's at High Street. But I want to make certain."

Then Ransom lit out north, running through deserted warehouse alleys until he had passed Lincoln Avenue and arrived at McKinley Avenue. Here there were a great many people on the street, and he slowed down to see if Dinsmore were one of them. He was surprised at how little winded he felt.

"Mr. Ransom!"

It was Nate's voice; then the boy, running around the curving wall from Grant Street so fast he rushed right into Ransom's arms and had to choke out his news. "I saw him. He's up at the Lanes' house."

"Find the marshal. Do you know who he is?" As the boy nodded that he did, Ransom went on. "He ought to be down at the Lane Hotel. Tell him where I'll be. Then get Judge Jackson too. Do you know where he lives? Yes? Good. Run, now, boy."

Ransom ran too, right up the service road of the Hill, between Grant and High streets. Only when he had come within view of the back of the Lane house did he slip off into the trees and bushes, shunning the road and moving Indian fashion from bush to building until he was at the garage.

Both motorcars were in, not surprisingly. They would be too slow for an escape, too much trouble. Dinsmore would ride out on a horse. But he might be gone already. After checking to be sure that no one was in the garage, Ransom crossed the yard and approached the stable more cautiously.

One door was slightly ajar. Was Dinsmore inside? Had Ransom been heard approaching? He stopped and listened. A horse snorted within, but there was no other sound. He slipped into the dark room and quickly hid himself in a corner. Still no one. No one but the horse. Didn't they have two horses? Had the other been taken already? Ransom went to the stable door and, grateful that it faced away from the back of the house, opened it for further illumination. As he had thought: only one horse, still unsaddled. And only feed and hay for one stall too. Good. Dinsmore must still be at the house.

Then he realized he hadn't any weapon. Nothing at all to defend himself with. Why hadn't he gotten a gun from the sheriff or the marshal? Ought he to take a pitchfork? Absurd.

Closing the stable door and pushing the bolt locked to make sure it would take longer to open it, Ransom crawled through the bushes to the back of the house. As he reached the edge of the back porch, he heard a short, dull-sounding stroke from within. What could it be? Then another stroke followed, sounding a bit more metallic.

When he raised his head to look into the small side window, Ransom realized where the noise came from. Dinsmore stood some three yards from the window, at the other end of the kitchen, his head and chest curved back, his wrists straight out in front of him, flat down on a butcher block. Opposite him, with a wood-axe raised in her hands, about to strike down with it, was Mrs. Ingram, looking very frightened and tense.

"Careful," Dinsmore warned between his teeth. "Aim well. Now!"

The axe fell and this time the manacles split apart and flew off in several directions.

"Excellent, Harriet! You've done much to improve my attitude toward you," Dinsmore said, rubbing his wrists. "Now get all the pieces and hide them. Remember. You never saw me. Do you understand?"

She nodded timidly. Then she asked, "When will you be back?"

"How do I know? Possibly next week. Possibly never. Go get my clothing. Hurry. Go!"

He pushed her into the corridor and Ransom lost sight of them, although he could hear her heavy, rapid steps as she ascended the backstairs. Where had Dinsmore gone? And where was Carrie? Had she not driven in from the ranch after all?

Ransom moved along the length of the porch to the other side of the house. The office ought to be near. Dinsmore was probably in there, getting money and whatever documents he needed. Ransom hoped Braddaugh had sense enough to come up the back road quietly. Someone armed was needed to stop Dinsmore from leaving. He turned to check the service road. Empty.

Mrs. Ingram was back in the kitchen with a small travel bag in her hands. Then Dinsmore was back too, putting a small leather wallet into his waistcoat pocket. He almost caught sight of Ransom when he approached the back window to see if anyone was coming.

"Strap it up, Harriet. Hurry! I know you'd like nothing better than for me to be caught, now wouldn't you?"

"No, Frederick. I . . ."

"Don't lie!" he said, pulling her head back, grasping her braid of hair and almost spitting into her face. "You're one of them now. Even you, Harriet. You bitch!" He gave her hair another tug that made her cry out. "I really ought to kill you. But I haven't the time to do it as I would like." He let her go and